Imogen Parker was born in Hertfordshire in 1958. She is the author of *More Innocent Times* and *These Foolish Things*. She lives in London with her husband and son.

D0587830

Also by Imogen Parker

MORE INNOCENT TIMES
THESE FOOLISH THINGS

and published by Corgi Books

THE MEN IN HER LIFE

Imogen Parker

CORGI BOOKS

THE MEN IN HER LIFE
A CORGI BOOK : 0 552 14658 7

First publication in Great Britain

PRINTING HISTORY
Corgi edition published 1999

Set in 10/11¼pt Plantin by Kestrel Data, Exeter, Devon.

Corgi Books are published by Transworld Publishers Ltd,
61–63 Uxbridge Road, London W5 5SA,
in Australia by Transworld Publishers
c/o Random House Australia Pty Ltd,
20 Alfred Street, Milsons Point, NSW 2061,
in New Zealand by Transworld Publishers,
c/o Random House New Zealand,
18 Poland Road, Glenfield, Auckland
and in South Africa by Transworld Publishers,
c/o Random House Pty Ltd,
Endulini, 5a Jubilee Road, Parktown 2193.

Reproduced, printed and bound in Great Britain by
Cox & Wyman Ltd, Reading, Berks.

Acknowledgements

Every writer dreams of a reader who will laugh at the jokes, cry at the sad bits, and generally offer constant, undiluted enthusiasm. Luckily for me, that reader is my sister. Thank you, Becky, for all your incredible support, friendship and love. I write all my books for you, and this one's dedicated to you too.

For
Becky

PROLOGUE

'Once upon a time there were two little girls.

One lived with her mother in a tower in the middle of a big city where the lifts did not work and the garden was made of concrete. Every day, after school, she would climb one hundred and eighty-two steps to their flat, and let herself in with her key. She would throw down her satchel and gaze out of the window at the chimneys and rooftops below, and the great grey river that shone in the sun like a trail of silver, dreaming of being rich and famous.

The other lived with her parents in a big white house that looked like a castle. Every afternoon she would lie on her bed in her smart school uniform listening to the rustle of the leaves in the tall trees that lined the street outside, dreaming that one day a prince would come to rescue her . . .'

PART ONE

1st May 1997

Chapter 1

'How's the man in your life?' Holly's stylist enquired.

He always asked, and she never could remember what she had told him the last time. Had she invented someone, or had there actually been a man in the picture who she thought might still be around by her next appointment? Each time she promised herself she would write down what she had said as soon as she left the salon, but somehow the relief of breathing fresh air after the farty smell of perm always made her forget. Some people had the kind of relationship with their hairdresser which allowed them to talk about a sporadic affair with a married lover. She wondered whether to mention it, to have something to fill the frozen, expectant silence but decided against. Danny was always telling her that he was a bit psychic. So he should bloody well know how the man in her life was, she thought, or perhaps he was just testing her.

'No-one special at the moment,' she heard herself saying, with the unspoken implication that there were plenty of not-special-enough queuing for the opportunity, but the feigned nonchalance came out sounding slightly forlorn. She wondered how it was that she could be perfectly at ease telling the head of a Hollywood studio to piss off with his offer of a hundred thousand dollars for a script one moment, yet reduced to a panicking wreck of insecurity by a simple question from a man she paid to cut her hair just half an hour later.

Danny grasped a handful of her curls and stared at them with a kind of suppressed despair. Holly's hair was uncompromisingly ginger. Sometimes people tried to describe it as flame, or auburn, and that always made her feel worse about it, as if ginger was such a terrible colour you couldn't even mention it. She had the same sinking feeling when told she didn't look her age. That wasn't meant to start until you were old. And thirty-five was not old. Was it?

'Right, let's get you washed.' Danny thumped her briskly on the shoulder.

Holly loved having her hair washed. She closed her eyes as the pretty male assistant's thumbs dug hard into her scalp and decided that if she ever became really rich she would have her hair washed and her head massaged every day. She would book an appointment each morning before work, or after work, or both, if she were really rich. If she were really rich, her mind began to apply logic to the fantasy, it would probably be more sensible to have the masseur on call throughout the day: a quick massage at noon to clear her mind before an important lunch, a quick massage in the afternoon just as the West Coast was waking up. If she were that rich, she might even get herself a massage table and a speakerphone and negotiate while being massaged, like sleazy movie moguls did in the movies. Was it just in the movies, or did they do that in real life too? Was the studio boss she had just spoken to lying on a white towel as he made his offer, the folds of his skin shining with aromatherapy oil? The thought made her slightly nauseous. In her mind she cancelled the massage table.

'Voted yet?' Danny asked her, scissors scrunching through her hair.

'I was there when the polling station opened,' she said, 'what about you?'

'I'm not very political.'

'That in itself is a political statement,' Holly began to say, then stopped herself, sensing that her hair would be the loser in any argument.

'What are we going to do today?' Danny sighed audibly.

'Just a trim,' she replied meekly.

Holly's hair was shoulder-length and so curly that there came a point, once every six weeks or so, where it changed from bob to explosion overnight. Danny was always urging her to have it short, but she resisted, mainly, she now realized, because instinctively she didn't trust him, and she finally understood why. He must be a Tory. People who said they weren't very political always were.

'Touch of the Jane Ashers.' Robert Preston gave his uninvited opinion when Holly returned to the office.

'Is that a compliment?' Holly wanted to know.

'Not sure,' Robert walked a circle around her in the small kitchen. 'I'm told some men find her sexy because they dream of ruffling those sleek feathers, but you're a bit ruffled already.'

'Charming.'

In every job she'd ever had, Holly had made a best friend at work. At the local Odeon, where she'd been an usherette on Saturdays, it was the box-office lady who wore a bright blond wig and had a husband who hit her. In the promoter's office where she'd had her first typing job, it was the Australian girl who answered the phone and had bonked most of the roadies. A best friend at work was a safety-valve. She was the person whom you went to when something made you so angry you wanted to cry, or something was so funny you had to share it. She hadn't found one at Louis Gold Ltd until Robert turned up. He had seemed the most unlikely candidate when he arrived, being rather snooty and effete, and she was sure that if she had still been a secretary he wouldn't have given her the time of day. But after exchanging exasperated looks at a couple of the interminably dull agency meetings that took place in the boardroom every Tuesday morning, she realized that at last she had found a kindred spirit. They took to sitting next to one another passing notes like naughty children at the back of the class with Louis Gold giving them stern looks, but unable quite to bring himself to tell them off since he was always banging on about encouraging youth and freedom of expression in his company. Robert worked on the book side of the agency, representing novelists. His clients were mostly beautiful young gay men like himself. They lolled about in reception and in Robert's office, distracting the secretaries and giving rise to mutterings by the older staff about the office becoming a cappuccino bar.

If only it were, Holly thought, pouring herself some of the bitter brown liquid that boiled away all day on the hotplate. There was a cleaning rota pinned above the machine with people's names with dates and boxes to indicate when descaling duty had been completed, but there hadn't been any ticks since the New Year, Holly noticed. She took a sip and wondered how many million micro-organisms had just entered her mouth.

'Fancy a fag?' Robert asked her.

'You should be so lucky,' Holly responded as she always did. Some of their jokes were really childish but they still laughed. Robert was a giggler. Sometimes he came into her office with a pained expression on his face and Holly would just be about to ask him what the matter was when he would bang the door shut and bend in half as the laughter gurgled out of his body.

'Oh, go on.' Robert's voice was wheedling.

'I've got a meeting in five minutes,' Holly replied.

The office had recently instituted a no-smoking policy which meant that having a cigarette entailed getting the lift to the ground floor and standing outside in the street to display your vice like a criminal in the stocks.

'Smoker?' Robert asked. The no-smoking policy was only relaxed when clients who smoked were in.

'Yup!' Holly said, triumphantly.

'He's not thinking of writing a novel?'

'Sorry.'

Sometimes Robert would get Holly into his office on the pretext of talking about film possibilities when one of his smoking novelists was in, but talking to screen-writers about the possibility of writing novels just didn't work in the same way.

'Bitch,' Robert said, amiably enough, and started on the long walk towards the lifts.

The view from Holly's fifth-floor office was a horrible abstract of brick and pipes encrusted with stalactites of city grime, but if she craned her neck she could see a triangle of blue sky at the top of the ventilation shaft. Holly opened the window. In between the fatty blasts wafting up from the fast-food outlet below the air felt summery for the first time that year.

'I've got another one I'd like to run past you, only an idea at the moment, but I like it . . . it's a kind of *Men Behaving Badly* meets *Mars Attacks*,' Jeff was telling her.

Ever since some clever git had pitched *Alien* as '*Jaws* in Outer Space', no proposal for film or television could be described except in terms of something else. Holly and Robert had a competition for the most ridiculous pitch each week and whoever won had to pick up the bill for their regular Friday drink. The previous week Holly had won with a script whose author had described it as '*Godzilla* holidays in *Howard's End*'.

Jeff was one of her least favourite clients. He was perfectly competent at trotting out episodes for various long-running drama serials, but his ideas for original screenplays always struck her as slightly less than original.

'Go on . . .' she said, cautiously, and pushed an ashtray across the desk, hoping it would encourage him. She had already let him overstay his welcome by half an hour in the expectation of a legal Marlboro.

'Well, it's two blokes sharing a flat, right, but one of them is an alien, right?' Jeff was unable to stop himself chuckling at his own wit, 'so . . . all he knows about human behaviour is what he's seen on TV. Like, he doesn't know what the toilet is for, because people never crap on TV, so he just pours Frish down the whole time and buys a labrador puppy to run around with the bog roll . . .'

Holly smiled weakly. Only half an hour to go before she was meeting her best friend Colette for a drink. Surely she could last without nicotine until then?

'Great, look, Jeff, there are a couple of calls I've got to make . . .'

'And then,' said Jeff, warming to his theme, 'he gets this can of deodorant but he has to find a leaf with a V in it before he sprays it on his back!'

'Don't you think we've had aliens in flats in *Third Rock from the Sun*?' Holly interrupted him sharply.

'You may be right,' Jeff conceded, 'I've got a couple more . . .'

'Jot them down and fax them over, OK?' Holly stood up and walked to the door.

Jeff got to his feet, slightly bewildered by his sudden dismissal.

'Have you given up smoking?' Holly asked him as he walked past her.

'Three weeks ago,' he announced with the absurdly triumphant smile of the recent ex-smoker.

'Good for you!' Holly said, smiling broadly as he left.

Holly dialled her voice mail. In the time Jeff had been talking, she had missed eleven calls. She looked at her notepad. Below Jeff's name and the date she had written Men BB + Mars - crap, loo roll, dog. She tore off the sheet and threw it in the bin, then picked it out again, suddenly feeling rather heartless. When she had first become an agent she had been grateful to people like Jeff for providing her bread and butter, and now she didn't have time to listen. When she had first joined the company, Holly reflected, her ultimate goal had been to have an office of her own. She closed the window as the early evening frying sent up thick clouds of burger. Now her ambition was to have an office of her own with a view, air-conditioned, preferably in a building with a gym and a swimming-pool in the basement. Ideally the building would be beside the river, within easy walking distance of some terrific restaurants. There would always be a line of cabs outside and she would be so successful nobody would dare to object to her smoking. And then there was the masseur . . .

Holly called her secretary in.

'Messages?' she demanded.

'None,' said Jemima with a sheepish smile.

'So what have you been doing for the last hour? I've got eleven on my voice mail. I should have thought you could have fielded one or two.'

'I was filing . . .' Jemima blushed with guilt.

'Oh, for God's sake . . .'

Having risen from the secretarial ranks herself, Holly was well-known as the worst boss in the building. She was the only one who knew every excuse in the book because most of them she had invented herself.

'You're a bit like a child-abuser,' Robert had once told her, 'people who abuse have always been abused themselves. You'd think they'd know better.'

'I don't mind people lying to me,' Holly had defended herself, 'as long as they put some effort into making it a good lie. Otherwise, it's insulting.'

'It's a class thing,' Robert had teased, stepping out of the way of a friendly punch, 'you common people just don't know how to treat servants . . .'

Jemima's dressing-down was interrupted by Holly's phone ringing. Holly picked it up, dismissing her secretary with a glance.

'Anji, hi!'

Anji was one of Holly's brightest stars. Her self-help book *Single File* had been the previous year's surprise bestseller and her writing was so witty it had generated a lot of interest amongst producers. She had a sitcom in development with Channel 4, and she was working on ideas for feature films. She was also one of Holly's nicest and most modest clients.

'Do you have a moment?' Anji asked, 'it's just I came up with this idea in the bath last night and well . . .'

'Go ahead.'

'Well,' Anji began very tentatively, 'I'm calling it *The Men in her Life* and it's about how you think that there must be someone out there with your name written on . . .'

Holly had a fleeting vision of a man with a tattoo on his arm that read HOLLY.

'Go on . . .' she said, uncertainly.

'. . . so it's about this woman, thirty-something, she's had boyfriends, but never found the One, you know, and then, like waiting for a bus, suddenly three come along at the same time. They are everything you'd ever want in a man . . . except divided by three. One is rich, one is good-looking, one is really funny. She can't decide, so she comes up with some tests . . .'

'God, I like this,' Holly interrupted, 'I'm thinking feature film with Julia Roberts and three guys . . .'

'Four guys, because there's her next-door neigh-bour . . .'

'. . . who's always loved her and yet she's never thought . . .' Holly went on.

'How did you guess?' Anji laughed. 'Do you think it could work?'

'Yeah . . . I mean for once it's not about men choosing between madonna or whore, mistress or wife . . . I mean this is Girlpower. At last we get to bloody choose between randy or reliable, hunk or husband . . . I love it . . .' Holly always knew she was onto something when the pitch seemed to speak itself.

'Great!' Anji said, 'I'll have a go at it, then.'

'I think you should call it *The One*,' Holly suggested, 'it's got more of a ring to it.'

'*The One*,' Anji tasted the words, 'OK. I'll write something for you to have a look at in the next few weeks . . .'

Holly put down the receiver feeling excited. This was the part of the job that she loved. Being in at the start of things, the thrill of pitching an idea, then selling it for a fortune and finally seeing something she had helped to create up there on the screen, although, usually, by that time, the work had been the subject of so many rows and tantrums it had rather lost its thrill. Generally, she preferred seeing films and television programmes that she hadn't been involved with. Even the best scripts lost their capacity to surprise and delight when you had read all fifteen drafts and acted as a buffer between the writer and the producer.

She was about to call Jemima back in for some dictation when her phone rang again.

Colette was waiting for her in reception.

'So, where shall we go?' Colette asked in the lift down, 'I'm dying for a drink.'

'I'm dying for a cigarette,' Holly said, putting one in her mouth and holding her thumb on the flint of her lighter ready to light up as soon as the lift touched down. 'I can't get drunk,' she added.

'Why not?'

'Louis's election party tonight. Doesn't start till half past nine, goes on all night. I can't be drunk before I arrive.'

Her boss, Louis Gold's, election bashes were the North London intelligentsia's version of the parties Swifty Lazar used to host after the Oscars.

'Well, what are we going to do?' Colette wondered.

'One glass of wine and then a meal?' Holly suggested.

'Don't be daft . . . we've never managed to stick at one bottle, let alone one glass.'

'They do great martinis at Odeon and they're so expensive you feel guilty having more than one.'

'The Odeon?' Colette asked.

'Not the cinema, the restaurant, but that's a thought . . .'

'What?'

'We could see a movie. We couldn't get drunk then, not unless we snuck in a bottle and I'm not that desperate . . .'

'All right . . . what?'

'I've seen everything, but I don't mind seeing most things again. You choose.'

Colette decided on *The English Patient* because she was one of the three people left in London who hadn't seen it and because Holly was the only person she would admit that to. There was an early evening show which would get them out by nine, giving Holly just enough time to pop home, change and grab a cab to Hampstead. They calculated they could have one cocktail and two cigarettes beforehand if they missed the adverts and previews.

'What do you want?' Colette asked her.

'Champagne cocktail – no, hang on, make that a

vodka martini.' Holly noticed Colette's surprise. 'I just don't want to do anything that feels like premature celebration,' she explained.

'I don't think that drinking a glass of champagne is going to determine the result of the election, if that's what you mean,' Colette said, 'anyway that sounds a bit superstitious for you . . .'

'I'm always worse after a haircut.'

'I can't see what difference it will make anyway,' Colette opined.

'I just don't want to live in a country where everyone is so tired or frightened that they elect a bunch of rotten old sleazebags again . . . it's more about style than anything else,' Holly said, staring out of the window.

The table in the Odeon bar looked over Regent Street. The early evening light was golden. Shoppers and office workers were strolling rather than hurrying, with jackets slung over shoulders, occasionally looking skywards as if unable to believe that the sun was still shining. There was definitely a different atmosphere in the air. Maybe things were really going to change tonight.

'It looks nice, very sleek,' Colette gave her assessment of the haircut.

'Really? He put pomade on it, whatever that is. I thought it was the stuff men put on before Brylcreem was invented. Feels like a helmet. Every turn of my head, the hair goes too. Should I have it all cut off?'

Colette appraised her again as if for the first time.

'It would suit you, but it'd be different,' was her considered opinion.

Holly sipped her martini. It was so cold the vodka was slightly viscous. She lit her second cigarette and relaxed back into the armchair feeling almost completely happy.

Chapter 2

Fifty feet away, almost directly beneath Holly and Colette's table, although she did not know it, Holly's mother Mo sat in a stationary Piccadilly line tube reading the paper. Everyone was so sure that Labour were going to win she wondered whether there was any point in voting. But she didn't think she would forgive herself if she didn't vote and then they lost in her constituency, although that was unlikely, since it had always been a safe Labour seat. And if Labour did win, as everyone was saying they would, then she would feel bad if she hadn't participated in it. If Holly found out she would never hear the last of it.

Mo turned to the recipe. She never made any of the dishes described but it was her way of reading the paper, just as she noticed other people turned straight to the television listings or the stars. The train started up again and slid into Piccadilly Circus. Crowds of people got on. Mo tucked her legs in as near to the seat as she could but someone still trod on her foot. She peered down at the toe of her black patent court shoe which was now decorated with the ghostly imprint of a trainer's sole. It was too much of a squeeze to bend down and buff it up.

At times like this Mo wished that she lived a bit nearer to the department store where she worked. It wouldn't have been so bad if the journey hadn't taken her right across the busiest part of town, from Knightsbridge to the East End. The trains seemed fuller than they had been, or perhaps she was just getting older. Lots of things that had floated over her head when she was younger irritated her now, like the way that all the foreign kids seemed to raise their voices a few decibels as soon as they got into the compartment. When she first arrived in London she remembered thinking how unfriendly everyone was, sitting silently in their tube train seats, staring into space, avoiding eye contact, let alone a chat. After thirty-odd years, she had almost become a Londoner herself.

Mo tried to visualize what she had in the fridge for tea. There was a cod in butter sauce in the freezer which she could do with peas, but Eamon had said he might pop in and that wouldn't be enough for both of them. There was a little supermarket near Holly's old junior school where the polling-station was. She could pick something up there. Or perhaps they could have fish and chips. Mo stood up and pushed her way out to change at Holborn.

The Central line was less full and there was room enough for her to open the paper again. She glanced at the television listings to see if there was a good film on that evening. She didn't think she could be bothered with all the election-night swingometers and polls and things. When Holly lived at home she had always insisted they watch it. The last couple of elections, just out of habit, Mo had dutifully stared at the screen for as long as she could, but she didn't really see the point. It didn't change anything whether you watched or not. The only thing that was different was whether you woke up the next morning after a nice comfy sleep in your bed, or slumped in the armchair with a cricked neck and a mouth tasting of last night's food.

Mo flipped idly through the news stories. It was all

election stuff. She thought everyone would be glad when it was all decided. The campaign had been going on so long the papers were really scraping the barrel for new angles. There was an article entitled Luvvies for Labour about famous people in the arts who were voting for Tony Blair. Mo sighed and was just about to turn over when her eyes fell on the photo at the bottom of the page. Under the headline 'I'm all Left, Jack!' was a picture of Jack arriving at Heathrow. Unusually, he was smiling. Mo couldn't help smiling too. The California sun was doing him good. He looked relaxed and a bit weather-beaten, as if he'd been spending his days on a yacht. He had a pair of sunglasses in one hand, a cigarette in the other, and he had obviously just made a joke at the expense of the photographer because he had that look of his that was slightly shy and triumphant at the same time. Mo read the paragraph beneath.

'Arriving at Heathrow yesterday evening, Jack Palmer joked, "When I heard that Andrew Lloyd Webber said he'd leave if Labour got in, I had to come home." The director, whose new film *Paying for It* is set to open later this year, added, "On a more serious note, I've done what I want to do in Hollywood for the moment, and there are lots of exciting things going on here. It's good to be back. Of course I'm voting Labour, as I've always done." '

Mo doubted very much whether that was really what Jack had said. It didn't sound much like him, but she supposed it was difficult to get his distinctive brand of dry sarcasm onto the page. It was a complete lie about voting Labour. She remembered being shocked when he told her he was going to vote for Thatcher in 1979. Or maybe he'd been lying then and the joke was on her. She'd known him nearly all her life, and she'd never been able to tell when he was teasing. Mo looked at the photo again, allowing herself to wonder just for a second whether she'd be seeing him this time he was home. He usually turned up just before he was about to leave again. She never knew whether the visits were supposed to be for her benefit, or for his, but she never told him to go away. She could tell herself a million times that he was a selfish, ruthless bastard, but she melted every time he stood in the door-frame with his sheepish half-grin – his sinner's face, she called it – and she always forgave him.

Chapter 3

As Clare dropped her vote into the black metal ballot-box, she closed her eyes and made a wish.

'It's no use praying,' Joss told her, 'you don't believe in God.'

'I was just wishing,' she told him, ashamed that he had noticed her childish gesture. She could not tell whether his tone was hostile or indulgent. Even after eighteen years of marriage, she sometimes found it difficult to read her husband's mood.

'Do you still wish?' he asked, very gently and incredulously. 'Am I really married to the last dreamer in England?' Then he put his hand on her waist and drew her body to his, and for a moment she felt utterly cherished.

To a casual onlooker they would appear a perfect family, Clare thought, as they walked back up the hill from the two-room school building that had become a polling-station for the day: a tall, handsome man, his wife, and between them, asleep in his buggy, a beautiful little boy with his father's face and his mother's golden hair. Even the teenager who walked a sulky couple of paces behind them was exactly as a teenager should be. Their daughter Ella wore black, and had a nose ring. Together they opened the gate and walked up the flagstone path to their Cornish stone cottage with its view of the sea and its garden crammed with orderly lines of vegetables and bean rows.

They had always voted together. It was one of the first things they had done as a couple in 1979, the first time she had been old enough to vote. Clare recalled exactly the shiver of excitement as she dropped her ballot-paper into the box, and the sensation that she was now truly an adult, responsible for her own destiny. Later there had been the enormous weight of disappointment as they watched the results come in. It had felt like losing her innocence twice in one day.

At every election since then her natural optimism had flared briefly in the run-up, then fizzled away on the day as the results confirmed inescapably that they were swimming against the tide. The rest of the population busied itself with the pursuit of wealth while she and Joss struggled to live on as little as they could. Without exception, her old schoolfriends in London had spent the Eighties obtaining qualifications, careers and suits with shoulder-pads. Clare had raised a child and turned their little smallholding into a source of food. Her peers whiled away their evenings networking in metropolitan wine bars, while Clare washed nappies and patched clothes. Sometimes one of them would remember her and ring for a chat, but she could not afford to make long and gossipy calls back to them, and anyway, they had very little to talk about any more. It had not worried her then, because she had felt so lucky to have Joss and Ella, but recently she had begun to find it increasingly difficult to believe in a way of life that no-one else seemed to value. Joss thrived on being different from everyone else, but she began to yearn for the normal. It was one of the many ways they had grown apart.

'Do you think Labour will really win?' she asked, taking his arm as they approached their door.

'The question is, will it make any difference if they do?' he replied.

When she had first known him, the habit he had of rephrasing everything she said had made her think him profound, now she just found it deflating.

'At least the mood will change . . .' she suggested, letting her arm drop again.

'Will it?' He put his key in the front door and ducked his head to step in.

Clare fell silent. Surely things were going to change, she thought. They must.

In the garden, as she tugged at a handful of dark green crinkly leaves, she thought how ironic it was that their way of life seemed to have become fashionable at the very moment she had begun to grow dissatisfied with it. The papers were full of stories about women of her age who had put all their energy into careers which they were now giving up to raise their children. There were endless articles about middle-class people deciding to live in poverty, which the journalists called down-shifting. Organically-grown food, like the spinach in her hand, fetched extortionate prices in supermarkets, and the latest health advice extolled the benefits of antioxidants from fresh fruit and vegetables. Clare stooped to pick a bunch of parsley. People were actually choosing to come to Cornwall from London so that their children could grow up in fresh air and go to a village school. It was perverse to dream about leaving now.

In any case, there was no way they could ever afford to go back to London, she told herself, even if Joss wanted to, which he did not. Life in Penderric suited him.

Clare tried to shake herself into a more positive mood. There was a party on the beach later, and before that she had to make supper, get Tom bathed and into bed, and change. She straightened up and paused for a moment to look over the fence at the view. It was the first real summer day that year and the sky was cloudless and blue. A small fishing-boat, as tiny in the distance as one of Tom's bath toys, chugged towards the harbour, and following it the white wings of gulls glinted in the late afternoon sun.

Somewhere on the other side of the bay she could hear tinny blasts of the campaign theme tune wafting from the Labour candidate's car like the jingle of a distant ice-cream van.

'Things can only get better!'

Clare put on clean black jeans and a sleeveless black T-shirt and went into the bathroom to look at herself in the mirror above the sink. That morning, in a fit of whimsy, she had sewn tiny roses she had made out of narrow red ribbon round the neck of the vest. It worked surprisingly well. She brushed her hair, feeling suddenly excited at the prospect of the beach party.

'How do I look?' she asked Ella as she came down to the kitchen.

Ella was preparing supper for herself and her boyfriend. They had volunteered to babysit for Tom.

'Lovely.'

Even though Ella wore Doc Martens and heavily distressed clothing all year round, she had good manners.

'Where's Joss?' Clare asked.

'He said he'd see you there,' Ella said, stirring the saucepan of pasta that was bubbling on the cooker.

'Oh . . .' Inside Clare's tummy, the little burst of optimism she had allowed herself to feel collapsed like the centre of a too-little baked cake. 'I made some leek and bacon sauce, if you fancy it,' she told Ella, trying not to let her feelings show.

31

'Matt's vegetarian.'

'Of course he is. Well, I'm sure there are tomatoes. And some cheese . . .'

'Just go, Mum. We'll be fine,' Ella told her.

When Clare and Joss had first arrived in Penderric there seemed to be parties every night of the week, simple impromptu get-togethers fuelled by rough red wine and dancing. Sometimes Pepe had played flamenco guitar. Clare remembered making huge bowls of spaghetti *aglio olio* that people would fall upon at two in the morning, ravenous from enjoying themselves so much. It had been unlike anything she had known before.

At home, in London, parties had been catered and waiters roamed around with trays of champagne flutes, but most of the time the large Hampstead house stood like a fortress, empty except for its three inhabitants, the windows and doors wired with devices to screech at uninvited intruders.

Here nobody locked their front door. *Tu casa es mi casa*, Pepe had told them when they arrived. Clare had loved that closeness then, enveloping her like the family she had never had. She could not remember exactly when it was she had started to feel that the embrace of the community was stifling her.

Clare walked slowly down the hill into town. It was a bit of a dead end, not really pretty enough to be a day-trip destination, and too far off the beaten track to become much of a resort. Nothing ever seemed to change. Recently there had been an influx of camper vans parked along the North Beach each weekend, but the surfers who owned them kept themselves to themselves. In the school holidays, families who had been coming to Cornwall all their lives filled the few empty cottages, spent their days pottering around the rock pools in rolled-up jeans and plastic macs and treated themselves to clotted cream teas at Amelia's tea shop, but it was a long way to come down from London for the weekend, even a bank holiday.

Clare knew every crack in every paving stone, every faded postcard advert on the post office notice-board, every tacky souvenir in every shop window. The day before, she had found herself telling Ella with some excitement that the jardinière in the shape of an elephant they had jointly voted most hideous artefact 1996 must have been sold since it was no longer in the window of The Kiln, and they had speculated for a good ten minutes about who could have been the purchaser before Ella had sighed and said, 'Enough. We're as sad as they are if this is all we can talk about!' She had meant it as a joke, but like so much of what Ella said, it was almost chilling in its truth.

Clare forced herself not to think about how she would cope without her beloved daughter. After her A levels, which were just starting, Ella was taking a gap year in the States, and then she was going to medical school in London. Despite looking the embodiment of disaffected youth, Ella was hard-working, clever and ambitious. Clare knew that there was no point in pretending that she would come back home in the holidays, because she would not. Ella despised all the things that constituted the town's attractions – sailing, surfing and particularly the exclusive group of writers who had chosen to make Penderric their home in the Seventies and were known in the town as the Poets, but whom Ella usually referred to as the Wankers.

'They're nothing but a bunch of middle-aged wankers living off their wives and fantasizing about bonking the girls on the beach. I don't know why you put up with it,' she had told Clare, throwing down that spring's edition of *Penpoetry*, the pamphlet the poets published twice a year. And they had both burst into fits of conspiratorial laughter that stopped abruptly when Joss had walked in.

When Ella left, she would be leaving home for good. America would change her. She would be able to be exactly who she wanted to be. When she came back she would be different, just a little, or maybe a lot, and it was odd to think about that. If you were a good mother, you had to trust your child to have the strength and resources to make herself happy. Letting go was going to be tough, but she was almost looking forward to it on Ella's behalf. For a moment Clare visualized herself in America, on her own in a new land, creating a new identity for herself. She was driving a convertible across the States, losing herself in the vast landscape, and when she reached the other side running down the beach to leap into the salty spritz of the Pacific. With a stab of guilt she realized that she had not included Tom in her fantasy, so she immediately put a car seat in the back of the convertible and a baseball cap on his head and repeated the journey with him behind her, singing along to the song on the radio.

'You look happy,' Amelia told her when she arrived at the party.

'I was miles away,' Clare replied.

Chapter 4

In the kitchen of a large house in Hampstead, Philippa Palmer poured herself a glass of Chablis from a bottle that was chilling in the fridge and picked up one of the little wooden bowls of Japanese rice crackers her housekeeper Lucinda had lined up on the breakfast bar in the kitchen.

Apart from lighting a flame under the new potatoes, there was nothing left for her to do. She knew it was considered slightly *de trop* these days to serve poached salmon, but Lucinda assured her that it was wild, not farmed, and Jack had always loved fresh salmon, rather sweetly believing it to be the ultimate upperclass food.

It was warm enough to sit on the terrace. Philippa settled herself on a sun-lounger and began to leaf through the brochures her secretary had sent over by messenger. The previous evening, exhausted after his flight, Jack had agreed to her suggestion that they take a holiday, and she wanted to have something booked before he had a chance to change his mind. The nearest they had come to having a holiday for many years were the weekends they met up in New York, halfway between her work in London and his in Hollywood.

She tried to remember the last time they had been on a proper holiday together, or if they ever had. The very first summer they had intended to go backpacking round Europe, but when she became pregnant she had felt too sick to go. After that there had been family holidays but it wasn't the same as being together, just the two of them, and by the time Clare had left home they were both too busy to take real time off. Jack always went skiing for two weeks in Whistler and she collapsed somewhere hot in the Caribbean, but for the rest of the year they were both travelling so much betweeen London, the States and the various locations of Jack's movies, that evenings together just hanging out at home had become as rare and exotic as nights in the most luxurious hotels of the world.

Now, for an unlimited stretch of time, neither of them was working. The coincidence of their individual decisions to take a breather was too glorious an opportunity to miss, but she knew that the liberating freedom they both felt now would never last unless they were challenged in some way. Jack especially had such a low boredom threshold he practically itched when unoccupied.

Philippa was astonished by the variety of cultural holidays available. The Artistic Traditions of Japan, White Nights in St Petersburg with special access to the Hermitage, a tour of the archaeological sites in Libya, or Syria, the indigenous history and culture of Zimbabwe, for heaven's sake. There was even a trip to Yemen which carried a health warning because of the high altitudes and off-road driving. Philippa tore that page out and threw it in the kitchen bin when she went to get herself another glass of wine. She wanted to be intellectually engaged, not utterly exhausted, and it was exactly the trip that Jack would get fixated on if he were allowed to see that it existed. There were gentler tours, and courses. They could learn to paint in the South of France, or to cook in Tuscany. There were opera festivals in Verona, Bregenz, Vienna and Prague.

Philippa rather fancied the Italian cookery. She had never learned to cook. Her one act of rebellion in the Sixties had been to refuse to go to finishing school in Switzerland, as her older sister had done. In the Seventies she had refused to cook as a matter of political principle, in the Eighties she had simply been too busy. Now, suddenly, in the Nineties, cooking had become a revered skill that she did not possess. She liked the idea of learning how to make those deliciously crisp little pizzas that had become so popular recently, or to roast a pigeon. Her one attempt at roasting had been in the early days of marriage to Jack. Nobody had told her that you had to take the little plastic bag of giblets out of the chicken before putting it in the oven. At least it was the last time Jack had complained that they never ate a proper Sunday lunch.

As she wandered back into the kitchen for a refill, she debated where she would install the wood-fired oven that seemed essential to modern Italian cuisine. She would ask Lucinda in the morning, she thought, when she came to clear up after the dinner party.

Philippa had decided on a dinner party rather than a full-scale election party because Jack would still be jet-lagged, and she didn't want the house full of people at breakfast. Most of the people Jack would want to see were anyway already going to Louis Gold's bash down the road. So she had invited six people for dinner who were bound to be invited to Louis's do, and hoped that they would be gone by ten o'clock, leaving her and Jack alone together. The sale of her management consultancy company and the problems he had had editing his new film meant they had not been together for six weeks, the longest they had been parted in all their years of marriage. She wanted to touch every inch of his skin, to feel his weight upon her and his breath damp in her hair. She wanted her body to melt on the warmth of his.

She heard his key in the front-door lock and his footsteps along the hall. One of the pleasures of knowing someone so long was being able to tell from the rhythm of their footfall what kind of mood they were in, and she knew that Jack was happy. His meeting with the distributors had clearly gone well. Now he would be able to relax and enjoy the time that stretched before them. She went to greet him.

Chapter 5

'Would you rather be Kristen Scott Thomas or Juliette Binoche?' Holly asked Colette as they emerged from the cinema into Leicester Square and walked diagonally across the little patch of park. It was beginning to get dark and a great cloud of blackbirds swirled around the tops of the trees, filling the city air with birdsong.

'Juliette Binoche,' Colette answered without hesitation.

'Why?' Holly demanded to know.

'Because I loved that scene with her swinging around the church looking at the frescoes. I thought it was the most romantic bit . . .'

'Give me steamy afternoon sex in Cairo with Ralph any day.'

'But she dies . . .'

Colette could be infuriatingly rational about these things.

'The trouble with you is that you want it all,' Colette went on. 'You want the silent, difficult, handsome man and yet you're always moaning on about men being bastards . . .'

'There's not a lot I wouldn't do for Ralph Fiennes,' Holly said.

'Even with his face all burned?' Colette asked.

39

'God, no! No, then he looks like ET and I was the only person in the world who didn't think that ET was cute.'

'You can't love someone when they look all right and then go off them when they're in trouble . . .'

'Who can't?' Holly asked.

They started walking in the direction of Holly's flat.

'Who would you prefer . . . Ralph Fiennes before the burns, or Robert De Niro?' Colette wanted to know.

'I'd have Robert De Niro in *Godfather II* above anyone, but he's got a bit paunchy recently, so if I had to choose today, it'd have to be Ralph Fiennes . . . Who would you have?' Holly asked.

'For me it'd be Ralph every time.'

'But I'm not prepared to share . . .'

'Well, that's not fair because if Robert De Niro came along looking like he did in *Godfather II*, you'd drop Ralph just like that,' Colette argued.

'Why d'you have to have one of mine anyway? I thought you fancied George Clooney. Why can't you just have him and leave me alone? I wouldn't touch him . . .'

'That's because you don't fancy him, but I do fancy both of yours . . .'

They had been playing the same game since their childhood, although the men in question had changed over the years. There had been a time, Holly remembered, when they had almost come to blows over which one of them would get off with David Cassidy if he ever turned up in the concrete playground at the foot of their block of flats.

'Well, for God's sake get a grip of yourself,' Holly burst out laughing, 'lucky we never meet any men otherwise we'd be in trouble.'

They stopped outside the wrought-iron gate that led into the courtyard where Holly lived.

'Are you coming up?' Holly asked, putting her key in

the lock of her front door. Her flat was on the first floor and her front door led straight onto a flight of stairs.

'We do meet men,' Colette said, following her up, 'just not the right men. Do you think that's it, or do you think we're emotionally unavailable?'

Colette was a receptionist for a Harley Street dermatologist. She read all the women's magazines and always had the latest psychological jargon. Colette could make a syndrome out of a vague anxiety in the time it took to say *Cosmopolitan*.

'Emotionally unavailable?' Holly asked, throwing her bag onto the kitchen table and opening the fridge to see if there was any wine. 'Is that the same as accidentally celibate?'

That had been last year's way of saying on the shelf.

'No, accidentally celibate is all about having so much in your life you just don't have time for a relationship. Emotionally available is about being open to love and commitment. I mean, we tell ourselves we are, but are we really putting up barriers to intimacy?'

'What do you mean?' Holly couldn't help asking as she poured them each a glass of Pinot Grigio. Colette's theories were a bit like astrological predictions. Your first instinct was to dismiss them as ridiculous, but something made you just have a quick read (for a laugh) and by the time you got to the end you couldn't help wondering how they knew that about you.

'Well, take you and your married man . . . you're always saying that it's the perfect relationship 'cos he's bright and you have great sex and you never have to pretend to feel sorry for him when he's got a cold, but maybe you're just using him as a kind of shield against a real relationship . . .'

'I sometimes wonder what I'd do with a real relationship if I had one,' Holly said, dismally.

'Settle down, have children . . .' Colette suggested wistfully.

'You've done all that once,' Holly responded.

Colette had married her first boss, a plastic surgeon. It had been an unqualified disaster.

'We didn't have kids . . .'

'Well, that's what you want to do,' said Holly, 'it's not what I want to do. I hate people just assuming that every woman once she reaches thirty-five can only be fulfilled by children. It's like in movies, as soon as you see in the script the description "she is an ambitious career woman", you just know that by the end of it, she's going to be dead or pregnant.'

'All right, all right, you don't have to bang on,' Colette protested.

'Well, why can't women be fulfilled by something else?'

'Such as?'

'Well, I don't know, housing the homeless, or something,' Holly said, feeling rather pleased with her example.

'I'm sure some people could be.' There was a definite trace of sarcasm in Colette's voice.

'Meaning?' Holly asked.

'Well, I just saw you look the other way from that *Big Issue* seller.'

'Well, I've never noticed you buying it,' Holly shot back.

'No, but I've never said I wanted to house the homeless.'

'Oh, piss off.' Holly wandered into the room where she kept her clothes. 'So what's it to be, little DKNY black dress or long Nicole Farhi black dress?' She held up two hangers.

'Short.'

Holly began to strip.

'Perhaps there's no such thing as a real relationship?' she called from the shower.

'Well, why does it bother us both so much that we

don't have one then?' Colette answered, lying back on Holly's bed and staring at the paper tropical fish that dangled from a nail in the ceiling. She loved Holly's bedroom. It was so different from her own home, like a magical cave, full of brightly coloured bits and pieces: the patchwork quilt Mo had made of all Holly's childhood dresses, a string of Indian elephants for a light-pull, beads slung over the corner of the mirror and the dressing-table cluttered with lipsticks and earrings. Holly emerged from the shower with a towel wrapped round her head. 'You washed your hair!'

'I know, I only remembered I'd had it done after I'd slapped on the shampoo. I don't think I'm very good at sleek,' Holly said, pulling on a black jersey dress with an asymmetric neckline.

'VPL,' Colette warned, pointing at Holly's bum.

'You see what I mean?' Holly bent and pulled off her knickers. 'Better?'

'Yes. Aren't you going to wear tights?' Colette asked as Holly slipped her foot into one chisel-toed suede pump and hopped round the room in search of the other.

'Black is out and flesh-coloured never looks anything like my flesh. What? Do I need a wax? Well, why are you staring then? Come on. I'm going to miss the Exit poll unless we get a move on. Are you going home?'

Colette lived in the suburbs, in the colonial-style house she had shared with her husband. They were still arguing about the divorce settlement. The house had five bedrooms, a patio and a pergola. It cost a fortune to keep up, but her ex was still responsible for half the bills. Colette had a bloody-minded side to her.

'No, I think I'll stay in town. D'you think anywhere will have a television on?'

'Bar Italia does. You could stay here, but don't fall asleep on my bed because I'm feeling lucky . . .'

Holly kissed Colette on both cheeks and clattered down the stairs.

Louis Gold's was the kind of house that had framed posters by David Hockney in the kitchen, but when you looked closely you realized that they weren't posters, but originals. It was a house just like her father's, which she had visited only once as a child but dreamed of living in ever since.

'White or red?' Louis asked.

'Oh, I think red tonight,' Holly smiled at him.

The kitchen was a balcony overlooking a spacious airy living area filled with modern furniture, art and plants. Most of the guests were crushed together around a small television. In a far corner, standing slightly aloof from the party, she spotted the man she was having an affair with looking up at her. She took a step back, trying to work out whether the angle was sharp enough for him to have seen up her dress. A cheer went up as the screen went red.

'We're predicting a landslide . . .' the presenter announced.

Everyone started grabbing each other's hands, dancing and kissing as if it were New Year. Holly was dragged down the steps and into a ragged conga. As she passed him, Piers indicated with an almost imperceptible shake of his head that he would like to leave. She frowned at him and let herself be pulled by the kicking, singing snake of people through the open door and down more steps into the garden. A tall apple tree was suddenly ablaze with coloured lights, all red, as if luscious, glowing fruit had miraculously appeared. There was a collective gasp, followed by a hush, as each person felt a pang of unease, a flashback to 1992, that they might be celebrating too soon, tempting fate.

'The Exit poll couldn't be that wrong, could it?'

Holly said to Louis, as people began to push back into the house to watch the television again.

'One hopes not,' he said. 'Holly, do you know Freddy?' He introduced her to one of his most illustrious producer friends.

Holly smiled and held out her hand.

'Holly O'Mara,' she said.

'How nice to meet you at last. I've heard so much about you . . .'

The boss's election parties were a good barometer of the progress of her career. In 1987, when she had joined the company as secretary to the director of the media division, her invitation had been issued with the request that she come along early and help with the preparations. Handing round nibbles is such a good way of meeting people, Louis's wife had told her, dropping a very heavy silver tray into her arms and pointing her towards the throng. It sounded good to Holly, until she realized that nobody who goes to election parties in large houses in Hampstead, even if they have the most impeccable left-wing credentials, expects to engage in conversation with the girl who's offering the chicken satay. By 1992 she had become an assistant agent selling film and television rights in the books the agency represented. At the election party Holly had been free to mingle, but she had found it so difficult to engage with any of the tight little groups of people that she had been almost tempted to grab a tray of tapenade crostini to make it look as if she had a function. It had been a dismal evening, with everyone leaving stunned by the revelation that it wasn't time to change after all.

Now a director of the agency, Holly knew how to work a room with confidence. But although she had become adept at handling small talk with the movers and shakers in the media, she had not forgotten the women who had stared over her shoulder when she had

45

nervously tried to join in their conversation, and the men who had waved away her platter of canapés, dismissing her like a servant, who now shook her hand warmly and loudly expressed their delight in meeting her at last.

As Holly took a scallop wrapped in bacon from a passing tray, Piers sidled up beside her.

'Why don't we slip away somewhere more comfortable?' he whispered, an inquisitive finger trying to ascertain whether she really wasn't wearing knickers.

'No, I've only just got here and, anyway, I want to see the results coming in,' she said with her mouth full and shifted her bottom away from his furtive grope.

'They're all safe Labour for the first couple of hours. If we slipped away now, we could be back in time for Edgbaston.'

'Edgbaston?'

'It's the first key marginal.'

'You're such a sweet-talking guy,' she hissed and wandered away in search of Robert, who was talking to a very handsome Irish actor who had recently appeared in a film one of her clients had written.

'Ruffled again,' Robert said, looking at her wild hair and leaning forward to give her a kiss, 'piss off, eh, darling, I rather fancy my chances,' he whispered before straightening up.

The swing in Sunderland South was eleven per cent. It was real. There was going to be a change of government. There was going to be a landslide. Even the Tory ex-cabinet minister on the television looked despondent as he insisted they reserve judgement until some more results were in.

Champagne corks started popping all over the room. For the first time in her life, Holly felt as if she were participating in a moment of history. In the future, people would ask each other what they were doing the night the Labour government swept to power and she

46

would remember this room, these people, the faint smell of red roses and cigarette smoke, this moment. Under the cover of all the celebratory kissing and hugging, Holly found herself in Piers's arms.

'Why are you crying?' he asked, stepping back quickly, as if there were a danger of contracting emotion.

'It's the first time I've voted for the winning party,' Holly told him, brushing away the tears that had surprised her as much as him. 'I think it's the first time I've had a sense of democracy being something to do with me . . .' she tried to explain.

'Do you mind if I use that?' Piers took out his notebook.

'Are you writing this party up?' She couldn't believe he wanted to lift something she had struggled to articulate and use it in an article.

'Well, the editor did ask me to do a kind of how-was-it-for-you column . . .'

'And how is it for you?' Holly demanded to know. The sharpness of her tone made several people glance in their direction.

'Well, as I said in my column last week, practically, I don't think it will make a great deal of difference,' Piers said, over-loudly, as if he were talking to a stranger.

His coldness had always both repelled and fascinated her. When she first met him, a couple of years before, at one of the lunch parties the agency occasionally threw, to which they invited a selection of current opinion-formers, she had thought him amusing, in a conceited kind of way. He had a brilliantly sharp mind but the icy, untouchable beauty of a statue.

The lunch had gone on until late in the afternoon. When the last of the other guests had drifted away, and her colleagues had gone back to their offices to pick up their messages, she had suddenly found herself alone in the circular boardroom with him. He had picked up the last claret bottle and, finding it empty, asked her if she would like to go for a drink somewhere else, and even though she instinctively did not like him, she was paradoxically flattered that he found her interesting enough to want to spend more time with.

They found a musty basement wine bar and drank a lot of armagnac, laughing a great deal at each other's wit, and a few hours later, when she took him home, at whose suggestion she had never been sure, she discovered that under a white shirt that smelt deliciously of starch his skin was smooth and warm, his body pliable, responsive to her touch.

'I'm going to get another drink,' Holly said. Piers followed her up to the kitchen at a suitably discreet distance.

'Have you noticed that everyone has a least favourite cabinet minister they're betting will lose his seat?' she asked him, pouring herself another glass of claret. 'My personal choice is Malcolm Rifkind, but there's a lot of money on Ian Lang and some optimistic punters are even having a flutter on Michael Portillo.'

'That's good,' he said, taking out his notepad again, 'that's very good.'

She wondered why, after nearly two years, she still got a buzz when he praised something she said. It was so illogical. She was a successful woman, old enough to know better, young enough to do better, a feminist for God's sake, enslaved in an affair with an arrogant, sexist shit, someone she knew was bad for her, but she couldn't seem to give up. It was a bit like smoking.

'Can I have a cigarette?' she asked Piers.

'I thought you were quitting.' He looked round quickly to check that no-one was within range of hearing such an injudiciously familiar comment.

'I am, if Labour win,' she told him.

The Labour candidate in Edgbaston was making her victory speech.

'When the people elect a German woman in a relatively safe seat, the Tories know their time's up . . . enjoy this, it may be your last,' Piers said, offering her a Marlboro, then, bringing his voice down to a whisper, 'shall we go?'

'You go if you want. I'm enjoying myself,' Holly found it gave her rather a kick to see him denied, 'anyway, I thought you were meant to be writing something about it.'

'We could always watch the television at your place . . .' Surreptitiously, he ran a finger down her spine.

'I want to be with people . . . just another hour or so,' she compromised.

The mood at the party changed from excitement to euphoria. People had become so disillusioned, Holly thought, they had not even dared to hope for a better life. And now it was being offered, they did not yet know how to greet it. It was fashionable to be negative, to say that things wouldn't change much anyway, to talk of the global economy and the powerlessness of government, but at some point between ten o'clock and one o'clock in the morning there was a subtle change of style and people started using words like renewal and regeneration as if they really meant something.

'Extraordinary evening,' Piers remarked, as they finally left the party in the early hours of the morning.

'It's like fantasy Election night,' Holly said. 'You start off thinking you'd be grateful for a narrow majority, then you're looking at a landslide, things really are going to change . . .' her eyes sparkled. 'I feel empowered . . .'

'Really?'

The short, dry sneer that normally made her feel stupid merely disappointed her. For the first time since she had known him, Piers's acute mind had failed to read the *Zeitgeist*. There had been a slight shift in the world's axis. The country had exchanged a man who spoke in a flat grey monotone for a man who grinned like a cartoon cat. In his minimalist black suit, Piers suddenly looked out of date.

They stepped out of the cab in the narrow street by the National Gallery where Holly lived. She put her key in the entrance gate then paused before turning it.

'Hey, why don't we go down to the South Bank and join the party? You could include it in your piece.'

'We haven't got invitations.'

'We can crash . . .'

'We've let the cab go,' Piers argued.

'For God's sake, it would only take us ten minutes to walk!'

'But I've only got a couple of hours before my copy has to be in.' Piers clasped her waist in his hands and kissed her there in the street.

'All right,' she said, half-annoyed, half-flattered by his open desire to have sex with her.

'Did you hear a rustle?' Piers asked as they walked up the stairs.

They both stood still and listened for a moment.

Silence.

'Maybe you've got a mouse,' Piers suggested as they continued.

'Don't,' Holly said, 'I hate mice.'

'Or a rat . . .' he said.

'Oh, I know I've got a rat.' She turned and kissed him.

They went straight to her bedroom and stripped. It seemed colder inside the flat than out. Holly jumped into bed and pulled the covers right up to her chin.

'Aren't you going to put something on?' Piers asked, pulling back the quilt, staring at her bare, goosebumpy flesh.

He meant underwear. He had started to buy her underwear just after the episode where she had threatened to stop seeing him if he couldn't promise that she was the only woman he screwed apart from his wife. It was as if he needed to assert his power again after her small victory.

At first, she had quite enjoyed receiving high-quality silk and pure cotton in pale feminine colours, wrapped in tissue paper and nestling in boxes with designer names on. She had been slightly shocked to realize that there was something erotic about putting on a slip of satin from Janet Reger costing a hundred pounds and having it ripped off ten minutes later with passionate urgency. Instead of making her feel cheap it seemed to have the opposite effect, conferring on her a curious kind of status as a high-class mistress. Now, as she rose wearily from the bed, stepped into camiknickers and hunted around in a drawer for a pair of clean stockings, it seemed a ridiculously tawdry ritual for two grown-up people to be enacting.

She got back into bed shivering with cold. Piers rolled her over and tied the corset laces tight, squeezing her ribcage, pushing her small breasts up like a serving-wench in a costume drama. He rolled her over again and began to lick the exposed flesh above her stocking-tops. Holly relaxed, waiting for the usual electric shocks of desire, but feeling nothing. After a few minutes she looked down dispassionately at her cleavage, her lace-encased tummy, Piers's head bobbing with the effort of giving her pleasure, then suddenly she pulled herself up to sitting, leaving his nose pressed against the bottom sheet.

'Piss off, Piers,' she told him.

He looked up and smiled, his eyes sparkling at the idea of a new game.

'No, I mean it. Just get out.' Her voice was calm, not aggressive, but firm. She got out of bed and pulled on a pair of jeans. 'I want to go down to the South Bank. I want to celebrate. The country's had enough of the Tories, and I've had enough of you. It's New Labour,

New Lover, I'm afraid,' she continued, rather pleased with the alliteration.

'How much have you had to drink?' he asked her, disbelievingly, suddenly looking rather vulnerable with no clothes on.

'Surprisingly little,' she told him, 'but I'm sick of sleaze,' she handed him his underpants, 'and I deserve better . . .'

Chapter 6

There was a sunset and even when the sun had dropped beyond the horizon, the sky remained red and the air retained its clement warmth. It seemed like a good omen for Labour. As it grew dark, Pepe turned the music up, and the air was filled with the smoky, aromatic smell of charcoal and marinade. Everyone was in a good mood. Even the disagreement about what colour the lights strung along the front should be – supporters of red forced to compromise with supporters of yellow on alternate bulbs to reflect the balance of political views – seemed to have floated away on a breeze of *bonhomie*. The only thing that had been overlooked was access to a television, but Mr Chan, who owned the takeaway on the front, had agreed to stay open until two and was doing brisk business.

There weren't many takers for the hamburgers Clare was turning on the giant barbecue, but her shift was almost up. In the waving orange light of a burning torch, she watched Joss flirting with her friend Olivia in a manner that suggested they had very recently had sex, or were about to. Olivia was giggling and fiddling with her hair in a way you just don't do when you have known someone many years, unless the chemistry between you has changed. She kept glancing in Clare's direction to see whether she had noticed. Odd, Clare

53

thought, spearing a charred burger with a long-handled fork, that she should be so concerned for her feelings, or perhaps it wasn't that. Perhaps adultery lost some of its pleasure when the wife was looking.

'I love your top.' Vivienne came and stood just a little bit too close to her as she always did.

'Really? It's just a T-shirt, I sewed some bits on. Had to do something . . .' Clare smiled, her eyes still fixed on her husband.

'I know what you're thinking, and I'm sure you're wrong.' Vivienne followed her gaze.

'Well, if anyone should know, it's you.' Clare meant it as a casual remark, but Vivienne flinched.

'I thought we'd got over that,' she said, in a little hurt voice, 'I thought we'd talked it all out long ago.'

Vivienne was the kind of person who thought that any problem could be solved by talking about it or applying tea tree oil.

'We did talk about it and it is a long time ago, but that doesn't cancel the fact that you slept with him,' Clare said, quite reasonably.

'I thought you'd forgiven me . . .'

'I did forgive you.' Clare was slightly irritated by the ease with which Vivienne had taken on the mantle of the wronged one. 'I'm sorry,' she said, wondering why on earth she should be the one to apologize, except that part-time work in Vivienne's shop was one of her only regular sources of income. 'I should be used to it. I should probably be flattered that my husband is so very attractive to other women . . .'

She could not hear what Joss was saying but she could see his face and she knew what it felt like to be Olivia at that moment. Sometimes, rarely these days, Joss could still make her feel like that. He could conjure a compliment from the simplest thing. He could make you feel privileged to be in his company.

'Time for me to clock on,' Vivienne suggested

over-brightly, bringing Clare abruptly back to the party.

'Are any of the results in?' Clare asked, wiping her hands.

'Yes and it really does look like a landslide, and the Liberals are doing brilliantly.'

'That's great!' Clare slipped the halter of the plastic apron over Vivienne's head as if awarding her a medal. She walked away from the barbecue, then stopped and watched the crowd from the shadows by the harbour wall, not quite knowing what to do next. She wanted someone to hug and celebrate with. It should have been Joss. Their marriage had spanned almost exactly the years of Tory rule and now it was over. But even at this most significant moment, Joss was not available for her. For a moment she felt almost unbearably lonely, then she took a deep breath and walked up the stone steps towards Mr Chan's.

'Could I just have some egg-fried rice? And a Diet Coke?'

Tending the barbecue had made her very thirsty. She sat down on one of the hard chairs to wait for her order, drinking from the can. On the television, the great and the good were arriving at the Festival Hall for the Labour victory party. The reporter was interviewing Richard Branson. Clare stared at the screen, not really seeing or hearing anything. The reporter began to wind up and the camera panned the crowd. The screen suddenly leapt sharply into focus as Clare noticed a youngish woman with a cloud of red hair tap the man in front of her on the shoulder. The man spun round, his face glowering with impatience, but when he saw who the woman was the hug he gave her was so powerful, it lifted her off her feet. They kissed each other on the cheek and walked into the building arm in arm.

'That's Jack Palmer and a companion just arriving,'

the reporter said, 'and now back to the studio . . .'

'One rice,' said Mr Chan, 'you OK?' he added, seeing the expression on Clare's face.

'Yes,' Clare said, collecting herself, '. . . I just saw my . . . someone I . . . I used to know . . .'

'You from London?' Mr Chan asked uncharacteristically warmly.

'Well, yes, a long time ago,' Clare smiled at him.

'Me too,' he said, shoving a paper bag of prawn crackers into her carrier as a kind of acknowledgement of their shared origins.

Clare thanked him and walked along the front munching the crackers, feeling stupid for ordering the rice which hung heavy in its warm foil container. She wasn't hungry, she just felt it was rude to watch his television without buying something, but the Coke would have been enough. She could have gone home to watch television, but she didn't think it was fair to accept Ella's invitation to babysit and then return hours before expected. Clare leant against the railings overlooking the beach. Most of the crowd had moved into the disco tent.

The thing that most annoyed her about Joss's infidelity, now that she had become numb to the pain, was the way it made people regard her. If she went into the tent now and he was dancing with someone, everyone would feel embarrassed on her behalf. If he wasn't there, it would look as if she was looking for him, and if she decided to dance with someone else, it would look as if she was trying to compete. Stranded between good manners and pride, Clare let one solitary tear drop, then brushed it away. It would be even worse if someone saw her crying.

'Do you think I'm the kind of mother who makes jam?' Clare asked the next morning, wiping her fingers on a tea towel.

On the kitchen table there were two dozen miniature jars with tiny linen covers tied with string. Unable to sleep, she had come down at five, after she heard Ella's boyfriend leave the house, and begun cooking while she listened to the last election results on the radio.

Ella laughed, her eyes bright and sparkling as if she had just woken up from twelve hours' sleep, not three.

'You do make very good jam,' she said, 'but no, I don't think of you like that, if that's what you mean.'

'Thank heavens for that!' Clare said, smiling at her daughter, 'Philippa had a thing about mothers who made jam. It was the ultimate put-down to be the kind of woman who made jam . . . I'm not sure why . . .' she tied the last knot and stood back to assess her work, 'what do you think?'

'I'm wondering about the string . . . I thought you usually did them with gingham.'

'Not fashionable any more, according to Amelia. Everything's got to have a natural undyed look about it. Lots of twigs, sacks, raffia, that kind of thing . . . can't make an exception for jam.'

'I'm not sure that the customers will want twigs with their cream tea.'

'Nor am I, but Amelia is my customer, and she is always right,' Clare said, lining the jars up inside a shallow cardboard box, with wodges of kitchen towel to stop them clinking together. Each customer at Amelia's tea shop received a pot of Clare's jam with their clotted cream and scones. At the height of the season that meant a hundred a week, but in early May, twenty-four would last several days. Clare ladled the rest of the jam into a large jar and stuck a date label on it.

'How was the party?' Ella asked, opening the fridge and pouring herself a glass of orange juice.

'Fine,' Clare started to wash up. When she had returned the night before, she had opened the front door into the kitchen as noisily as she could to warn the teenagers of her arrival, then dumped the rice on the kitchen table and gone straight upstairs.

'Matt said thank you for the rice. He had a terrible attack of the munchies . . .'

'Yes, I thought there was rather a distinctive smell . . .'

'You didn't mind him having a joint here?'

'It would be pretty hypocritical since Joss offers him one whenever he's around . . . do you smoke dope too?' she asked her daughter.

'Not much. I hate the way it makes you think you're saying something interesting when you're talking balls. You were home early, didn't you want to stay out?' Ella put a piece of bread under the grill to toast.

'Isn't there something slightly the wrong way round about that question?' Clare laughed.

'Didn't you want to watch the telly?'

'I thought you might want to . . .'

'Not on the sofa!'

Ella could sometimes sound incredibly prudish, which was odd for someone with a nose ring.

'Did you have a good time, anyway?' Clare asked.

'Not bad.' Ella wiped her toast round the jam saucepan and put it in her mouth.

'Things all right between you and Matt?'

'Not bad . . . actually, I think I'm a bit bored with him, does that sound terrible?'

'Not at all.' Clare knew it was best to remain neutral in such conversations. She liked her daughter's boyfriend well enough, although the fact that he had recently bleached his short hair peroxide blond made her think him rather vain. Ella was so very levelheaded, so very unlike she had been at seventeen, she never worried about her getting carried away by a boy who looked as if he should be singing with Boyzone.

'He just didn't get it last night . . . says he's not

interested in politics . . . how can you not be interested in politics?' Ella demanded to know, with the righteous zeal of the newly converted. She had been furious that she was not quite old enough to vote in this election. 'Actually, I rather fancy Tony Blair . . .'

'You and half the women in the country,' Clare teased her.

'Including you?'

'No, I think I've got past fancying men with curly hair and shiny white teeth who think they're simply marvellous . . .' Clare stopped. She hadn't meant to make so direct a comparison.

'Where is Dad, by the way?' Ella asked.

'I don't know.' Clare struggled to remain loyal. Your daughter could be your best friend in many ways, but you could not discuss her father's infidelities with her.

'I wish you'd leave him,' Ella said.

'It's not that simple, El.'

'You make most of the money in this household anyway,' Ella argued.

'It's not just a question of money,' Clare said.

'I just can't bear to think of you being miserable when I'm away . . .' Ella said.

'I won't be. I've become immune, I think,' she said, trying to make a joke.

'But it's awful for a woman of thirty-five to be immune, whatever that means,' Ella said, unwilling to be jollied away from the subject. 'You've got to get a life . . .'

'I do have a lovely life with you and Tom.'

'But that's not enough . . . and it's not fair. You have to have your own life, not just mine and Tom's,' Ella said, matter-of-factly. She picked up her bag and left for school. Upstairs, Tom woke up and started shouting.

The inadvertent cruelty of Ella's observation stung. The great irony of motherhood was that if you did everything you could to bring up your daughter to want

59

more than you, to expect better, to have the confidence to demand it, and if you were successful, your daughter despised you. But at least that was proof that you'd got something right, Clare thought, running upstairs to tend to her two-year-old son.

'Mar Me, Mar Me, Mar Me,' Tom chanted like a miniature football hooligan, leaning over the rails of his cot.

'I'm here!' Clare told him.

'Want my digger!'

'Not in bed. Let's get you up first . . .'

The moment of the day she most enjoyed was when she lifted her son, all warm and smelling of baby wee, from his cot and held him against her chest. He was just at the stage of turning from a baby to a little boy and she knew that soon he wouldn't be so willing to lie with his head upon her shoulder, his little arms tight around her neck, saying 'Hello Mar Me, how are you Mar Me?' over and over again because he liked the sound of the words. Each day she had to remind herself not to be in too much of a rush to treasure those few minutes.

Vivienne had once asked her whether Tom was an accident, and Clare had responded, with a spontaneous righteousness she had been rather proud of afterwards, that nobody who was a parent would talk about a child like that, which was slightly disingenuous, because had she known there was the slightest chance of conceiving she might well have taken precautions to prevent it. She had always wanted more children, but in one of those strange twists of fate, although she had become pregnant with Ella almost the moment Joss smiled at her, her next pregnancy miscarried, and the third and fourth were ectopic. The consultant at the hospital told her that it would be virtually impossible for her to become pregnant again naturally, and that verdict, which she had initially disbelieved, was confirmed by the barren years which followed. As Joss had put it once, 'The one thing you're good at, you can't do.'

It seemed so unfair to have given up everything to have a baby, and then not to be able to have another. She had dealt with it by channelling every ounce of her energy into being a good mother to Ella. If she was only going to do it once, she was going to get it right. Sometimes she had wondered whether it was her fault that Joss had started to be unfaithful. Ella had always been her priority.

By the time she became pregnant with Tom, conceiving another child had not even occurred to her as a possibility until one day in the hypermarket on the edge of town, she realized that she had not been down the aisle where the tampons were for several months. The odd thing was that Joss had been as thrilled and excited as she was when she told him, confounding all her expectations. The only thing you could rely on Joss to be was unpredictable, she had thought with a smile, briefly entertaining the thought that things could again be wonderful between them.

It was going to be a hot day. Clare was light-headed from lack of sleep, and feeling unusually lazy. Friday was normally her cooking day, but having already made a batch of jam, she was ahead of schedule.

'We've got a new government today,' she told her son, as she pulled off his Postman Pat pyjamas, 'so I think we ought to celebrate. Would you like to go to the beach?'

'Tom don't want to go to beach,' he said.

'Oh, I'll just have to go by myself then.' She dressed him in a stripey T-shirt and shorts.

'No, Tom want to go to beach.'

'Oh good,' she laughed and kissed him on the nose.

The tide was out, the wet sand shimmered like a mirror in the sun. The town was still asleep after the previous evening's celebrations. It felt as if they were the only people in the world. Clare sat down on the sand and tried to interest Tom in building a sandcastle next to her but all he wanted to do was run.

'Tom running!' he shouted.

She kicked off her shoes and chased after him, splashing through the shallows, until eventually they both fell down, panting.

'Mar Me laughing,' Tom said delightedly, and she realized guiltily that her face looking happy was a sight unusual enough for him to remark on. Tom looked around, as if searching for the single thing that would make the moment perfect, and announced, 'Want my digger.'

'Well, let's just see whether . . . oh, that's a bit of luck.' Clare delved into the plastic carrier bag she had brought and pulled out his favourite toy, a yellow and red digger with a shovel at the back and a bulldozer at the front. Tom's face lit up with pleasure at finding the revered object in unfamiliar surroundings. He began to scoop up sand, frowning with concentration.

A voice behind Clare said, 'Shall we build a dam?'

'Daddy!'

Neither of them had been aware of Joss approaching.

'Got a new guvvermen, Daddy,' Tom told him solemnly.

'That's right,' Joss smiled and took his son's hand and walked closer to the water's edge looking for a suitable rivulet to block.

'Here, Daddy.'

'There's no water there,' Joss said, 'I'm sure we can find a better place.'

'No, here a very good place . . .'

Men never understood that small children weren't amenable to reason. Joss seemed to think that if he argued coherently enough, Tom would suddenly see sense and agree with his choice of location. Clare lay back in the sand, pretending not to listen.

'Oh, all right then,' Joss finally capitulated, 'we'll build the damn thing here . . .'

'Tom and Daddy building dam thing,' Tom informed his mother, which made her sit up and exchange a complicit parental smile with Joss over their child's head. She found herself blushing, as if he had tricked her into inadvertent intimacy. She looked away quickly.

'I went for a long walk,' Joss said to her.

'It's a lovely morning.'

He sounded on the verge of confession and she didn't want to hear it. Especially not in front of Tom.

'I was drunk last night, I was stupid . . .' he went on.

Olivia couldn't have been what he wanted in bed, then. Clare had heard so many apologies over the years, she was weary with cynicism. Silently, she frowned at Joss, nodding significantly at Tom.

'I wanted to say I'm sorry,' he continued, oblivious to her attempts at discretion.

It made her furious that he had engineered a situation where she couldn't be angry with him because he knew she wouldn't want to upset Tom.

'I think I'll go for a walk myself,' she said, jumping up, 'will you look after him for the morning?'

'Of course.'

She walked away before either of them could see she was crying. She didn't know whether she was crying because he still had the power to hurt her, or whether they were just tears of frustration with herself. Ella was right. It would be simple enough to leave him, so why, whenever she started to think about it, did she seem to find it so frightening? There was no need to be the humiliated wife when she could be a free and independent woman.

From the railings that edged the sea front, she

watched Tom pick a stone out of the wet sand and show it to his father. Joss knelt down to inspect it and then he stood up and skimmed it out to sea. Tom needed a father. It would not be fair on him to move away, and anyway she had no money. What she managed to earn from seasonal jam-making, odd bits of cleaning and decorating other people's houses and two afternoons a week in Vivienne's shop just about kept them all. She had worked so hard on the house and the garden, it would not be easy to give it up. Alone, she could not be lonelier than she already was, but there was always the nagging doubt that she would be happier.

She had always been lonely. Her favourite fairy story when she was little had been Rapunzel. The house in Hampstead had the unusual feature of battlements at the top of the stucco front, and in her room on the top floor she had often imagined that she was in a castle. Her hair was very long, and sometimes she would try hanging her plaits out of the window to see how much longer it needed to be before a prince could use it as a golden rope to scale the building and claim her. An only child of parents who loved each other so passionately there seemed to be no love left over for her, she had dreamed of being rescued by someone who would be just hers. Years later, the moment she saw Joss with his dark curls and his sparkling eyes, her first thought had been that he looked like a prince in a book, and her fingers had automatically started twirling the long golden hair that fell around her shoulders, wondering if fairy stories really did come true.

There were still moments with Joss that glittered, then disappeared like shooting stars, tantalizing her with the thought that things might be as they were again, and making her believe that it was only her lack of understanding, or generosity, that had failed them.

In the distance Tom picked up another stone and

threw it into the sea, bending his knees and hurling it with such force in an effort to copy his father that he fell over. Joss picked him up and hugged him, brushing sand from the palms of his hands and kissing them better. What was the point of leaving him? For what? Just for the possibility of starting again with someone else who would love her more? There was no-one else who remotely interested her. The way the couples in the town periodically mixed and matched repelled her. They called it open marriage, but to Clare it had the insularity of inbreeding. She had never wanted anyone but Joss. She knew that thirty-five was too young to write herself off as a failure at love, but she was sapped of emotion. Joss had taken it all.

Chapter 7

'I've discovered the secret of going to the hairdresser,' said Holly from the doorway.

'And . . . ?' Colette was eating Harvest Crunch in Holly's kitchen.

'You have to be drunk . . .'

Colette looked up.

'You went and did it! Looks fantastic.'

Holly's curls were cropped to within an inch of her scalp.

'I went to the victory party and I bumped into Jack. We had bacon rolls at this kiosk where taxis stop for snacks . . . then he had to get home and I was walking past my hairdresser and I just went in on the off-chance and the first appointment had cancelled. Normally you have to wait three months . . . what do you think?'

'It's fantastic,' Colette said, 'it really suits you . . . I never knew you had a beautifully shaped head.'

'Thank you,' Holly touched her head, still unable to believe what she had done. 'New Labour, new haircut. Everything's changed, so I thought I would too . . .'

She was riding high on champagne and the exhilaration of being up all night. Suddenly her spirits bumped back down to earth as she registered Colette's presence properly.

'You haven't been here all night?' she asked.

Colette smiled wickedly.

'Piers,' she said, in a fake posh accent, 'no wonder you wouldn't tell me . . .'

Holly had always refused to reveal the name of her lover to anyone, preferring not to mention him at all to most people and to refer to him only as the married man or MM to Colette. She knew that if his name had been something less pretentious like Peter or Paul, she would have found it harder to be so unusually discreet.

'You were here?' she asked, unnecessarily, trying to gather her brain together to figure out what Colette must have heard.

'Fell asleep. I dashed into the bathroom when you came in. You can't hear much in there. Promise. Well, well, well, Piers eh?'

'Why didn't you go into the spare room? What would you have done if one of us had wanted a wee?' Holly wanted to know.

'I was hiding behind the shower curtain. I just bolted. I didn't have time to think of the sensible option,' Colette defended herself.

'But you can see behind the shower curtain from the loo . . .'

'Only if you're a girl . . . think about it . . . or is he the sort of man who doesn't mind having a crap in an unfamiliar bathroom?'

'What do you mean?' Holly couldn't help asking, even though she knew Colette was deliberately diverting her from her justifiable outrage.

'Well, I never do. Not until I know someone really well. Do you?'

They had been friends since they were children, but there were still things they didn't know about each other, Holly thought. Didn't want to know.

'Anyway. I finished with him,' Holly said, helping herself to cereal and looking at her watch. The euphoria of the victory, the party, the unusually hot sun outside had made her lose all sense of time. It seemed long ago that she had said goodbye to Piers, almost another life.

'I thought it was over rather rapidly . . .' Colette remarked waspishly.

'No, really finished. That's it. Finito. I really feel as if things have changed. D'you know what I mean?'

'Today is the first day of the rest of your life,' Colette mocked.

'No, really. Something *has* changed. I suddenly feel as if life is full of possibilities . . . the Tories conned us into thinking we had to just accept things as they are. But we don't. We can do something about it. I've got an in-tray this high, but I've decided to take today off work and devote it entirely to celebrating.'

'You're getting a worryingly evangelical look in your eye. Have you taken E or something?'

'No. And another thing . . .' impatiently Holly tried to think of another example. 'I'm not going to spend the rest of my life knocking back Australian chardonnay and moaning about men. I hate chardonnay as a matter of fact.'

'Why?'

'That horrible resin taste . . .'

'I meant men.'

'I'm sick of being negative. I don't need a man to make me happy. If one comes along, fine. If not, fine too.'

'Have you ever considered dating agencies?' Colette asked in a confidential tone of voice.

'God no, have you?'

'You say it like it's taboo. Apparently there are half a million people in the country who belong to them.'

'No. Half a million? Have you then?'

'In a way . . . I wondered if we should do it to-gether . . .'

'No way.' Holly's response was categorical.

'You just said you were open to anything.'

'I didn't . . . I said . . . well, I can't remember what I said quite, but I didn't mean . . .'

'But it'd be fun. We might meet someone . . .'

'We might meet some bloody weirdo . . .'

'Says the woman who's been fucking a bloke called Piers . . .'

'Oh piss off . . .'

' "Life is suddenly full of possibilities . . ." ' Colette quoted her.

'Oh shut up! Now, if you'll excuse me, I'm going for a swim. I'm going to get fit and follow a regular skincare routine.'

'All in one day?'

'I think you'll find when you get off your arse, out of my flat and onto the streets, that your attitude is completely out of date. Cynicism is very April 97 and optimism is very May. You heard it here first.' Holly slung her swimming bag over her shoulder and marched down the stairs.

The one disadvantage of living where she did was temptation. It was quicker to pop out for a cappuccino than wait for a kettle to boil, spoon in the Gold Blend and then find that she'd got no fresh milk in the fridge. Why waste time cooking when she could go out to dinner, eat better food and leave the washing-up? These were expenses that Holly found easy enough to justify to herself, and even though she did it every day, the sheer glamour of eating in restaurants had never lost its thrill for her.

Buying a new white shirt because she had forgotten all the ones that lurked in the pile of ironing waiting to be done was a bit more difficult to justify, and abandoning a swim because she happened to walk past a shop window full of clothes the colour of Love Hearts was really pushing it. But she hadn't bought anything

69

for summer yet. It hadn't been the weather for it. She fancied a pair of lilac jeans. New Labour, new wardrobe. It wasn't as if it was New Year, Holly told herself, wandering into the shop. She hadn't made a *resolution* to swim every day, so she wasn't exactly breaking it. By the time Holly got to the changing-room she had turned her initial whim to buy a few clothes into an absolute necessity.

People sometimes referred to Holly's body as rangy, which she liked because it sounded sexy, or lanky, which didn't. She was tall and slim but appeared to have a lot of angles. Even though she bought clothes almost every day, she nearly always ended up wearing jeans which suited her best.

'So you're taking the grape and the papaya,' the shop assistant's eyes widened as Holly put another pair on the pile.

'Not the kiwi?' she asked.

'Kiwi? It's not a bit like kiwi, more pistachio ice-cream,' Holly remarked, knowing exactly what the assistant would say next.

'. . . goes beautifully with your colouring . . .'

They could never resist telling a redhead to wear green. Holly had been dressed in green all her childhood. The colour made her feel sick in the same way that blackcurrant cheesecake had ever since the afternoon she had defrosted and eaten a whole one.

'I'm buying the rest of the bloody fruit bowl,' Holly said, sharply.

So that was casual sorted out, she thought, perched on a stool in a coffee-shop. Now all she needed for summer was work clothes and something for the evening. And shoes. She drank her coffee quickly, checking in the mirrored wall in front of her to see she hadn't left powdered chocolate in the corner of her mouth. There was something funny about the light, she thought, leaning closer to her reflection. It made her look as if she had very fine lines under her eyes. Holly sat up straight on her tall stool and smiled insincerely at herself in the mirror a couple of times. The lines were where her face scrunched up when she smiled. Laughter lines. The trouble was that they didn't entirely disappear when she wasn't laughing. She had never noticed them before. How long had they been there, she wondered. Maybe the haircut had not been such a good idea after all. Without a mass of curls blowing around it, her face felt very exposed. Holly gathered up her carrier bags and hailed a taxi to Knightsbridge.

'I've come to take you out to lunch.'

Mo hadn't noticed Holly walk into her department, or at least she had been keeping a watchful eye on a tall young woman with short red hair hanging around the Calvin Klein but had been too busy folding her customer's Mani suit to recognize her daughter with a new haircut.

'Turn around,' she made a circle with her hand.

Holly twirled in front of her.

'It's gorgeous.' Mo's voice was decisive.

'You really think so?' Holly's face broke into a broad grin.

'You should have had it done years ago.'

'Well, thanks.' Holly's face fell dramatically. She wanted people to like her new haircut, but was slightly alarmed by the implication that she had not looked her best for most of her adult life. 'I haven't slept, too excited, and it's so hot outside,' she began to explain her presence in the department store where Mo worked, 'so I awarded myself the day off in honour of New Labour, and I decided to change my life . . . and get some clothes for summer while I'm about it . . . trouble is – everything seems to be linen. What's the point of linen?'

'It's cool and natural,' Mo said in a helpful shop-assistant kind of way.

'It creases as soon as you look at it, and then it goes shiny and out of shape,' Holly pronounced and Mo knew better than to argue.

'I do like your hair,' Mo said, as they walked towards the escalators, 'makes you look very young.'

The haircut transformed Holly from Crystal Tipps to supermodel.

'That's one of the things I need your advice on.' Holly linked her mother's arm.

'What's that?' Mo asked.

'I think I may be getting wrinkles. I mean, how old do you have to be to start using Revlon's Age-Defying foundation?'

'Well,' Mo considered the matter carefully as they glided down to the ground floor, 'I think we should go and talk to my friend Sonya in Perfumery. But let's have lunch first.'

They went to a crowded sandwich bar in a side street just off Knightsbridge.

'I'll have Parma ham and mozzarella on grilled ciabatta,' Holly said to the nice Italian man serving.

'What a palaver for a ham and cheese toastie,' Mo joked. 'Prawn and advocado, for me, on white.'

'Mum, it's avocado,' Holly told her.

'No, is it?'

'You always say that and you never take any notice. I mean, look, where's the d?' She pointed at the menu painted on the wall above the counter.

'Well, it's Italian.'

There were some words that Mo always got wrong and it didn't seem to bother her. It didn't bother Holly like it used to. She had spent the first few years after leaving home trying to improve her elocution, then East End accents had become fashionable.

'I bumped into Jack,' Holly said, as they pushed

72

back through the queue towards a little round table on the pavement outside, 'he flew back to London to celebrate . . .'

'There was something in the paper about people who said they'd leave if Labour won and people who said they'd come back – as if anyone cared what he'd do!' Mo said. 'Still, that never stopped him telling anyone who'd listen . . .'

'Well, he is one of the most successful British film directors ever,' Holly rose immediately to Jack's defence. 'I think people do care. I think it was an important thing to say . . .'

'Oh well, if you say so,' Mo said, taking a bite of her sandwich and looking at her daughter. At times, Holly was so much Jack's child with her fiery colouring and the temper to go with it. She had exactly that way he had of swinging from pleasant to outraged in one go, with no build-up through irritated, annoyed, angry, on the way, and her blue eyes had exactly the same gleam, challenging anyone who dared to contradict her.

'He's asked me out to dinner with him tonight at the Ivy,' Holly announced.

'Oh good,' Mo remarked neutrally.

'Want to come? He said to ask . . .' She leaned forward and took Mo's hand across the table.

'No, I don't think so. Nice of him though. Send him my best . . .'

'Why won't you come?' Holly demanded to know.

Mo was sure Holly would have stamped her foot if she had been standing up.

'There's a Country and Western evening at the club . . .'

Mo's social life revolved around the Irish club. She taught Irish dancing there once a week and her boyfriend, Eamon, who was a postman during the day, was the bartender a couple of evenings a week.

Sometimes Holly could almost understand why her

father had abandoned Mo all those years ago. It wasn't just that she was ordinary, it was that she was so content to be ordinary. Not that she didn't have many extraordinary qualities, she reminded herself guiltily.

'Oh go on, you'd enjoy it . . .' she tried to cajole.

'No, and I can be just as stubborn as you,' Mo said, wiping the corners of her mouth on a paper napkin. She never saw Jack in public. What could he have been thinking of, inviting her too?

'Why?' Holly demanded a better explanation.

'I told you, I'm going to the club. There's a Country and Western evening . . .'

'Honestly Mum . . .'

'You said you liked Country and Western . . .'

'Only ironically . . .'

'I don't see the difference. How can you like something ironically and not like it really?' Mo wanted to know. 'Seems silly to me.'

'But you can go there any time,' Holly said, trying another tactic.

'You can go to the Ivy any time, but it doesn't stop you going.'

'True,' Holly admitted. The logic was irrefutable if you left out the fact that the Ivy did great food and Jack Palmer was very good company, unlike the club and Eamon. But she knew Mo also knew these things.

'I'm not going to argue with you,' she said, resignedly.

'Bloody hell!' Mo teased her, 'you must be getting old!'

'Just a few crow's-feet and we should be able to arrest the development of the wrinkles with this cream,' Sonya said, smearing some onto Holly's tilted face, 'it's got fruit AHAs . . .'

Sonya was wearing a white coat. She looked like an over-made-up dental nurse and she spoke several decibels too loudly because she was used to doing demonstrations on willing victims with nothing better to do than kill half an hour on the ground floor of a department store.

'If I just give you some of the night cream, a simple cleanser and moisturizer, and an exfoliating scrub to use once a week, you should be fine . . .'

The trouble was, she wasn't giving it. The sub-total was over eighty pounds, Holly calculated, and rising.

'And just because it's you,' Sonya added with a bright coral smile, 'I'll give you the complimentary vanity bag, exclusive to this store, that really goes with two purchases from the make-up range. It includes a weekend-size eye-refreshing balm, two matt shadows and a mini-mascara.'

'How generous,' Holly said, wishing she had never sought advice.

In her heart she knew that she would use the miraculously non-greasy contents of the frosted bottles once or twice before abandoning them on the top of the cupboard in her bathroom where they would gather dust until the contents began to separate and either Mo, or Colette on one of their exasperated unsolicited cleaning binges, would throw them away.

'The trouble is they never do seem to make the visible difference they say they will,' Holly whispered to her mother as they escaped from Sonya's singsong mantra.

'Perhaps you never use them long enough,' Mo argued.

'This morning I was absolutely determined to, you know, New Labour, New Skincare and all that . . .'

Mo looked mystified.

'. . . but Sonya's made me a bit depressed. I mean crow's-feet? I've gone straight from youthful com-plexion to crow's-feet without passing laughter lines. I thought these were laughter lines,' she wailed, pointing at the corners of her eyes.

'As a matter of fact, I couldn't see what she was talking about . . .' Mo said, as they reached the escalator.

'Even under that Nazi interrogation lamp?'

'No.'

Holly hugged her mother so tight, she almost picked her off the ground.

'Every girl should have a mother like you,' she said, 'it'd put the cosmetics industry into recession.'

'What are you going to do now?' Mo asked, blushing pink, but clearly pleased to be so publicly loved.

'I thought I might drop my bags back at the flat and go visit the new incumbents of Number Ten, cheer them in, I mean,' Holly said, kissing her mother good-bye.

When Holly had first moved into the flat, after answering an ad in the *Evening Standard*, two other people lived there too. She had been at the bottom of the hierarchy with the smallest room and bathroom-cleaning duties. The other tenants came and went, but Holly stayed, and after a couple of years she had the biggest room along with the responsibility for paying the bills and advertising for new flatmates. As her career progressed, she found she could afford not just the biggest room, but the little one at the back too, which became a kind of cupboard for all the stuff she didn't want in the big room. And when that filled up, and yet another flatmate moved out to take up a mortgage on yet another dingy one-bedroom flat in Tooting, Holly took over their room too, and so, without really thinking about it, she had the whole flat to herself. Most of the time she liked living on her own, knowing that the grime on the draining-board was her grime and that if there was no toilet paper it was because she hadn't bought any, but just sometimes, when she put her key in the lock at the end of the day, she longed for someone inside to call out 'Hi! Had a good day?' and offer her a glass of terrible white wine.

Holly dumped her cardboard carrier bags in the middle of her bed and changed out of her blue jeans into the pale orange ones the assistant had called papaya. She pulled a white Gap T-shirt over her head, and clipped a pair of enormous plastic daisies onto her ears. She had bought the earrings on her last trip to Los Angeles, but never worn them because, she realized, with long hair, they had made her look like an overgrown seven-year-old. With short hair and a pair of white plastic sunglasses they looked rather American retro, she decided, doing a hand jive in front of the mirror.

A quick flick through the TV channels showed that Tony Blair's car was on its way to Downing Street. She wasn't sure whether she could hear the sound of crowds cheering outside, or on the television. Holly grabbed a couple of notes from her purse, shoved them into the back pocket of her new jeans, slammed the door behind her and hurtled down the stairs to the courtyard, almost crashing into Simon in her haste.

'You're home early,' she said breathlessly, not wanting to stop and chat.

'Is that label meant to be sticking out at the back of your neck?' he asked.

'No.' Holly craned her neck as Simon manfully wrestled with the stubbornly strong plastic filament that attached the price tag to her new T-shirt.

Simon had lived in the courtyard almost as long as Holly had, both of them refusing to join the mad rush to buy property that had left almost everyone else in their age range with negative equity and a subsiding house in Willesden or Stoke Newington, or some other area of London that was supposed to be on the point of coming up, but never somehow did. Holly had never wanted to move because she thought you only got that lucky once. A flat right in the centre of town, within spitting distance of the best Chinese restaurants and all the major cinemas, just didn't happen in London. It happened in New York and in the movies. She sometimes felt she was living in a kind of 1990s *Breakfast at Tiffany's*, the film after which she had been named. Except that unlike Audrey Hepburn, none of the men she slept with gave her money for the powder-room.

Simon was the George Peppard character in the film. Simon was the boring guy downstairs (except that Simon lived across the courtyard). Simon was Holly's sensible, good-looking-in-a-conventional-kind-of-way admirer, who always had a sachet of Resolve to help her with her hangover. Simon had not joined the property-buying lemmings of the Eighties because he had bought a small yacht and he spent most of his weekends sailing. Simon was what Mo would call 'lovely boyfriend material'.

'Where are you off to?' he asked.

'Downing Street!'

'Why?'

'The Blairs are about to arrive. I want to be there. I don't know why exactly. I just want to be part of it . . .'

'Oh, I see what you mean. Mind if I come along?'

'Of course not,' Holly told him, wishing there was time for him to change out of his very old Conservative-looking suit and into some New Labour jeans, but there wasn't.

'You've had your hair cut!' Simon suddenly exclaimed as they strolled across Trafalgar Square, as if he had been trying to figure out what the difference was.

'Like it?' she asked, pirouetting in front of him.

78

'It's very short. But I expect I'll get used to it,' Simon said with a smile, and the fact that he thought that even approached an acceptable response was proof, if proof were needed, that Simon was most definitely not a man Holly would ever dream of dating.

Chapter 8

On the top of the cliffs there was a strong breeze that blasted Clare's hair away from her face. The sea was deep blue and choppy, with white horses appearing and disappearing like random brush-strokes of bright white paint on ink. On the horizon there were three yachts with white sails, triangle boats as Tom called them. Close to the shore a windsurfer was struggling to pull his bright pink sail out of the water. Looking at the sea gave her a rush of confidence. The sea changed all the time and made her think that she could change too.

Today everything seemed to be touched with a kind of momentousness. The whole nation had decided on change. And she had been part of that. For the first time in eighteen years, she realized, her vote had meant something. The childish wish Joss had teased her for had been granted. And then her father had popped up on television like the materialization of a thought she had not been aware of thinking. Curiously, she had not felt anger, or resentment, when she saw him, only a sensation that welled then disappeared, and felt oddly like fondness.

Clare walked along the clifftop path. There were dandelions in the long grass and soon red campion would dance in the hedgerows. In Cornwall at this time of the year two realms of beauty touched one another:

the minutely detailed world of the wild flowers, tiny pink-dipped daisy petals, speedwells like pinpoints of bright blue light in the pale wheat-grass, and above, the huge dome of sky, where vast clouds metamorphosed in the blue drift of wind.

Clare sat down on a hillock tufted with clover absorbing the magnificence of the sky.

After a few minutes she became aware that someone was walking up the field behind her.

'I thought you might be up here,' Ella said.

'Oh?' Clare patted the ground next to her.

'It's where you come when you want to think,' Ella said, sitting down.

'Is it? No lessons this afternoon?'

'It's only lunch-time. I had a yoghurt.'

'Is it only lunch-time?'

'Get a grip, Mum.'

'It's because I've been up so long today . . .' Clare laughed and lay back in the springy turf.

'What were you thinking about?' Ella wanted to know.

'I was thinking about my father, actually. I saw him on television last night.'

Ella looked around at her as if she had gone completely mad.

'No, really. Just for a moment. He was going into the Labour victory party.'

'I thought he lived in the States.'

'I thought so too.'

'I was worried about you,' Ella said, lying back beside her mother.

'I'm all right, El,' Clare said, staring at the sky, her arm across her forehead to shade the brightness, 'I know it's not perfect, but we have a good life. You mustn't worry about me. I'm responsible for the choices I make . . .'

Ella was almost exactly the same age as she had been

81

when she left home. In some ways her daughter was so much more mature than Clare had been then, but in others she was still young, young enough to think she had the power to make things right if she wanted to enough. Clare hoped that life was not going to be too much of a disappointment for her. Ella was going to be a doctor. She would be a marvellous doctor, but people in her care would die, through no fault of hers. It was going to be hard to watch her fierce idealism give way to the blunting disillusion of experience.

'How did you feel?' Ella asked.

'About what?'

'Seeing your father.'

'I was trying to work that out, just now. I don't really know what I felt . . . a bit strange . . .' Clare said, 'he looked softer than I remember. He was with a woman and he looked, well, happy. I don't remember him as ever looking spontaneously happy. Triumphant, yes. Perhaps he's mellowed . . .'

'Perhaps you've mellowed,' Ella suggested.

'What do you mean?'

'Well, you must have been pretty spiky to just walk out . . . it was a very confident thing to do.'

'Was it? I suppose it was. I certainly didn't think of it like that at the time . . .' Clare had always thought of herself as a coward for not standing up to him. She remembered standing in silence absorbing his rage like a punchbag, and when he had finished, picking up her canvas bag and walking out of the house for ever.

'Who was the woman?' Ella asked.

'What woman?'

'You said your father was with a woman,' Ella sighed impatiently, 'honestly, Mum, you're just not with it today . . .'

'I don't know. Much younger than him . . . I wonder if Philippa knows . . . I wonder what she thinks about the new government . . .'

'I bet she loves it.'

'Do you think so? She was a great supporter of Margaret Thatcher, you know.'

'Philippa loves whatever's in fashion,' Ella said.

It was a perceptive remark. Clare remembered Philippa's reaction when she told her she and Joss were going to live in Cornwall on a smallholding and try to be self-sufficient.

'But it's the beginning of the Eighties,' she had said, dismayed, 'people did that in the Sixties . . .' The rights or wrongs of the way of life had not concerned her, it was out of date and that was a cardinal sin.

'I'd better be getting back,' Ella said, looking at her watch.

'Me too,' Clare said, linking her arm through her daughter's.

By the time she reached the house, Joss and Tom were back and were eating chips in front of the television.

'Your mother rang,' Joss told her.

'Philippa?'

'How many mothers do you have?'

'How weird,' Clare said, 'we were just talking about her.'

She sat down on the sofa watching the crowds outside Downing Street.

'Isn't it lovely?' she said, delighting in the joy on people's faces as Tony Blair pressed hands with the enthusiasm of a novice and the camera-awareness of a well-trained professional.

'They're all New Labour plants, you know,' Joss told her, 'they've been given those flags by the PR guys.'

The Blairs posed on the doorstep of 10 Downing Street. They were the perfectly proportioned family. Watching them waving to the cheering crowd brought a lump to Clare's throat. She picked up Tom and his digger from the floor and hugged him tight.

'That's our new Prime Minister,' she told him, pointing at the television.

'I wonder how long they debated what clothes the kids should wear,' Joss remarked, 'to make them look so relaxed and informal . . .'

Oh don't spoil it, she wanted to say, but she didn't think she could bear to get into an argument. Joss was so critical she often wondered what would happen if he ever got what he wanted. He wouldn't know what to do. His whole *raison d'être* was negative. It occurred to her suddenly that Joss did not after all want to change the world, he just wanted to criticize endlessly.

Her father had known what Joss was like immediately. Clare wondered why her thoughts kept going back to him.

'He's the sort of man who thinks the world owes him a living,' he had told her, after their one and only meeting, 'and he won't make anyone happy . . .'

'He does make me very happy,' she had replied, smiling triumphantly, and for a long time after that she had not let herself admit that she was anything else, unable to bear the idea of her father being right.

The Blairs gave a final wave and stepped over the threshold of their new home.

'Philippa sounded a bit upset,' Joss suddenly remarked.

'Oh?' That was unlike Philippa. Even if she was capable of being upset, she would never allow her voice to betray it. Perhaps Jack was leaving her. He had looked radiant with that young woman at the Festival Hall. But she doubted her mother would even ring her to tell her that. Every couple of years or so, Philippa booked herself a weekend in the best hotel in the area and dropped in to see them for a day. At Christmas, and on the children's birthdays, a Federal Express van would stop outside the cottage and the driver would walk up the garden path to deliver large boxes containing presents and clothes for the children, like hugely expensive aid packages from Hamleys or Harrods. Even more rarely, Philippa rang, but they never discussed Jack or what their relationship was these days. He lived most of his life in LA and Philippa in London but they always appeared together at film premières. Clare assumed that they were as besotted with each other as they had ever been. If you had money, then distance didn't really matter these days, did it? It had never even occurred to her they might now have other people in their lives.

Clare went into the kitchen and picked up the phone, hesitating for a second before dialling. Afterwards, she realized she must have somehow known that the call was going to change her life. At the time she put the strong sense of presentiment down to the events of the day.

'Philippa, it's Clare.'

'Darling, he's dead,' Philippa said. Her voice was surprised, as if she had said the words over and over but could not make them sound true.

'Who?'

'Jack. He died this morning.'

Chapter 9

'Well,' said Holly, 'that was fun. Completely staged of course, but this lot really know how to put on a good show . . .'

The cheering had finally subsided and the crowds with their Union Jacks and red roses were beginning to wander away dazed, not quite knowing what to do next.

'D'you fancy a drink before dinner?' Simon asked, as they pushed their way back up Whitehall.

'I'd love a drink . . . where?'

'I've got a bottle of Bollinger in the fridge.'

'Have you?' Simon occasionally had a few cans of Stella Artois. Bollinger seemed so unlike him. 'Well, let's go and drink it immediately,' Holly said.

Simon rewarded her with a huge smile. He really looked nice when he smiled like that, Holly thought, with his eyes all scrunched up.

'So how's things in the world of broking?' Holly asked him ten minutes later as she lolled in his comfortable but beige sofa.

'It's underwriting. I haven't been a broker for over five years.'

'But it's still Lloyds, isn't it?' Holly tried to cover her mistake. She had never really understood what Simon did and whenever she asked him she found her mind wandering around about the second sentence of explanation.

'Well, yes, but . . .'

'All right, perhaps I should have said how's the world of insurance?'

'It's fine, thank you. More champagne?'

'It's a bit unusual for you, champagne, isn't it?' Holly asked.

'It's my birthday,' Simon said.

'Oh God,' Holly reeled with guilt, 'I am so sorry . . . what with the election and everything . . . oh no, we were meant to be going out for dinner, weren't we?'

'We were . . .'

'It's just that my father's in town and, oh, look, can we just forget today and pretend it's your birthday next time we see each other . . . please . . . I'll take you out to any restaurant you want?'

Simon looked at her very crossly, and then his face softened and he smiled.

'All right,' he said.

'You're thinking I'm incredibly selfish, aren't you?' said Holly.

'Yes,' he said, 'but it's OK.'

Afterwards Holly didn't know how she would have heard the news if she hadn't been unable to resist turning on the television to see whether she and Simon had been picked out by the cameraman in the celebrating crowds outside Downing Street. How long would she have waited for Jack at his table in the Ivy? Would a waiter have taken pity on her, or would they simply have asked for the table back for the second sitting? If she had to be told by someone who didn't know her, better an anonymous newsreader than an embarrassed *maître d'*, she thought later, with the weird hypothetical reasoning of the bereaved.

The ironic thing was that she *was* on television, four

times in all that evening, although it was only on the third playing that she recognized herself. The same clip of the moment she had surprised Jack the evening before was shown again and again. It was incomprehensible to see him so alive and yet to keep being told that he was dead. At one point she thought that she must have died as well, as she sat in her darkening bedroom watching herself embrace her father on the flickering screen.

'And finally, some sad news tonight. Jack Palmer, film director and prominent supporter of New Labour, died today of a heart attack. Palmer, pictured here at the South Bank in the early hours of this morning, began his career in advertising but moved on to directing films in the early 1980s. He was fifty-nine . . .'

Holly picked up her handbag and took out a packet of cigarettes. As she lit up she realized that it was her first of the day.

Chapter 10

'I simply cannot understand why you're going,' Joss said later, as Clare hunted for a sponge bag in the chest of drawers in their bedroom.

'Well, nor can I exactly, but I just feel I need to,' she replied.

'Middle-class guilt.'

'Joss, there's absolutely nothing middle-class about it, and even if there were, so what? We are middle-class, actually. I know you don't like to be reminded of it, but you're a vicar's son.'

Your father is still alive was the unspoken implication, don't tell me what to do about mine who is dead.

'Are you all right?' Joss asked, more kindly, surprised at the firmness of her tone. 'I mean, how do you feel about it?'

Clare sat down on the bed and pushed her hair back from her forehead.

'I feel very peculiar,' she told him honestly, focusing on the photograph of Ella in a meadow of ox-eye daisies that she had taken of her when she was about five, 'not exactly sad. It's more selfish than that. I feel that my life was one way, and now it's completely different. It's as if my history has changed. I used to wonder what I would feel if he died, not recently, long ago . . . I didn't think I would feel anything. I do, but I'm not certain what it is . . .'

'I feel rather guilty myself,' Joss said.

'You? Why?'

'I took away his only child,' he said, 'I saw Ella looking at me this evening and I thought I knew how Jack must have felt. You know how she sometimes looks just like me? It was like holding a mirror to my face and hating what I saw . . . she is the age you were when I . . .'

'You didn't take me away. I left,' Clare interrupted, impatiently, surprised by how much she resented the denial of her personality contained in his melodramatic statement of guilt. Why did everything have to be something to do with him? Except the things he did wrong, of course, which were always, somehow, the fault of irresistible urges that swept him along in their wake.

'I wonder how I'd feel if someone took Ella away,' Joss went on, oblivious to her annoyance.

'Ella is her own person. If she went, then it would be her decision. Anyway, she is going. I don't know why we're talking about it.' Clare got up and pretended to be looking for something in the chest of drawers, hoping he would leave their bedroom. His presence seemed to fill the room and she wanted to be by herself. She felt brittle, as if she would snap if touched. Don't you notice how she ignores you, she wanted to ask him. Don't you realize that your behaviour has driven her away already?

'When are you going then?' Joss stood up.

'Tomorrow. I'll stay till the funeral.'

'That's nearly a week.'

'There's everything you need in the freezer . . .'

'I meant that we will miss you . . .' he protested, and as she turned, flustered, he hooked his forefinger gently under her chin and tilted her face towards him.

90

She felt herself blush.

'You will take care of yourself . . .'

Sometimes his voice sounded just the same as it had in the darkness of the student common room after they had made love for the first time. Joss was very attractive to look at, but it was the softly resonant masculinity of his voice that made him irresistible. An unrequested warmth began to spread through the lower half of her body and, as if he could sense the ebbing of her resistance, he kissed her mouth, pushing her gently back into the pillows, and kissed her again. Then he knelt on the counterpane, his legs astride her waist, and looked at her, his eyes exploring her as thoroughly as if they had just met.

Chapter 11

The Central Line carriage was empty until Bank, when three sweaty young men in suits got in and flopped into the seats opposite Mo. It was only then that she became aware that she had been staring at her own reflection in the dark glass of the opposite window, watching the woman she saw there without recognizing herself.

The men were drunk and happy.

'New Labour, new bloody bonus, mate,' one of them said, eliciting a cheer from the others. They were Thatcher's boys, but a record day on the Stock Exchange had converted them to Blairites in less than twenty-four hours.

'Cheer up, love, it may never happen,' the one with cropped hair bleached like Gazza's said, not unkindly, leaning towards Mo.

To her surprise, she found herself laughing.

'It just bloody has,' she said.

They laughed along too.

Stop it. Mo tried to control herself. She was feeling everything wrong. Sitting there paralysed by pent-up anger then laughing like a bloody hyena. Jack is dead. It's not bloody funny. The laughter stopped as abruptly as it had begun and the anger flooded back. Why did he have to die? Why was he always leaving her?

Mo decided to get off at Tottenham Court Road and walk to Holly's flat. It wouldn't take much longer than changing onto the Northern Line and she needed some air. The City brokers blew her vodka kisses as she stepped out of the carriage.

Underground, London was more or less the same as it had been when she and Jack had arrived at the beginning of the Sixties. The escalators and ticket halls were all in the same places. The adverts were different now, of course. Bolder, funnier and that was partly down to Jack. He'd seen the potential of it like nobody else, probably because he and Mo had come down from Manchester, where there was no underground. It's the ultimate captive audience, he'd explained one evening, rehearsing a campaign strategy for her as she ironed his shirt for the next day: you've got bored people, half-asleep, who want a bit of entertainment. If you can engage them, make them laugh, they're going to like you.

Jack was good at getting people to like him. Jack was the man who put a strawberry on the bowl of cereal in the picture on the packet. Nobody really eats their cornflakes with strawberries, he'd said, but then nobody has a sunny balcony where they have their breakfast either. The point is they like to think that one day they will attain that sort of life, and in the meantime, they can afford to have the cereal that goes with it.

Above ground, London had changed. The department store where Mo had first worked was now a mall with neon lights, artificial palms in pots and the same shops that appeared in every mall all over the country. Tie Rack, Next, Gap. You could buy the same here as you could in Manchester, which seemed a bit sad to Mo although she wasn't sure why. She always felt nostalgic when she walked past the place that had been Bourne and Hollingsworth. It hadn't been much of a job, demonstrating worksavers for the kitchen, but she had been so excited to get it, and there had been plum crumble and custard in the staff canteen.

Now, what on earth had made her remember that? Mo shook her shoulders, trying to pull herself together. Jack was dead and all she seemed to be able to concentrate on were silly things. Plum crumble! Jack was dead. It couldn't be true, could it? She wanted to stop someone and ask them, am I dreaming? There were crowds of young people and they all seemed to be talking into mobile phones. They wouldn't know. They would think she had gone mad.

Mo turned off Oxford Street and walked through Soho Square. The tall trees made it very dark. The square had always frightened her, she didn't know why. She remembered running across it, hearing the clatter of her steps echoing round the deserted office buildings, reaching the top of Greek Street breathless and relieved, as if it were home in a game of dare she played with herself. Now she walked calmly, but she could still feel her heart racing at the slightest movement in the shadows.

Soho had changed. Better really. It was full of cafés that smelled of freshly-ground coffee and sold cakes that made you fat just looking at them. No more porn shops and dodgy-looking derelicts in raincoats. Just beautiful young men these days and restaurants. Mo stopped at the end of the street where she and Jack had lived. It was a tiny street. Most people never noticed it even if they walked past every day. They had a room with bare boards, a bed and a Baby Belling, but you could squeeze out of the window into the gulleys between the pitched roofs and see all the tops of the theatres. It was a make-believe life. They had pretended to the landlady that they were married. They had pretended to be warm when they had no money for the meter. They had pretended not to hear the mice at night. But they had been happy. She had, anyway. She had never known when the exact moment was that Jack had decided to go nor how long he had lived with her, making love to her, knowing he was going to be leaving. It was something she always meant to ask him later, but never quite got up the courage. It would have been worse to hear that he didn't remember, and she wasn't sure whether she would have trusted his answer if he did. And now she would never know. Mo stared up through the orange vapour of neon into the darkness. The building was still there but you couldn't see their window. It was at the back. Perhaps it wasn't there at all, she thought. Perhaps she had made that up too.

Mo crossed Shaftesbury Avenue and walked through Chinatown, breathing in the steam of broth and the wafts of hot air perfumed with five-spice. There were so many people milling around these days. At the beginning of the Sixties there had only been a couple of Chinese restaurants. Nowadays, people casually dropped fifty pounds for a meal for two. Then it had been an event. She remembered precisely the moment she had savoured her first morsel of sweet and sour pork, her surprised remark that it tasted like jam and vinegar. Then the look of dismay on Jack's face as his colleagues from the agency sniggered into their chop suey. It was one of those moments of acute embarrassment when she had wondered how it was that Jack just knew what to say and she hadn't a clue. Years later, she had felt a tiny jolt of triumph when she discovered from a recipe in *Woman* magazine that her guess about the ingredients had been almost exactly right.

Mo stopped walking, shaking with shame and anger as she stared at the bundles of pak choi outside a Chinese grocer's shop. Why couldn't he have stuck by her about the sweet and sour pork? He was always pulling rank with his bloody working-class background, but truth be told he hadn't been able to leave it behind fast enough.

He had said sorry, she reminded herself, breathing deeply, trying to calm herself as she continued on down Wardour Street. Sorry for the way he had behaved, but not until years later. And she had replied that it was all right, she understood. But now she regretted giving him a blanket of absolution to cover all the little wounds he had inflicted so casually, which had taken so long to heal. And she was angry with herself for being so weak, even though it didn't matter any more.

'I wish I'd shouted at him. I wish I'd given him bloody hell,' Mo said as Holly let her into the flat. She sat down on a hard kitchen chair, her handbag on her lap.

Holly was taken aback. It wasn't like Mo to swear.

'I wish you'd told me he died,' Holly said quietly, sitting down opposite her.

Both held their backs stiffly upright, as if trying to make their bodies impenetrable against pain.

'I didn't know until the ten o'clock news . . .'

'Not now, I don't mean today,' Holly said impatiently. 'Then. When I was little. I wish you'd told me he was dead . . .'

'I thought about it,' Mo admitted, 'it just didn't seem right.'

Holly shot an infuriated glance at her mother, but seeing how pale she was, how debilitated, she felt the tension of anger subside. It was Mo's loss too, she reminded herself. She got up to put on a kettle. She wasn't sure she had a tea bag in the house, but she needed something to do, some ritual to perform. They couldn't just sit there.

'I used to make up the dad I wanted,' Holly said, turning on the tap, 'he was always changing when I discovered something more exciting for him to do . . . one week he would be an astronaut, the next a film director. And then I met him. And then he *became* a bloody film director. I could never get over that. Sometimes it was like I *had* really made him up . . . and now it doesn't seem like he ever existed really. I hear about his death along with millions of other people and I'm there on television like bloody Forrest Gump appearing in a bit of newsreel as a bystander to a historical event . . .' Her voice, which had been calm and controlled, began to wobble. She stretched her hand behind her and Mo took it.

'I didn't want to lie to you,' Mo told her, 'and there was always that chance that I'd run into him or you would . . .'

Jack had left Mo just before Christmas 1960, the Christmas she had spent crying and wandering by the river trying to decide whether to jump in. He had appeared in her life again at Christmas eleven years later.

She was working in Children's Clothes. They'd moved her up from Haberdashery because they were short-staffed. She had often wondered whether she would have set eyes on him again if she had stayed at her usual counter. She couldn't imagine Jack ever buying a card of hooks and eyes, or a reel of cotton.

It was so busy in the department, she hadn't noticed him until he came to pay. She was on the till and there was a queue. There was no way of avoiding him.

'Mo?' he'd said, unbelieving.

'Hello Jack.'

'I thought . . . I assumed . . . you'd gone back home . . .'

'Well you were wrong.' Mo placed a piece of tissue paper on the dress, and began to fold it. It was an expensive rustly dress of ice-blue satin with a net crinoline and a sash.

'Well, what do you think?' Jack asked her, trying to appear unruffled.

'About what?' Empowered by his obvious discomfort, she looked him directly in the eye. She could sense the manager of the department hovering behind her, waiting to pounce on any further slide towards insolence.

'The dress,' Jack said, looking down at it.

'It's beautiful,' Mo told him, sweetly, unable to resist adding, 'not at all what my little girl would like of course, but very pretty, very *appropriate* . . .' She knew the word would annoy him. She felt rather pleased with herself. She had often rehearsed all the things she would say to him if they ever had a chance encounter, but she had never imagined them in a situation where other people might be listening. In the circumstances, she thought she was doing rather well.

'You have a little girl? How old is she?' Jack asked pleasantly.

'She's ten,' Mo replied without thinking.

'What would she like then?' he enquired, handing over the cash.

'Oh, something fashionable, you know how they are . . .' She gave him the receipt and change and swung the bag over to his side of the counter.

'Right.'

'Can I help you, sir?' Mo had turned to the next man in the queue who handed over a miniature green and red tartan kilt with a matching red jumper.

Jack had been waiting for her outside the staff entrance that evening. It was freezing cold. The thin soles of her court shoes stuck momentarily to the pavement with each step. His smile was so dazzling it turned her insides upside down for a second before caution returned.

'You're looking good, Mo,' he said, falling in with her step.

'Why are you here, Jack?' She wouldn't look at him.

'Could we have a coffee somewhere?'

'I don't think so.'

'A drink?'

'No.'

'Oh come on, Mo,' he grabbed her arm. She stopped walking for just one moment, staring at his hand on her coat. He withdrew it.

'Are you married, Mo?' he asked, looking at her gloveless, ringless, left hand.

She should have known not to underestimate Jack, she realized then.

'There's a pub up there,' she pointed across Knightsbridge. 'Not very nice. And I'm only having one,' she told him, trying to regain control of the situation.

She told him about Holly over Britvic Orange topped up with lemonade. There was no point in pretending. He'd already guessed, and if he hadn't, then he soon would. In the moments that followed her revelation, his expression changed from angry to delighted to ashamed.

'You should have told me,' he said eventually.

'And what would you have done?' she asked him.

'I don't know,' he said, sighing and putting down his empty pint glass, paying her the compliment of not lying, 'I just don't know.'

'Well, here we are then,' Mo had said, surprised by how good she felt. It was a relief that he knew, 'And now I must be getting back.'

'Yes,' he said, putting up no fight.

She left him sitting staring at the little round table with its puddle of beer, but at the door he was behind her again.

'When can I see her?'

'Jack, you can't. It wouldn't be fair on her . . .'

'I don't agree.'

'Think about it.'

He had let her be for a week. She was surprised. It made her feel more kindly towards him. Then, when he appeared again, she kicked herself for forgetting how he could break down your defences when he wanted to.

'I've thought about it,' he had said, simply, categorically. Mo could lay down the ground rules, but he was not going to be denied access to their daughter.

'If I had said you thought he was dead, it wouldn't have made any difference, Mo told Holly, 'it would just have made him more determined.'

She looked up and saw her daughter nodding.

'I wonder when the funeral will be,' Holly said.

'We can't go . . .' Mo said.

'I'm going,' Holly said. She shot Mo a glance that was pure Jack. She had the same pale blue eyes.

PART TWO

One Week Later

Chapter 12

Jack Palmer's funeral had given everyone who was anyone the excuse to go out and buy the season's little black suit and the weather was perfect for the kind of wide-brimmed black straw hat that would have been over the top in winter and disastrous in rain. The women were wearing bright red lipstick and tragic expressions, the men skulked around in charcoal grey, exchanging tight little smiles of relief that they had not been the first of their generation to die.

Holly stared at the coffin and its flawless arrangement of white lilies as the pallbearers dragged it out of the hearse, trying to feel appropriate emotions, but her mind kept returning to the troubling thought that he might not be in there at all. How often did undertakers cock it up, she wondered, how often did they bury people who wanted to be cremated or take the wrong box to the wrong funeral?

She stood holding the little hand-tied bunch of bluebells and ivy in front of her like a bridesmaid, then swapping it into her left hand, casually, so that it wasn't quite so visible. It was her first funeral. She hadn't known that you sent flowers, you didn't bring them along with you. It didn't matter, she told herself. She wanted to feel that she was giving them to him. They were his favourite flowers. It was one of the things he had told her the first day they went out alone together in his red E-type Jag. Holly had phoned six florists before finding one who was prepared to get them for her, and they had cost a fortune.

One of the crematorium officials, a rotund man with a nice smiley face, took her aside as they were going into the chapel and asked her if she would like him to put the posy with the other floral tributes. She smiled gratefully at him.

'Not with,' she whispered, 'just a little bit apart, so they don't get swamped?'

'They'll have pride of place,' he whispered back in friendly conspiracy.

An actor Jack had worked with several times did the oration. It was further proof, Holly thought, that Jack wasn't in the coffin at all, because if he had been, however dead he was, he would have bellowed 'cut!' after the first sentence. The actor wasn't talking about Jack. You couldn't say Jack was marvellous, generous and visionary, without also saying he was difficult, mean, and bloody-minded. The actor was playing his role rather well, pitching it somewhere between *Julius Caesar* and *Four Weddings*, Holly thought, but, just like the white lilies, it had nothing to do with Jack. But perhaps Jack, when he was with his posh friends, had not been the Jack she knew. Perhaps that was what he had meant when he had said that he only felt real with her and Mo. Great, Holly thought, he feels real with us and ignores us most of the time. Mo was right, Holly thought. There had been no proper place for them in his life, and there was no place for her here. Many of the guests were the same as those who went to Louis Gold's parties, but there were no canapés for her to hand round.

It was only when the coffin began to crank out of sight that she suddenly wanted to scream, no, don't go. Not yet. I haven't finished talking to you.

The widow walked out to a recording of organ music. Philippa Palmer had been undeniably beautiful in her youth and she had aged well. She knew just how to soften the neck of her black suit with a silk scarf the colour of pearls and to dab away her tears before they smudged her make-up. Just behind her walked a much younger woman with hair that shone like a cornfield in late summer sun, and a complexion as pale as the moon. She was thin and slight, and her bare arms were goosebumpy in the chill of the red brick chapel. As the widow walked past Holly she missed her step, and the younger woman reached out to steady her, but the hand offered in compassion was shrugged off in a gesture subtle enough to go unnoticed by everyone except Holly, who was only a foot away. The younger woman's stricken eyes met Holly's and her face was instantly transformed by a smile, as if she were greeting a long-lost friend. Then the smile suddenly faded and she lowered her eyes again, bewildered.

Clare was not feeling as she thought she ought to feel. She had expected the funeral to be a kind of watershed after which everything would be different, but oddly it only seemed to be confirming her place in the world, rather than offering her a new one. Occasionally she would recognize a face she knew among the mourners, but when her smiles were met with bemused, even slightly irritated, frowns, she realized that these were people she had seen only on the television or while flicking through the magazines in the doctor's waiting-room. They did not know her, and in the dress she had bought from Dorothy Perkins, they did not want to. It was as if she had a label round her neck saying chain store.

The whole party repaired to the cloisters and stood around not quite knowing whether to be silent or to talk in hushed tones. She overheard one woman whisper 'beautiful service' and thought how inappropriate a description that was. There had been nothing beautiful about it. Golders Green crematorium was a hideous collection of dark buildings designed to give an artificial sanctity to the send-offs of non-believers. The chapel was as cold as a real church but contained no warmth of spirituality in its secular walls. 'Jesu Joy of Man's Desiring' rang out from the CD player, filling the space with the recorded echo of a cathedral.

Amid the quiet murmur of condolence, a mobile phone began to ring, and Clare watched as the men reached into their jacket pockets, the women flipped open their handbags to see if it was theirs. Eventually a long, lean man with floppy hair guiltily answered the call.

'I'm at Jack Palmer's funeral,' he hissed, shaking his jacket sleeve back from his wrist so that he could check the time, 'can I call you back in ten minutes?'

The flowers were all extraordinarily tasteful. Amelia would approve of all the twigs and raffia, Clare thought, which made a kind of ersatz harvest festival in this fake religious setting. Just below the name-plate, where a card with the words Jack Palmer had been slotted in, there was a small bunch of bluebells. The sight of the flowers touched her as nothing else had done that day. She had known that she knew what his favourite flowers were, but the memory drumming like a forgotten tune somewhere in the back of her consciousness had refused to offer up the word. Bluebells. Her father had taken her once to Epping Forest at about this time of year and as they wandered through the blue shade he had asked her whether she liked it there. 'Yes,' she had said, shivering, frightened by the vastness of the forest and wondering how they would ever find their way out. 'It is where I come when I want to hear silence,' he had told her, after which she had not dared to utter a word.

A couple of men filleted themselves away from the

crowd in the cloisters and went walking across the well-manicured lawn side by side, looking straight ahead but clearly talking, taking up a negotiation they had started in the cab on the way, Clare imagined, that had been put on hold for a respectful half-hour. Business as usual. Still, why not? It was what Jack would have wanted. Isn't that what people said at funerals, with great solemnity, certain in the knowledge that they wouldn't be corrected?

Clare had no idea what he would have wanted. She didn't even know whether he would have wanted her to be there. It felt faintly ridiculous now to have trekked all the way up to town in a black dress she didn't like and would never wear again in order to look at a box. She had not seen him in person for eighteen years and the irony was that had he been alive Jack would probably have glanced at her curiously when she tried to smile at him, then flicked his eyes away from hers, as these other famous people did.

'Shall we round everyone up?' Philippa whispered beside her, 'Do you think there'll be enough food?'

Back at the house, there was a buffet lunch, a splendid affair that had been arriving since seven o'clock that morning. Clare wondered how soon after Jack's death her mother had got on the phone to the caterers. How much notice did you have to give for food for a hundred of your closest friends? Did you consult a menu, or were Dublin Bay prawns with chilli and coriander and tiny marinated goat's cheeses what one ate these days at the best funerals?

'Of course there will,' Clare said, but her mother had not waited for an answer.

She watched Philippa sweeping the crowd of people towards the long line of limousines and black cabs, and wondered when her mother would allow herself to be sad. She had clearly made a stylistic decision to be the strong woman coping admirably, rather than the

107

grieving widow. Clare was aware that for some reason her own presence was not helping. The house was big enough for a dozen people to live in without interfering with one another, but whenever she met her mother in the kitchen or wandering round the walled garden at the back Philippa would make a little cough of annoyance, as if there were something stuck inside her throat that she couldn't quite bring herself to say.

A woman with cropped red hair was lolling against one of the cloister arches. She was one of the youngest people there, and one of the tallest. Her height seemed to magnify her awkwardness. She was wearing the regulation black suit with a skirt that looked shorter on her than the other women because of her long, slightly knock-kneed legs. If she had been wearing lipstick, she had bitten it off. Drawn to her by an invisible thread, Clare traced the line of the woman's gaze.

'Did you send the bluebells?' she asked her softly.

'How did you know?' the woman asked defensively.

'I just saw you looking.' Clare stepped back, nervously. 'They were his favourite flowers. Did you know?'

Holly shot Clare an angry glance, but saw from the way that she shrank away that she had only been trying to make her feel comfortable.

'Yes. I knew,' she said.

'Are you coming back to the house?' Clare asked her.

Who was this gentle person in the baggy dress, Holly wondered, a half-memory ringing like a distant alarm in her head.

'I'm not invited,' Holly told her, standing up straight. She wished the woman would just go away so that she could have a few minutes alone with her father before leaving.

'Well, I'm inviting you,' Clare said, pointing towards the taxis. In the distance she thought she saw Philippa shake her head as she got into the limousine.

'OK then,' Holly said, picking up the handbag by her feet. What did it matter now, she asked herself. She smiled at her companion and saw her do a double take.

'Oh, I know!' Clare said, delighted to have recognized her, 'you're the one on the television! On election night. You were at the South Bank. I didn't . . . you've cut your hair. Oh . . .' she looked towards the cars, 'oh well perhaps . . .'

'What?' asked Holly, defensively, seeing the invitation disappear as rapidly as it had materialized.

'Well, I mean, your . . . your relationship with Jack . . . not that I care, it's just my mother . . .' Clare stumbled, embarrassed.

The funeral cortège pulled away.

'Relationship? I'm his daughter.' Fortified by hearing herself saying the words out loud, Holly retaliated, 'Who are you anyway?'

'I'm Clare. I was his daughter . . .' Thinking how odd that sounded, as if she were dead, not he, she added, 'I am his daughter.'

Somewhere in the back of her mind, Holly saw herself in Hackney public library looking Jack up in *Who's Who*. Married Philippa Harper-Smythe 1960, 1 d. She had known what the annotation meant, and even though she had desperately wanted it to, she had known that it had not referred to her.

The two women stared at each other.

Although she had no reason to believe her, Clare somehow knew that Holly was telling the truth. She looked like a finer version of Jack. The eyes were not hooded as his had been, but they were the same pale azure. Like milled steel, Joss used to say.

'But how old are you?' she asked.

'Thirty-five,' Holly said.

'No!'

'It's not that old.'

'No. No, it's just that I am too . . .'

'Really? You look much younger.'

'So do you.'

The two women smiled at each other, each knowing she was being truthful and hoping that the other one was too. Even in the midst of the most momentous revelation of your life, Holly thought, it's nice to know you could pass for twenty-eight.

'But how? . . . I never knew . . .' Clare said, grappling with the logic of it. Of course it was physically possible, but how could he have done it? He never seemed to have enough love for her. How could he have had enough for two? Or perhaps the reason was standing in front of her. He had loved this daughter who looked so much like him. Oddly, her first feeling was relief. At last there was an explanation for the way he had written her off.

'Nor did I,' Holly said. Then, feeling bad about lying at a funeral, she qualified that to 'Or maybe I did . . .'

They stood side by side in silence, watching the last of the funeral cars pull away, with Holly wishing that she could just rewind the last ten minutes and erase it from her life, and Clare trying to think of a way to continue their conversation.

'Look, do come back to the house, if you'd like,' Clare said eventually, 'I've no idea whether Philippa . . .'

'No. I don't think she does.'

'I'd like to get . . .'

'. . . very drunk.' Holly finished the sentence for her.

'Well, I was going to say, get to know you . . . I'm Clare,' she held out her hand. It felt as risky as asking someone to be your best friend on the first day of school.

'Holly.' She looked at Clare for several long seconds, before shaking her hand. 'OK then, why not?'

They walked away from the looming red brick edifice in silence, down towards the main road. There were no taxis now. Clare waited nervously beside Holly on the corner of the street, wondering whether to suggest the tube, not wanting to do anything to disturb the delicate accord between them. She could sense Holly's agitation and felt she might at any moment walk away. When they eventually hailed a cab, they did not speak, except to discuss where to go. Wandering round the streets of South Hampstead the day before, Clare had found a small Polish wine bar where she had eaten a meal for less than five pounds. It had been open all afternoon even though there had been little custom. Holly said that sounded perfect.

The windows were misted over and inside the steamy air smelled of boiled sausage. A couple of men who looked like shabby intellectuals were drinking black coffee and brandy at one of the tables. Clare and Holly sat down in a hard wooden booth and simultaneously picked up their menus, grateful for something to hide behind.

It was a blind date, Holly thought. She knew so much about this woman and yet nothing at all. She could not even decide whether she liked her. Clare was fragile and pretty and her skin was fresh. Since she had found lines on her own face, Holly had started obsessively searching other faces for signs of ageing. Clare had none, but her eyes looked as if they had suffered pain, which made it difficult to hate her instantly for the looks and the smooth complexion.

'I'll have pierogi and red wine. A bottle. Is that OK with you?'

Clare nodded. 'I'll have the blinis with apple and sour cream.'

It was one of the cheapest items on the menu. Holly looked at her companion's dress again. Either she was very mean, or poor. How could she be poor?

'Tell you what,' Holly said, drinking a glass of wine very quickly when it came, 'the only way to do this is like a job application. Describe, briefly,' she put heavy emphasis on the word, 'your education, work and hobbies.'

Clare laughed nervously.

'You first,' she said.

'OK,' Holly launched in, 'Holly O'Mara. Born 1961, June 1961, star sign Gemini, if that means anything to you, mother Mo, short for Maureen, father unknown until later. Lived on eleventh floor of tower block in Limehouse. What an awful place to grow up!' she put on an upper-class accent, 'says everyone now, before spending half a million on a loft in a converted warehouse in Docklands.' She looked up to see how her story was going down so far. Clare smiled at her. 'Spent most of youth reading, going to movies and staring out of the window dreaming of being rich and famous. Wrote film reviews for school magazine under the name Holly Wood. Worked as usherette in the Odeon on Saturdays. Left school with ten O levels and did a secretarial course . . .'

'Didn't you go to university?' Clare asked, amazed that someone who seemed so confident had not.

'They told me I could've. I got really good results, but I didn't want to waste time with all those posey students when I could be earning money. Mo said I couldn't go wrong with a typing qualification, which was the best piece of advice I ever had. So Colette and I . . .'

'Colette?'

'Best friend . . . Colette married her first boss, I got a career. Lucky in life, unlucky in love, or however that one goes . . . now I'm a screenwriters' agent, busy, busy, busy . . .' Holly took a deep breath and drank another glass of wine in one. 'Shall we have another bottle?' she asked.

Clare nodded, although she had yet to finish her second glass.

Their food arrived.

'What does a screenwriters' agent do?' Clare asked.

'I represent people who write screenplays, and television. I sell what they write,' Holly explained.

'And are you rich and famous . . . like you dreamed?'

'Well, put it this way, right, I always wanted to work in the movies, but I wasn't much of an actress, and how many female film directors are there? So, in a way, I've got exactly what I wanted, and relatively quickly . . .' Holly sounded as if she was listing her achievements for herself as much as Clare. 'To answer your question, I'm probably as rich and famous as I ever dreamed I'd be at sixteen, but as you know more about how things work your ambitions grow, don't they? . . . Like, I buy real designer clothes now instead of Wallis and Next versions, and so I still have an Access bill I can't pay. I used to think that doing something, anything, to do with films would be enough, but now I'd like to represent an Oscar-winning screenplay writer . . . d'you know what I mean?'

Her accent sounded more East End the more impassioned she became, Clare noticed.

'Come on,' said Holly, aware that she was going on a bit, 'CV time. You've got to do your CV.'

Why? Clare asked herself. Why do I have to do it like a CV? I'm not sure I can. She was about to protest, but when she looked up Holly's face was so eagerly awaiting her participation in this game she had devised, she felt she had to join in.

'Clare Drummond,' she began.

Holly frowned, not understanding.

'Born 1961, July. Star sign Cancer, and I don't believe in it either,' Clare looked up and saw that Holly's face had softened. 'Lonely childhood with parents usually out and a series of depressed Scandinavian au pairs. Did everything wrong as a teenager, including conviction for possession of dope, expelled from nice girls' direct-grant school and scraped into further education college, almost immediately got pregnant by English lecturer and poet Joss Drummond,' she looked up. Holly clearly did not know the name. 'Left home, married, moved to remote Cornish town, gave birth to Ella when I was nineteen, and then Tom two and a half years ago . . .'

'What did you do in between?' Holly interrupted, calculating a gap between children of almost fifteen years.

'Gardened and cooked, mostly. We have a small-holding. We had this dream about living off the land . . .'

'The Good Life?'

'Sort of. Except it's hard work.'

'Bloody hell!' said Holly, 'and?'

'That's it,' Clare said.

So what became of the dream? Holly wanted to ask but sensed it was too soon.

Now what, Holly wondered. They had both said their pieces and she was sure they had both been honest, but everyone knew that the truth lay in what you left out of a CV, not what you put in.

'Perhaps we could do blurbs,' she suggested, 'you try to encapsulate the flavour of your life in less than a hundred words . . .'

'How do you know all these games?' Clare asked.

'I go to a lot of dinner parties,' Holly told her, 'this is the sort of thing I mean: Holly is thirty-something,' she interrupted herself, 'I'm really sick of that thirty-something stuff, d'you know what I mean? Usually it means getting pretty close to forty . . . so, Holly is thirty-quite-a-lot, with a bustling, busy life and a brilliant career. Parties, premières and something else beginning with p – there are always three things on the list – may be fun, but sometimes, in the small hours of the morning, Holly lies awake wondering whether there's more to life than champagne and hang-overs . . .'

Clare clapped her hands.

'Now you,' Holly encouraged her.

'No, I couldn't, you do one for me . . .'

Holly thought for a moment.

'It sounded like the perfect life: a cottage in Corn-wall, a husband who wrote poetry and dug potatoes, two beautiful children . . . so why did Clare look so wistful when she spoke of it . . . ?'

'Hmm,' Clare said, 'as a matter of fact, I don't think Joss would know a potato from a beetroot. I think I'd better have some more to drink . . .'

Holly couldn't work out whether Clare's reticence was because she was shy or unwilling to trade in confidences so soon.

'So, you left home when you were seventeen?'

Clare nodded.

'More precisely, I got thrown out . . .'

'For the dope, or being pregnant?'

Holly was so direct, it was proving difficult for Clare to sidestep her questions.

'The dope was the main thing,' she began, 'the pregnancy just added insult to injury, although I didn't really see why it was so significant before, but now I do . . .' She looked at Holly. Because of you, she seemed to be saying, but without malice.

'I suppose I can understand now that Jack was insecure and he couldn't let anything go wrong in his house,' Clare continued, looking at her hands that fidgeted and twisted as she spoke.

'He was always going on about "my house" this and "my house" that and actually, it wasn't his house, it was my mother's, but that made him behave as if it was his even more. It made her behave like that too, because she was so determined that he must not feel inferior because of her class and her money and all that. I understand all that now, but I didn't then, you see,' Clare said. 'He wasn't even a film director then, he was still directing adverts. Maybe he got more relaxed when he had real money and acclaim?'

Clare looked at Holly as if expecting an answer. Holly didn't know what to say.

'I've seen all his films,' Clare said, 'so it sort of felt as if we were in touch . . .'

'Isn't it funny how you and I are so different?' Holly asked, trying to leaven the intensity of Clare's analysis, 'must prove something.'

She knew there was an obvious phrase but she couldn't locate it.

'I know, nature over nurture or something . . . no, the other way round . . .'

'Do you think we're so unalike?' Clare asked her, 'I was thinking that we're rather similar.'

'Well, that just proves how unalike we are, because I think we're unalike, and you think we're similar, if you see what I mean . . .' Holly heard her words and noted that she was getting drunk.

'What do you mean, similar?' she asked, trying to quieten herself down and resist the urge to step in and control the conversation. She was swamping Clare, she realized. Simon had once told her that she could be too much of a good thing, and when she had demanded that he explain, he had said that she had a tendency to overwhelm people on first meeting. When Holly had protested that she only did that because she was nervous, he had said that he knew that, but it still had the same effect.

'Well, we're the same age, same colouring . . .' Clare began to list their similarities.

'Wrong,' said Holly. 'Your hair is long, glossy, strawberry blond and mine is a ginger Brillo pad . . . I'm ambitious, and you're . . .' Holly was going to say not, but stopped herself. Perhaps she was assuming too much.

'I used to think I wasn't,' Clare said, 'I saw what ambition did to people, you see. Jack and Philippa are, were, so ambitious, living with them was like having ambition aversion therapy . . . but now I don't know. I sometimes feel like I'm waiting for something to happen . . .'

'It just did. Our father died,' Holly said, gloomily.

'Yes, that's another way in which we're alike, and another way is that we've just met one another.'

Holly didn't say 'so what?' but her expression did.

Clare didn't know whether it was the wine that was making her so undaunted in the face of someone who could sometimes look as contemptuous as Jack at his worst, but she pressed on, determined to explain what she meant.

'I didn't know I had a sister, and I don't know how it's going to affect my life, but even after knowing you for an hour, I know it will . . .'

'I think I did know about you, you see,' Holly decided to confess, 'but I didn't want to. I'm the most competitive person in the world . . .'

'No wonder Jack liked you,' Clare said.

'How do you know he did?' Holly was instantly suspicious.

'I told you I saw you on television on Election night, just a glimpse, and I saw his face. I wondered who it was who made him so happy . . .'

'Really?' Holly divided what was left in the second bottle between their glasses, beaming. 'How do you think Jack would have felt about us meeting?' she asked.

Clare thought for a moment.

'He would have hated it,' she said.

Holly's face fell.

'You're right,' she said, picking up her glass and

chinking it against Clare's, 'well, he can't do anything about it now, the old bastard . . .'

Clare looked shocked.

'I hate all this reverence just because he's dead, don't you?' Holly said.

And suddenly they were both laughing together.

They spent the afternoon exchanging stories about their father, tentatively piecing together a jigsaw of half-forgotten memories and attempting to find a chronology into which they fitted in relation to one another.

'I went to your house once,' Holly revealed, 'I thought it was like a castle. I didn't get a guided tour or anything, just in the kitchen bit at the back . . .'

'When? Why did he take you there?'

'I suppose I was about twelve. We were on our way somewhere. He'd forgotten his wallet. You must have been out with your mother . . .'

'We spent summer in the Hamptons once. Philippa had a project in New York. I had a wonderful time . . .' Clare thought that it was the summer between primary and secondary school. 'I remember kissing a boy on the beach. It was probably the beginning of my downfall,' she joked.

'Mo stayed in the car, but I insisted on going in. I didn't know he was my dad then. I wondered how come Mo had such a rich friend.'

'But why did he take you in?' Clare asked.

'Maybe he wanted to show me the life I should aspire to,' Holly said.

'Who did your mother tell you he was?' Clare wanted to know.

Holly was surprised by the question. Most people would not have thought to ask that.

'She said he was a friend from back home, old schoolmates, you know . . . which was true. She never lied, you see, but she didn't tell me all the truth, and I was too thick . . . I even remember asking her when we were really poor one Christmas why we didn't touch Jack for a loan and she was furious with me . . .'

'I don't think you were ever thick,' Clare said, smiling.

They had both been to Epping Forest in his E-type Jag, but neither could remember which year. Had he taken them one weekend after another, or had there been longer in between? It was a little spooky if you started to think about it like that, and Clare remembered the silence and the coldness under the canopy of trees. Why Epping Forest anyway, Holly wanted to know. They both pondered that for a while until Clare suggested that he might have filmed a shampoo advert there.

'You know, one of those "natural" products,' she said, 'before Body Shop and all that, with essence of silver birch or something . . . they all smelled like pine toilet-cleaner . . .'

'Perhaps it was a commercial for toilet-cleaner,' Holly said. 'He was one of the first people to think about the image of the product as opposed to the germs under the rim . . .'

Holly talked about Jack with pride, Clare noticed. She had bought the fresh-scented image he had created of himself, whereas Clare had only seen the nasty bits lurking beneath.

When they emerged from the wine bar, Holly expected it to be dark. She had the same kick of exhilaration that she always felt after seeing a matinée, that made her feel as if it were wrong to be caught enjoying yourself in daylight. She was in the happy, floaty stage of drunkenness where she wanted to go on drinking, chatting, anything to delay returning to reality for a few hours longer, but she was still sober enough to understand that Clare was beginning to suffer from sensory overload. They began to wander in the direction of Philippa's house. Holly knew that she wasn't going to go in, even though Clare had issued an invitation for tea. At the junction with Haverstock Hill, seeing the orange light of a free cab, Holly's arm suddenly shot in the air.

'You will call me before you go back?' she insisted, grabbing Clare and kissing her on both cheeks.

'Yes. Yes. Of course . . .' Clare looked confused and lost now that Holly was leaving her so abruptly.

As the cab lurched away, Holly instinctively turned round to see Clare waving, her thin bare arms looking like a child's as the distance between them grew longer.

'I didn't want you coming back to an empty home.' Mo was sitting in the kitchen when Holly arrived back at the flat. Why did everyone sit in the kitchen when they came round, Holly wondered. It was the least comfortable room in the flat, the chairs were hard and it stank of Ajax liquid because Mo hadn't been able to resist giving the floor a once-over.

'Did you take the afternoon off?' she asked Mo.

'Took the day off. I wanted to pay my respects, in my own way . . .'

For people like Mo who were not confident in their use of words at the best of times, death turned love into deepest sympathy, flowers into floral tributes, and tears into paying respects.

'What did you do?' Holly asked.

'I wandered round a bit. Sat in the park. That didn't feel right. Then I thought of the river boat. I haven't done that since we first came down . . .'

It made Holly sad to think of her mother dressed in her smart black suit sitting on the deck of a river boat, surrounded by Americans in Burberry raincoats, the incessant crackle of the captain's commentary filling her ears as she tried to mourn the man she had loved.

'Greenwich or Richmond?'

It was the only thing she could think of asking that wouldn't make her cry.

'Hampton Court. It's quite pretty down that way,' Mo replied, thinking how strange it was that you could live in a city for nearly forty years and still not know bits of it. 'How was the funeral?'

'Funeral itself was all wrong. You would have hated it. But I had an interesting meeting afterwards with my half-sister . . .' Holly watched her mother's face. Mo's blush proved beyond doubt what Holly had already suspected. She had known.

'Why didn't you tell me?' she demanded.

'Don't keep going on at me like I did everything wrong,' Mo sighed, 'I only tried to do what I thought was best . . .'

'I didn't mean . . . it was just a shock, that's all . . .'

'I suppose if it hadn't been for your half-sister, Jack and I would probably never have seen each other again . . .'

For the first time Mo related the incident with the ice-blue satin dress to Holly.

'I never understood why you didn't want me to know he was my father,' Holly said, a few minutes after Mo had finished.

'D'you know what it's like to be nineteen, unmarried and pregnant, living in a city where you don't know anyone, and you can't go back to the city you do know because you left in disgrace and went to live in sin down south?' Mo asked her, suddenly eloquent in her exasperation.

Holly shook her head, ashamed. Just because Mo never made a big deal about it didn't mean it wasn't a big deal.

'Well, think about it,' Mo said, 'you manage some-how. You get through, then just as you're breathing a sigh of relief because your daughter's almost grown up, you've got a decent job, you're even starting to think you might have a bit of a life again, the man who abandoned you turns up out of the blue and expects you to fall in with his plans. How was I to know he wouldn't just be off again?'

'But you never told him you were pregnant when he left,' Holly protested, 'you never gave him a chance to look after you . . .'

'Jack Palmer did not look after anyone except himself, whatever he told you later,' Mo said wearily. 'If you're so keen to have the truth, let me tell you something. He loved that Philippa Harper-Smythe getting pregnant because it made leaving me so much easier. He had his proper excuse then. He could tell himself, and whoever else wanted to know, that he was doing the decent thing. If you think that he would have chosen us, given a choice, you're stupider than you look . . .'

It was the nearest Mo had ever come to anger with her daughter. She was shaking as she said it.

'I'm sorry, Mum,' Holly said, enfolding Mo in her arms.

'No need to be sorry,' Mo sniffed, 'I got the best bargain. I got you . . .'

There were a few goat's cheeses still sitting on the layers of dark green vine leaves that covered the wicker platter. Somebody had dropped a wedge of potato and aubergine tortilla on the rug and there were omelette footprints leading through the French doors into the garden. A waiter with a white jacket and black hair parted in the centre was collecting plates and cutlery on a huge butler's tray, and a girl with a tea towel tied round her waist which was almost the same length as her black micro skirt had her arms in bubbles washing up glasses.

'What time did it all finish?' Clare asked the waiter.

'Most people had gone by three.'

She had no idea what the time was. She asked him, and he told her it was nearly five o'clock.

The air was still warm outside. The recent hot weather had brought out all the blooms on the pale apricot rambling rose that covered the right-hand wall. It looked like the backdrop for a wedding, not a funeral.

'Oh, there you are.' Philippa was lying on a sun-lounger, looking over the pool. Her skirt had ridden up leaving an undignified expanse of stockinged leg on display. The sombre black of her outfit looked strange against the flowery chintz covering of the plump cushions. 'Did you enjoy yourself?'

The question issued in an even voice fooled Clare long enough for her to reply, 'Yes, thank you.'

Philippa looked round, her body suddenly transforming from a sleek and house-trained Burmese into a feral cat.

'How dare you?' she spat. 'How dare you come back here drunk?'

'I'm not drunk,' Clare said calmly.

'How dare you be so rude to our guests?'

'Philippa, they were not our guests, they were your guests. I didn't know any of them and I'm sure nobody even noticed I wasn't here . . .'

'How dare you . . .'

Clare looked at the jug on the paving beside the sun-lounger. It could have been water, but she suspected it was dry martini.

'How dare you . . . ?' Philippa asked, following Clare's gaze.

'Oh do stop saying that,' Clare said, turning away, 'it was bad enough when I was eighteen, but it is really silly now.'

It was as if the intervening years had never happened. The only thing that had changed was the colour of the lining of the swimming-pool. Clare had stood in exactly the same spot vowing that she would never say 'how dare you?' to anyone.

'I don't know why you bothered coming back,' Philippa said.

'No,' Clare replied, walking away, 'nor do I.'

She walked back into the house and up two flights of stairs to the guest-room. The room next to it had been her room. It had been quite a shock when she first arrived to find that the Mucha posters had been stripped down and her matching pine Habitat chest of drawers and bookcase removed. She had wondered briefly what had happened to the battered Penguin editions of D. H. Lawrence that had lined the shelves alongside the trendy Picador editions of Richard Brautigan. There had been no reason for her to imagine that her room was standing like a shrine to a lost child, untouched and undusted for all these years, but it had chilled her to see that her memory had been so comprehensively erased from the house. Even in the kitchen, the picture she had painted when she was about ten, that Jack had said was better than a Picasso, had been replaced by a genuine Picasso.

The guest-room had Pompeian red walls, sanded boards and black and white curtains by Timney Fowler with a design of Roman emperors' heads. Clare took the sheets off the bed. She collected her toothbrush from the *en suite* shower room, pausing before slipping two of the roughly chopped cubes of guest soap into her sponge bag. She had enjoyed the sheer expensiveness of the scent, and she knew that they would only be thrown away after she had gone. She took off her dress, rolled it and put it into the woven African shoulder-bag she had bought in Vivienne's shop, then put on the vest, jeans and jeans jacket she had arrived in. She glanced around the room, checking to see that she had everything, then went over to the window. Philippa was still lying beside the bright blue rectangle of the pool, like an intruder on a David Hockney painting. It felt awful to be leaving again in just the same way as she had left before, and yet part of her was glad. It gave a weird kind of justification to the intervening years. Clare thought of the hugs she would give to Ella and Tom when she arrived back, and to Joss who had taken her away from all this. She swung her bag over one shoulder, smiling, then she stuffed the sheets under her other arm and walked downstairs to the laundry. She loaded the machine, tipped powder in and started it, then walked back out into the garden.

'I'm going now,' she told Philippa.

Philippa was staring into the middle distance. She did not turn round to say goodbye.

Clare shut the front door behind her and walked down the steps and through the front garden to the street. At the gate she turned back. The imposing white-fronted house was like a fortress and she had been its prisoner for too long. Now she was finally free.

It was only when she was sitting on the tube that she looked at her timetable for trains back to Truro. The last one went at six thirty. She had twenty-five minutes to get it. She counted the stations left to Paddington and thought she would just make it in time. Belsize Park, Chalk Farm, Camden Town, Euston, King's Cross then change. Clare looked at her watch again. Come on. At Camden Town, she allowed herself to think that she was going to make it with minutes to spare and immediately, as if in answer to her complacency, the doors opened a second time and clunked shut, the train started, moved an inch, but an automatic brake came on and stopped it. The doors opened again and shut. Minutes ticked away. Open, shut, brake. A waft of irritation blew through the carriage as other people checked their watches and shifted in their seats. Open, shut, brake. Open, shut, move. They were moving. Clare exchanged a smile with the man opposite. If her train was just a little late, she would still get it. Surely the last train was always a little late? At Paddington she ran up the flight of steps from the Circle Line and stood panting as her eyes scanned the departure board. Just as she spotted her train the numbers began to whirl. She dashed to the platform to see the last carriage a hundred metres away and moving at speed. Then, quite unexpectedly, she sank to her knees, her face in her hands, and wept.

Holly was trying to decide whether or not she was hungry. She felt empty, but she had no appetite. She stared into the fridge as if there would be an answer inside if only she looked long enough, but there was only an unopened jar of chocolate spread and a bag of salad that she was about to open when she saw that half of it had melted into yellow slime. Picking it up by the corner, she dropped it disdainfully into the swing bin, thinking that she should have taken Mo out to dinner. She had put her mother into a cab and given her two ten-pound notes for the fare, knowing full well that Mo would wait until the cab turned the corner before stopping it and getting the tube. Or perhaps tonight she would not. It had been a strange day.

When the phone rang, Holly was certain it would be Mo informing her that she was home. Instead there was a hollowness at the other end which told her immediately that the caller was speaking from a public phone.

'Hello?'

'Hello? It's Clare . . .'

By the time Clare arrived, Simon was there too. He had come round to check that Holly was OK, as he had done every evening since Jack had died. His presence eased the heightened awareness of having somebody in your home for the first time, which makes you see all

the dust and cobwebs that are usually invisible. Holly
made her bed and she and Simon sat on it whilst Clare
sat in the collapsed armchair with the seat that slumped
to the floor. Simon had brought a bottle of red wine,
which the sisters drank while explaining their relationship to him, and then he volunteered to go out for
more.

'You are lovely to me,' Holly told him, as he put his
shoes back on and stood up.

They sat in silence for a few seconds listening to his
footsteps on the stairs and the slam of Holly's front
door.

'Is he your boyfriend?' Clare asked.

'Simon?' Holly said unnecessarily, 'no. No, he is
not.'

'He seems very nice,' Clare said.

'Yes, he is. Very. Far too nice for me in fact . . .'
Holly laughed.

'Hmm. I always went for bad boys too,' Clare said.

She seemed so sweet. Holly couldn't quite believe
that.

'So, your husband, Josh is it?'

'Joss.'

'Joss. As in stick?'

Clare laughed, 'Yes, I suppose so. It's short for
Jocelyn. I remember thinking Joss was a tremendously
romantic name when I first met him . . .'

'Like all the blokes in *Jackie* were called Rick or
Jake?'

'Exactly.' Clare's eyes shone in recognition of a
shared girls' culture.

'So, is he bad? Joss?' Holly wanted to know.

Clare thought before answering. If Holly had asked
that afternoon, she might well have said yes, but now
she only felt grateful to him for taking her away from
London.

'He can be,' she said, cautiously, 'what about you?'

Holly sighed.

'I've been having an affair for a while, but that's over, and I don't know what's next. Sometimes I think it would be nice to have someone around, but I usually only think that when I'm struggling back from Tesco Metro with loads of bags . . . maybe what I really want is a shopping trolley . . .'

At this point Simon appeared again with three more bottles of Burgundy in a plastic carrier, and looked slightly alarmed when both women fell about laughing.

'There's sex, of course . . .' Holly continued, as Simon said that he had some phone calls to make, and disappeared again. '. . . tell me something, is it different after eighteen years or does it get a bit boring? I don't think I've managed to have sex with the same person for more than six months ever . . . except Piers and that was different because sex was all it was, if you see what I mean . . .'

Clare thought of the night before she had come up to London.

'Oh, for heaven's sake,' said Holly, 'you're blushing! Well, I don't think I want to know any more . . . bloody hell, how come you got the cottage by the sea with the roses round the door, a naked bloody poet in your bed, and I just got a flat full of clothes . . .' She waved her hand round the room.

'I think it's lovely here,' Clare said, looking at the mess and jumble with unfeigned envy.

'Mo would say that the grass is greener,' Holly said.

'Mo?'

'My mum.'

'Right. What is the story about your mum? Was she my father's mistress?'

'No, she was his first love,' Holly said, dramatically.

'Tell me . . .'

'It was a bit like one of those Angry Young Man

movies, you know, like *Room at the Top* or *Saturday Night and Sunday Morning*?'

Clare nodded, not wanting to interrupt the flow of the story.

'. . . in fact it's so like one of those films, whenever I think about it, I imagine Mo and Jack in black and white. You know how the story goes: bright, working-class lad wants to better himself and leave his background behind him. Well, that was Jack, in the Laurence Harvey, Albert Finney type of role. But the girlfriends in those films are not really characters, they're symbols of the world he wants to leave behind and the world he aspires to. Mo represented the working-class bit, and your mum the aspirational bit . . . the working-class one always gets dumped of course, or killed . . . except it wasn't a movie . . .' Holly said, looking suddenly sad.

'So she came down from Manchester with him?' Clare asked.

'They came down from Manchester in 1960. Jack got a job in an advertising agency, Mo demonstrated irons and things in a department store. They were poor and happy at the beginning of swinging London. Must have been great. Jack became a bit of a star at the agency because of inventing Farmer Fred. Did you ever eat Farmer Fred's Wonderbread?'

Clare shook her head.

'No, it wasn't the sort of thing posh families in Hampstead had for their tea, was it? A miraculous triumph of branding over nutrition . . .'

Clare laughed. Holly's perceptions were astringent and she delivered them with an intimidating confidence, but she was so honest it was impossible to feel threatened by her. She could see why she was good at her job. She could weave a yarn and sell you a story with complete conviction. It was something she must have inherited from Jack.

'. . . then Jack meets Philippa,' Holly went on, 'a beautiful débutante with brains and ambition, far more appropriate for the life he's chosen for himself. Then you were conceived. And that's the end of the story. Or, it would have been if Mo hadn't been pregnant too. Too proud to tell him, too Catholic to have an abortion, and not Catholic enough to go home to all that guilt and recrimination, so she stayed down here. Everyone likes my mum. She managed.' Holly's final sentences were clipped.

'I don't think that my mother knew about your mother,' Clare said, wanting to offer some comfort, 'I hope she didn't . . .'

'I don't really blame her. It wasn't her fault that she had looks and money,' Holly said sharply.

Clare felt suddenly guilty for her earlier reticence.

'My life isn't really roses round the door,' she admitted, wanting to repay Holly's honesty in some way.

'Do you think we're going to be friends?' Holly asked, the emotion making her voice sound aggressive.

'Oh yes . . .' Clare replied instantly, adding nervously, 'don't you?'

Chapter 13

Holly had heard that one American agent was so arrogant he didn't even bother speaking to prospective purchasers of his clients' work until the figure they offered was somewhere near what he was looking for. Instead he kept a buzzer on his desk, like the MISS button in *Juke Box Jury*, that he would press occasionally just to let the hapless individual at the other end of the line know that he was still there. Holly didn't know whether the story was apocryphal, but as the producer who was trying to option the new crime novel she had offered him droned on with excuses about why his initial offer would be low, she wished she had the buzzer herself. The inside of her head felt like a lottery machine full of marbles.

'Fifteen hundred against five thousand an hour . . .' the producer said, 'but that is absolutely as high as I can go.'

'Can you get the typescript back to me by messenger then? Bye . . .' Holly went to replace the handset on the phone, enjoying the squeals she could hear as he realized what she was doing.

'Sorry, did you say something?' She spoke into the mouthpiece again.

'What figure did you have in mind?' he asked.

'I want five up front, and I'm not going to consider

less than ten thousand an hour plus repeats and re-siduals . . .'

'You've got to be joking . . .'

'I'm deadly serious.'

She wondered why he laughed, then remembered that *Deadly Serious* was the title of the novel they were talking about. Her hangover had put a kind of time-lapse delay on her brain.

'Can I think about it?' he asked her.

'No. You've had it exclusive for a fortnight and there's a buzz about this book. Think about it if you want, but I'm going to be sending it out to six other people this morning . . .'

'Three thousand against ten thousand an hour full buy-out . . .' he said.

Holly thought for a second or two. He was obviously very keen indeed and she wondered if she could press him for more, but since she had had zero interest in the book from anyone else, she thought that might be greedy. The few occasions she had come unstuck in a negotiation had happened when she had started to believe her own sales pitch.

'You just got yourself a deal,' she told the producer and put down the phone with a satisfied smile.

'Jemima!' she called as she saw her secretary trying to sneak past her door unnoticed, 'if I gave you a quid would you go round the corner for a cappuccino for me . . . tell you what, make it two quid and you get one for yourself . . .' Holly knew that she was tough to work for, but she didn't want to get a reputation as com-pletely unreasonable.

Jemima stepped forward and took the two pound coins. Then Holly changed her mind.

'Take a fiver,' she said, scrabbling around in her purse, 'and get me two cappuccinos, one for yourself and a cinnamon Danish . . . oh to hell with it, I'll go, I need a cigarette . . .' she snatched back the money, 'and while I'm out can you draw up the contract for this,' she handed Jemima the notes of the telephone conversation she had just had, 'I want to get it on his desk before he changes his mind . . .'

Holly picked up her bag and walked towards reception.

'I just made a deal for *Deadly Serious* . . .' she told Robert as she sauntered past his office.

'You're joking?'

'No, I'm . . . not . . . Three thou option . . .'

'You're a genius,' Robert told her.

'Fancy a coffee?'

'It's raining . . . oh, all right.'

Sitting on high stools in the chrome-lined coffee bar, neither of them spoke for the first heady drags of the first cigarette of the morning, then Robert said, 'You're a sly minx . . .'

'What do you mean?'

'First she's escorting Jack Palmer on the telly, and then she's spotted at his funeral . . . so what's the story?'

'You won't believe me if I tell you,' Holly replied, grumpily.

'Try me . . .'

'He was my father. You see, you didn't . . .'

She had never consciously hidden her parentage, but she had grown up without a father, he had never really been part of her vocabulary. Even when she had found out who he was, she had never called him Dad, and she saw him so sporadically, it had not really occurred to her to talk about him except to people who knew her really well. And though they had never exactly discussed it, she had somehow known that Jack would not have liked it if she had used his name at work. He had told her once that he was proud that she had come from nowhere, just as he had. It meant that no-one could take away the achievement, he said,

133

and she had basked in the warmth of his praise.

'Good God, you mean it!' Robert said, delighted with an unexpected piece of gossip, then he remembered himself. 'I am sorry,' he said, formally.

'That's all right,' Holly said automatically, and then realized that you weren't supposed to say anything when somebody offered their condolences and anyway, it was a stupid thing to say because it sounded as if she didn't mind that Jack was dead. It was an awkward moment.

She sipped at the large paper cup, but the coffee beneath the froth was still too hot to drink.

'I didn't know him very well,' Holly tried to explain, 'I was illegitimate, and well, it's a long story, but we had become quite close recently. I used to see him a bit when I went to LA.'

'How extraordinary!' Robert said.

Her headache was too painful to get into a discussion about why he found it so odd.

'I'd rather you didn't tell everyone,' Holly told him.

'Of course not,' he agreed, but she knew that by the end of the day the story would be all round the office.

It didn't matter, Holly told herself, because Jack was dead. A lot of things didn't seem to matter nearly so much any more.

The suburbs of London were endless: Acton, Southall, Uxbridge. Rows and rows of red-brick streets interspersed with increasing greenery as the train trundled further away from the centre of the city. Clare stared at the gardens which backed onto the railway and told a certain story about the occupants of each house. A well-manicured lawn bordered with standard rose trees indicated an elderly couple of diligent gardeners, the shed and heap of rusting doors a car-repair enthusiast, a climbing frame and several faded plastic pushalong toys spoke of toddlers who were growing up. Each rectangle of land encapsulated its own small world. All those lives going on every day. All those breakfasts and school runs and arguments. Outside, lives collided, and serpentine trails of kinship and friendship threaded through society, but inside, in each little home, family dramas unfolded like plays without an audience, and nobody really knew what went on in another person's life.

Clare was hungover. Her pummelled brain did not feel capable of focusing on anything for very long, but from time to time a thought would shoot painfully to the front of her forehead and seem almost terrifyingly profound. But as soon as she tried to retain it for the future it eluded her, and she found herself holding onto the sensation of revelation without a clue as to what the thought had been.

When she was little she had fantasized about having a sister. Lone heroines like Susannah of the Mounties and Anne of Green Gables interested her for a while, but it was only when she discovered *Little Women* that she really understood the escapist pleasure of reading. Friends were OK, and she had as many as anyone else, but there had never been a special best friend in whom she could confide that her life, even with all its privilege that her father reminded her of daily, was desperately lonely. It would have seemed too ungrateful.

The sister she imagined was someone like her, but naughtier. They would have adventures together. She was the sort of person who would suggest and build a tree house on the Heath. The sort of person with whom she could run away to the seaside and survive in an upturned boat on the beach.

Perhaps that was why she had been so insistent, the previous afternoon when they were sitting in the wine bar, that she and Holly were similar. Now that she thought about it, it seemed a pretty hollow claim. It was strange to think that all those times she had wished for an urchin to materialize with scuffed knees and a cheeky look on her grubby face, Holly had been only five or so miles away.

Outside the train window there was a cemetery that seemed to go on for miles. Clare closed her eyes and let herself drift, but when she opened them again, it was still there. When she was a little girl she had wished for parents who would do normal things like go to the park at the weekend, or teach her to swim. But she could not even imagine her mother in the public pool, her thick shining hair flattened and dripping with chlorine water. The week before Clare's birthdays, Philippa would ask Clare to make a list of four or five friends and invitations would be sent out for tea at Harrods. The girls would all arrive in party dresses and white ankle socks and dutifully eat their ice-cream with long-handled spoons. Philippa and Jack would sit a little distance away, drinking coffee, smoking, and occasionally glancing at their wrist-watches, waiting for the first moment when the interminable boredom of the occasion could be politely brought to a conclusion. Clare had once overheard Jack joking about it afterwards at one of the cheese and wine parties her parents used to throw on Saturday nights during the early Seventies.

'I've spent most of my life trying to find adults I could have intelligent conversation with. I find it almost impossible to revert to talking to children . . .'

And his companion had roared with sycophantic laughter as people always did when Jack made one of his pronouncements, half-shocked, half-admiring the iconoclastic sentiments he dared to express.

Jack had the great gift of making everything he said sound spontaneous. It was why his most famous commercials ran and ran, for there was a fresh simplicity about the words that people could not tire of. His best lines became part of the language. 'Taste the dream,' people said to one another with a knowing smile, when they tried a new food they liked. 'We're on the road,' they said when they switched on the engine and released the handbrake at the beginning of a car journey. It was all the more remarkable that Jack could claim no interest in children when everyone knew that he had come up with the immortal line, 'Here's Farmer Fred who makes your bread.' Farmer Fred was so successful that the spin-off merchandise and books about Farmer Fred and his dog Bran became bestsellers the Christmas they were released.

Sometimes, lying in her room at the top of the big white house, Clare had wished her parents were dead, so that she could be adopted into a big happy family who would sit around a great wooden table at mealtimes, laughing, throwing their food around, then rushing out to play in barns and wheatfields, returning with straw in their hair and smiles on their ruddy faces. Ironically, this vision of family happiness derived solely from the sun-drenched adverts for Farmer Fred's Bread.

Clare shuddered. The peculiar coincidence of seeing Jack for the first time in many years on television, and then almost immediately hearing he was dead, kept making her think that she had had something to do with his death, and she remembered her wish guiltily, trying to suppress the giddy feeling of panic that her hangover was so keen to escalate.

'Do men constitutionally lack the bit of the brain that deals with folding up dry washing and putting it away, d'you think?' Ella said later as they chatted together in the steamy kitchen.

It felt very nice being home.

'. . . I only ask because it would be unfair to criticize Dad over something that he can do nothing about . . .'

'Oh dear, has it been that bad?' Clare asked.

She was frying eggs in a large blackened frying-pan, suddenly ravenously hungry. Ella was sitting at the kitchen table with a picture of a human skeleton in front of her, testing herself on the names of the bones.

'Dad told me on day one that he would do everything and I was not to do anything at all except revise for my exams,' Ella looked up and registered Clare's look of surprise, 'yes, he was really nice. He was great at putting all Tom's washing into the machine,' she paused and chewed on a pencil, 'I'm sure he would have been great at doing the washing-up in one huge load at the end of the week, which is obviously what he intended, except he didn't seem to notice that we'd run out of plates by Tuesday. Still, that's poets for you . . . I realized the poem "Broken Crockery" wasn't as I'd previously assumed a metaphor for a failed marriage, but in fact a simple description of what would have happened if he'd added one more cup to the tottering pile on the draining-board . . .'

Clare winced at the savageness of Ella's wit.

'Then, when I actually did the washing-up, and hung out Tom's wet clothes, and took them in again and folded them up and put them away, Dad looks up from his paper and says crossly, "I *said* I'd do that" . . .'

Clare threw back her head and laughed. She turned the heat down under the frying-pan, wiped her hands and sat down opposite Ella.

'I've got something to tell you.'

'Oh no, you're not pregnant again . . .'

Clare was shocked at the degree of despair in her daughter's eyes. It made her slightly nervous about what she was about to say.

'No, nothing like that, although I suppose it is an addition to the family. I have a sister. Well, a half-sister, called Holly. She's almost exactly the same age as me . . .' Clare outlined the history as Ella listened intently.

'What's she like?'

'She's . . .' Clare tried to think of a word to describe the combination of vivacity and quick-temperedness, 'fun, well she is, but that's not enough . . . I suppose she's kind of tremendously fearless . . .'

'Sounds great,' Ella said eagerly, and Clare suddenly realized who Holly had reminded her of. Not Jack, although she looked a lot like him, but her forthright daughter.

'I think you'd like her,' Clare said.

'Do you like her?' Ella asked.

How wonderful it was that Ella had such a clear idea of her own identity that she did not automatically assume that she and Clare would feel the same way.

'Very much,' Clare said.

'And would Dad like her?'

'I don't think so,' Clare said, wondering why she thought that, but her brain was still too fuzzy to figure it out. 'When I was little I used to wish for a sister, and I didn't know that all the time I had one living on the other side of town . . . So I got my wish, I suppose. I should have wished that someone would *tell me* I had a sister. You have to be so specific with wishes, don't you?'

Ella looked at her to see whether she was joking. Clare smiled. She was. Sort of. Ella's disapproval of childishness could be rather intimidating.

'So I'll have an aunt in London when I go to medical school.'

In London, Clare had imagined her life in Cornwall in a kind of sealed capsule. The two places had no connection except the train journey between. She had not thought of Holly as Ella and Tom's aunt. She did not think she had talked much about her children to Holly, but she couldn't remember everything they had said. They had spent the previous evening getting more and more drunk together until Clare had fallen asleep in the battered old armchair, and been woken by the fizz of an Alka Seltzer next to her face. Holly was dressed and made up for work. They had compared hangovers and then Holly had gone, leaving Clare to let herself out. After making herself a cup of black tea with a stale tea bag she found in an almost empty box, Clare had walked along the top of Trafalgar Square to Charing Cross tube station, her grip on reality returning a little as she breathed in fresh air after the smoke-soaked atmosphere of Holly's bedroom.

'Anyway, I'm glad you're back,' Ella said, leaning over the table to kiss Clare on the cheek.

'I'm sorry I left you for so long, just before your exams.'

'It was fine. Did you get what you wanted out of going?' Ella asked with her usual directness.

'I think maybe I did,' Clare said smiling.

Philippa could not stay in the house any longer. Every corner of every room was full of him. In his office, she twirled in his chair, pushing herself round with the toe of her shoe until his bookshelves spun around her head. She could still smell the scent of him there. It was as if he had just wandered out into the kitchen to get a cup of coffee or a glass of wine and she was waiting, mid-sentence, for him to return. Her nails dug into the padded leather arms, grasping at something physical to embody his continuing presence. He knew that she hated it when he walked out when they were in the middle of a discussion. He knew it. He had done it to punish her. Come back, you bastard, she screamed inside her head.

There was a downpour outside. The weather had been hot and unusually summery up until the funeral, as if it had no respect for her feelings. Now, the rain fell on the roof of the conservatory like machine-gunfire, so loud she could not think. She called her secretary, Yvonne, who assured her that everything was fine without her, but she knew that already. Since she had sold her company she had become extremely rich and more or less redundant.

During the years she had worked day and night to build up the management consultancy, she had, just occasionally, stopped to wonder whether there would ever be a time when she would be able to let go. The moment came without warning one day in a black cab on her way to see an interior designer when she suddenly realized that she had spent most of her waking hours the previous month vacillating between an ornate or minimalist style of decoration for her office. Philippa had turned the taxi back and by the end of the same afternoon had set in motion the sale of the company to her chief competitor for a ludicrous price. She had taken the honorary title of chairman of the newly-merged company only as a sop to her vanity and an irritation to the man who had been her rival for so many years. On the phone that evening, Jack had promised her that when he was done with editing, they would take time off together and travel the world before it was too late.

'Too late for the world, or for us?' she had asked him.

And after the slightest pause from the satellite link, his laughter had gurgled down the line.

'You've never lost your edge, have you?' he said, 'that's what I love about you.'

Why couldn't those have been his last words to her? Why had he left her with anger still in the air that wouldn't seem to go away however much she opened the windows?

'Can I do anything for you?' Yvonne asked, breaking the long, thought-filled silence.

Philippa stared at the rivers of rain pouring down the windows.

'Book me one of those holidays. Take the one that leaves soonest. I don't care where.'

Chapter 14

Simon's boat was moored in the Marina at Brighton, along with dozens of other boats that looked just the same to Holly as she walked back along the boardwalk from the clubhouse, searching the white hulls for identifying marks. It was the first time she had been aboard, even though he had owned the boat for several years. He often asked her if she would like to spend the weekend sailing and she had made excuses because even wearing a Guernsey sweater, Dockers and espadrilles, she didn't see herself as a sailing kind of person. This weekend, after the emotional upheaval of the last week, she had jumped at the opportunity to get out of London and feel the wind on her face. She was enjoying it more than she had thought she would, even though it was raining so hard it was impossible to tell where the sea ended and the sky began. Playing cards in the cabin reminded her of being in the caravan Colette's family had taken every summer at Camber Sands. It felt safe and cosy drinking beer out of cans and chatting about nothing in particular with Simon.

'Did you find it?'

'Yes, thank you,' Holly ducked her head. The boat was fun in a cramped, Wendy-house kind of way, but she drew the line at peeing in a chemical toilet.

'If it brightens up tomorrow, I thought we might

wander down to Littlehampton.' Simon was looking at a navigational chart.

'Right. Great!' Holly replied, privately hoping the sky would continue to throw it down. The slight rocking motion of water beneath them was quite relaxing, but she wasn't sure she would be as happy bobbing about on the swirling grey mass beyond the Marina walls. Simon folded his chart and dealt another hand of gin rummy. She took up the cards slowly.

'Did you know there's a floating Chinese restaurant? D'you fancy going? Or I saw a poster for a karaoke evening in a pub . . .'

Simon grimaced.

'You're not serious?'

''Course I am. Come on, it'll be fun. Scampi and chips in the basket, lots of lager and I promise I won't make you sing.'

Holly had all the gestures and the power, but her voice was approximately a semitone flat and 'Memories' was a difficult song at the best of times. The packed audience divided between booing and cheering as she returned to the table, her face pink from the exertion and heat.

'Was I OK?' she asked earnestly.

'You were brilliant,' Simon said, making room for her next to him on his chair.

'I'd love to be able to really sing. Did I ever tell you that the first day I got given a dictaphone at work, I brought it home that evening and taped myself singing along to Patsy Cline? I wanted to know how bad I sounded, and you know, it wasn't that bad . . .'

She remembered herself standing in the colourful fall-out that was her bedroom, can of Stella in one hand, dictaphone in the other, singing 'Crazy'.

'Your turn,' Holly said, taking a slug of lager and pointing at the stage. They were calling for volunteers.

'No way,' Simon said.

'You must. You've got all the words on the screen. Go on. You couldn't be worse than that . . .' she pointed at the elderly Teddy boy with boot-polish quiff who was slurring his way through 'Always on my Mind'. 'Go on, I dare you . . .'

'I suppose if I don't, I'll never hear the last of it . . . ?'

'Correct . . .' Holly drained her glass.

'As a matter of fact, I used to do Sinatra after about fourteen pints when I was at college . . .'

'Well then . . .'

'But I've only had three . . .' he pointed at his empty glass.

'I'll get another round in while you're up there.' Holly was unrelenting.

Simon walked unsteadily towards the stage and within seconds was standing in the spotlight singing 'Strangers in the Night' to a full orchestral accompaniment.

'You bastard,' Holly said, sticking her tongue out at him when he came back to the table, 'you never told me you could really sing.'

At closing time they walked along the sea front, bought hot dogs from a van and ate them leaning against the railings. Beneath them a row of discothèques pounded out Seventies hits. A gaggle of women wearing L-plates queued on the lower promenade giggling and shrieking.

'Hen party,' Holly said, as Simon stared bewildered.

The rain had stopped but the sea was still heaving. They had to shout to hear each other above the Bee Gees, the crash of waves and the football-rattle drag of pebbles.

'I could be perfectly happy living by the sea,' Holly cried.

'Me too . . .'

'I don't mean somewhere peaceful and nice, like

where Clare lives, I mean somewhere like this, with all the tackiness and sleaze. I'd be in my element.'

'You'd probably get bored with karaoke every night . . .' he joked.

'Well, I could always take up Bingo, or bowling . . .'

'Some of us from work sometimes go bowling on Friday night,' Simon said as they turned to walk back to the Marina.

'Where?' Holly demanded to know, 'why didn't you tell me?'

'Finsbury Park. I didn't think you'd be the slightest bit interested,' he protested.

'Well, that just shows . . .'

'What?'

'Oh, something or other, I don't bloody know . . . come on,' she began to run towards the blur of flashing lights at the end of the promenade, 'I want to go on the dodgems.'

Later that night they lay in their separate berths chatting in the dark. The funfair had been a shot of adrenalin, sobering them up. Holly had insisted on going on every ride and she was the most aggressive dodgem-car driver Simon had ever had the misfortune to sit next to.

'Thank you for a lovely day,' Holly said, between creaks as she tried to turn over. 'God, these beds are narrow . . .'

'They're called berths . . .'

'That doesn't make them any wider.'

'It was a pity about the rain,' he said, apologetically.

'Well, it was different . . .'

'Hmm. Let's hope it clears up tomorrow.'

A long loud yawn filled the space between them.

'I like Brighton,' Holly said suddenly, as if she had just woken up again.

Simon sighed.

'So do I,' he replied softly.

'Did I ever tell you that Brighton is where I discovered that Jack was my dad . . .' Holly asked casually, as if she was just remembering a trivial detail that had slipped her mind.

'No,' he replied, abandoning his effort to encourage sleep. 'No, I never knew that.'

'It wasn't exactly in Brighton, but afterwards,' Holly remembered. 'We came down here for a celebration, just after I got my O levels. Me and Mo and Jack. Once every couple of months he would turn up in some flash car and I'd watch him from the balcony, standing by the driver's door, waiting for us. I don't think he wanted to leave the car for a second down there, and I couldn't blame him . . . I suppose he must have phoned beforehand, but Mo never told me, although I began to notice that whenever he came she would've insisted I wash my hair the night before . . .' Holly's voice trailed away, then picked up again, '. . . so we came to Brighton for the day and Jack had bought me a camera as a present, because my results were so good. He sometimes did that. Bought me something. Not every time, but when he did, it was always really expensive. We went on all the rides. Me and Jack. Mo wouldn't. She took some pictures of us, and when we got them back from Boots, there was this one of me and him on the Whip and we were both laughing, and you know how you see yourself differently in photos . . . I looked at it and then I looked at Mo, and she tried to skip onto the next photo, and I just said, Jack's my dad, isn't he?'

She fell silent, lost in thought.

'Were you upset?' Simon asked nervously, as if striving to find something neutral to say in the midst of such a powerful revelation.

'I was bloody furious. With both of them. It was like I'd lived my life up till then believing that people told me the truth and they hadn't . . . I was crosser with Mo than Jack. Took us a long time to get over it . . . I mean, I know she thought it was for the best in the beginning, in case he went off again and left us. I can see that she was frightened of me being disappointed . . .'

'And I expect she was frightened of losing you . . .' Simon added.

'What do you mean?' Holly sat up abruptly.

'Well, perhaps she thought that if you knew, you might want to be with him because he could give you more than she could . . .'

'But . . .' Holly began to protest then stopped, 'I've never thought of that,' she admitted, 'isn't that weird? I've never even thought of it from her point of view. You are clever.'

Lying back down she smiled, pleased with Simon's observation. He wasn't normally very good at this sort of conversation. In the darkness she stretched out her left hand, found his right hand, and gave it a quick squeeze before turning over and drifting into sleep.

'What do you think?' Joss asked when Clare returned from working in Vivienne's shop on Saturday evening. The products of Tom and Joss's afternoon were pegged out like washing on a piece of string Joss had strung across the kitchen.

'Late Matisse,' Clare replied, wondering why Tom's paintings always looked so much better when Joss was in charge, suspecting that Joss directed the paintbrush rather more than she did.

'Perhaps we could persuade Vivienne to have some in her shop? Primitive art. I'm sure she'd love it if you told her it was done by Andean Indian children . . .' Joss said.

'. . . with paint made from ground-up beetle and the sap of an endangered tree . . .' Clare added.

They smiled at one another, enjoying the easy digs at their friend's obsession with alternative products.

'Couldn't you get Amelia to put them up in her tea room? Thirty quid each framed, two for fifty?' Joss asked.

'Trouble is, I want them all myself,' Clare laughed, 'you are a clever boy.' She bent down and scooped Tom up from the floor.

'I've been working on something, while you were away . . .' Joss said suddenly.

'Oh, that's marvellous,' she began to enthuse, then stopped herself, knowing that the slightest mistake in tone could send him into a mood. If she was too encouraging he would almost immediately stop what he was doing, if she pretended not to be very interested, he would rage about nobody understanding how hard it was for him. He always made her feel that she was somehow to blame for his writer's block.

When she first met him, his future had looked as bright as any poet's ever did. His poems were published in magazines. One had even made the pages of the *Observer*. Then a small, but highly-regarded, publishing house had published his volume *Women*. In retrospect, the title had been a mistake because although the review coverage had been wide, much wider than for most first collections, most of it had been very negative. Literary editors had not been able to resist giving such a title to leading feminists to review, and, to a woman, they had hated it. Since most of the poems were obliquely about her, Clare had felt responsible for that too. Joss had sunk into a kind of beleaguered gloom and had not written any poetry for several years.

They had been busy then, doing up the house and garden, with Ella a little girl. Clare remembered it as a happy time. Then he had written a novel, which had been rejected by his publisher, and a couple of others. And after that he had retreated into poetry again, but in the interim he seemed to have lost touch with the *Zeitgeist*. Now, when poetry was enjoying a popularity it had never before achieved, Joss's work was not read. In the Seventies he had been a young lion and his voice had spoken to a generation, but now his roar seemed anachronistic among the knowing, quirky voices of the young post-modernists.

'What's it about?' she asked, trying to sound neutral, but engaged.

'All this newness that's around,' Joss replied.

He never let her read his work until it was finished. Sometimes not even then.

'You seem new too,' he told her, 'you've changed.'

'Have I?'

' "All these years I thought I knew you, but I did not know this new you . . ." ' Joss quoted a line.

Clare still experienced a girlish thrill when he wrote about her.

'So, what do you think? Can we renew? A modern relationship for the Millennium? What is Clare's vision of the future?'

She laughed at the pun. All the Sunday newspapers seemed to carry supplements entitled 'Blair's Vision of the Future'. She wasn't sure whether he was reciting, or asking her a question.

'What do you mean?' she finally asked, realizing that she was supposed to say something.

Joss sighed heavily and impatiently.

'I suppose I realized when you were not here how much I take you for granted,' he said almost sheepishly, adding, with sudden anger, 'you shouldn't let yourself be taken for granted . . .'

Like most of what he said, there was a germ of truth that made him impossible to dismiss as merely selfish. She had never been very good at asking for what she wanted, and that was not something she could blame on him.

'OK then,' she said to him, making a feeble joke, 'you can do the washing-up for a week . . .'

'I'm not talking about the bloody washing-up,' Joss said, suddenly angry, 'for God's sake, you shouldn't think of yourself as a washing-up machine. That's what I'm talking about. I'm talking about you recognizing your needs as a woman . . . you constantly undervalue yourself . . . I'm talking about what you want from life, where you see yourself in ten years . . .'

She wanted to say that if she undervalued herself it was because her confidence had been eroded not just by his fucking other women, but the way he jumped on everything she said. If he would just give her time to collect her thoughts, she might be able to make some kind of sense. She wanted to say that she tried not to think about where she would be in ten years in case that meant facing the prospect of still being in Penderric, still serving in his former mistress's shop two afternoons a week, still making jam. But she knew him well enough to know that he wasn't really interested in hearing what she wanted to say. The silence that had fallen between them was charged with his impatience. Tom started to grizzle. Clare shot Joss a glance that said, don't go on.

He turned back to the sink and the task of scrubbing paint from his nails and then asked with studied indifference, 'I don't suppose he left you any money?'

'There was no will.'

'Which means that Philippa gets the lot.'

'I suppose so.'

'Surely you're entitled to some of it?'

Suddenly the direction of the conversation became clear. Joss was so bloody clever. He had dangled the carrot of talking about their future so that she would ask him what it meant and he could ask about Jack's money without appearing grasping. How was it that he always managed to sneak up on her tangentially? In a curious kind of way, she admired his ingenuity, wondering, as she had wondered on many occasions before, whether he had planned their conversation in advance, or whether he was just effortlessly manipulative.

Mo had seen her before, many times. Even if there hadn't been the name on the credit card, she would have recognized her. Philippa had not changed much since the day that she married Jack Palmer and was pictured in the *Tatler* standing outside the registry office in King's Road wearing a short white couture dress. She came into the store once or twice a year, at the beginning of the season, and spent several thousand pounds on what she called her basics. Sometimes Mo had tried to imagine how many yards of cupboard space Philippa's basics must occupy: an aircraft hangar always came to mind. It was a bit of a shock to see her so soon after the funeral.

Philippa was wearing a black trouser suit, but the summer clothes she had picked out and hung over her arm were mostly orange and lime green, the year's bright citrus shades, which only someone with the right colouring could get away with. Philippa had had the right colouring, Mo thought, bitchily, once upon a time. Usually, Mo let someone else attend to her, but she was standing in the middle of the section clearly expecting service and there were no other assistants around.

'Can I help you with those?' Mo approached, taking the hangers from her one by one and showing her to the changing-rooms. 'Lovely bright colours,' she hung the clothes on a hook, unable to resist the urge to say something.

'I'm going on holiday,' Philippa replied, with a faint patronizing smile.

'If there's anything you need . . .' Mo said, tightly, swishing the curtain across the cubicle.

Philippa began to strip. She had often meant to find

out where department stores bought mirrors with subtly distorting glass that made you look far better than you ever looked at home. She stepped into a loose dress made of orange linen, turned round and smiled at her reflection but the dress hung unflatteringly from her shoulders and threw a horrible yellow light onto her neck and face. Quickly, she took it off and put on a trouser suit of white linen which made her look like an inmate at a psychiatric hospital. She inspected the labels. Everything was her size but it was all too big. She had always lived by the adage that you could never be too rich or too thin, and now she had more money than she could ever spend, and she was so thin that clothes looked like sacks. With rising panic, she tried a belted sleeveless Versace dress the colour of a geranium, but neither the stylish simplicity of the garment nor the outrageous charm of the mirror could flatter her neck and arms. There was too much skin and too little flesh. Recent rapid weight loss had made her look suddenly old. She had come to the store to cheer herself up, but had looked in the mirror and seen her own mortality. Trembling, Philippa drew back the curtain.

'Can you get me these in a size 8?'

'Everything?' the assistant asked.

'Not the orange. Nothing orange. Or white . . .' her voice was rising.

Mo looked at the hangers she was being handed, and then at Philippa's face poking through the curtain, the selvage clasped tightly to her cheek. The look in her eyes was not arrogance but sheer terror. Mo recognized suffering and understood. For a moment she allowed her eyes to meet Philippa's and acknowledge her pain, then she looked away quickly.

'Cerruti has some lovely dark navy separates,' she said, breaking the charged silence.

'Right,' Philippa said, anxious to re-establish the

hierarchy with the assistant after the strange moment, 'perhaps you could choose some for me?'

It was like in the movies, Mo thought, flipping through a rack of jackets. Two women from opposite ends of the social spectrum meet. They have nothing in common except the man they both love. In the movie they would become friends, even plot against the man, he would get his comeuppance and everyone would live happily ever after. A romantic comedy. In real life, Mo would continue to watch Philippa from a distance once or twice a year when she came to buy her spring and autumn wardrobe, and she would size her up, as she had done ever since the first time she spotted her in the department, measuring her decline against her own: number of grey hairs, firmness of bottom, drop of breasts, except that now there would be no small victories like the time she had spotted a varicose vein behind Philippa's left knee, because she could no longer think of her as a competitor. All they now shared was loss.

Chapter 15

Was there any point in continuing to take the Pill? Holly was staring at the posters Sellotaped to the wall beside the receptionist's hatch. If she really believed that condoms worked, she reasoned, looking at the helpline number for HIV/AIDS, then she should not need to be on the Pill anyway. If she trusted a condom to stop her getting a terminal disease, she ought to trust it to stop her getting pregnant. The way things were going it would have to be an immaculate conception anyway, and she didn't know whether the Pill was effective against that. The doctor was running half an hour late, and Holly was sure that she was contracting TB from the disgusting old man who leered a yellow smile at her in between death-throe bouts of coughing. The moment she made up her mind to walk out of the crowded waiting-room, the receptionist called her name far too loudly for the distance that separated them and Holly jumped.

It wasn't the health risk involved in taking the Pill as much as the summation of her life in the doctor's notes.

Age: 35.

Weight gain? NO (at least that wasn't a problem)

Are you in a stable relationship? NOT REALLY (sounded so final to say just NO)

Do you smoke? YES (but I'm cutting down)
How many? ABOUT 10

Holly bought ten cigarettes each morning, and ten each evening for the next day. She didn't know any smoker who actually smoked ten a day. She was surprised that the computer wasn't programmed automatically to compensate for the underestimation and come up with twenty when the doctor tapped in ten.

My life, Holly thought, taking the prescription for another six months' supply. If she decided to put in a personal ad, as Colette was so keen for her to do, it would read:

'Thirty-quite-a-lot female smoker, slim, seeks man to make taking Pill worthwhile.'

It seemed such bad value to take potentially dangerous hormones each night without actually getting the pleasure they were designed to give you, like paying a year's subscription for an expensive gym and never getting round to going, or not using up the monthly free bit on your mobile-phone bill.

Holly picked up six slim boxes from the pharmacy counter at Boots, one slightly bulkier packet from the newsagent, and a giant cappuccino on her way into the office.

Putting the shake-sized coffee down on her desk, she decided to ring Colette before she opened her post.

'It's me. Fancy a drink tonight?'

'A quickie. I'm going out at eight. I could always shower at your place.'

'Not another date?'

'Yeah, you ought to try it.' Colette was in Soul Mates, Eye Love, and regularly left messages on the answerphones of strangers. She had taken to contemporary methods of dating with the zeal of an Open University student studying for a business degree, and her conversation these days was all about hit rates and personal interfacing.

'So far you've had three who wouldn't even reach up to my tits and a trainspotter . . .' Holly reminded her.

'He was not a trainspotter, he was interested in transport policy.'

'Oh, right, excuse me for not knowing the difference.'

'You're so judgemental.'

'So what else is new?'

Holly put down the phone. Colette's attitude had definitely changed. She couldn't work out whether it was just the obsessive blind-dating, or the fact that she was slightly jealous of Holly's discovery of a sister. Colette and Holly had always been like sisters. They grew up in the same tower block, Colette and her five brothers in a flat on the fifth floor, and Holly on the eleventh; they went to the same schools; they had even performed an exchange of blood when they were twelve, although Holly had never thought that Colette's pricking herself with a pin involved quite the same commitment as the gash she had sliced into her forearm with Mo's Kitchen Devil.

Perhaps Colette was getting serious about a man. She had always been a bit odd about men. As soon as she'd been to bed with someone, she'd lose the use of the first-person pronoun and start every sentence with we. You only had to think about her ex-husband to see that she had a few neurotransmitters missing in the relationship area of her brain. Yes, he was rich. Cosmetic surgeons usually were. Yes, it was comforting to know that you could have your bottom lifted for free, but to actually marry someone who spent the honeymoon measuring your breasts up for enlargement and insisted that you give up your job on your return?

'We think I've got quite enough to do looking after the home,' Colette had announced proudly on their return from a Caribbean cruise.

Hadn't she seen *The Stepford Wives*, for God's sake?

Holly opened her diary. The visit to the GP had taken so long it was almost time to leave the office for lunch with an independent producer called Charlie Prince, who was a friend of Robert's.

'What's Charlie Prince like?' Holly said, leaning on the door-frame to Robert's office.

'Clever, arrogant . . . very like you in some respects.'

'Oh thanks . . .'

'Very sexy too,' Robert conceded, 'but not my type.'

When she had called him to make a lunch-date, he had had an extremely sexy telephone voice, she remembered. She had made it a rule never to mix business with pleasure, but sometimes she wondered whether she shouldn't lapse just occasionally. It wasn't that she couldn't imagine going to bed with some of the men she dealt with, it was the thought of negotiating with someone whose penis had been inside her. At least there wouldn't be that endless waiting for the phone to ring like after most one-night stands, but it might be worse. He would call and then feel obliged to say something, or not, she couldn't decide which would be worse, and then there would be all the comments as people found out. They always did find out. *He's really screwed a good deal out of her. Who did you have to fuck to get this?* Whatever happened she would regret it.

Charlie Prince was as sexy as his voice. Sexier even. She liked men with dark curls, and there was mischief in his eyes. They spent the first course gossiping, the second discussing films they had loved, and even though he was slightly keener on Tarantino than she was, which was really a gender thing, she decided, they were almost perfectly compatible. They were drinking coffee and she found herself telling him about her current favourite property, which was the script her client Anji was working on entitled *The One*.

The way to sell something for a lot of money, she had discovered after years experimenting, was to tell potential buyers that you weren't going to sell it to them. Even better than that, tell them that you weren't even going to let them see it.

'I'll read it this afternoon if you get it sent over . . .' Charlie Prince was saying as their second double espressos arrived at the table.

'She's still working on it. I haven't even read it yet.'

'Can I have first look when it's ready?'

'Certainly not.'

'Why?' Charlie smiled at her. Very naughty smile. Holly almost forgot why not.

'Because I'm sure it's for Hollywood,' she told him.

'But I'm fixing up a development deal at the moment. Can't tell you who with, but I think you'll like it . . . listen,' he said, leaning across the table, 'I know we've only just met, but are you free for dinner one Friday evening?'

What was this man not prepared to do to get first look at the script? Did she care? Holly threw caution to the wind.

'Friday, which Friday?'

'I'll call you. My wife and I are trying to arrange some dinner parties. You'd really get on with her, I think . . .'

What are you doing married, she wanted to ask him. You're years younger than me and miles trendier.

'She's writing a script herself. Needs a good agent,' Charlie winked at her as he signed the bill with a flourish. 'Maybe you could bring *The One* with you.'

'Maybe,' said Holly, feeling as if she had just been run over.

Eamon was the only teetotal Irishman Mo knew and he was all the more unusual because he was a barman. It wasn't that he didn't like drink, he told anyone who asked, it was that he liked it too much. If only someone would perfect a way of taking the alcohol out of

Guinness and making it taste the same, like they did with decaffeinated coffee, he'd be a happy man. But he was a happy man, Mo thought. He was the happiest man she had ever met. And as a matter of fact, decaffeinated coffee was never as nice as the real thing.

'There were a lot of them tonight,' he said, pouring some lime cordial into the pint glass of mineral water she was drinking.

'It's *Riverdance*,' Mo said, 'every little girl wants to be in *Riverdance* now. If the class gets much bigger I'm going to have to split it and do two a week.'

She had been running an Irish dancing class for years. It was the only part of her heritage that she had brought down south with her. Her mother had taught her when she was a girl, and she had won prizes. When Holly was little, she had started to teach her on Saturday mornings, when nobody could object to the tapping on the floor. Then some of Holly's friends wanted to learn after they'd seen her showing off in the playground, and that was how the class had started. Holly had dropped out at eleven when she grew. In just over a year she shot up a foot, and suddenly her long legs seemed to get tangled up in the steps, but the class continued. Recently it had become so popular Mo had had to hire the whole hall at the Irish Club rather than one of the rooms, which was better really, because the hall had bare wooden boards and the girls could really hear the thud of their shoes. She enjoyed the class. It meant there was more to life than work, tube and home every day. It brought in quite a tidy sum of money these days too. Enough so she didn't have to save for a holiday.

Eamon wanted her to go to Ireland with him for two weeks in July. He said she looked as if she needed a holiday, and he was right. The past few weeks had been draining.

Mo hadn't been to Ireland since she was a little

girl. She remembered soda bread, donkeys and the Connemara landscape which couldn't make up its mind whether to be land or sea. Eamon came from County Mayo.

'There is a little golf course just across from Achill Island,' he was telling her, a faraway look in his grey eyes, 'and sometimes the wind is so strong it blows the best-hit ball right back at you.'

Mo couldn't see the attraction of that, but then she'd never understood golf.

'You wouldn't be playing golf all day, though, would you, Eamon?' she asked him.

'Of course I would not,' he protested with a wink, 'I'd have a break for my dinner and my tea . . .' He leaned forward over the bar, sensing a weakening of her resistance.

She couldn't make up her mind. She and Eamon had been together years, but they had never been on holiday together. It would put the relationship onto a different plane. They had always been equally reluctant to get serious, Eamon because he had married too young and been through an acrimonious divorce which had brought shame on his family back home, Mo because of Holly, or so she told herself. Even though they got along famously and they slept together once or twice a week, Mo had never wanted to live with him. She'd become used to having her own key to her own front door. But it was stupid to waste the opportunity of having a good time for a couple of weeks, just because she was afraid of getting in too deep. They were both in their fifties, not teenagers. There was no-one she was more comfortable with than Eamon, except Holly, and Holly was too busy to have holidays with her nowadays. Mo had been on enough bargain breaks to Tenerife with the girls at work to last her a lifetime.

'All right, then,' she heard herself saying, 'I'll go up

to the travel agency tomorrow and see about some brochures.'

'But Charlie Prince is quite famous,' Colette said, taking the glass of wine that Holly offered her. She had a large white towel wrapped around her head and was wearing Holly's cherry-blossom kimono. 'There's a feature on him in this month's *Arena*.'

'So?' Holly watched as Colette touched up the varnish on her toenails.

'Well, I mean, why can't you just set your sights a bit lower?' Colette suddenly threw her head forward and began to towel dry her hair vigorously.

'Why should I?' Holly responded automatically.

The look on Colette's upside-down face said, well, you're not exactly successful this way, are you?

'The trouble with you is that you want too much,' Colette tried to be helpful. 'You want *An Officer and a Gentleman*, but you want to have a conversation about nuclear disarmament with him afterwards. You see *Truly, Madly, Deeply* and you want Alan Rickman. The whole point is that he's dead.'

'You wanted Michael Maloney and he's so boring.'

'He's not boring. He turned a Russian novel into a pigeon, don't you remember?'

'So you want the guy who turns a book into a bird and I want the dead one. What's the difference? I'll tell you the difference. Alan Rickman is sex on legs . . .'

'But he's got a moustache . . .' Colette said, thinking that she'd at last caught Holly out.

'But his voice is just so . . . brrr,' Holly shivered with pleasure, 'frankly, if he wouldn't shave it off, I'd close my eyes and pretend. I'd make an exception for that voice.'

'He's still dead,' Colette said, straightening up. Her dark brown wavy hair fell prettily round her face.

'Why don't you put in an ad?' she asked, as if for the first time.

'They're just so desperate,' Holly said. 'Worst of all are the ones who say "OK, so I've placed an ad but I'm not a sad old git, it's just that as a company director I don't have the time . . ." I think I'd prefer one that started "Sad old git seeks . . ."'

'Not that you ever look at them, of course,' Colette said.

'OK, just supposing I did do a personal ad, or something, what would I say?'

Colette made an O with her mouth and painted on mulberry lipstick using a lipbrush. She was the only person Holly knew who used a lipbrush.

'You can go for the straightforward type, like, "Vivacious, slim redhead seeks tall man, GSOH" . . . keep it simple, you know . . .' Colette blew herself a kiss in the mirror.

'Yes, what is GSOH anyway?'

'Good Sense Of Humour,' Colette enunciated clearly, then blotted her mouth with a clean tissue she took from a packet in her handbag. Holly always forgot to blot.

'Oh, for God's sake! Anyone who puts GSOH doesn't have one at all . . .'

'Or you can go for the more roundabout ones, like, "Emma seeks Mr Knightley" . . . maybe that'd be more you . . .' Colette said.

'I'm nothing like Emma and I don't want a Mr Knightley.'

'I saw one the other day that might suit you. Very simple, it just went, "Harry. Why don't we meet? Sally."'

'But the whole point of *When Harry Met Sally* was that they *had* met and were best friends. Isn't it asking a bit much to meet a best friend, who then turns into Mr Right, thereby telescoping at least ten years' human communication into one line in a news-paper?'

'It was only an example . . . you just think of your favourite heroine . . . anyway, I've got to run,' Colette looked at her watch, 'meeting yet another Heathcliff in All Bar One in ten minutes . . .'

'How many Heathcliffs have there been so far?'

'This is my third. Number one still lived with his mother, and the other had an artificial foot. I mean I know it shouldn't matter, but . . .'

'What did his ad read, Long John Silver seeks parrot?'

'Or you could try an agency,' Colette continued, ignoring her. 'That's what I'm going to do next, when I've saved up the joining fee.'

'You've made it sound so attractive, I can hardly wait,' Holly told her.

'I'm trying to compile a list of things I want and things I don't want in a man,' Holly announced later to Simon, 'but I only seem to be able to come up with things I don't want . . .'

They were sitting on the roof terrace of Holly's club in Soho. Her encounter with Colette had made her feel depressed, and the only thing to do about it, she told Simon when he opened his door to her, was to drink a lot of champagne.

' . . . I mean, you don't like someone because they like the same things as you, do you? Whenever I look at those personal ads . . . just for a laugh,' she qualified quickly, 'about the biggest turn-offs are the ones that say "likes cinema", I mean for God's sake, who doesn't like cinema? The fact that you use two expensive words to state the obvious shows how boring you must be . . .'

Simon chuckled.

'It's almost as bad as "I'm considered attractive . . ."'

I think that means he's bound to be bald. Who considers him attractive? His mother? I've decided the best ones are the ones you phone and leave a message. What you have to do is get drunk and listen, then if you fancy one just blurt out enough to get them to ring you . . . Then, you see, you have this list of questions by the phone for when they call back . . .'

'What sort of questions?' Simon asked.

'Do you have or have you ever had a beard?' Holly answered immediately.

'What about if they'd been on a trekking holiday, or something, and they didn't have access to water?' Simon asked.

'Exactly. I could never sustain a relationship with someone who'd thought for one minute about going on a trekking holiday.' She picked up the empty bottle and held it up in the air, hoping that a waitress would see and bring them another without the tedious process of having to get up and go downstairs to the bar.

'Is that it, then?' Simon asked.

'God, no. My list is enormous. Almodóvar – genius or warped pervert?'

'So?'

'Genius, of course . . .'

'Go on . . .'

'Have you ever sent a round-robin letter at Christmas . . . ?'

'Oh yes, I really loathe those things,' Simon agreed, 'especially the ones that start with a disclaimer, like, "I hate these as much as you do, but there never seems to be the time to write to everyone I know . . ." '

'Exactly,' said Holly, 'with lots of exclamation marks. It's like, no, you don't even register on the hating-these-things scale, mate . . .'

'What else?' Simon asked, warming to the theme.

'Have you ever sung along to the chorus of "Lady in

Red?" What a dirge! I can't stand it. And I think Chris de Burgh is short . . .'

'What difference does that make?' Simon attempted to introduce a note of logic, 'I mean, you're hardly likely to come across Chris de Burgh himself in an ad . . .'

'It just makes me hate the song even more and his soulful expression . . .' she pulled a face.

'Enough,' Simon held up his hands, 'I'm beginning to feel sorry for the guy.'

The waitress uncorked another bottle of champagne.

'Here's another one . . . have the words "Maybe we've had enough champagne for one evening" ever crossed your lips?' Holly said, drinking a glass in two gulps, 'OK, so what would yours be?'

'Who's your favourite Beatle?' Simon said.

'Ringo Starr,' Holly replied.

'No, I meant that would be one of my questions.'

'Oh, and did I pass?'

'As long as you didn't say John Lennon. I can't stand people who worship John Lennon. I mean, I preferred the Rolling Stones anyway, but John bloody Lennon, with his silly glasses and his smug bloody "Imagine all the People". Imagine all the people who could have lived good lives on the money he put up his nose. It's not that I particularly care what he did. I just hate the hypocrisy . . .'

Holly stared at Simon. It was the first time she could remember him getting heated, apart from the time he was convinced the waiter in a Chinese restaurant had given him a draught Carling in a glass as opposed to the Tsing Tao beer he had requested. What a thing to get worked up about. She'd never really thought about John Lennon like that, although, now that she did, she remembered having been very tired of all the candlelit vigils and stuff that surrounded his death.

'This is my whole point,' she said, feeling the wonderful *bonhomie* of a shared prejudice.

'Surely you don't need to do this sort of dating?' Simon said, slurring his words slightly, 'you're always meeting men.'

'But nobody ever takes me seriously, usually because they've already got that part of their lives sorted out. I'm a bit on the side, for recreational purposes only. It's my fault just as much as theirs, as Colette points out all the time, it's the image I project, and I've done such a good job of convincing everyone else, I almost convinced myself . . .'

'So why the change of heart? Why do you suddenly want something different?' Simon asked.

'New Labour, New Lover . . . I don't know. I suppose it must have something to do with my father dying. About the last thing he told me was that I'd never find anyone and it's just about the only thing I've got left to prove to him . . . I don't know. Meeting Clare, who's married with two children, and we're the same age, well, you know how competitive I am . . .'

Simon laughed.

'At least with an advert there's not a lot of doubt about what you're saying. You're saying, I want a relationship, and presumably they're saying that too . . .' Holly went on trying to persuade herself.

'But isn't that half the fun?' Simon asked, 'I mean all that will she, won't she stuff is quite a turn-on . . .'

'Is it really?' Holly thought about some of the girl-friends Simon had had over the years. Most of them had looked as if they had kept him guessing for quite a long time. 'Trouble is,' she said, 'I never get that bit because generally I will. Not confident enough to run the risk of missing getting laid in case he doesn't call again . . .'

'Biological clock,' said Simon.

'Oh don't start,' Holly said, 'why is it when you're a

woman of my age you only have three choices – mother, broody or sad? I'm not a mother, and I'm not broody, I'm just open to the idea of maybe having a sustainable relationship. That's not sad, is it?'

Simon held up his hands in protest.

'You're right, it's just not me . . . so where the hell am I going to find this man?' Holly demanded to know, finishing off the champagne, 'shall we have another?'

'I daren't say no, now,' Simon said.

'Will you marry me, then?' she asked him.

She always asked when she was very drunk. It was so much part of the routine now, she didn't think twice about it, but this time she noticed the briefest stricken look flash across his face. Perhaps it was a bit mean, she thought, to imply that she'd only settle for him because she'd been so bloody unlucky in love.

'I'm afraid I once had a beard,' he confessed, smiling again.

'Oh well forget it then,' she said, cheerfully.

Mo wished that Holly would not ring her when she was drunk. Sometimes it was difficult to tell at first because Holly just sounded happy and talkative and they would chat along for a few minutes, but then she would start repeating herself, telling the story she had started off with as if for the first time and by the end she was sounding like a stuck record and usually crying a bit, and Mo would have to tell her gently to go to bed. There was an awful lot of drinking in Holly's world, and everybody smoked, which made them drink all the more. Mo had never met a drinker who didn't smoke. Her most vivid memory of her father was of him lighting his first bleary cigarette of the day, taking in a great draught, then coughing sour breath at her over the chequered oilcloth on the kitchen table. She hoped Holly wasn't drinking too much. They said it ran in families. Mo had read articles about it in women's magazines. It bothered her to see Holly recklessly ignoring all the health warnings, but she could never work out whether it was just how everyone behaved these days, or whether Holly was like that because she was unhappy underneath all her joking.

'Mum? I just called to see how you were.'

Mo looked at the dull green glow of the radio alarm beside her bed. It was after midnight. They'd always gone to bed later than most people, but as she grew older she found she needed her seven hours' sleep each night. Next to her in the bed, Eamon shifted. She didn't want to wake him up.

'I'm in bed,' Mo whispered.

'Oh, sorry, I didn't wake you up?'

'No,' Mo answered truthfully, turning onto her side. It didn't seem right to be talking to Holly when Eamon was there. It felt as if there were three of them in the bed.

'How are you?' Mo whispered.

'Fine. Went out with Simon . . . I thought I'd see if you were all right . . .'

'I'm fine . . .'

'I meant to ring you earlier, but I've only just got back . . .'

'Right,' Mo said, 'so are you all right?'

'I'm fine.' As the conversation went on, Holly sounded less ebullient. 'Mum, do you think I'll ever find the One?' she suddenly asked.

'The One?'

'You know, a man with my name written on.'

For a moment, Mo had a vision of a man walking down the street with sandwich-boards with HOLLY painted on in large black letters. She wanted to scold her daughter because Holly was always proclaiming loudly that she didn't want to be in a serious relationship. It made people boring, she said, and Mo felt certain that that attitude would put any likely men off.

'I'm sure you will,' she told her now, not having the heart to criticize at this time of night.

'Was Jack the One for you?' Holly asked her.

The image Mo had of him was always the same. He was standing in the bitter cold outside the shop waiting for her that Christmas. When she caught sight of him her heart had leapt as she allowed herself to believe for a fraction of a second that he was there to reclaim her. After all those years he had realized that only she could make him happy.

'I thought he was,' she told Holly, as, next to her, Eamon began to snore softly.

At the other end of the phone she wasn't sure whether Holly had begun to cry.

'Go to sleep now, love,' Mo said, 'you'll feel better in the morning.'

PART THREE

June

Chapter 16

There *were* roses round the door, the colour of lemon fondant icing, but the rain had battered their soft petals, turning the edges to brown paper and scattering them on the path like confetti. It was the wettest June ever recorded. Typical, thought Holly, that this is the moment I choose to go away for a long weekend. The taxi sloshed away from the gate and she watched it disappear into the misty streets. The little grey town looked more like a deserted mining village than a resort. Holly knocked on the door.

'Is it you?' a very young, surprisingly loud voice asked from the other side.

'Yes. At least I think so,' Holly replied.

'Can you come in?'

'I hope so.'

'MAR ME!' shouted the voice, 'it YOU.'

'It's her,' Clare's voice corrected. 'It's Holly.'

'It Holly,' came the echo.

The door opened and there was Clare, her sleeves rolled up and flour all over her hands, and, at about the same height as her knees, a perfect little grinning cherub with curls exactly the same colour as Clare's.

'Hello, you must be Tom,' said Holly.

Suddenly shy, he turned his face into his mother's legs.

The two women bent forward to kiss each other on the cheek then stood up straight and looked at each other, smiling.

'You're getting wet. Come in,' Clare said, breaking the silence of friendly appraisal, 'mind your head. The doors are all quite low.'

'Have you got a present for me?' Tom suddenly regained his confidence.

'Yes. How did you know?' Holly asked him laughing.

'Where is it?'

'I am sorry to have promised him something on your behalf,' Clare apologized, 'it was the only way I could get him to stop demanding to go out and jump in puddles . . .'

The front door opened straight into the kitchen, which was warm and smelt of cakes baking. While Clare made coffee, and Tom brought his toys, one by one, to show her, Holly sat down at the big wooden table taking in her surroundings. The chipped white porcelain sink was deep and rectangular, the draining-board made of wood that had seen many years of scrubbing. There was a fridge covered in bright plastic letters which seemed to be the only relatively modern item there. Above the wooden cupboards a frieze of children's paintings, some burnt with age, served as wallpaper. It was the kind of artless, primitive kitchen that would have cost a fortune if it had been ordered from a contemporary designer. A door led into the back room where there was a chair, a battered old sofa, a television, and a great deal of poster-coloured plastic.

Seeing her house through a stranger's eyes, Clare began to make excuses.

'Tom rather dominates down here, I'm afraid,' she said, 'he doesn't really have a bedroom of his own, his cot's in Joss's office, so we let him run riot down here. As soon as Ella goes away, he'll have her room,' Clare saw the expression on Holly's face, 'it's OK, the sofa makes into a bed. I'll make it up later. This is why I invited you when Joss was away. It's a bit crowded . . .' She didn't add that she had been pleased Holly had suggested a weekend when Joss was not there. She did not think the two of them would get on.

'Where is Joss, by the way?' Holly asked.

'At a poetry festival. He does about two a year, you know, readings and seminars and all that. They pay his fare and put him up in a nice hotel.'

'I'd like to have met him,' Holly said untruthfully. From what Clare had told her about Joss she had gained the impression of a lazy git who probably had a beard.

'I'm sure there'll be other times,' Clare put an enamel jug of coffee on the table between them.

Now that the pleasantries had been exhausted, they had come to a break in the conversation and Holly found the silence uncomfortable. Seeing Clare in her home made her realize just how little they had in common. This was the house of a poor family in a godforsaken outpost miles away from the things Holly thought of as civilization – cinemas, shops and Italian coffee-shops with steaming Gaggia machines and great discs of *torta de noci* on the counter. What on earth would they find to talk about? Suddenly the three days that stretched ahead of them seemed a very long time.

'I hope the weather gets better,' she said. The weather was what strangers talked about at bus stops.

'The forecast is good,' Clare replied, offering her a flapjack.

'Forecast good,' Tom confirmed from the back room.

'How's work?' Clare asked.

'Fine thanks. Well, the usual roller-coaster, but it's fine. I've got a couple of really good scripts in at the moment and my prestige in the agency seems to have gone up now they've discovered who I am. Or at least, who my father was . . .'

'You told them?'

'It was that bloody clip of me and him going into the party. I kept noticing people giving me funny looks and then I was spotted at the funeral. Gossip's like a virus at my place. One day someone sneezes, the next everyone's got a streaming cold. So I explained, and then they were all so bloody impressed . . . Do you think about him?' she asked Clare.

In their phone conversations since the funeral, they had not discussed Jack. She imagined that they were going through a similar process, each trying to reassess her history in the light of the other's existence.

'Quite a lot,' Clare replied, 'I sometimes wonder why I didn't make more of an effort to see him, for my children, if not for me. And I see him in Ella sometimes, and I'm sad that they did not meet . . . but my primary feeling is a kind of disbelief that he didn't tell me about you.'

'It's weird, the genetic thing, isn't it?' Holly said, 'I sometimes wonder whether there could be a gene for loving films that I inherited from him. No, seriously, I knew I wanted to work in movies long before I even met him, and then someone at work said something about having movies in my blood . . .'

Holly stopped talking as the front door opened and a sulky-looking girl with long, almost black, curly hair walked in, closely followed by an extraordinarily beautiful young man with spiky hair which looked as if it had been dipped in gold. At first sight they looked not unalike the couple in the recent version of *Romeo and Juliet*, although she was more knowing than Juliet, and he a slightly stockier, more masculine version of Leonardo di Caprio.

Clare stood up.

'This is Ella,' she announced.

For an instant, Holly tussled with envy. In spite of all the things she had that Clare did not – money, career, clothes – she knew she had never looked as radiantly proud as Clare did, standing with her arm around her daughter.

'Hello Ella.' Holly got up and, not quite knowing whether to shake her hand or commit herself to a kiss, they ended up in a brief, embarrassed half-hug.

'Matt,' said the young man, holding out his hand. She shook it, wondering how he got his hair to go like that, and whether he looked at everyone with the same smouldering insolence. She felt herself blushing. 'Tom, come and get your present,' she said over-loudly.

The little boy came pelting into the kitchen.

'What it is?' he asked, turning the parcel over in his hands.

'Open it and see,' Holly said.

'He's too young to open it himself,' Ella told her, crouching down, 'here, Tom, d'you want me to help you?'

It was a pop-up book that had a 3D cardboard pirate ship inside.

'It a boat?' Tom asked uncertainly.

'Yes.'

'Take it in sea?'

'Well . . .' Holly looked to Clare for help.

'Not really,' Clare told him, 'but we can sail it round the kitchen when it's too rainy to go to the beach, can't we?'

'Ah, that OK then,' Tom said.

Holly smiled, relieved. 'I bought something for you too,' she told Ella, 'Clare said you had a pierced nose, so I assumed your ears were, too . . .'

'Mum!' Ella shot Clare an exasperated look that said, what are you doing talking to strangers about my nose? Wearily, she flicked back her hair to reveal three studs on one ear and four on the other.

'Oh. Only got you one pair, I'm afraid,' Holly said.

Matt laughed. Ella scowled at him but took the box Holly was holding out towards her and opened it. The earrings were tassels made of fine jet beads. Holly watched the girl's face and knew that she had chosen well.

'Oh . . . oh . . . they're really beautiful,' Ella said, 'they're like tiny pieces of coal . . .' the wide, unexpectedly dimpled smile changed her face from glum to beautiful, 'sorry, that didn't sound right . . . the way that the edges of coal are sometimes like a mirror . . . I really love them . . .' she added, taking a pair of studs from her lobes and fastening the jet earrings in place. 'Matt?' she asked.

'Wicked!'

Clare and Holly exchanged grown-ups' glances and Clare breathed a sigh of relief. It wasn't like Ella to be rude, but there had been a distinct *froideur* in the room when she came in that had now thawed. It had not occurred to her that Ella might be put out by her new-found closeness with Holly. She remembered how she herself had felt when Ella was at the stage of talking to her best friend on the phone every night for hours, laughing at jokes that Clare could not hear as she wiped down the surfaces in the kitchen doing her best not to eavesdrop.

'Right,' she said, looking at her watch, 'it's nearly six. I'm going to give Tom his tea and I'll make supper for us at eight. It's not raining too hard. D'you guys want to show Holly round? Borrow a pair of boots,' Clare advised, looking with concern at Holly's shoes.

Holly had bought a pair of cream suede trainers with lots of eyelets and bright white laces specifically for the holiday. It was about as casual as she had intended to get. The only wellingtons that fitted her in the pile beside the door were a pair of giant green things farmers wore. Reluctantly she jammed her feet in, hating the cold space around her feet and the dank sweatiness of the rubber.

It wasn't really raining any more but the air was soft and wet like a cloud. She and Matt and Ella clomped silently down the road.

'Are there any good pubs around?' Holly asked, pulling a packet of ten Marlboro out of her pocket. She would have stood in a downpour for the chance to smoke.

'A couple,' said Matt.

'Smoke?' she offered Matt.

'Not cigarettes,' he told her, looking right back into her eyes.

Ella just shook her head.

Cupping her hands round the flame, Holly lit up and inhaled deeply. Her feeble attempt to be cool had shown her up as distinctly the opposite. It wasn't cool to smoke any more.

'So what do you do round here for fun?' she asked, 'you've just finished your exams, right? How did they go?'

'Not bad,' Ella replied.

'She'll get straight As,' Matt told Holly, 'she's very clever.'

'Matt!'

'What about you?' Holly asked him.

'Did mine last year.'

'Oh.' For some reason, it was a relief to know that he was slightly older than Ella. 'So, what do you do?' Holly asked him, hearing herself sound like a London dinner-party hostess, something she never quite managed in London, even when she was hosting a dinner party.

'I play in a band,' smiling, he mimed playing a guitar for her.

Holly watched his fingers pick out imaginary notes very close to his denim-covered crotch, then looked away quickly.

'He's having a gap year,' Ella interrupted, 'he's going to university in September.'

'Or maybe not. Depending on the band . . .'

'I wouldn't hold your breath,' Ella told Holly, only half-joking.

'But it doesn't matter how you sing these days, does it?' Holly interjected. 'Only how you look . . .'

How middle-aged she sounded. She had a fleeting memory of Colette's mother who used to ask without fail 'Is that a man or a woman?' every time a long-haired singer came on *Top of the Pops* during the Seventies. Even when the singer had a beard she'd still have to say it, and Holly and Colette would exchange exactly the same conspiratorial look that was passing between Ella and Matt.

They walked past a small supermarket, a green-grocer, a post office and, as they approached the sea front, several souvenir shops. Everything was shut. It was like a ghost town, Holly thought.

'Has everything closed down?' she asked.

'Only till Monday,' Ella said.

'Oh, right.' Holly wasn't used to opening hours. In her neighbourhood, nothing closed before midnight, and lots of places didn't even open until then.

The pub had an unpolished wooden floor that was gritty with sand from fishermen's boots. There were nets draped across the ceiling, dotted with dusty sea-urchin globes. It smelled of beer and a stale sea tang like the inside of a mussel shell. Holly lit another cigarette and bought a round. They sat together at a circular table so small their three pint glasses barely fitted onto it. Matt and Holly were drinking bitter, Ella mineral water. Holly thought it was a bit goody-goody of her until she realized that in a town as small as this the bartender was bound to know that Ella wasn't yet eighteen. She wondered whether the weather-beaten men at the bar who were staring at her could tell that she was a generation older than Ella and Matt. People were always telling Holly that she didn't look her age, but, beside these two, she felt positively raddled.

'Does everyone round here stare?' Holly asked loudly, trying to shame the men into looking away.

'Only at grockles,' Matt told her.

'Grockles?' Holly repeated.

'That's our word for tourists,' he said.

'Not exactly welcoming, is it?' Holly said. 'I'd have thought that tourists were the only thing that kept the economy of this godforsaken dump going . . .' She said it without thinking, her brain unable even to contemplate the notion that the people who lived here might actually like it.

There was a short shocked silence and then Ella laughed out loud.

'Cheers!' she said, clinking her glass against Holly's, 'oh come on, Matt, she's right, it is a bloody dump. We're always talking about how to get out of it.'

'You are,' he corrected. 'It's better when the sun's shining,' he informed Holly.

'So, what's it like where you live, Holly?' Ella asked.

It was the first time she had used her name.

'You'll have to come and see,' Holly instantly responded to the overture of friendship, 'you're coming to live in London, aren't you?'

'Yes,' said Ella, 'and I can't bloody wait.'

'How did you get on with Ella?' Clare asked Holly later that evening, as they stood side by side washing up the supper things. Ella and Matt had gone to Matt's house to watch a video.

'You know what we were saying about genetics? Well, she reminds me of me,' Holly said, 'at that age. She doesn't make it easy. But then, why should she? I like her a lot. She seems to know herself very well . . .'

'Yes, doesn't she? Far better than me, I sometimes

think. Perhaps it's just her age. Maybe we had that kind of certainty at that age . . .' Clare suggested.

'I don't think so, although I probably looked as if I did. Maybe Ella only looks as if she does . . . she's extraordinary-looking, isn't she? Really beautiful when she smiles and almost ugly when she's pissed-off . . .'

'What did you think of Matt?' Clare wasn't sure she liked discussing Ella with Holly, even though she was the one who had initiated it.

'Sexy,' Holly said immediately. 'Lucky Ella. I'm assuming that "going to watch a video" means bonking . . . Can you imagine him in bed?'

It hadn't even occurred to Clare to imagine it.

'He's half your age . . .' she said, slightly shocked.

'Yes, but I get worse as I grow older. I wish I'd never read that men reach their sexual prime at eighteen.'

'I certainly don't remember any evidence of that,' Clare said, recalling embarrassed fumblings at muddy gigs before she met Joss.

'No,' said Holly, thinking about it, 'no, but it might have been our fault because we're only just coming into our prime right now . . .'

'I thought our prime was supposed to be thirty . . .'

'I'm having a very long prime,' Holly snapped back and they both began to giggle.

'Don't tell me you haven't looked at Matt and wondered what it would be like,' Holly said, as they sat down again at the table with mugs of tea.

'I have not. I really have not,' Clare told her.

'And is that because Ella's your daughter, so he's out of bounds, or because you're a happily married woman?' Holly asked, trying to establish whether it was marriage or children that deadened sexual attraction.

'Maybe I just don't find him attractive,' Clare suggested, skirting the question.

'Impossible!' Holly replied, then suddenly yawned. 'It's only half past ten and I feel shattered. Must be the sea air. Now that really does sound middle-aged. Doesn't it make you feel old being the mother of someone who's old enough to bonk?'

'Not as old as it does looking after a two-year-old,' Clare replied, 'why don't we turn in. We're bound to be woken up at six in the morning . . .'

'Jesus,' said Holly, 'who'd have kids?'

Was Holly really so concerned about sex and men and growing old, Clare wondered as she washed her face. Was she really so very unkeen to have children? She never quite knew when Holly was being serious and when she was being ironic, and the line between the two appeared to be fairly fine. Sometimes it looked as if Holly were tossing thoughts into the air like cards, watching how they fell, bringing out the joker if she found she had dealt herself a duff hand. Was it true that there were no men around that an attractive single woman in her thirties could fall in love with?

She squeezed toothpaste onto her toothbrush, and stood holding it in front of her mouth as if it were impossible to brush and think at the same time. Why was it that she had never thought about Matt in a sexual way, she wondered. Was it because he was Ella's boyfriend, as she had told herself when Holly asked, or was it because she didn't seem to think about men like that any more. Did that mean she was frigid, or just unbelievably naïve? You couldn't exactly be naïve after eighteen years of marriage to an extremely sexual man, and yet she was inexperienced compared to Holly, who had probably had at least a different man for each of those years. Sex was simply not something she thought about as a separate element of her life in the way that Holly seemed to, it was just there as part of the continuum. Holly could talk about wanting some sex, or having great sex without a relationship, and Clare could not imagine what that would be like. Perhaps she should try, she thought as she began to brush her teeth. Perhaps if she had separated the act of sex from the loving of Joss, she would not have felt so wounded when he slept with other women. Perhaps that was what he meant when he said it didn't mean anything.

Clare crept in beside Tom's cot as she did every night to watch him sleeping. Sometimes he was so peaceful she had to stop breathing herself in order to hear the whisper of his lungs. He was beautiful, lying on his back, both arms stretched up behind his head, dreaming the innocent dreams which made him smile and which he sometimes described the next day to her as if they were just part of his waking life. She was filled with an anguished love for him that she could not remember feeling for Ella when she was a baby. She had loved Ella differently. She had known how Ella's life would be and she had done everything she could to try to make it easy for her, but she did not know in the same way how Tom's life would be. It was impossible to imagine the soft skin on his face growing stubble one day, or the beam of his guileless smile becoming an expression that he would manufacture to manipulate and charm. And sometimes she feared the day when he would stop prattling on about Fireman Sam and Tinky Winky and Ella and Daddy and Mary Poppins as if they all existed on the same plane of reality, and the day his feet would begin to smell, as he began to turn into a man.

'Are you awake?'

The voice was exactly the same height as her ear.

Holly put her hand up to the side of her face as if she'd been smitten.

'I am now,' she said.

'Holly AWAKE!' Tom shouted up the stairs.

'Is that right?' Clare answered with weary patience as she was woken for the second time.

'I want to wee on the toilet,' Tom informed Holly, clambering onto the bed.

'Be my guest.' Holly turned over and pulled the sheet and blanket over her head. Suddenly realizing that if she didn't want a bed that smelled like a nappy, she had better do something about the small person who seemed so eager to become intimate with her, 'Let's go up and see Mummy,' she added hastily, jumping up and taking him by the hand.

'I'm sorry.' Clare was at the top of the stairs wearing a long nightie. She led him into the bathroom but he refused to go unless Holly watched, so Holly ran a bath while Tom arched his back and peed like a putto in a fountain. Then he insisted on watching her get into the bath, and since she'd seen him pee, she didn't feel able to refuse, and so she lay soaking and listening to him telling her about someone he knew called Ted Glen, while Clare went down and made them a cup of tea.

'He's quite a conversationalist,' Holly said, when Clare returned.

Clare put down the toilet lid and sat on it. They both listened to the stream of consciousness issuing from the child's mouth.

'Is Granny Dryden Joss's mother?' Holly asked, trying to keep up.

Clare threw back her head and laughed.

'Not exactly,' she said, 'she's a character in *Postman Pat*. You'll know all the inhabitants of Greendale by the time you leave.'

And Holly was surprised to find herself thinking, I don't want to leave. I like it lying here up to my neck in warm water, a cup of tea in my hand, and my family around me.

The weather had improved overnight. The surface of the tarmac road steamed gently in the silver sunshine. For the first time since she arrived, Holly could see the horizon. It was a fantastic view. She stood on the doorstep taking in the vast expanse of sea and sky while Clare wrestled Tom into his buggy behind her. He had to be bribed with a cardboard steering-wheel that Clare had obviously made for such occasions and for the entire walk into town their conversation was accompanied by revving and brmming sounds as Tom maintained a Grand Prix-style commentary on his drive.

'I'll show you round town and then, if it dries out, we'll go for a proper walk this afternoon,' Clare suggested.

It was the first time she had walked down the street with a friend who was just hers, she thought, glancing sideways at Holly and feeling rather proprietorial about her. She had left her old schoolfriends behind in London along with the rest of her life. When you were married and in a new place, you made friends as a couple. They had chosen other like-minded couples such as Pepe and Vivienne, Jeremy and Olivia, Richard and Joni, all poets and poets' wives. Richard was the reason they had moved to Penderric in the first place. He had been a colleague of Joss's at the college. They had come down here to stay with him one weekend soon after Clare had discovered she was pregnant, and he'd mentioned there was a dilapidated cottage just outside the town that was up for sale. Joss had been flattered. Richard had already published several volumes of poetry. To be invited to move to Penderric was like being asked to join an exclusive club. The men worked out that the mortgage on the property would be less than the rent Joss was paying on his flat, while Joni and Clare cooked the Sunday lunch. That afternoon she and Joss went along to see it alone. The ramshackle little house with its fenced front garden had reminded her of the Wendy house she had played in at nursery school. She felt safe there.

'What do you think?' Joss had asked as they stood in the flagstone kitchen with its dripping standpipe. She could see by his expression that he meant to buy it.

'I think I'm dreaming,' she had replied, smiling at him, and as if to seal the decision, Joss lifted the dress she was wearing and fucked her standing with her back against the woodwormed ladder that led upstairs. At the time she had thought the silent urgency with which he had freed his cock from his jeans and pushed it up inside her passionately Lawrentian. She had only just finished A level English.

After Joss's affair with Joni, Richard moved away to another remote grey stone village somewhere in Scotland. His cycle of poems entitled *Cuckold* had been shortlisted for a number of awards. Joss ran into him occasionally at poetry festivals. They seemed to get along fine again now. Joni had since married a German with a caravan business. It gave the men something to laugh about together.

All the women whom Clare had befriended in the town had fallen to Joss for a night, or a fully-fledged affair over the years, except Amelia, who was too fat for his tastes.

'What's the point of espadrilles?' Holly asked, kicking at an empty Coke can that had fallen out of a full litter-bin, 'I bought these to go on Simon's boat and I thought they'd be great for the seaside, but they've soaked right through, so I've got wet feet and they weigh about a ton . . .'

'I think they've got rope soles to grip the deck,' Clare said.

'I'm not planning to go on any more boats,' Holly told her, 'I was so sick I left a trail all the way along the south coast . . .'

'How is Simon?' Clare asked.

'Fine. The same as ever,' Holly said, 'good at cleaning up sick . . .'

They stopped to look in the window of Vivienne's shop.

'I work here two afternoons a week,' Clare told her, 'and, over there,' she pointed at Amelia's tea shop, 'I make the jam . . .'

'How does that pay?' Holly asked.

She told her and Holly's face contorted with disbelief.

'I know,' Clare said, 'I'm quite looking forward to the minimum wage. It couldn't be less than I earn . . . tell me about your job. I mean what do people actually do in Cannes, say?'

'I didn't go this year. It's no good when you haven't got a film in competition, or being launched, unless you've got something hot to sell. I love it, of course. I'm such a star-fucker, I still get a kick out of bumping into Robert De Niro, or more accurately, getting pushed out of the way by his bodyguards on the way back from the loo in the Majestic. It kind of makes you feel you know someone when you realize that they've had a slash only yards away from you.'

Clare's laughter pealed down the street.

'Of course you do business, you talk up projects, you drink, you see, you're seen. One of the weirdest things is it's like the exact opposite of the Oscars, or something, because everyone is desperate to be as dressed-down as possible. It's all T-shirts and shorts, and I had to buy a load of stuff when I first went, because I'd brought a suitcase full of cocktail dresses. Of course, the usual morals of society don't apply. You get all these people thrown together and they party, and then they go back to normal . . .'

'So what's normal?'

'A normal day? Lots of phone calls . . . if I've made a deal then drawing up the contract . . . reading, talking, I don't know . . .'

'But what do you actually do when you make a deal?' Clare was curious.

'Well, it starts with a client . . .'

'But how do you get your clients?'

'These days, they mostly approach me, but if I like somebody's work, I pester them until it's easier to say yes to me than to keep saying no. A lot of my screen-writers write books too, and they come to me through my colleagues in the agency . . .'

'So then?'

'Let me think of a good example . . . I've got this script just in which I read on the train down. It's by Anji Johnson, you know, who wrote *Single File*?'

Clare's face registered no recognition. How could anyone not have heard of *Single File*, Holly wondered, the bible of the single metropolitan woman? But Clare was neither single, nor metropolitan, she reminded herself.

'Well, she's quite famous, but she's got no ex-perience of writing full-length drama, but it is really good. Wish I'd had it before Cannes because I would have gone and got a buzz going . . . How do I sell it?' Holly had never really thought about the process before. 'I suppose I just talk a lot about it and try to get my enthusiasm across.'

Clare suddenly understood how it worked. Holly's enthusiasm was infectious, like laughter. When she talked about something she liked, there was an animated aura around her that was almost tangible. She had total belief in what she was selling and it made you believe her. Clare already wanted to read the script herself.

'What's it about?' she asked.

'It's called *The One*. It's about a woman in her thirties with four suitors. She sets them a kind of test to discover which is the One for her . . . it's frothy, romantic fantasy stuff, same kind of area as *My Best*

Friend's Wedding. I haven't shown it to my colleague in LA yet, but I expect we'll be talking to the major studios . . .'

'How exciting,' Clare said, 'sounds the perfect project for you because you love games, and tests and things . . .'

Holly looked at her with great affection. They were from different worlds, and Clare had about as much idea about pitching a film proposal as Holly had about cooking a five-course meal, but she was interested, and supportive, and that made such a change from all the cynical people she normally associated with.

'Was Joss the One?' Holly suddenly asked her, 'the man with your name written on?'

'Oh yes . . .' Clare said, 'when I met him,' she qualified.

'But everyone's the One when you first meet them,' Holly said, impatiently, 'you start off with someone and it's gorgeous and you can't eat because you're so happy and then after a few months it splits up and you think what did I do? We were so perfect at the beginning. And then you work out that you only got along so well because you didn't know each other . . .'

'I'm the One!' Tom shouted from his buggy, reminding them that he was there.

'So who wins?' Clare asked.

'In Anji's script? You'll have to wait and see . . .'

'Oh, tell me,' Clare said.

'OK, well, I won't tell you which, but it's the guy who most improves her life by putting a coat hook up on the back of her front door . . . there's been this kind of running gag . . .'

'So the moral of the story is that love is about honesty, simple things . . . ?'

'The moral of the story is the way to a woman's heart is through your screwdriver . . . what would your tests be?'

'I've never had three men vying for my attentions.'

'I bet you have,' Holly said, looking at her. Clare's skin was like a child's creamy complexion with no open pores, blemishes or other give-away signs of adulthood, and her eyes were really dark blue. She was genuinely beautiful.

'I used to think that the most romantic thing was to have poetry written for you.'

'And now?'

'And now . . . I don't even think about it. D'you fancy a coffee at Amelia's?'

'Treacle tart,' added Tom, eagerly.

At lunch-time, Tom insisted that Holly sit next to him. He was so excited by all the extra attention he refused to eat, so Holly went to the toybox and found a battered old glove puppet lion who took Tom's spoon in his paws and helped him.

'What that lion called?' Tom asked her.

'I don't know. It's your lion,' Holly told him, exchanging raised eyebrows with Clare.

'What he called?' Tom asked again.

'Perhaps you'd like to give him a name, Holly,' Clare suggested.

Holly thought about it.

'Well, when I was a little girl there was a programme on television called *The Herbs* and the lion was called Parsley. So perhaps he's called Parsley too. Do you remember that, Clare?'

'Yes. I loved it.' Clare smiled at her, delighted to see Holly and Tom becoming such good friends. Holly was natural with children. She didn't shout, like so many childless people did in a loud voice they reserved for old people and infants, nor did she talk in baby language.

'Prap he called Parsley too,' Tom said, uncertainly.

'He knows parsley from the garden,' Clare explained.

'Well, I'm called Holly and that's a tree, so this lion can be called Parsley even though it's a plant.'

'Holly a tree, Mummy!' Tom said, as if that suddenly explained her great height.

When Clare came down from putting him in his cot for a nap, they ate the rest of their lunch together. It was a lasagne made with roasted vegetables and feta cheese.

'How did you learn to cook like this?' Holly asked, helping herself to seconds.

'It's very easy to cook well. All you need are good, fresh ingredients, God, now I sound like Delia Smith! Force of habit, I suppose. And I always took a certain pride in being good at cookery at school because it annoyed Philippa so much . . .'

'Have you been in touch with her since . . . since the funeral?' Holly asked.

'I got this from Spain. She's in Seville. I didn't even know she was going away.' Clare removed a postcard from under a magnet on the fridge.

On the flip side of a view of the Giralda, Philippa had written,

'Jack never wanted to come to Spain because of Franco, but it is beautiful, and better to be somewhere we never were together. The orange season is over. Apparently they ship them all to England and cannot understand us wanting such bitter fruit. I am sorry we parted as we did. Big kiss to Ella and Tom. P.'

Holly handed it back without saying anything.

'Not exactly overwhelming,' Clare said.

'Do you care?'

'Not really.' Clare got up and put the kettle on, turning her face away so Holly could not see she was fighting tears. 'Actually yes, I do seem to,' she admitted, as they dribbled down her cheek. 'I don't know why she has to be like that,' she sighed, wiping her face with her sleeve. 'I expect she's embarrassed.'

It was as if she had spent her life making up excuses for other people's behaviour. At times, Clare had a defeated quality that made Holly want to shake her.

'Why are you so nice?' Holly asked suddenly, 'I mean, your mother's been a bitch to you, and your father for that matter, so what makes you so understanding?'

'I don't know if I am, really. It takes two people to have an argument, and it takes a lot of pride to keep it going for so long. I think I'm much more like him than I would like to admit . . .'

'There you go again,' Holly said, 'the difference is that you weren't much more than a child and he had a responsibility to you.'

'Did you think Jack had a responsibility to you?' Clare asked.

'No,' Holly said immediately, 'but that's different. I thought Mo had . . .'

'Well, anyway . . .' Clare said, sniffing and trying to put on a cheerful face.

'You're not happy, are you?' Holly suddenly saw the depth of misery in Clare's eyes. 'Why aren't you happy? I can't see how anyone could be happy living in the back of beyond, but it's not that, is it?'

'How do you know when you're happy?' Clare asked. 'How do you know that what you think is unhappy isn't what other people would think is normal?'

Clare was very practised at avoiding direct questions, Holly thought.

'What I do is divide my life into sections and give it points out of ten,' she told her, 'it's a method Colette and I devised when we were kids. You think of the five things that are most important to you and then you give them marks out of ten, then you double your final score to make a percentage . . .'

Clare looked at her disbelievingly.

'I haven't done it for a while . . .' Holly said. 'Work:

Nine, could even approach ten if I sell *The One* to a Hollywood studio. I feel as if I'm on the cusp of something at work, as if I just need one more push to get really successful and then . . . and then I won't have to worry, or maybe I'll do something different. Anyway. Nine. Or eight. Something in that area. Family: difficult one since Jack died, but I've found you and I've got a lovely mum, so let's say nine. Men: zilch. Friends: eight. Simon's great, but Colette's been a bit funny recently. Flat: ten. So add up the categories. I should have a maximum of fifty but in fact I've scored thirty-six. Which means I'm seventy-two per cent happy. It's only a rough guide . . .' she said, 'although, funnily enough, however I do the figures, it always seems to come out at about seventy-two . . .'

Clare just threw back her head and laughed. Holly loved it when she did that. Her laughter was like a child's, and it was the only time that she didn't seem to be holding something back.

'Come on, your turn,' Holly cajoled.

'I can't . . .' Clare said, still laughing.

She had opened up to Clare and Clare had to open up to her, otherwise it wasn't fair, Holly thought. But then she had to ask herself whether that was true. Had she really opened up to Clare or had she done her usual brilliant act of appearing to say everything she was thinking, but never quite admitting to her worst fears? Sometimes, late at night, especially when she had drunk too much, Holly would lie awake wondering whether everything she said and did was a front, or whether the fact that the act was so convincing meant that it really was part of her. Mo had once told her that people were like onions with lots of different layers, but Holly thought of herself as more like a water melon. There was a very hard outside and a load of sweet pink pulp inside, but there were also even harder black pips that you had to spit out before you could enjoy the nice pink stuff. When she had tested this metaphor out on Mo, Mo had said that was getting a bit too complicated for her. Holly found herself explaining this to Clare.

'What would you be?' she asked her.

'Maybe I'm a Seville orange,' Clare said, picking up Philippa's postcard and sticking it back under its fridge magnet, 'I look sweet, but I turn out to be sour.'

'You're not sour,' Holly protested, 'now you're doing exactly what I do, you're seeing only the bad bits and not giving yourself any credit . . .'

'I'd give my marriage three out of ten,' Clare suddenly stated, 'there, now I've said it. I'm not very good at confiding, I'm afraid, because everyone I've ever confided in has almost instantly jumped into bed with Joss . . .'

'But . . .' Holly couldn't believe what she had just heard. Clare was so pretty and she had lovely hair and she was sweet and slim. But her shocked reflex reaction gave way to the knowledge that men did not seem to need good reasons to cheat on their wives.

'That's the part I don't like about living here,' Clare went on, 'I don't mind it being the back of beyond, but it's so familiar. Everybody knows, you see, and they feel sorry for me. At least the ones who don't still have the hots for him do. It's humiliating. There you see, I am proud, and isn't pride one of the seven deadly sins?'

'If you believe that crap. But so are greed and sloth and I've never understood what's deadly about pigging out and then having a bit of a lie-in. Why don't you leave?' Holly asked.

'Because it's not that easy when you have kids.'

Holly thought about it for approximately a second before saying, 'You could stay with me . . . I really like Tom, and Ella's going off anyway. I don't mean I don't like her, I just don't know where I'd put my clothes . . .' She was already envisaging the scenario. They could take it in turns to babysit and Clare could get a life. She felt easy with Clare. She knew they could work it out. In her mind she was already getting Simon to put up another towel rail in the bathroom, when Clare said, 'Thank you. But that's just not a solution. I mean, I'm really touched, really. It's the nicest offer I've had in a long time, but it's more complicated when you have kids. You haven't seen Tom with Joss, but if you did, you'd know that you couldn't just take him away. It wouldn't be fair . . .'

'But don't you have to think of yourself too? You're no good to your children if you're miserable . . .'

'I know that argument,' Clare said, cautiously, 'and I don't buy it. I've brought the children into the world and I should do my best by them.'

'But you can't sacrifice yourself . . .'

'That's what Ella says. It's what people who haven't got children always say. And then I feel guilty for moaning in the first place because it's not that bad. It's not intolerable. I would leave if it were. That's what I meant by how do you know you're happy. Everyone makes choices. You've chosen not to have children. I chose to have them and I expect if I did one of your calculations I would probably come out at about seventy per cent too . . . and I suppose this is why I don't talk about it.'

'I haven't chosen not to have children,' Holly suddenly said, 'it just hasn't happened . . .'

'Yet . . .'

'No, no I don't think so. I've never met anyone who wanted to . . . wanted to do anything serious with me. Jack said that he didn't think there would be any men strong enough for me . . . At the time, I thought it was a compliment . . .'

'I'm sure it was meant to be . . . you give a pretty good impression of not caring about men and babies and all that . . .'

'I think I probably say I don't because I can't face the

possibility of admitting that I might, and then not getting it . . .' Holly stopped talking abruptly. Put like that, it sounded ridiculous to deny yourself the opportunity of something so big just because you might feel a bit of a failure if you didn't get it.

Upstairs, Tom woke up and Clare went to get him.

'Let's get our coats on and try to run off some of his energy while the weather holds,' she said, when she came down. 'It would be nice to talk some more later,' she added, slightly alarmed by Holly's thought-filled silence.

'I sometimes think it's a bit like having a dog,' Clare went on, forcing Tom's reluctant arms into his jacket, 'you have to take them out for a good walk twice a day.'

'I hate dogs. I was bitten by one when I was four.' Holly stopped to turn her back to the wind and light a cigarette as they walked along the clifftop path. 'Children kind of dictate the pace of your life, don't they?'

It wasn't a criticism. It was just something she had never thought of before. On the rare occasions she had imagined herself having a baby, she'd thought about how she would look pregnant, and the scene in the hospital with baby all wrapped up in a cellular blanket in her arms, flowers all around them and a beatific smile on her face. She'd thought about how nice it would be to have someone that didn't have a choice about loving you, and then, to stop herself getting soppy, she'd tried very hard to imagine the smell of a full nappy. She had never got to the stage of thinking that the baby would grow up and become a child who asked you questions all the time, and determined whether you went out, or stayed in, or talked or listened. That was much more scary than any amount of baby poo.

'Did you mean it when you said we could visit you in London?' Ella asked Holly in the pub that evening.

'Of course,' Holly replied, leaning back against the panel that divided the public and saloon bars. The place was growing on her. It reminded her of the pubs she and Colette had frequented in their teens. You couldn't find a real pub in London any more. They were either pseudo-Irish bars or part of pub chains as homogeneous as McDonald's but with sillier names.

'It's just that there's a gig we both want to go to before I leave for the States . . .'

'No, that'd be great,' Holly said.

'Can we stay?' Ella asked, just to make sure.

'Yes,' Holly said.

'Last time I slept with some dossers near Waterloo,' Matt told her.

Holly didn't know whether she was meant to be impressed or sympathetic.

'I stayed with Philippa when I went up for my interview,' Ella said, 'but she was too busy to show me round. She took me for lunch at this health club she goes to and bought me some treatments for the afternoon, but it wasn't really my scene . . .'

'Have you only been to London once?' Holly asked, astonished.

'Yup,' Ella said, 'pathetic, isn't it?'

'Twice,' announced Matt, proudly.

Both women looked at him pityingly.

'Oh well, that changes everything,' Holly said, 'I'll show you round.' She felt quite excited at the prospect. 'If you want me to . . .' she added quickly.

When Matt went to the toilet, Holly found she couldn't resist asking Ella, 'What's Philippa like?'

'About as different from Mum as you could imagine. I mean Mum's tough in her way, she's the iron fist in the velvet glove, but Philippa's iron through and through,' said Ella.

Holly remembered how smart and contained she had looked at the funeral, as if there were some magnetic field around her that would bounce away unwanted intruders.

'What about you?' Ella asked.

'Me? I'm the velvet fist in the iron glove,' Holly told her.

Ella laughed. 'Mum still doesn't know whether Philippa knows about your mother. Isn't that weird?'

Then Matt returned to the table and Holly had to suppress the urge to tell him to piss off. She would have liked to have talked some more.

Holly's last day in Cornwall was her birthday. With a little help from his mother, Tom made her a card. They had a cake with three candles which he blew out at tea, and in the evening Holly bought three bottles of very expensive Barolo to drink with supper, thinking that Ella at least would join them, but she was babysitting for Amelia. Clare had baked a leg of spring lamb with rosemary and garlic from the garden. It was as good as anything Holly had ever tasted.

'It almost makes me think I should get a garden and grow my own food,' Holly said.

Clare laughed. Holly frowned at her.

'Sorry,' said Clare, 'it's just that I can't see you knee-deep in mud and mulch . . .'

'I know,' Holly said, dispiritedly, 'Simon once bought me a window-box for my birthday. It was already planted with those pink things and that blue stuff, but I still couldn't keep it going. It became a giant ashtray. When it rained, I almost expected to see tiny little tobacco plants germinating out of the dog ends, you know, like cress on a flannel. Did you grow cress on a flannel at school?'

Clare nodded. She loved the way that after a few glasses of wine, Holly would veer off, Walter Mitty-like, from the most mundane conversation.

'It stank, didn't it? I mean the flannel? The only way

I could have a garden would be if I was rich enough to have a gardener,' Holly said, 'or a husband, I suppose.'

'Husbands aren't necessarily much help,' Clare said, sharply.

'Tell me something,' Holly said, emptying the remains of the first bottle into her glass, 'what does Joss actually do? I mean, correct me if I'm wrong, but you work two days a week, you look after Tom, you cook, you clean, you do the garden, you make jam, for God's sake. Is his sole contribution to the household a few lines of poetry?'

Holly decided that she hated Joss, and whatever Clare said about the children, she was going to make it her mission in life to persuade her of the many good reasons to leave him. Anyone could see that he was doing her in. It was mad for someone of Clare's looks, brains and charm to be mouldering away in a hole like this. The view was great, but man could not live on view alone, and even if he could, woman couldn't. Clare had to leave him. He was a puffed-up, arrogant womanizer who'd been allowed to have his own way far too long.

'Sometimes he does a bit of carpentry . . .' Clare offered.

'Jesus Christ!'

'No, even he doesn't have that big an idea of himself . . .' Clare joked.

'Are you sure about that?' Holly asked, 'what with the beard and everything . . .'

'He doesn't have a beard,' Clare said, mystified.

'Doesn't have a beard?' Holly repeated surprised.

'Well, I don't notice his looks like I used to,' Clare said, 'but I think I would have noticed that . . .'

'He sounds as if he has a beard to me, which is just as bad. He's a closet beard and they're the worst sort,' Holly pronounced.

'He sometimes does some decorating . . .' Clare suddenly felt the need to defend Joss against Holly's increasingly irrational criticism, 'and he is quite good at making things. He made Ella a dolls' house . . .' As soon as she said it she realized how long ago that had been. Ella had not played with dolls since she was about seven.

It wasn't that he couldn't do things, because he could. He had converted the house from a ramshackle cottage to a home. In the beginning, his ability to do real work, like constructing a staircase was one of the things she had so admired in him. It was a terrible cliché, but masculinity was attractive. She had come from a house where everything was done by paid help. The garden had a gardener, the redesign of the ground floor was done by an architect, a decorator painted the stucco front with white matt and the front door with black gloss once every three years. She had found sensuality in Joss's dirty hands and the smell of turps and wood shavings.

Holly did not trust herself to speak.

'Another bottle?' she asked, her lips black with wine.

'I don't think . . .' Clare began.

'It's my birthday,' Holly said, 'my bloody thirty-sixth birthday. I'm nearer forty than thirty . . .'

'All right, all right . . .' Clare gave in.

Finding a sister at the age of thirty-six was a bit like falling in love, without the sex bit, which always fucked it up anyway, Holly thought as she tried to brush the taste of red wine from her tongue the next morning. You meet someone, you like the look of them, you test them out with a few targeted probes to see how they react, you find you like them more, you laugh, you reveal a little of yourself, you sense they like you, and suddenly you're telling them everything you've ever thought and dreamed, and they still like you and you can't believe your luck. You talk till dawn, fall asleep and the next morning they're still there.

They had finished two bottles of wine and talked long into the night, so long that both of them had been too tired and drunk to make up Holly's bed, so Holly had slept next to Clare in her bed, and they had chatted in the dark until at some point Holly had realized that the only sound in response to the last two questions she had asked was Clare's even breathing.

'Taxi's here,' Clare shouted up the stairs.

Holly spat the third squeeze of toothpaste out of her mouth. It still tasted like the inside of a wine keg. She grabbed her bag and clattered down the wooden steps. Clare was at the bottom with a mug of coffee in her hand.

'I put some cold water in so you wouldn't burn your mouth,' she said, as Holly gulped hastily, and handed her a family-sized tetrapack of orange juice and a brown paper bag. 'Sandwiches,' Clare smiled.

Holly was about to protest when she thought of the alternatives. Anything that Clare had made was bound to be better than what she could get on the train.

'Tom, come and give Holly a kiss.'

The little boy charged Holly's legs and clung on for dear life. She bent down and kissed the top of his head. Everything about him was soft, his skin, his glorious curls, but his grip was like iron.

'You look after your mummy,' she told him. 'It's been lovely,' she said, enfolding Clare in a hug.

'It has, hasn't it?' Clare said, her eyes filling with tears.

'Tell Ella to call about her weekend.'

'I will.'

'And you take care . . .'

'*You* take care . . .'

They exchanged significant looks.

In the cab, she craned her neck waving until they disappeared out of sight, her sister and her nephew.

Chapter 17

When the tour left Seville, Philippa stayed on. She
found she had not wanted to visit monuments with
guides, nor eat companionable meals with other well-
educated, early-retired people in five-star hotels with
air-conditioning. She wanted to be by herself in a place
where she would not be alone, and this city with its
stark contrast of light and shade seemed as good as
anywhere. She would go on to Cordoba and Granada
in her own time. Or not. There was nothing to hurry
her, or to take her home. If she wanted to, she thought,
she could live the rest of her life in the room she had
taken, in a whitewashed house in the Barrio de Santa
Cruz. It was as simple and dark as a prison cell, but
when she stepped into the courtyard outside each
morning, the sunlight was blinding.

In the mornings, Philippa sat in a nearby square
drinking thick china cups of *café con leche*, watching from
behind sunglasses the first groups of hungover tourists
wandering through the quarter. No-one noticed her.
There was a harshness about the city that she found
almost comforting. The citizens bore the cruelty of the
past on their shoulders with defensive pride, like blood
on a matador's suit of lights. There was no pity here save
for the great outpouring at Easter, when the Virgin La
Macarena cried crystal tears for her crucified son.

Sometimes, in the afternoons, Philippa went to the bullring, La Maetranza, and sat alone in the shade under pretty white arcading, mesmerized by the orchestrated brutality of *los toros*. No-one there had any interest in trying to cheer her up as Lanny and May, an American couple on the tour, had done, insisting she sit with them at dinner, making extensive well-intentioned efforts to turn her into a merry widow. The rest of the day she wandered until it was too hot to wander, seeking sanctuary in the gardens of the Alcázar or the deep shade of the Parque de Maria Luisa. She took with her one of the paperbacks she had bought in the departure lounge at Heathrow, and sat on a stone bench staring at the open page. Nobody disturbed you if you were reading. She was not reading, but the book was like the insect repellent she sprayed all over her body each night, keeping unwanted intruders at a safe distance.

Very slowly her head began to empty. Since Jack's death it had felt crammed, as if a whole log-jam of thoughts had gathered, all bobbing and jostling to find their way out of her brain, and she had pushed them down, fearing that if one were allowed to surface then they would all follow with uncontrollable force, knocking her down, perhaps even drowning her. Now, freed by the anonymity of a strange city, she began to be able to think and remember.

Her mind kept flitting back to the day he asked her to invest in his first movie. She had inherited a tidy sum from her father, and the management consultancy she had set up on leaving advertising was far more profitable than she could have ever dreamed. They were in bed one Sunday morning. You'll get a good return, Jack had told her cockily, flirting with her for her money, even though they had been married many years. I just need you to trust me, he said, rolling on top of her pinning her to the bed and staring close into her face, his pale blue eyes sparkling with sport. Trust me.

He had repaid the money ten times over, but not the trust. Not the trust. And then he had died before she could find out whether there was anything left without trust. He had left her without a future. And without a past, she suddenly thought, because what she had thought was their past turned out not to have been.

Every memory she had of their life together was now tainted with not knowing.

She was angry with him for lying and angrier for dying, leaving her with her life half-answered. Why? Why me? What did I do to you, Jack, to deserve this? Lying on her hard, narrow bed in the afternoons with a damp flannel on her forehead and the rhythmic breeze of the electric fan she had bought in *El Corte Inglés* blowing up and down her body, she would try to relax the anger out of her body, but it kept her stiff like an effigy on a tomb.

In the evenings she drank two glasses of fino in her breakfast café, chewing on a few olives and little scraps of *jamon*, watching passers-by from the shadows. Then she moved on to a dark tapas bar where the natives ate, tasting the little plates of peeled broad beans, roasted potatoes with sharp chilli sauce, and prawns, their shells burnt and glistening with olive oil and salt. And she drank sufficient red wine to anaesthetize the pain and allow her to sleep.

The bartender nodded his recognition of her, but that was as far as familiarity extended. If anyone else noticed her she did not see it, until, one evening, after she had been in the city several weeks, a couple sat down at the opposite end of the bar. A middle-aged but handsome man, and a much younger woman. At first she thought they were lovers, and that the rise and fall of their rapid conversation was the cadence of a lovers' tiff, but when an older woman joined them, Philippa realized that the younger woman was their daughter. She was rather beautiful, and spoilt, and although she was wearing jeans and simple T-shirt, Philippa could imagine her in full Sevillana flounces of satin and black lace, with a fancy tortoiseshell comb in her lustrous dark hair and a fluttering fan. The lovers' row she thought she was witnessing, she now heard as a dispute about the daughter's being allowed to stay out, and the coquettish look she had mistaken for flirting was not flirting, she realized, it was just the daughter's way of reassuring her father that he would still have a place in her heart, even though she would love other men. The three of them suddenly stopped bantering and stared at Philippa, and only then was she aware of the tears streaming down her face. Fumbling in her handbag, she flung some notes onto the bar, slipped off her stool, and fled from their questioning gaze down the darkened alleys, through the courtyard, to the safety of her room. There she stood with her chest heaving huge breathless sobs and the memory of her last conversation with Jack, which she had kept dammed up, flooding over her in a tidal wave of lamentation.

She had been waiting downstairs in his study when he returned from the election party that night. She had showered, dressed and reapplied her make-up, wanting to look her absolute best for the confrontation. A quick search through his address and diary files had established nothing. It made her feel tawdry tapping into his PC, like a woman going through her husband's pockets in an increasingly frantic search for the credit-card slip that betrays a dirty weekend or an unreceived bouquet.

'Who is she?' she demanded as soon as he walked in, trying to keep her voice as level as possible.

'Who?'

'I saw you on the television, along with half of

London, I expect . . . if you have to have an affair, you could at least be discreet. No wonder you were so keen to go to the party. No wonder you weren't in the least bothered that I was too tired to come . . .'

'I don't understand,' he had offered weakly.

'You were on television, Jack. Kissing a redhead. Advertising your affair to the world.'

She could see that Jack was frightened, and then she knew it was true. It was so rare for him to be frightened, he did not know how to disguise it.

'It's not what you think,' he finally said.

'Oh, spare me your corny dialogue!'

'Sit down . . .'

'We're not in a movie now, Jack,' she said witheringly, 'anyway, why does the woman always have to sit down to hear the bad news? Do you think I'm going to faint? I've never fainted in my life . . .'

'I have a daughter,' he looked at her face, 'not Clare, another daughter . . . I've meant to tell you. I was going to tell you . . . You have to believe . . .'

'A daughter . . . ? You've meant to tell me?'

'Yes,' he smiled at her. It was the silly look of relief that angered her most.

'And you think that makes it OK? It wasn't my mistress, it was my daughter.' Her mind began to work with the information. 'So you don't just have another woman, you have a whole other life . . . .?'

'Let me get us both a drink.'

'I don't want a bloody drink . . .'

He had walked out of the room and she had stood stiffly waiting for him to return. To follow him would weaken her moral superiority, she decided coolly. It was up to him to come back to her. She heard the cellophane-crackle of ice-cubes being pushed from their trays and then she heard a loud thump like someone jumping off a chair, but at first she was still too angry to wonder what it was. She had waited, beginning to wonder whether she should after all follow him into the kitchen. This way she was only giving him time to get his story straight, and as the silence continued she started to feel a little anxious. She called his name, the first time in anger, the second a question, the third a scream.

He was lying on the polished wooden floor with ice-cubes all round his head, glittering in the kitchen spotlights like the Macarena's tears. He looked so frightened, she found herself saying, 'It's all right,' as she knelt beside him and felt for a pulse. The warmth of him steadied her, but there was no movement of blood in the veins, and no rise and fall of his chest. Suddenly she began thumping his ribcage, frantically pushing up and down, not knowing what she was doing, only copying what she had seen people do in *ER*. Then she grabbed the cordless phone from its hook by the cappuccino machine and stabbed out three nines, already knowing that it was too late.

In the still heat of her room in the Barrio de Santa Cruz, Philippa knelt, howling her despair, doing penance for everything she could have done differently, and as she wept, her anger melted into grief for the man she missed so terribly.

After shock came anger, then grief, and after that, curiosity. Shock, Anger, Grief, Curiosity. For some reason Philippa thought of the whiteboards they used in the first days of management consultancy, writing acronyms in coloured pens to make difficult processes sound simple, like POP which stood for People Off the Payroll. SAGC. If curiosity had begun with an E then the emotions would have spelled SAGE, but it didn't, and she couldn't think of a synonym which did. In any case, abbreviation didn't seem to make the process of bereavement any more straightforward.

She was sitting under the bright yellow Schweppes umbrella of one of the cafés near the cathedral in a daze of strange unconnected thoughts. Suddenly, she snapped back into consciousness, wondering whether she had been staring blankly, or twitching, or even sleeping, and for how long. A second, an hour? She had thought there would come a day when she would wake up feeling miraculously better, like the beginning of recovery after a long illness, but she was beginning to dread waking up at all.

Her mind ran and reran over and over again the embrace she had witnessed on the television screen. She saw a cloud of red hair and a hug that was joyous in its fervour and then the memory collapsed into jealousy. She was his daughter. Slowly the image of the hug became almost tolerable. The woman was tall, but not a model, she had red hair. Given the location, she must be a Labour party supporter, Philippa realized, with a faint smile of self-congratulation for her powers of detection, but that was all she knew. How old was she? Philippa tried to date her, trying to think of bad patches in her relationship with Jack when he might have taken a lover. And gradually the man she thought she knew so well became more and more of a mystery.

When they met, they were both junior copywriters at the advertising agency. He had been brought into an account that she was working on. Her first sight of him was his tall silhouette against the window of the sixth-floor conference room, looking out over the river Thames, his shoulders square, arms akimbo, the air charged with his determination. He turned, his eyes met hers, there was a split second of attraction like a glint of sun on the glass of a revolving door, and then the pale-blue eyes became opaque, unreadable. She had found herself twisted between resentment and longing.

It was a campaign for a Swiss brand of butter. She had come up with the slogan 'Better butter, *bitte*' which she was rather pleased with, but Jack's reaction was contemptuous.

'That's German, isn't it? People don't want Germany in their kitchen. The nearest Germany can come is the garage . . .'

It was 1960, long before a German name became the acceptable byword of quality for freezers and washing-machines and practically all the white goods that aspirational families kept in their kitchen.

'We'd love to hear your ideas,' she told him, matching his rough northern bluntness with the pure, disdainful sweetness of breeding.

I wanted to fuck you right there on the boardroom table, he had told her later, but his face had betrayed nothing.

'It's from Switzerland, right?' He paused for a moment, letting her think that she had outmanoeuvred him with her challenge.

He admitted afterwards, a long time afterwards, that he had been handed the account on the Friday afternoon and spent all weekend working on it, but, at the time, the thoughts he came up with looked utterly spontaneous.

'I see an Alpine meadow, flowers, a couple of cows with bells and "Taste the cream".'

'Oh I say, that's good. I think they'll like that,' the account director said, in a triumphant voice that had made Philippa regret all the times she had turned down his invitations to the opera.

She had made a graceful enough exit. Philippa was good at dignity.

'Class,' Jack said to her as they lay in bed a couple of weeks later after the first time they'd made love, 'I thought, she's got class.'

'And what would you know about class?' she had

asked him jokily, but trembling with the risk, knowing that she was already in love with this man with his accent like a steel cable, his one good suit and his hard blue eyes.

The look he gave her was fearful in its intensity.

'I know what you want,' he told her, rolling on top of her again, effortlessly pinning her arms outstretched beneath his so that their bodies made a cross on the bed, 'you want a bit of rough, don't you? Shall I be your bit of rough and you be my bit of class, and together we'll take over the world?'

He had looked at her as she struggled not to show the electrifying desire his latent violence aroused, then suddenly he had lowered his mouth onto hers and kissed her with such profound tenderness that she felt for a delirious second that she owned him in all his complexity of strength and gentleness. Nothing she had ever experienced came close to the mind-blowing feeling of seeping into him and having him seep into her. It was as if there had been no other men. At that moment, she had known with certainty that all of him was hers and all of her was his.

So when was it that she had become not enough?

Chapter 18

'Going on holiday with Eamon? Why didn't you tell me?' Holly asked.

'Well, I am telling you now,' Mo replied.

'Is that wise?'

'I need a holiday, so does he . . .' Mo defended herself.

'Oh well . . .' Holly said, resignedly. She had never been able to see what Mo saw in Eamon. He was a big, jolly man with a red nose, who said jolly, inconsequential things, the same jolly, inconsequential things, every time she saw him.

'I wondered if you would have Frank Cooper . . .'

Frank Cooper was the name of Mo's cat. She had wanted to call him Marmalade, but Holly said that every ginger cat was called Marmalade and it was boring. She'd suggested Frank Cooper as a joke but it had stuck.

'No, I can't,' Holly said.

The last time she had taken the cat, when Mo went to the Canaries with the girls from work, he had howled all night pining for Mo and crapped in her best pair of loafers. Mo said it wouldn't have happened if she had bothered to clear out his litter tray, but cleaning out a litter tray was almost as horrible a prospect for Holly as having to throw away a pair of navy blue suede shoes.

'I'll see if Sonya will have him,' Mo said, 'otherwise it will have to be a cattery . . .'

'If that's meant to make me feel guilty,' Holly told her, 'it doesn't.'

'You're very selfish, sometimes,' Mo said.

'Still not feeling guilty,' Holly told her breezily, 'have a lovely time.'

She put down the phone feeling a bit odd. Mo hadn't even asked her this year whether she would like to go on holiday with her. Usually Holly said no, but this year she thought it would have been nice to have been asked. Everyone around her was in a couple, and now Mo too, and she couldn't even go out for her usual drink with Robert to moan about the lack of men in their lives because she had agreed to go to dinner with Charlie Prince and his bloody wife. Holly scowled at herself in the Ladies mirror as she slicked on her most scarlet lipstick.

Charlie Prince's house was in a white crescent off Ladbroke Grove. The door was opened by a woman so elfin she made Holly instantly feel huge and ungainly.

'Hello, I'm Pic,' she said, with a broad, welcoming smile that put Holly slightly more at ease, 'Ginger's just feeding Rose.'

Holly followed her along the high-ceilinged hall and downstairs to the basement kitchen. It was ground level at the back and had French doors onto a decked area, beyond which was a gate which led into a large communal garden canopied with tall trees. Sitting in a low chair on the decking was a woman so exactly like Pic that Holly looked around to see whether Pic was still standing by the door behind her, or if she had magically jumped in front and sat down. The only difference was that the seated elf had a baby attached to her chest.

'Oh!' said Holly.

'Hello. I'm Ginger,' she said, with the same broad smile and in the same upper-class accent.

'You're twins!' Holly said in astonishment.

'Sorry, didn't Charlie tell you?'

'No. Which one of you is Charlie's wife?'

'Oh God, did you hear that, Pic?' Ginger stamped her very small foot. 'He is the absolute limit. I am, although I won't be much longer if he keeps on forgetting that I have a name . . .' She huffed and puffed as much as was possible sitting down breastfeeding, then suddenly focused on Holly and asked, 'You don't mind Marks and Spencer, do you? I've got a friend who throws away the packets and pretends she's done it herself, but nobody would eat dinner with us if I told them I'd cooked it.'

'I love Marks and Spencer,' Holly said, sitting down in a wicker chair, feeling suddenly at home, 'where's Charlie?'

'Charlie's going to be late. He just rang from his mobile. I'm afraid I couldn't hear where he said he was, and anyway, there's no way of knowing that someone's telling the truth, is there? Mobile phones must make having an affair so much easier. "I'm just at the office, darling, switchboard's closed for the night, but you can always reach me on my mobile . . ." Ooops,' Ginger looked suddenly ashamed, 'sorry, Pic. My sister has just split up with her filthy bastard two-timing husband . . .' she explained.

'I'm sorry,' Holly said, nodding at Pic with embarrassment and sympathy.

'. . . which is why she's here tonight. Charlie and I never go out now that we've got two babies and we were getting so bored with each other, we thought we'd have people round on a Friday evening. This is a kind of trial run. I don't see why there always have to be equal numbers of men and women, do you?'

'Oh Ginger, do shut up,' Pic said.

'I'm sorry. I think I'm worse after having a baby,' Ginger said, 'other women get post-natal depression and I get post-natal verbal diarrhoea. It's because I have so little adult conversation, you see. Guy's very grown-up for his age, but he is only one and three-quarters . . . my son,' she explained to Holly.

'Oh. How old is Rose?' Holly looked at the tiny infant in Ginger's arms.

'Rose is six weeks old. She was born on 1st May, which is why she's called Rose, although it's a nice name too, don't you think? Charlie wanted her to be called Red Rose. Can you imagine, Red Rose Prospect Prince? Poor thing. Anyway, people would call her Red and I've had enough trouble explaining all my life why I'm called Ginger when my hair is blond . . .'

'Nobody who was ginger would call themselves Ginger,' Holly said.

'Do you hate having ginger hair?' Ginger asked her sympathetically.

'Yes I do.'

'At least you haven't got freckles,' Ginger pronounced, 'there was a girl at school, wasn't there, Pic, who was absolutely covered in freckles . . .'

'Ginger!' screamed Pic.

'Sorry. Oh look, Rose is asleep. What well-behaved children I have. I'll just go and put her down. Pic, pour us all some wine.'

Holly watched as Ginger went inside with her baby. Sometimes, very rarely, you discovered someone you knew instantly was going to be a friend, and Ginger was one of those people.

'Do you have a sister, Holly?' Pic said, looking for sympathy as they heard Ginger walking upstairs to the nursery.

'Well, yes, I do. Sort of . . .'

'You say it as if you were surprised . . .'

'Well, I only met her recently,' Holly began to

explain. She wondered whether all pairs of sisters had a bossy one and a reticent one, as she and Clare, and Ginger and Pic seemed to be.

When Ginger returned they decided they were all too hungry to wait for Charlie, so they went into the kitchen and sat down at the large rectangular table to eat the first course of poached salmon terrine, and focaccia bread that Pic had warmed in the oven.

The twins took it in turns to quiz Holly about her recent history.

'How amazing,' Ginger said, 'it sounds like a film script. Far better than any of my ideas, but then the truth usually is. I'm always thinking of plots and Charlie says to me, no, that's just not realistic, and yet I never would have thought of having a twin I didn't know about.'

'She's not my twin, just nearly the same age,' Holly corrected.

'Well, of course, in a film, she would have to be. Then you could have the titles rolling over little clips of their birthdays – sepia at the beginning when they're still babies, becoming black and white as the Sixties roll on and then flower power . . . The working-class one gets a fairy cake with a couple of candles and the upper-class one has a whole party with paid entertainment and little girls in dresses from Harrods, but guess which is the happier?'

'Ginger, it's Holly's life you're talking about,' Pic said sternly.

'Well, then, Holly should write it . . .' Ginger said.

'No,' said Holly, 'you write it. I'm too close. I'm so bloody close, it hadn't even occurred to me. I can't believe it. I spend my whole bloody life reading other people's plots . . . you will let me know how the story turns out?' she asked Ginger, laughing.

'If I get beyond the first page . . . I expect Charlie told you that I'm trying to write a script. Trouble is, it's a romantic comedy about how I met him, you see, and I think I'm just *too close*,' she put deliberate, serious emphasis on the words, 'hmm, that sounds so much better than I'm too undisciplined, or just not very good at writing. I'm too close. What do you think, Pic?'

'You don't concentrate,' Pic said.

Sisters could say that sort of thing and get away with it, Holly thought. That was what made them different from friends.

'She's right,' Ginger admitted, 'I've got the concentration span of a moth. I'm good at first pages, and titles, especially now that I read so many nursery rhymes. They all sound like titles because they all have that thing, like Charlie always says . . .'

'What do I always say?'

Charlie appeared at the door, kissed all three of them on the cheek and grabbed a piece of focaccia from the board in the middle of the table.

'You say that titles have to sound like you've heard them before . . . and of course they do if they're nursery rhymes because you have heard them before, and some of them are really sinister . . .' Ginger said, lowering her voice. 'Fee, fi, fo, fum, I smell the blood of an Englishman . . . The Blood of an Englishman . . . I mean, it's a great title, isn't it?'

'I'll just pop up and see the sprogs,' Charlie interrupted.

Ginger made a face.

'I hate that word,' she confided to the women.

Holly was thinking about nursery-rhyme titles.

'We could play a game,' she said, 'one of us has to say a title and the rest have to pitch the film . . .'

'Brilliant. I'm so glad Charlie invited you. It's turning into a real dinner party with games and everything,' Ginger said, 'Charlie can award us points. You start.'

'*Three Blind Mice*, starring Morgan Freeman, Tommy Lee Jones and Danny Aiello. Three detectives on the trail of a serial killer they call The Cat . . .' Holly improvised.

'Shouldn't the serial killer be called The Farmer's Wife?' Pic interjected.

Ginger and Holly just looked at her and dissolved into laughter.

'*Lavender's Blue, Dilly, Dilly,*' Ginger said, '. . . marriage of convenience turns sad as husband gets AIDS.'

'There's a film about a marriage of convenience being released next year,' Holly told her, 'a romantic comedy.'

'Well, this is the weepy version. This is *Philadelphia* meets *Love Story*, but for God's sake, not Tom Hanks.'

On that basis Holly was prepared to allow it into competition.

When Charlie came down he wanted to join in rather than judge, and so it was left up to Pic to choose. After many suggestions and much serious thought, she awarded first prize to *Little Miss Muffet* – thirty-something arachnophobe finds romance with a man from Rentokil, which was, in everyone else's view, one of the weakest entries.

'Did you bring that script?' Charlie asked Holly, as Pic took two trays of bread-and-butter pudding out of the oven.

'It's in an envelope on your hall table,' Holly told him.

'I'll get back to you on Monday.'

'Fine,' Holly said. She had been enjoying herself so much she hadn't really thought about why she was supposed to be there. She sat up straight trying to remember how many glasses of wine she'd consumed.

'Did you always want to be an agent?' Charlie asked her.

'I didn't even know what an agent did until I was in my twenties. I always wanted to be in the film business.

I was an usherette, and when I left school I learned to type and worked in the music industry and then somebody told me about the *Guardian* on a Monday, Creative and Media, and there was this secretary's job at Louis Gold. So I got it and as soon as I'd worked out what my boss did, I thought I could do it just as well, so I just worked on them until they let me.'

'That's pretty unusual, isn't it?' Charlie said.

'Yeah, I suppose so. There are loads of Oxford graduates swanning about who have a daddy in the business,' she laughed drily, thinking of the irony in that, then looked up.

'Oh, I suppose you're now going to tell me that you're an Oxford graduate . . .'

'Yup.'

'Shit.'

'But Charlie was the first person from his terrible East London comprehensive to go to Oxford. Surely he's told you that? He tells absolutely everybody,' Ginger said, 'he's the biggest inverted snob in the business . . .'

'I thought you were genuine East End,' Holly told him.

'And not just some poser putting on the voice?' he said.

'Yeah . . .'

They began to swap anecdotes about their school-days.

By the end of the evening Holly was aching with laughter. Charlie called a cab for her, and when the doorbell rang, Ginger said, 'Holly, before you go, come and see the most beautiful sight in the world . . .'

Holly followed her up the stairs. The walls in the nursery were painted as a panorama of sky with clouds and hot air balloons drifting across towards a sunset, and on the side of the room where the cot was, it had grown dark and there were stars and a crescent moon.

'What a fantastic room!' Holly said.

'Come and look,' Ginger whispered, peering over the top of the cot.

Her little boy was fast asleep. Around his head a halo of black curly hair fanned out on the mattress and in his sleep he was smiling. He looked a bit like Tom. She wondered if all little boys were so angelic, and when it was that they changed.

There was obviously some sort of conspiracy going on, Holly thought as the cab sped down Ladbroke Grove, to make her want to have a relationship. Until recently she had found that her friends who married became instantly dull. Not just Colette and Dr Implant, but all the ones who had wedding lists and then got you round to see their soft furnishings and said things like 'I expect you find all this very boring' and never invited you back when you said yes.

Holly sometimes envied people having a relationship, but she never wanted to have the relationship they actually had. She had never fancied one of her friend's men. But she did want Ginger's relationship. In fact she wanted Ginger's life, house, children, husband, everything, but she couldn't seem to think of any reasons why Ginger shouldn't have them and she should. Too much wine. Charlie was the One for Ginger and vice versa, and there was something just so right about that.

What was so strange was that seeing Ginger and Charlie had actually made her feel optimistic rather than depressed. Ginger was the chaotic and opinionated sister who wasn't supposed to live happily ever after, she thought. Pic was the sensible, feminine one, the sort of person who followed the washing instructions on her underwear, and yet Pic was on her own. In an odd sort of way the thought gave Holly hope.

Chapter 19

'Is Ella taking her computer, do you know?' Joss asked Clare on one of the rare mornings they had both woken up before Tom. He had made her a cup of tea and they were sitting in bed together passing the time of day under the companionable warmth of the duvet. It was like a scene from a domestic drama, Clare thought. On television, couples were always sitting up in bed together talking. In real life, there was always a small child in there with them, or calling proudly from the landing that he was just about to jump all the way down the stairs, or a teenager shouting up from the kitchen unable to decide what to take to school for lunch.

'Her computer? I don't think so. Why should she?' Long experience had taught her to look for a subtext in everything Joss said, but she couldn't for the moment second-guess what he was after.

'She guards it so jealously here . . .'

The state-of-the-art Powerbook had been Philippa's most recent Christmas gift to Ella and she spent many hours shut in her room with it. Clare thought of it as the 1990s equivalent of the teenage diary she herself had kept, except that Ella's thoughts were more secure because no-one else in the household had the first idea of how to use the machine.

'Why do you ask?' she asked, suddenly defensive on

Ella's behalf, wanting to protect her daughter from having Joss surfing around her secrets, as Jack had done in hers, mocking her adolescent confessions, using her own words as ammunition to humiliate her with in their final battle.

'If I could just use the word-processor part, I feel I would be more productive . . .'

'Why don't you ask her, then?' Clare suggested.

'It would be better coming from you . . .'

Clare was torn. She wished that either Ella or Joss would grow up enough to speak to each other properly without her having to be the go-between, and yet she wanted to encourage him. She had always thought that their fortunes might change if he would just set his mind to working rather than using his intellectual abilities to create more and more elaborate reasons why life as a writer was impossible. Since he had returned from the poetry festival, he seemed more at ease with the world. She was always looking for a turning-point and she must not let the possibility of one slip away just because she felt uncomfortable about using her influence with Ella on his behalf.

'All right, I'll ask her,' she said.

'You're a good woman,' he said, putting down his mug and looking at her.

It was a long time since she had seen his face when they were making love. At night, she sometimes suspected that he did not want to see her as he pushed himself into her in the dark, whispering into her ear and yet never speaking her name. My love, my beauty. They were transferable blandishments acceptable to any woman, whatever her name.

'Clare,' he smiled at her now, pulling back the duvet, looking at her as her white flesh turned goosebumpy as it met the colder air of the room.

'Still beautiful,' he said, running his large hands over her body.

She smiled nervously, feeling strangely as if she were being rewarded for falling in with his plans, like a dog being stroked on the head after retrieving a stick. As Joss climbed on top of her, she was almost grateful to hear Tom's voice yelling out his morning call.

'MAR ME!!'

'I'd like to take some photographs of you before you leave,' Clare said to Ella later that day.

'I'm not leaving yet,' Ella said grumpily.

'But it's a nice day. It's a pity to waste it.'

'Mum!'

'Oh, just indulge me, just this once,' Clare said.

They walked up along the top of the cliff together arm in arm. Ella would be leaving in just a few weeks and however much she told herself that she must get on with her life, find new interests, work harder, Clare couldn't persuade herself that she wasn't going to be desperately lonely.

Ella stood at the edge of the cliff surrounded by sky, posing awkwardly, then hamming it up, blowing Clare exaggerated kisses, pretending she had lost her balance over the edge. Clare dropped the camera and was halfway across the distance that separated them before she realized it was a joke.

'Oh you . . .' Clare lunged, and Ella squealed and then Clare chased her all over the top field just as she used to when Ella was a little girl and eventually they fell down in the grass together giggling.

'Are you taking your computer with you to the States?' Clare asked, when their laughter had subsided.

'No,' Ella said, clearly mystified by the question, 'why?'

'I don't suppose you'd let Dad use it, would you?'

'I don't see why not . . .' Ella said.

Relief flooded through Clare as the confrontation she had been anticipating suddenly evaporated.

'You're marvellous, did you know?' she said to her.

They lay on their backs looking at the sky for a few minutes.

'We thought we'd stay a couple of days with Holly before my flight . . .' Ella said a little warily, and Clare was suddenly conscious that her daughter too had been waiting for a good moment to ask something tricky.

'Oh . . .' Despite her best efforts to pretend otherwise, it hurt. She had assumed that she would go to the airport to see Ella off.

'Good idea,' she added quickly, trying to adjust the picture she had imagined of herself crying at the airport after Ella disappeared through the departure gate, to a picture of herself crying at the station as her train pulled away.

'There's a gig that Matt wants to go to . . . might as well end on a happy note . . .'

'Yeah, what's going to happen with you and Matt?' Clare asked.

'Not sure. He's all right, you know, but I can't see how we can survive with me there and him here, and I'm not sure I want to anyway. He's talking about reapplying to colleges in London and I really don't want that, but I don't know how to tell him without hurting his feelings . . .'

'Better now, than if he gets a place and then . . .'

'I suppose so. It's just, well, he's nice, you know, and he really likes me, and I sometimes wonder whether anyone else ever will.'

'They will.'

'You think so? Even though I'm moody and difficult?'

A thought of Holly still single in her thirties flitted across Clare's mind.

'Of course,' she reassured her daughter, hoping she was right, 'you're really not that bad.'

'I want to have lots of men, and I don't want to love any of them,' Ella said.

I'm not going to make the same mistakes as you, she seemed to be saying.

'Sometimes you don't have a choice,' Clare said.

'Oh come on . . .'

'No, really, when I fell in love with Joss that is what it felt like – free-falling, like I imagine doing a bungee jump is – totally exhilarating and really frightening too . . .'

'And then you had me and all that stopped . . .'

Something in the tone of Ella's voice made Clare turn her head on the grass. There were tears in Ella's eyes.

'Then I had you, and it was even more wonderful . . .' Clare said, sitting up.

'Oh, come on, Mum. Having me stopped you doing anything . . .' Ella sat up too.

'I didn't do nothing, I did something very important. I don't know why everyone these days attaches so little value to bringing up children . . .' Clare said. 'I mean, you and I are perfect examples,' she put her arm around Ella, 'I had a mother who resented the merest second of time that I took her away from her personal ambition and what happened? I fell into the arms of the first man who said he loved me at the age of eighteen. You've had a mother who was there at least, if nothing else, and at the age of eighteen you're going abroad, then to medical school, you're sussed about men, you know you can choose to do what you want when you want to. I was too insecure to allow myself that choice, even though I had known about a woman's right to choose from my cradle,' she gave Ella a squeeze. 'I'm not saying your achievement is my achievement . . . I don't really know what I am saying . . . but I'm glad you're like you are . . .'

In some ways she had never had to worry about Ella

because she was such a sensible and reasonable person, and yet she realized she had worried this last year about whether Ella, who had always coasted through her schooling, would raise herself to get the qualifications that would give her real options in her life. She had worried about not putting enough pressure on her, or too much. Ella had sailed through, having done enough before she even sat the exams to be offered a place at her chosen medical school, and still studying right up to the last minute in order to achieve perfection. It made Clare smile to think that she had set such a good example for her daughter: Ella was completely determined not to end up as she had done.

'I'm glad you're like you are too,' Ella said, giving her a kiss, 'honestly, Mum, I didn't mean . . .'

'I know,' Clare told her, embarrassed now by her outburst. She had wanted to say something for Ella to take away with her, but she had ended up talking about herself. It was all the wrong way round.

Chapter 20

A two-day-old English Sunday newspaper caught Philippa's eye on a kiosk at the bus station. Philippa was moving on. She had deliberated about having a car drive her across Andalucia but could not bear the thought of being enclosed with a stranger for so many hours. A cab-driver would be bound to ask questions which she had neither the language nor the inclination to answer. In a bus she would be uncomfortable but nobody would bother her, and she found she was quite enjoying slumming it. Her small Louis Vuitton case looked charmingly out of place slung in the space under the bus alongside turquoise and pink nylon rucksacks. It was bound to get stolen, but she did not seem to care. She found herself quite enjoying freedom from the pressure of material possessions.

The bus was hot and the seats were sticky leatherette. All the Spaniards were seated on one side of the aisle. Philippa happily chose a pair of seats on the empty side and it was only when the bus drew out of the station into the road that she realized why she had been left so much space. The sun was on her side of the bus and, even with the blinds down, it was impossibly hot. A sweat broke out instantly beneath the white T-shirt she had bought the previous day, and the baggy khaki chinos suddenly felt as tight as a newly-washed pair of jeans. Seeing her distress, an old lady shifted a pile of carrier bags from the seat next to her and beckoned Philippa over. The smell of garlic sausage that impregnated the old woman's clothing was almost less bearable than the heat. Philippa picked the Sunday newspaper from the plastic carrier bag that contained her provisions for the journey – a large plastic bottle of mineral water that was already warm, a banana, a small tin of olives stuffed with almonds – and held it around herself like a makeshift cubicle, grateful that the English newspapers still came out in broadsheet form.

It had been weeks since she had seen the news, but the world had gone on without her. Usually she was an avid reader of newspapers and now she wondered why she bothered. What was the point of cramming your head with facts and trivia and other people's opinions? Because it was easy, she realized. It gave you the appearance of being a thinking person without the bother of thinking. Thinking was the hardest thing.

A man the same age as her daughter had become Leader of the Conservative party. Philippa tried to examine why that news should make her feel peculiar. She was used to employing people half her age and respecting them. It was just that government was different. For a long time her own generation had held the reins of power, and now, all of a sudden, it was Clare's. On page two there was a picture of Princess Diana in New York with Mother Teresa. Even living saints were handing over the baton of caring, Philippa thought grimly. Jack, she said silently, you got out just in the nick of time. You died before you ever became past it.

She turned to the television listings for the week and noticed, with shocked synchronicity, that she had missed a screening the previous evening of his first film *All Parties*. A tribute to the late British film director, it said underneath, see Pick of the Day.

Beneath the superficial glitter of Jack Palmer's slick and sophisticated début lurk dark questions about class and misogyny. A haunting examination of glamour and illusion with subtle performances from . . .

Philippa read, proud and delighted as she always had been by his good reviews. She was about to tear it out to give to him when she next saw him when she remembered that she would not be seeing him again. It kept happening, this forgetting, and she wondered whether it was a sign of age, or grief, or both.

Jack's ambition had always been to direct a film of *The Great Gatsby*. She could remember the way he had told her, leaning forward over the coffee-bar table, as if honouring her with a great secret, after going to the pictures for the first time together. It had seemed an odd choice to her, until he had explained that cinema had been his only escape from the satanic mills of his dreary industrial home town and his local library happened to hold the complete works of F. Scott Fitzgerald. He had described the novel with such passion that she had gone straight to her bookshelf when she returned to her flat and reread the book that night.

In the mid-Seventies, Jack had been furious when somebody beat him to making the film. He had always referred to the Robert Redford vehicle as the chocolate-box version, but it had not deterred him. It was almost impossible to divert Jack from something he wanted. Several years later, none of the reviewers had spotted the resemblance of Jack's modern yuppie retelling of the story, *All Parties*, with its themes of glamour, rivalry and excess perfectly in tune with the mores of the early Eighties. Suddenly Jack was hailed as the man breathing life into British cinema. He had caught the *Zeitgeist* just as he had always done in his advertising campaigns – his films were always steamy enough to get the PR going, but not enough to present the censors with difficulty.

Philippa put down her newspaper shield for a moment and stared blankly at the headrest on the seat in front of her. In all of Jack's four films the central male character had a wife and a mistress, and yet it had never occurred to her before that he was writing auto-biographically.

On the night they married he had told her with pride that she was the least wifey person he could imagine. They were lying in bed in the Ritz. The first night of their honeymoon was a gift from her older sister who had bad memories of her own wedding night spent in the discomfort of the night-train to Italy.

'Wives are supposed to be angels in the kitchen and whores in the bedroom,' Jack had pronounced, lying on his back staring at the curlicues and cornicing of the stucco ceiling. His hands supported his head, his elbows were bent.

'But I've found myself an angel in bed and a whore in the kitchen, or the bathroom, or the hall, or . . .' he turned onto his side and smiled at her. Jack smouldered with charm. He was not generous with compliments but when they came they were each so much better than a dozen from anyone else.

'You won't change, will you?' he asked her, suddenly boyish in his fear.

'I won't change,' she promised him.

Had she changed, without being aware of it, so much that he had needed to find himself a mistress? The question tormented Philippa. And the not-knowing. She had been so sure, so arrogant in her possession of him.

The bus crawled through the baked-mud landscape. The old woman got off after an hour or two, leaving Philippa two seats. She shifted over to the window and stared out at the dusty road and the dusty houses, occasionally sipping warm water from her bottle, oblivious to time passing.

It was dark by the time she reached Granada. She asked a cab-driver to take her to the best hotel, longing to wash the sweat and smells of the journey from her skin. He looked bemused, asked a question, she repeated *el mejor*. He shrugged and drove up a steep road towards the Alhambra. The receptionist at the Parador looked at her suspiciously. The Louis Vuitton suitcase fitted, but the grimy T-shirt did not. Yes, they had a room. She swiped Philippa's gold visa card through the machine and waited insolently for Philippa's credit to check out before she would say whether she was prepared to let Philippa have it. Of course with a bath, she replied, as the positive response stuttered out of the machine. How long will you be staying? Philippa said she did not know. Time had lost all its meaning for her.

PART FOUR

July

Chapter 21

Clare had been saying for days that they mustn't leave everything until the last minute, but all her careful preparations meant that suddenly there was nothing to do but wait for Matt to arrive. His father was driving them into Truro to catch the train. Ella's rucksack was packed and she had said goodbye to Joss and Tom who had gone down to the beach. They wouldn't all fit in the car.

It would almost have been better to be rushing around, ironing, searching for passports than sitting, listening to the seconds tick away. There was nothing to say. It was not the time to embark on a long, soul-searching conversation about life, and little questions like whether she had remembered her toothbrush seemed to annoy Ella disproportionately, making Clare aware that she was very nervous too. Ella was so cool, so well-prepared, it was easy to forget that she was just a teenager who had never really ventured outside Cornwall.

Clare made coffee and the two of them sat in their usual places at the kitchen table cupping their hands like carol singers with mugs of hot chocolate at the end of a long cold evening's walk. It was a bit like she imagined it must be saying goodbye to someone on death row. She wanted to say something significant, something that would make Ella's parting OK for both of them, but she could think of nothing. She caught her daughter's eye and they both laughed at their unaccustomed embarrassment.

'You will come home if you don't like it? I don't care how much it costs. We'll find the money, OK?'

'Yes,' Ella said through gritted teeth. It was at least the tenth time she had answered the question.

Clare suddenly noticed Ella's unadorned nose. 'You've forgotten your ring.'

'Not forgotten. I've taken it out.'

'Oh?'

'It had to go sometime. I don't think it would have given my patients much confidence . . .'

'Oh.' For some reason, the absence of the nose ring and the grown-up reason for its disappearance made Clare want to cry. It was a rite of passage as significant as the day Ella had her first period.

'It was only a kind of protest,' Ella said, adding with a short laugh, 'I'm not even sure what I was protesting about.'

Outside, Matt's father sounded the horn of his car.

'You will write,' Clare said, feeling their time had run out and she had wasted it.

'I'll call,' Ella said, standing up.

'And write. There won't be time on a call to tell me what it's really like . . .' She knew the words were too eager as she said them.

'I will if I have time. It'll take me a while to settle in. You mustn't worry about me.'

'No.' I don't want you to go, Clare wanted to scream. Please don't leave me.

'I love you very much,' she said, fighting back tears.

'I love you too, Mum,' Ella said, and then as the horn sounded again outside she shouted, 'I'm outta here!' punching the air.

At the station, they simply hugged. Ella held on for a

236

long time, and Clare felt each second of her pressed warmth as a gift. Finally she let go and climbed onto the train. Clare forced herself to smile. She did not want Ella's last image to be of her crying.

'It's OK, Mum,' Ella pulled down the window and leaned out, 'I'm only going away for a year . . .' and then the train pulled out and Clare ran down the platform wanting to see her right up to the last millionth of a glimpse. And when she had gone, she exhaled, as if she had been holding her breath for an hour.

'As she says, she's only going for a year,' Matt's father said cheerfully.

Oh shut up, Clare thought.

'Matthew will miss her,' he continued. His tone implied that Matt was the only person in town who would. They didn't know each other very well. Just the occasional nod of recognition at parents' evenings. He was the assistant bank manager and didn't have a very high opinion of what he called artistic types.

'Not as much as I will,' Clare told him, brightly, trying to achieve a sort of closure by the time they got into the car. She didn't think she would be able to bear the strain of polite conversation all the journey back to Penderric.

The house was empty. She went upstairs to Ella's room and lay on her bed, trying to remember all the happy moments they had shared, but only able to see her daughter's waving arm going further and further away down the track until the point where she didn't know whether she was seeing or imagining it. As she lay staring blindly at the ceiling tears dripped from her eyes and down both sides of her face, filling her ears, then overflowing on to Ella's pillowcase.

'MAR ME!'

She didn't know how long she had been lying crying before Tom and Joss arrived home. She sat up quickly and wiped her eyes with Ella's duvet cover, then looked at herself in the mirror on the wall. She looked as if she had a bad cold, she thought, practising a smile for Tom.

'It's a kind of *Cyrano de Bergerac* of the Internet,' Jeff said.

Holly's heart sank. It was a very good idea, but she couldn't see Jeff having the finesse to pull it off. It was late on a hot summer's Friday afternoon. As she looked out of the window trying to think of a suitable response, he leant towards her and she caught a faint whiff of stale deodorant and sweat.

'Have you got a light?' he asked her.

She saw there was a cigarette in his mouth.

'I thought you'd given up,' she said, leaning casually back in her chair, fumbling as unobtrusively as she could in her desk drawer for her cigarette packet. With relief her blind fingers discovered that she had one left.

'My father died, so I took it up again,' Jeff said between sucks as she lit a match under his cigarette.

'Oh, I'm sorry.'

She lit up too and blew the match out.

'Yeah. It's a bit illogical since he died of lung cancer, but there we are.'

She meant she was sorry about his father, not his relapse, but it seemed too cruel to say so. Anyway, she reminded herself, there were no right and wrong ways to grieve.

'My father died recently too,' she offered, trying to show she understood.

'Right. Did he smoke?'

'Yes.'

They sat silently and gloomily filling the room with fumes.

'So tell me about *Cyrano of the Internet*,' she said with

238

fake enthusiasm, wondering how this slightly un-savoury man always managed to make her feel guilty.

'There's this girl, woman, right, who puts out an advert for a guy . . .'

'Can you do that on the Internet?' Holly interrupted, 'I mean personal ads . . .'

'Yeah . . .' Jeff looked rather uncomfortable.

'Sorry. Go on.'

Holly wondered whether Colette knew about In-ternet dating.

'. . . so her ad says she wants someone with a poetic nature, and there's this computer nerd who falls in love with her. So they strike up an E-mail correspon-dence, and he knows that he's going to have to do the poetry thing before he gets to meet her, so he gets in his friend . . .'

Jeff looked up for her approval.

'It is a good idea,' Holly said. 'Why don't you work up an outline and I'll have a look . . .' She was sure he could do the nerd bit convincingly, but she wasn't at all sure about the poetry or the romance.

'There's another one I'd like to . . .'

Holly's phone rang, on cue. She'd told the recep-tionist to interrupt if he wasn't gone after half an hour.

'Right,' Holly spoke to the dialling tone, 'I'm just finishing here . . .'

Taking his cue, Jeff said goodbye and left, and as soon as he'd gone Holly wished she'd let him stay. He had body odour and a dead father and he wasn't much of a writer, but there was a bulge near his groin that shouted almost full pack of Marlboro, and now she was going to have to last the next half an hour without one.

Holly's phone rang.

'I've got Charlie Prince for you,' Jemima announced.

Charlie Prince said that he didn't think he was the one for *The One*. He liked the script, but thought it needed work. At the moment the central character was too much like a dominatrix and the men looked too silly. It was only one man's view, he told Holly, adding, 'I'm sure you'll prove me wrong.'

'Yes, I'm sure I will,' she said, laughing, 'I already have a six-figure offer on the table.'

'I thought you said you were giving me first look,' Charlie objected.

'In the circumstances it's a good thing I didn't,' Holly retaliated, 'anyway, you said you'd come back to me on Monday morning. It's now Friday afternoon, three weeks later.'

'God, you're tough . . . you're my kind of woman,' he joked.

If only, Holly thought, without rancour.

'But you're right,' he conceded, 'I don't think I'm a romantic comedy person . . .'

'You ought to be. It's the only thing Hollywood thinks we do well here . . .'

'Yeah, I know. I need to team up with someone who is . . . do you know anyone who'd be interested? Who you rate, I mean?'

'I'll think about it,' Holly told him, putting her feet up on the desk.

'You wouldn't be interested, I suppose?'

'Me?' She wasn't sure whether he was joking.

'Think about it,' Charlie said, banging down the phone.

She didn't have time to think about anything, Holly realized, looking at her watch, because Ella and Matt would be arriving at her flat any minute, and even though she lived just a short walk from the office, she had never made it in less than five minutes.

They were standing by the wrought-iron entrance gates when she arrived, looking like a couple of young back-packers.

'You're not planning on moving in,' Holly exclaimed, kissing each of them on the cheek, and looking sceptically at the size of the rucksack on Matt's back.

'It's Ella's . . .' he said, 'she is going away for a year . . .'

'God, what a gentleman you are!' Holly said, putting her key in the lock.

They all tramped up the stairs.

'What a fantastic place,' Ella said, putting her head round Holly's bedroom door on their way to the kitchen.

'Could do with a bit of a clean-up,' Holly said. The sun was at the perfect angle to show up all the smudges on the kitchen window. She had never really noticed before how shabby the kitchen was.

'I would offer you coffee,' she said, 'except that I don't have any milk, or any coffee for that matter. We could go into Soho and have one or a drink . . .'

'Be great.'

'I'll just show you your room . . .'

Nobody ever stayed in the guest-room except Colette when she couldn't be bothered to go back to her mansion in the burbs. Holly didn't have friends who lived outside London, except the people she'd met in New York and Los Angeles through work, and she couldn't imagine any American wanting to stay in a dusty room on an old double divan wedged between two clothes manufacturer's rails of her garments and surrounded by piles of books. She was proud of the rails. She'd often seen clothes being delivered to the department stores on them when she walked up Regent Street early in the mornings, but she had never seen them for sale. One day she'd asked one of the guys trundling along a consignment of dresses where she could get hold of one, and after a short negotiation, he had turned up at her door that evening with two in exchange for five ten-pound notes. As it turned out,

Simon had had to take the castors off in order to get them up the stairs, and somehow Holly had never got round to screwing them back on, so they didn't trundle from room to room, in the way she had imagined, but stood in the spare room getting more and more weighed down with her purchases. Holly bought clothes like other people bought groceries, something almost every day and a big shop at the weekend.

'What's in there?' Ella asked about the little room at the back that had been Holly's first bedroom.

'Skeletons . . . and a few shoes,' Holly told her, 'I've got big feet and it's hard to get my size, so whenever I try some on that fit, I buy several pairs.'

'Hard to get your size?' Matt exclaimed, peering in.

'Well, other people buy lampshades and vases and sets of kitchen knives in wooden blocks and chrome toasters. Cherie Blair buys all of those AND shoes,' Holly defended herself, looking at the stacks of shoe-boxes then closing the door, 'as you can see, I don't. It's not exactly colour supplement, but it is home.'

'I think it's wonderful,' Ella said, 'it's the kind of place I've always dreamed of living in.'

'Me too,' Holly smiled at her, 'now it's seven o'clock and it's Friday and I want a drink. Shall we see if Simon's around?'

There was a floodlit statue on the top of the Palace Theatre that you couldn't see from the street. Holly had never been able to work out whether it was a royal figure or a neo-classical god but she liked to think of it as an angel who stood up there in a golden halo of light, silently watching over the flashing lights and milling crowds of showbizland.

'When my parents first lived in London, they had a room over there,' Holly pointed, 'in fact, that's where I must have been conceived. No wonder I feel so at home up here,' she said.

'You are where my two worlds meet,' she remembered Jack telling her.

She had sat on this terrace drinking beer or wine or cocktails a hundred times with friends, or colleagues, or clients and yet never thought about her Soho origins. That was the difference with family, she realized. What she shared with Ella was more like history than anecdote. It meant that Ella understood things about Holly without even mentioning them which, with strangers, would have needed conversations to explain. It was what they meant by blood being thicker than water, Holly suddenly appreciated, liking the feeling it gave her.

'How much older are you than Clare?' Ella asked.

'About a month. I've just been thirty-six. She's about to be, isn't she?'

'Oh no, it's tomorrow and I forgot,' Ella said, 'I can't believe I forgot . . .'

'You could send flowers.'

'Yes, OK. I just can't believe I forgot . . . Jack was a shit,' Ella returned to the conversation.

'No,' Holly felt compelled to defend her father, 'he didn't know about me.'

'He was still a shit to screw your mother and Philippa at the same time,' Ella insisted.

There was an uncomfortable silence in which Matt and Simon shifted around on their chairs and Holly stared at her niece.

'You're right,' she said at last, 'he was.'

The men breathed almost audible sighs of relief.

'Shall we eat Chinese?' Holly changed the subject.

'I don't like Chinese food,' Matt told her.

'You don't understand,' Simon advised him, in a man-to-man kind of way, 'that was a rhetorical question.'

'You only think you don't like it because all you've had is Mr Chan's version,' Holly told him.

'There's never any vegetables,' Matt whined.

In Chuen Cheng Ku, Holly ordered deep-fried bean-curd with pak choi and three kinds of mushroom for him, scallops, squid, Malaysian style Ho Fun and pork belly with yam for the rest of them. She closed the menu with a smack, feeling rather like a schoolmistress.

'So what are we going to do tonight?' she asked.

'Is that a rhetorical question too?' Matt asked.

When was it that men developed that inwardly fuming kind of look? Matt was not much more than a boy and yet he had it down to perfection. Holly remembered Tom's innocence and charm, and wondered when the moment would come that he folded his arms and closed down his face, threatening to sulk.

'Can we go to the Ministry of Sound?' Ella asked, stepping in to divert the stand-off from developing.

'Can people our age get into the Ministry of Sound?' Holly asked Simon.

'You don't look that old,' Matt told her, his eyes flicking for a second to her small high breasts.

She was wearing a short black T-shirt that just touched the waistband of her jeans. Infuriatingly, she felt the faintly erotic pull of her nipples contracting against the cotton fabric.

'I think I read that Peter Mandelson goes there,' Simon said.

'If he can, anyone can,' Holly said, 'although if he's there, maybe they wouldn't want to . . .' She was speaking fast to cover her embarrassment at the pure physicality of Matt's gaze.

Simon was slurping noodles, Ella was looking at the huge round table of Chinese people eating their dinner. Holly looked at the young man opposite her and wondered if his knee had just nudged between hers deliberately or accidentally. She thought she caught an infinitesimal trace of a smile as he put another forkful of greens into his mouth.

'Mmmm, this is good,' he remarked, and Ella turned her head and smiled at him, glad he had decided to be polite.

When Holly had seen the stockinette body with a Renaissance image of the Virgin Mary on it, she hadn't been able to imagine a time she would actually wear it. She had loved its combination of sexiness and blasphemy so much that she had told herself if the occasion did not arise, she could always hang it on her bedroom wall along with the three-dimensional postcards of religious images that Robert sent her from his holidays in Tuscany, creating a kind of shrine of religious kitsch beside her mirror.

Now she put it on with black jeans. She wavered about adding a large cross made of fake rubies, but decided it would be too much. In the room next door she could hear Ella whooping like a child with a dressing-up box as she tried on Holly's clothes.

Eventually they all emerged into the corridor ready to party, and Holly felt herself blush as she saw surprised approval register on Matt's face. He was wearing a black T-shirt that stretched tight across his chest and showed off the muscles in his upper arms. He was more stockily built than she had imagined, and she thought he had lined his sloping eyes with kohl.

'You look fantastic,' Ella said to Holly.

'So do you.'

Ella was wearing flared Pucci trousers with a Seventies Paisley pattern and a purple vest. The trousers were slightly too short for Holly. She knew that was how they were supposed to be, but she had spent so much of her life trying to get trousers long enough, she somehow could never bring herself to wear them. Anyway, she thought there was probably something a bit sad about someone who had been a teenager in the Seventies wearing teenagers' clothes again when the wheel of style turned full circle. She didn't know whether it was that, or the fact that she wanted to appear to be generous that made her say, 'Keep them. I never wear them and they look so much better on you . . .'

Ella's face lit up.

'It is so nice having an aunt. It's a bit like having a really cool fairy godmother,' she said, giving Holly's arm a quick squeeze.

Just as they were leaving, the phone rang.

'Clare, hi!' Holly said, 'we're just going out to a club, here's Ella.'

'Mum? Great . . . Yes . . . On time. We've had a lot to drink, we've eaten a lot of food and now we're all dressed up . . . Holly looks like a cross between a madonna and Madonna . . .'

This was a description Holly far preferred to fairy godmother, however cool.

'Oh, and Mum. Happy birthday for tomorrow!'

Chapter 22

'If I won the Lottery I'd buy a place out here,' Eamon said as they walked barefoot along the strand.

As dusk fell the western sky was a layered wash of pink and blue, and the opalescent light turned the sea to mother-of-pearl. The water was calm and flat. Small curls of waves at its edge lapped soothingly near their feet.

Eamon's words made Mo think of Holly. She was always saying that you couldn't get serious about a man without asking the Lottery question. If his answer involved anything to do with cars, it was off. Mo couldn't understand why Holly was so vehement about that, but that was just how Holly was. She had very strong opinions.

'It is beautiful,' Mo agreed, slipping her hand through his arm. Eamon squeezed affectionately with his elbow.

It had been the best holiday Mo could remember. They had rented a cottage just along the coast from Galway City. They'd had to take a place that slept six but it was nice to have a bit of room. Normally holidays meant living out of a suitcase with nowhere in the bathroom to put your toothbrush. Here they had three cupboards and three double beds with stiff white sheets and blankets that smelt of childhood holidays. In the mornings, Mo lay in bed enjoying the luxury of dozing warmly while Eamon cooked her breakfast, and the taste of buttered soda bread dipped in egg was as good as anything she'd ever eaten.

'It tastes better when someone makes it for you,' she told Eamon.

'I'll make it for you every day, if you'd like,' he replied.

She didn't know if he meant every day on the holiday, or every day of her life. Then she wondered why she was even thinking about it.

They'd had a few fine days and on one of them they had taken a flight to the Aran Islands in a little propeller plane that chugged along like a minibus in the sky and landed in a field. She thought it was the most wonderful place she had ever been. They hired bikes and cycled to the end of the island, past donkeys in tiny walled fields the size of rugs. Out here on the edge of the Atlantic with nothing but sea for thousands of miles until America, it was difficult to believe that London was going on just the same, that the tube was still filling and emptying its hordes of disconsolate commuters, and that shoppers were wandering through her department with its distinctive city smell of perfume and carpet.

Every night they went into Galway and listened to Irish music in a pub, and as the evening wore on people began to sing in turn, and, finally, Eamon persuaded her to dance, and even though she tried to make herself shy, she could not be. She stood and danced, her long hair loose around her shoulders, as happy as she had ever been in her life.

'You look like a native,' Eamon told her proudly as people applauded.

She looked at the other faces in the pub, listening, smiling at the fiddler, and she recognized herself in them – the blue eyes, the tawny, freckled colouring – and she felt as if she had come home. In London, everything was difficult, and people spent their lives hardening themselves to the stress, but it was different here.

Then she thought of the time she had been to Tenerife with the girls and Sonya, who had got off with a bartender, José-something, whining on the last day that she never wanted to leave and draping herself ridiculously over him at the airport. Mo had thought it a silly display. She was sure that José-something would be with another impressionable tourist by the end of the evening, or even sooner by the way he was looking at the Arrivals gate over Sonya's shoulder. Holidays were holidays and that was why everything felt so much better. There was no point in thinking it could go on like that for ever.

Arm in arm they watched the molten red wafer of sun stick on the horizon for just a second before disappearing. Gulls swooped around the harbour as the sky faded from pink and gold to grey. Two lovers on a beach at dusk, a sunset, the damp breeze just slightly tainted with seaweed, and the poignant cry of a seagull. It was so perfect it had made her feel powerful, as if anything could happen.

'Well, that's it for another day,' Eamon sighed.

Mo's spirits sank. Eamon was a good man, a kind man, but he was no poet, and poetry was what the moment had demanded. He stooped to tie his shoelaces and she put a hand on his back to steady herself as she slipped her feet back into her sandals.

'Lean on me, Mo,' he joked, and she was filled with such fondness for his cheerful good humour, it made her want to cry.

She had bought steak for the evening, his favourite meal, and a bag of oven chips, but as she was lighting the grill he came up behind her and put his hands around her waist.

'You're not cooking on our last night,' he told her.

'But the steak . . .'

'I'll have it for breakfast . . .'

'But where will we go? By the time we walk into . . .'

He pointed through the window. To her surprise, there was a mini-cab waiting outside. Then she was cross with him for not giving her time to get ready.

'That would have spoilt the surprise. Anyway, you look beautiful.'

'Ach you!' she punched him playfully as she went to change. She looked in the bathroom mirror as she pulled the fastening from her long pony-tail, shaking her thick curly hair around her shoulders. Her face was pink from their walk, and her eyes were shining. The holiday had ironed the frown from her forehead. She thought she did look pretty for the first time in months.

They had passed the restaurant on one of their walks in the rain and stood in the shelter of its porch reading the menu and wondering who could afford prices like that.

'But . . .' she said, when the cab drew up outside.

'Now, Mo, I don't want you spoiling your dinner by thinking of the price,' Eamon had read her thoughts. 'I won a few bob on the horses,' he told her, 'and you're going to start with a glass of champagne . . .'

For a moment Mo guessed that all the surprises and champagne were a prelude to a proposal, and she worried about what she would say to him, but after a couple of glasses she felt so relaxed she began not to care, and by the time she had finished her crème brûlée she became anxious that the evening was going to end without him saying anything. Why should he propose, she asked herself, when he had everything he wanted without marrying her and his independence too? And why was she even thinking about it? They'd survived so far without being married. Why tie themselves down now?

'Have you had a good time?' Eamon asked.

'I have,' she found that they had both reverted to the Irish cadences of their childhood. An English person would have said yes in response to his question.

'Would you really think about coming to live here,' she asked him, 'if you won the Lottery . . .'

'I would.'

'Maybe I'll buy a ticket myself so we'd have a double chance,' she was encouraging him to go further, she realized.

'I don't want to lead you into gambling,' he teased.

She blushed, and agreed to a brandy with her coffee.

'Would you live here, then?' he asked. Suddenly the conversation had become stilted and embarrassed as they simultaneously drew back from the brink of uncharted intimacy.

'I don't know. Oh, it's a dream, isn't it, Eamon?' Mo thought of Sonya and José-something. Maria, that was it, José-Maria, at Tenerife airport.

'Maybe we'll come back next year for a holiday. I'd like that.'

Chapter 23

Clare was sitting diagonally opposite Joss at Amelia's oval dining-table, watching him tell an anecdote. She had heard the story several times since he returned from the literary festival, but he had a way of engaging his audience, as if inviting them to share a wicked secret, that never failed to please. When he performed, he turned himself inside out, she thought. The mist of suppressed rage that usually hung around him became a bright radiance of charm.

'. . . so this Italian woman was talking to Richard and Richard said, "Do you know Joss Drummond? He was a neighbour of mine in another life . . ." '

Clare looked at the faces around the table, all smiling with the privilege of being in his company. She realized she had spent her life waiting for moments like this, when the sun broke through the clouds. Long, long ago, in the first few weeks of their relationship, it had been sunny all the time. She had been a tightly-furled bud opening and flowering under his warmth and light. And because she had seen the charm first, she had thought that the charmer was the man and the moods emanated from his acute awareness of the futility of life. As a poet, he felt these things more profoundly than she did, and she had thought her failure to feel equally deeply made her an inadequate person.

What Holly had said about love kept coming back to Clare.

'Everyone's the One at first . . . you start off with someone and it's gorgeous and you can't eat because you're so happy and then after a few weeks it splits up and you think what did I do? We were so perfect at the beginning. And then you work out that you only got along so well *because you didn't know each other* . . .'

At the time, Clare had thought that Holly had no understanding of marriage, and she had been slightly miffed at the implication that her own situation with Joss could be so casually dismissed. But the words haunted her like a prophecy, and she had found herself watching Joss since his return from the poetry festival, wondering whether she had got it all wrong all these years.

Could it be possible that she had long ago discovered what he was like but refused to believe it, because she so wanted him to be as he had first appeared to her, and not what he actually was? Could she have lived for so many years with an illusion? She stared at him as if he were a stranger as he recounted his story.

'So the Italian woman says, "Rilly, 'ow do you know zis?" So Richard and I exchange glances, and she sees us, and she says, "No, rilly, I am very interested in spiritual zings . . ." She couldn't understand why we roared. The poor signora thought that we really had met in another life . . .'

Had Joss fucked the hapless Italian woman, Clare wondered. Did he have harems of women at the poetry festivals he enjoyed so much? She couldn't imagine that he did not. He was always much nicer to her when he returned, which was probably as a result of guilt. She hoped he used condoms. Perhaps she should ask him. It would be perfectly reasonable, and yet she knew that his response would be a kind of wounded outrage that hurled the question back at her – don't you trust me? – and, panicking, she would forget to ask the crucial question: trust you to be faithful, or to protect yourself and me?

However calmly she prepared herself to challenge him, Joss always managed to get the better of her. It was as if their means of communication had stuck for ever at the point when she first met him, when she was a naïve student and he was her tutor. She had been happy then to have all her thoughts about literature or politics, or any of the things that students took seriously, dismissed by him as middle-class daydreams. She had been totally in awe of him, unendingly grateful for his attention, especially since her thoughts were so utterly trivial in comparison to his.

She stared at him now as he accepted the laughter of his fellow guests, basking in their admiration, and she suddenly saw that everything she had ever thought about him was wrong. She had mistaken his weakness for strength and his laziness for morality. In Penderric's small pond he was a very big fish, but in the outside world he would flounder. That was why they were there and she was the last person to have realized it.

In that lucid moment of truth she knew that she did not love him any more, or even like him very much, and it made her feel so guilty that she assumed everyone at the table must be reading her mind. Staring at the tablecloth she tried to occupy herself with the martini glass of prawn cocktail in front of her.

'This is very good,' she told Amelia, inadvertently interrupting Joss as he began to extemporize on the possible misinterpretation of figures of speech.

'. . . chip on the shoulder, what does it mean – does it mean that you're carrying a chip on your shoulder, or that you have a chip knocked out of your shoulder . . . ?'

'There's a tremendous revival of Seventies food,' Amelia said, just in case anyone had misunderstood the prawn cocktail as the old-fashioned variety instead of the contemporary one.

'I always assumed that it meant chip as in fish and chips . . .' said Olivia.

'What! A greasy potato chip?' Joss laughed dismissively, 'no, I'm certain it's not that.'

'What is chip on shoulder?' Pepe, who had never really mastered English, asked.

His wife, Vivienne, glanced at him contemptuously.

'Are you old enough to remember Seventies food, Clare?' she said.

From anyone else it would have been a compliment, but Vivienne made it sound as if she were addressing a child, and Clare knew that the main purpose of the question was to make Joss feel his age. Vivienne was quite aware of the age difference between them and the fact that Joss would certainly remember prawn cocktail first time round. Vivienne had never got beyond the stage of cattiness after Joss had finished with her.

'I'm thirty-six,' Clare said neutrally.

'Same age as Princess Diana,' Amelia remarked as if that were a compliment.

Pepe started singing Happy Birthday to You.

'No,' said Amelia, staying his arm, 'no, you must wait for the pudding.'

Oh for God's sake let him sing, Clare wanted to say. It was kind of Amelia to host a dinner party for her birthday, but her insistence on having things just as they would be in a magazine was driving any fun out of the occasion. The food and crockery and the arrangement of summer flowers in the centre of the table made it look as if Amelia was about to open the door to a camera crew, and the conversation was following the same route.

'A spoonful of plain yoghurt just takes that slightly cloying sweetness out of the mayonnaise . . .'

'Well, northerners always have chips on their shoulders, that's why I thought . . .'

'Olivia, you are the most terrible snob.'

'I really like the way you've used string instead of napkin-rings . . .'

'It was a bin end and I think I got a bargain . . .'

They had come to Cornwall to escape the inevitable slide into the middle-class rat race and nearly twenty years later they were sitting in the midst of *Abigail's Party*, Clare thought.

'I never would have thought of rosti with *coq au vin*. You are clever.'

'They're potato and salsify. I wasn't sure about the salsify, but I think it works . . .'

Nobody seemed to notice that Clare was not speaking.

'Black forest gateau,' said Amelia, depositing the chocolate and cream confection on the table. It had a candle burning in the middle. 'Now, you can sing!'

Later, Clare watched Joss undress, staring at his body as if she had never seen it before. She realized that she had not really looked at him for a long time. When they first met she had thought his body like an Olympian athlete, not just the shape of the triangular torso, moulded muscles and long, strong legs, but the solidity. Next to him, she had felt like a slip of something flimsy, a cobweb clinging to a rock. Physically, as well as intellectually, he had overwhelmed her and she had found the sensation of drowning in his power unbelievably sexy.

It was only when she became pregnant with Ella that she had experienced her body as something real and separate for the first time in her life. While other women hated the changes pregnancy brought to their bodies, Clare had enjoyed the sheer physicality of it. But even then she had been grateful to Joss for bestowing the gift of this condition upon her. In child-birth, the pain seemed to confirm her existence, but after Ella was born, things were never quite the same. Her body became something not just for his pleasure and hers, but for the sustenance of their child, and even though Joss claimed to approve of breastfeeding and wrote a long poem using the image of her as a madonna, she suspected that in reality he had felt diminished.

It was during that time that he had begun his affair with Joni. Clare always thought of it as his first affair, although of course it was not as far as he was concerned. Their own relationship had started off as an affair. He had been living with a female tutor at the college when she met him. The woman had been older than him and eager to have children. It must have been a terrible blow for her when he left her for a pregnant teenager. Clare was so very different from the tutor, it had not even occurred to her that Joss might do the same to her. Why was it, she wondered now, that every woman who takes a man from another woman believes that it will be different for her? How arrogant passion makes people, and how undifferentiated in their stupidity.

She watched Joss taking off an old checked shirt that she had ironed many times. When they were first married she had even loved ironing his shirts, enjoying the achievement of caring for him and the faint smell of his skin and washing-powder rising to her face in the steam. Now it irritated her hugely that he threw the shirt in the direction of the wicker washing-basket, neither seeing nor caring whether it went in.

The hair on his chest had become as grey as wire wool. His hair was greying too. When she had met him the long black curls and the sparkle of his eyes had made him almost magical to look at. He was still handsome now, and sometimes, lifted by a couple of drinks and the telling of a good story, the magic returned, but his resting expression had fallen, and the skin on his cheeks was pitted by years of shaving his black facial hair, not smooth and fine as it had been.

'Did you enjoy this evening?' Joss asked, jolting her out of her silent assessment.

'Yes,' she lied, her heart beginning to beat quickly, wondering if, after all, he had been reading her thoughts.

'You seemed rather quiet,' he said, climbing into bed next to her, 'there's nothing wrong, is there?'

His voice was filled with concern, and he put an arm around her, cuddling her into his chest. She switched off the reading-lamp beside her, not wanting him to be able to see her expression.

'Do you realize that I have known you as long as I haven't known you?' she asked him.

'As long as that?' he said, smiling down at her, 'are you having a mid-life crisis?'

She laughed weakly as his hand slid from her arm to her waist and began to caress her thigh. She did not respond, hoping that he would sense that she did not feel like it. But he was in an expansive mood, pleased with his performance as a raconteur, and she knew that he wanted a self-congratulatory fuck just as much as she didn't. He turned onto his side, his erection hard against her leg, then shifted down the bed to suckle at her breast. In the dim light of the moon she looked down at the mass of curls on her chest and thought how peculiarly big his head was. A hand pushed her legs apart, no more forcefully than it ever had, and yet she felt she was being prised open. She closed her eyes in an effort to remember what these same actions had felt like when she loved him, trying to relax her body as if floating on her back in water, but the act of releasing herself to him that had always been so sensual now felt like suffocation. Her body was nothing but a tool for his wank, her vagina a convenient receptacle for his semen. She just wanted it to be over so she could breathe again. She began to quicken the pace, to move him on to orgasm.

'Oh God, you're beautiful,' he cried out, 'my beauty, my love . . .'

'Say my name,' she hissed in his ear.

'Oh God . . . my love . . .'

Then he flopped down onto her. His chest hair itched against her breasts. She was clammy with his sweat and disgusted by her own complicity. This is what so many wives who no longer love their husbands trade for the sake of a quiet life for themselves and their children, she thought. But I cannot. Not for long.

'Clare?' Joss said, opening his eyes, as if he had just remembered who was beneath him.

'Yes?' she replied through gritted geeth.

'That was fantastic,' he said and kissed her on her nose.

For the first time in their relationship, she had faked it, and he had not even known the difference.

Chapter 24

At the beginning of the day, before the tourist coaches arrived, the Alhambra was almost silent. The air was cool and filled with the watery scent of dew on petals that reminded her of walking past expensive florist shops in Mayfair. Philippa lay on her bed listening to the occasional chink of breakfast crockery being set out on the terrace downstairs.

There was nothing up here apart from the ruins, the Parador and a couple of cafés, but it was green, like an oasis on a mountain top, and she felt curiously comfortable in the Moorish courtyards, as if her suffering was insignificant in the company of the unquiet ghosts of the Alhambra's tortured past. It was a place she was certain Jack would have liked, and that knowledge seemed to give her own existence purpose. In a kind of homage to him, she had ventured into the city of Granada to buy books to immerse herself in its history, and discovered, almost to her surprise, that she was interested in learning. Doing something that Jack would have liked seemed to bring him back into focus. Good conversations they had shared rolled agreeably through her mind, and the electric shocks of guilt from their last exchange became less frequent. Whatever he had done cast a new perspective on their life together, she realized, but did not negate it.

'*Café con leche, por favor,*' Philippa said, unfolding the large white napkin onto her lap. The waitress nodded. Sometimes she wondered what stories the staff of the Parador had made up to explain the Englishwoman who read and stared. Did they assume she was a widow, she wondered, or did they just think she was rich and mad? She did not know whether it was politeness, rudeness or inefficiency that made them so indifferent to her presence, but she was grateful. Her spoken words were confined to the choice of tea or coffee at breakfast. At dinner, she pointed at the menu.

On the other side of the terrace another lone woman was writing postcards. An American, Philippa thought, because you simply couldn't purchase shorts that size in any other part of the world. The woman looked up from under her coloured straw hat and smiled, but Philippa stared through her. Conversations with strangers could slide into intimacy in less than three sentences. She had only just begun to be able to tolerate her own company; she was not yet ready to talk to anyone else.

A Spanish couple at another table were reading the paper. Philippa glanced at the date with a slight shudder of *déjà vu*. During the night, she remembered, she had dreamed of Clare. She had wandered into one of the hotels at the foot of the fortification, and found Clare sitting by the swimming-pool. They had exchanged a few words, about the weather, she thought, and then Clare had got up to leave. She had to collect Tom from playgroup, she said, and Philippa remembered thinking in the dream how odd it was that Clare should be in Granada too. She had watched her daughter walk away, not stopping to turn and wave, and suddenly, just after she had gone, Philippa had remembered that it was her birthday and had run after her, but Clare had disappeared. None of the cabdrivers outside the hotel had seen her, and Philippa had stood helpless, not knowing where to begin to look. And then she had woken up with the tingle of bewilderment lingering into her waking moments only gradually soothed away by the silence and the watery scent of flowers.

Philippa pulled a flake of sweet pastry from her croissant. Strange that her dream should synchronize with the date of Clare's birthday, which she had not been aware of remembering, the pull of mother to child so strong it observed no boundaries of country nor distance, nor even the most determined barricades the conscious mind could erect against it.

She had found a spot where she liked to sunbathe. The top of a tower at the edge of the fortification was a terrace with a low wall. On the other side there was a sheer drop of at least a hundred feet, to some trees. The view over the city was panoramic and it was slightly off the beaten tourist route. From time to time someone else would find his way up to her terrace. They would exchange a word about the weather, but otherwise she was left in peace to bake in the sun. When it became too hot, she would gather up her book and bag and walk slowly over to the Generalife to sit on a shady bench listening to the soothing plop and trickle of the water garden and the lazy hum of dragonflies.

It was the hottest day yet. Stretched along the top of her wall, Philippa held one forearm over her eyes and the other in the air to peer at her watch. Still quite early in the morning, but she could feel herself beginning to burn. She sat up, blinking to accustom her eyes to the bright light reflecting off the pale sand surfaces of the fortification. She could hear the murmur of some English people making their way up to the top of her tower. Philippa put on her sunglasses and watched two heads grow into people as her visitors reached the top of the steps.

'Philippa! It is you, isn't it?' Serena Bean asked in a ridiculously loud voice.

For a moment Philippa was tempted to pretend not to understand. With her tan she could easily pass as a Spanish double, but she thought that her shoes and handbag would probably give her away.

'Yes it is.'

They were the first words she had spoken in English since leaving the tour in Seville and her mouth was dry from disuse.

'Hello Philippa,' John said, enfolding her in a big, comforting hug.

She liked John Bean, who had been Jack's cinematographer on all of his pictures. If her solitude had to be interrupted at all, she was glad it was by him, although neither she nor Jack had ever liked Serena very much.

'How are you doing?' he asked kindly.

'I don't really know, John,' she said, panicking at the idea of talking to people. 'God, it's hot up here. Would you like to come for coffee in my hotel? It's just over there.'

The terrace of the Parador was in the shade. They all sat exchanging guidebook pleasantries about how beautiful the Alhambra was, how much bigger and more intricate than they had imagined, what a difference a little running water made, how clever the Moors had been. John and Serena were touring in a hired car. They had wanted to stay in the Parador themselves, they said, but it was completely booked. They were going on to Almería in the evening.

Inwardly relieved to know that their meeting would soon come to an end, Philippa began to engage with a little more enthusiasm. It was as if she were learning to have a conversation again. You could exchange views for hours without saying anything at all, she discovered. Most people did not care what you were thinking. They only wanted to tell you about themselves. If you could think of a few questions to ask then you need not say anything at all. You could sit back as they talked and imagine the caffeine from the coffee you were drinking coursing through your veins, or consider how red the hibiscus lilies were.

'I think you were very sensible to get away from all of that,' Serena said, suddenly intimate when John excused himself to find the toilet.

Philippa's thoughts snapped back, alarmed by the change of tone.

'We had been planning to come away before . . .' she said neutrally.

'Must have been such a shock,' Serena said.

'It was,' Philippa replied.

'We hated all the gossip . . .'

'Gossip?' Philippa asked, knowing that she should not ask, but unable not to know something other people knew about her.

'Oh, not that anyone who knew him cared, or anything,' sensing Philippa's ignorance, Serena tried to back off, 'not that it's anything special these days, is it?'

John returned to the table.

'John, what's been going on while I've been away?' Philippa asked, turning away from his wife.

'When did you leave?'

'Two days after the funeral.'

'Bit of gossip about Jack's other daughter,' he told her straight, 'it just got everyone talking, you know how it is . . .'

'And what did they say?'

'Nothing really . . .'

'I see.'

After the brief loss of composure, behaviour learned over many years negotiating took over. You did not let people like Serena Bean know how you felt about anything that mattered. She did not mind that John had

264

sensed her distress and was clearly annoyed with his wife for raising the subject. Part of her would have liked to have talked to him, to find out the parameters of the gossip, and whether he had known about Jack's infidelity, and when, but she knew that she would not find it in herself to ask, not in front of Serena, and he would be relieved not to have to reply.

'We'd better be getting off,' John said, looking at his watch.

'Oh must you?' Philippa replied with formulaic politeness.

'We could have lunch . . .' Serena interjected, mis-understanding.

'No, we'll have lunch at the coast,' John said, standing up, 'it's about an hour's drive and then we'll follow it all the way round to the east . . . can I . . . ?' He picked up the bill and began to feel for his wallet.

'No, of course not. On me,' said Philippa, thinking how wonderfully useful good manners could be when things threatened to get uncomfortably personal.

'Well, if you're sure . . .'

'Quite sure. Lovely surprise seeing you,' she added, waving as they hurried away through the marble and tile lobby of the hotel, the smile dropping from her face as they disappeared from view and she returned to her steady contemplation of the hibiscus.

Who was Jack's daughter and how old was she? How many people knew about her? Her mind veered wildly from promising herself that she would never return to England to humiliate herself by asking these questions, to demanding to return straight away.

Chapter 25

Ella and Matt went to a concert at Wembley on their last night and the flat felt curiously empty without them. Holly decided to do herself a favour and go to bed really early, but it was warm and noisy outside and she could not sleep. She felt vaguely unsettled, as if something was about to happen but she couldn't remember what. The flat directly underneath hers had been empty for months, but someone had obviously moved in because she could hear a sound like distant sawing. Perhaps they were putting up shelves. It was an odd time to be doing DIY but Holly had been brought up in a tower block and she wasn't the sort of person who complained to the neighbours. Eventually she got up and pulled on shorts and a T-shirt and went to knock at Simon's door. When he finally answered he too was wearing shorts and a T-shirt and looking a little dishevelled.

'I was in bed,' he told her, 'what's wrong?'

'I'm bored. Do you want to go for a drink?'

There was something peculiar about the way he had his head around the door. Almost as if he didn't want her to come in.

'Actually, I was in bed,' he repeated.

'You're bonking!' Holly exclaimed, then whispered, 'sorry . . .' and tiptoed away with exaggerated discretion.

Back in her own flat, her embarrassment very rapidly turned to annoyance. It was very unfair of Simon to get himself laid without telling her, when she always told him everything about her love life. Sitting in the kitchen with a glass of water that tasted like a diluted swimming-pool, Holly weighed up whether she could be bothered to put on sandals and nip up the road to the off-licence for some cold Perrier and a bottle of white wine, decided she could not, went back into her bedroom and threw herself face down on the bed. It seemed less hot lying spreadeagled on the sheet than staring up at the ceiling. The sawing downstairs started again. Holly pulled herself to her feet and jumped up and down on the floor hard several times. The sawing noise stopped immediately. For a moment Holly wondered if her reaction had been too extreme. What if her new neighbour was a single, tall, good-looking man? Well, if he was, what was he doing putting up shelves on a summer Sunday evening? She didn't think she would be interested in someone who was both unpopular and fanatical about DIY, and even if they could get over those big hurdles, he would find out sooner or later that she had a temper, and if he thought that was unreasonable then they weren't going to last very long anyway.

Holly tried to empty her mind. She wanted to be asleep before Matt and Ella returned. It was bad enough that Simon was bonking his heart out only yards away across the courtyard, but she didn't want to have to overhear the passionate lovemaking of two young people about to be separated for a year.

It was two o'clock when they returned. Holly glanced at the five different faces of her alarm clocks to verify the hour before rising reluctantly and padding downstairs to open the door.

'We forgot our key . . .'

'I'm so sorry,' Ella said.

'It's all right,' Holly lied, trying her best not to wake up properly, but they were excited. They'd consumed a bottle of champagne and they talked about it as if it were a hugely extravagant treat. Their zest and giggling made Holly feel jaded and depressed.

'You'll have to allow at least an hour to get to Heathrow,' she told them, yawning, 'so when do you want to be woken?'

'Aren't you coming too?' Ella asked, crestfallen.

'I'll be at work,' Holly said.

'Couldn't you take the morning off?' Matt asked. It almost sounded like a challenge.

'I could,' Holly said, yawning again, but flattered that they both seemed to want her company.

'Oh please do,' Ella pleaded.

'All right then. Now go to bed.'

She heard the echo of Mo in her voice. As a child, Holly had often woken her mother in the middle of the night to ask questions about God and sex and stuff like that. How annoying it must have been.

At the departure gate, Ella kissed Holly on the cheek, and then Holly pretended to see something she wanted in Knickerbox so that Ella and Matt could have a few minutes alone together. It wasn't exactly private in the milling crowds of Terminal Three, but everyone was so busy saying their own goodbyes that nobody looked at the teenagers' extended, passionate kiss.

Why did kissing become so perfunctory as one grew older, Holly wondered, peering at them from behind a spinner of lingerie. She remembered the never-ending exchanges of saliva with boys round the back of the Irish club, and dancing to 10 cc at the end of discos, eyes closed, mouth open, drinking a boy's tongue as his hands made exploratory reconnaissance of her bra fastening. There had been very few boys tall enough for her to feel really comfortable smooching. Her idea of love in those days had been to be with someone on whose shoulder she could rest her head, without bending her knees.

'Do you wear this kind of stuff?' Matt was suddenly holding up a black teddy in front of her face, smiling his deliciously cheeky sideways smile at her.

'No,' Holly pulled herself up to her full height, which was an inch or so taller than he was, 'mine has to be much more expensive.'

He held her eyes, daring her to be the first to look away. It was a game she had played more often than he had, but he was good, very good, and she was on the point of capitulating when he finally dropped his gaze.

'Has she gone through, then?' Holly asked unnecessarily, since she had watched Ella go. She had not turned back to wave. Holly thought that she might be crying and she was sure Ella was far too proud to let it show.

'Yeah.' For a moment, Matt looked completely dejected.

'Shall we see if we can wave off the plane?' she asked him, trying to offer something to make him feel better.

'Could we?' His face brightened instantly, like a child offered a trip to the zoo after the dentist.

'Sure.' Holly had never been to the observation deck but she knew it existed. She had seen it in movies. She stopped a porter, who directed them to Terminal Two.

'It's quite a long walk. I think there's a bus,' he warned.

'Come on,' Holly said, 'we haven't got time to wait for a bus. Let's walk quickly.'

Outside in the stifling heat of the concrete tangle of roads, car parks and tunnels, what had been a fun idea became a challenge. Whoever designed the airport had not intended people to travel easily from Terminal Three to Terminal Two. The air was thick with exhaust fumes. They raced along trying to maintain a sense of direction, with time running out before Ella's plane was due to take off. The more difficult the assault course became, the more determined Holly was to complete it. When they finally reached the entrance to the deck, a notice announced that the lift was out of order. Pink with sweat and exertion, Holly shouted 'Race you!' and lunged at the steps taking them two by two. She just beat him to the top although he cried foul as, sensing him about to overtake her on the last flight, she had flung out her right arm to whack him in the chest.

At the top they stood bent over, panting, laughing and trying to catch their breath. Within seconds the jumbo jet containing Ella went thundering along the runway and they both screamed and waved for all they were worth as it lifted off and made its agonizingly slow ascent into the clear blue sky.

'Do you think she saw us?' Matt shouted, when the plane had finally disappeared. The noise up on the deck was so loud it felt as if they were inside the engine of an accelerating jet.

'Of course she did,' Holly screamed back, unable to entertain the possibility that their mad race had been in vain.

They looked at each other, laughing, then suddenly, surrounded by plane-spotters with binoculars and notepads, and families waving goodbye to their loved ones, in the deafening roar of aeroplanes taking off, Matt stepped forward, put his arms around her and kissed her, his face tilted upwards to hers, his eyes closed. For a moment she closed her eyes too, giving in to the *Casablanca* moment, and then she pulled away, not quite sure what had happened.

He began to walk back across the terrace to the steps and she followed him at a slight distance. They didn't speak as they started walking down again, but after the first flight, in the cool intimacy of the concrete shell where they could no longer be seen, he stopped, waiting for her to catch him up, and held out his hand. She took it. His palm was dry and firm. It was so long since she had held hands with a boy, and it was such an innocent, comforting thing to do, it made her want to cry.

They sat in silence side by side all the way back on the tube, and as they walked, still hand in hand, through streets teeming with tourists in shorts, his grip became firmer, and she felt as if he were leading her to bed.

'This is wrong,' she wanted to say, but she knew that words would put an end to the unreal spell that had been cast upon them, and even though she tried her best to think of reasons why she shouldn't, she couldn't persuade herself that it was wrong enough not to do it.

Her hand shook as she put her key into the lock of her door. They were greeted by the cool familiar air that smelled of dust and stale cigarettes. He closed the door behind them, then caught her hand again and shoved her gently back against the dirty carpet on the flight of stairs. Then he kissed her again, pushing the thin straps of her vest from her shoulders very deliberately, as if he had planned every move. His eyes were on her breasts as he unzipped the fly of her jeans. She lay still, powerless, unwilling to participate, but unable to stop herself wanting him.

He unzipped himself, took a condom from the pocket of his black jeans and rolled it on, and stood, faintly comical, with his jeans around his ankles and a hard-on like a shiny fist. She found herself kicking the jeans from her legs.

'Just stick that into me,' she whispered.

He slid his hands under her buttocks and tilted her hips towards him and when he had the position exactly as he wanted it, he bent his knees slightly and entered her in one giant push that made her scream. He paused, allowing her flesh to accommodate his, then he began to move just slightly, out a little, then in further, out a little, then in, further, harder, speeding the gentle rhythm to match her breathing, and as his thrusts grew stronger, her legs rose from the steps as if levitating, and finally the overwhelming mental and physical mixture of sin, secrecy and sex toppled her over the edge of orgasm. Her back arched and her pelvis jerked as she came until she had to scream at him to stop as the acuteness of the pleasure turned to pain.

As he withdrew, she saw that his erection was still huge and hard.

'You didn't come,' she said.

'There's plenty of time,' he smiled cockily, pulling her to her feet.

'I've got to go into work,' she said. 'My co-agent in Hollywood is conducting an auction for one of my scripts. I've got to be there . . .' she was trying to convince herself of the necessity as much as him.

'You can spend the whole afternoon thinking about what I'm going to do to you . . .' Matt smiled at her.

God, you're advanced for your age, she almost said.

'You need to shower,' he told her, as he followed her upstairs, 'your back has marks on it.'

Holly stood with her back to the bathroom mirror, craning her neck to see the lines where dirt on the corners of the stairs had met with her sweat, decided she must definitely hoover more often, and then pulled off her clothes and stepped into the shower. She hosed herself all over then directed the jet at her vagina to wash the smell of latex and sex away. The water stung deliciously, confirming exquisitely what had just happened. She began to sing, loudly.

Her co-agent in Los Angeles had rung to tell her that he had two bids of a hundred thousand dollars for *The One* and he hoped to come back to her with something substantially higher by close of business. Holly looked at her watch. Only another half an hour before the afternoon was over. She hoped that he had meant close of business her time, not his. She twirled lazily in her chair, thinking about what had happened and what was going to happen. Matt had told her to wear a dress and she had obediently pulled on the white cotton sundress he picked from the rails in the spare room. She couldn't remember the last time she had worn a dress to work. As she passed Robert's door he had remarked, 'You look very virginal today,' which made her shriek with a short gasp of laughter, as if she had been punched in the chest.

Come on, she said to the phone, willing it to ring with the final offers for the script. She didn't know whether to go straight home, or stop at Tesco Metro to pick up some essential supplies – wine, crisps, condoms, maybe a tub of ice-cream – so that they wouldn't have to go out later. She suppressed the stab of apprehension that told her it had all been a strange joke and she would return to the flat to find a note saying 'you didn't really think . . .'

Holly's phone rang.

'There's a Matthew Darling for Holly . . .' the receptionist trilled.

Holly was the agent who dealt with any unsolicited scripts that the agency received. From time to time a writer wounded by her rejection of his script would turn up demanding an explanation, or, on one occasion, a fight. Since then, the receptionist had strict instructions not to reveal whether or not Holly was in the building.

'I don't know any . . .' Holly began, and then stopped herself. 'Send him down,' she said.

She let him find his way down the long corridor. There were ten doors he would have to peer through before he got to hers and she wanted him to be slightly nervous so that she could regain control of the situation. Then after a minute or two, she went to the door of her office to rescue him.

'Matthew, darling!' she said, kissing him on both cheeks as she did most of her favourite clients. He looked endearingly lost. She showed him into her office and closed the door.

'Nice place,' he said, regaining his confidence.

'You've got a bloody nerve,' she told him, 'Matthew *darling* . . .'

'That's my name . . .'

Holly shrieked with laughter again.

'Oh God!' she said, as she saw that he was telling the truth. She didn't know which was more unsettling, having him prowling around her office, the fact that she had fucked a man whose name she did not know, or that she had mistaken his name for a brilliantly witty swipe at her luvvy ways.

'So this is where you work,' he said.

Holly's phone rang. She leaned on the corner of her desk and reached to answer it.

'Oh right, hello . . .'

Matt dropped to his knees beside her and pushed her skirt up around her hips.

'Yeah,' she yelped as Matt stuck his finger into her then took it out and licked it, staring at her with the insolence she found so disconcertingly appealing. He put his mouth to her clitoris and began to lap like a hungry cat. She looked down at the waxed spikes of gold-dipped hair and sighed as the pleasure he was creating filtered up her spine into her brain.

The agent in Los Angeles asked about the connection. There was a slight echo on the line, he said.

'Fine my end,' Holly said into the phone.

Matt looked up at her, then stood up and unzipped.

Holly gasped.

'No, don't know what that is . . .' she spoke into the phone.

'No, fine, shoot,' she said, unable to stop herself enjoying the *double entendre* and trying to disguise the sharp intakes of breath she took as Matt began to fuck her, lifting her bottom higher with every thrust. She clung to the edge of the desk with both hands to stop herself falling backwards, the phone wedged under her chin, trying to concentrate on the excited voice at the other end of the phone whilst staring over Matt's head and wondering what on earth she would say if someone were to open her office door.

'Two hundred and fifty thousand . . . ?'

Perhaps this was what they meant by fuck-you money.

'Final, final bids? . . . AHHH! . . . No, fine, echo on the line . . . DON'T STOP . . . that's great . . . two hundred and fifty you said . . . ? . . . THAT'S FANTASTIC . . . Yes, yes, yes, yes, YES!'

PART FIVE

August

Chapter 26

'Would you think of marrying me, Mo?'

Mo was standing in her kitchen just about to serve up dinner. Chops. Eamon was sitting at the table. Her back was to him.

'Pardon?'

'I said, would you think of marrying me?'

'What a funny way to ask,' Mo said.

'Ach, now I had it all planned and then I didn't want to spoil our holiday, and anyway, I didn't think it would be fair to ask you there, away from everything you know . . .'

'No, it's all right,' Mo reassured him. She levered the chops out of the frying-pan onto a plate and handed it to him, pointing with her fish-slice at the little bowl of new potatoes steaming on the table. Then she turned back to the cooker, looking out of the window over the rooftops of London towards the river, the view blurred out of focus by the memory of the last time she had been proposed to.

It must have been 1960, just after they arrived. They were on the river boat going down from Westminster to the Tower. It was a beautiful clear winter day and the river was huge and high. It hadn't seemed so dirty then, or maybe that was just nostalgia. There were just the two of them on deck. Everyone else was huddled sensibly inside. The wind was bitingly cold, but they were tough. They were from the north. She could still see Jack's face and hear him joking about it. It had felt as if it were their boat, and as they looked and marvelled at the expanse of the view – the Houses of Parliament behind and St Paul's in front, and the vast river, far wider than she had imagined and bustling with boats like a harbour – it felt as if it were their city, as if they owned it. She was standing in front of him at the prow, his front pressed against her back. It was the most exhilarating moment she had ever experienced, her cheeks burning with the cold and the bright sunshine making all the buildings glitter.

'Let's get married Mo,' Jack shouted, folding his arms tight around her waist, her body, enveloped in his, tingling with happiness and relief. It was like a dream where you knew suddenly that everything was going to be all right but you couldn't quite believe it. She was going to marry the man she loved, and her parents would forgive her when they found out. It had been worth all the risk. She wriggled round in his arms to face him, and before she could say anything he was kissing her, and she would never forget that feeling. Bliss, Sister Mary Lourdes had taught them at the convent school, was the state of being blessed. And at that moment she had known that God was smiling on her.

In the midst of dreams you woke up.

'You don't really want to get married, do you, Mo?' Jack had asked her the next morning as they lay in bed, treasuring a few moments' warmth before they split for the day for work. 'All that fuss. We're all right like we are, aren't we?'

It wasn't really a question, so she hadn't answered, not trusting herself not to say something that would give him an excuse to leave her. It wasn't that he had changed his mind, she told herself, it was just that Jack wasn't the marrying kind. On a perfect day in a perfect place he knew how to say the perfect thing and she had been a fool for reading more into it. Jack made you dream you had a different life. He put strawberries on your breakfast cereal.

Mo turned around and looked at Eamon who was eating his chops as he waited for his answer. She knew that if she said yes, he would not withdraw his offer the next day. He was reliable and trustworthy, and you knew where you were with him. He was kind and they had a good time together. There would be no strawberries with Eamon, but that wasn't such a bad thing. Truth be told, strawberries always brought her up in a bit of a rash.

She thought about their last night in Ireland, the mini-cab and the dinner. That had been a surprise. Not a sparkling, quicksilver promise, but a treat all the same. Eamon would look after her and they would grow old together and maybe retire to Ireland and she could dance away her fading years in the company of people who looked like her.

If she said no, she knew she would lose him. It had been brave of him to ask, and he was too much of a man to accept rejection and go on as if nothing had happened. That was why he had not asked her on their last night in Galway, she understood now. It would have been too horrible to sit next to each other on the plane the next day, knowing that they would go their separate ways after they touched down.

'I will marry you, Eamon,' she told him, solemnly, putting the fish-slice back in the frying-pan.

The words took a second or two of chewing to register, then he put down his knife and fork and stood up.

'Are you sure?'

'I'm sure.'

In one jump he was on his chair and then he leapt onto the table with an agility she had never seen before, jumped down and lifted her off the floor with the enthusiasm of his embrace.

'I love you,' he told her, kissing her neck.

'And I love you,' she replied, laughing with the joy of it, her feet in the air. And only as she spoke the words did she know it was true, and she was glad.

Holly picked up the ten-pound bowling ball and frowned at the skittles at the end of the lane. If she got a strike, her relationship with Matt was going to last, she decided. One, two, three, four steps, swing the ball and bowl. The ball rolled spinning down the centre of the lane and clipped the first skittle beautifully. They were all going down, they were, they were. No. One skittle remained standing.

'Try a heavier ball,' Matt urged her, 'that was almost perfect, but you didn't quite have the power . . .'

Furiously proud, Holly ignored him and picked up another ten-pounder. She threw it recklessly and it veered off halfway down into the gulley.

It was ridiculous to wager the outcome of a relationship on the throw of a bowling ball, she thought grumpily as she sat down and picked her lit cigarette from the ashtray in the arm of the padded seat. It was as childish and meaningless as picking the petals off a daisy reciting 'he loves me, he loves me not'. But the time she spent with Matt was so straightforward and uncomplicated, compared to her usual tortured agonizing about men, that she found herself needing talismans to cling onto. She could not tell whether he liked her or just liked having sex with her, and she couldn't bring herself to ask him, so she had to rely on signs.

Matt hurled a sixteen-pound ball down the lane and got a strike. He spun around like a winning-penalty kicker, punching the air with both fists. She stood up and hugged him in congratulation.

'Now you,' he said, 'come on, I know you can do it.'

She waited for the sixteen-pounder he had used to roll all the way back down the side of the lane, then picked it off and pretended almost to drop it, it was so heavy. Matt stepped forward to help her, then back as he realized she was teasing. One, two, three steps, swing the arm, if this lot went down she would have him for the rest of the summer, she bargained, releasing the ball and following through with her arm as he had instructed her. The ball thundered down the polished wooden lane and smashed into the skittles. STRIKE. The television screen lit up with her name and a cross and she leapt triumphantly in the air. The strike had given her as good a feeling as any deal she had ever made. She was born to bowl.

As she sat down again she wondered why she hadn't bet more on the roll of that ball. Why just for the summer, why not for ever? With Matt she could enjoy the simple pleasures of life. Sex, food, and bowling. Sod the career, sod the age difference. At one o'clock in the morning in a seedy bowling alley in Finsbury Park, with a Budweiser in one hand and a cigarette in the other, Holly felt as happy as she had ever been.

'If you wanted me to get you a muffin, you should have said,' Matt said as he slid into bed beside her later that night.

'What?' Holly opened a bleary eye.

He had discovered a place called the Canadian Muffin Company and bought three or four muffins in brown paper bags every day.

'They're not a bit like real muffins,' he would tell her, biting into a double chocolate chip, or macadamia nut fudge, 'more like cakes really.'

The excitement he derived from something so

ordinary delighted her. He had a very sweet tooth. Whenever she popped out for cigarettes and enquired whether she could get him anything, the reply would always be a Twix or a Yorkie, and it made him sound so young, she would wish she hadn't asked. It must be the difference between boys and girls, she thought. Girls grew out of chocolate and into diets and cigarettes at puberty. He was always getting up in the middle of the night to eat. At first she had thought it quite amusing that he was burning off so much energy with her that he had to keep refuelling, but persistent lack of sleep was making her less tolerant.

'I just wish you'd eat something properly, not take a bite and discard it when you fancy a cigarette . . .' He propped a pillow behind him and sat with his arms folded.

'I don't know what you're talking about,' Holly told him, turning over.

'You never finish a meal. It's the same in restaurants. You order all this food and then you pick at it and then you light up. I've never been out with anyone who smoked,' he added.

Holly couldn't decide whether to be angry with him for giving her a hard time, or flattered that he considered they were 'going out'.

'I've never been out with anyone who didn't,' she said, 'can we please go back to sleep?'

'I'm not tired,' Matt told her.

'Well, go and walk the streets, or go to a club, or buy yourself some more food, but let me get some rest . . .'

'All right, I will,' he said, scrambling out of bed and pulling on jeans and a T-shirt. He said it as if it were a threat.

She smiled, listening to the exaggerated noise he made stomping downstairs and banging the front door behind him, then she turned over and closed her eyes, seeing him sauntering around an almost deserted

Trafalgar Square, kicking at imaginary stones on the pavement in that spoilt boyish way he had when something wasn't quite to his taste. She sighed, tried to relax. Were they going out? Seemed such a silly teenage phrase for it. Was he living with her? Were they having a relationship? Was she being a complete fool? Did she care?

Chapter 27

Holly wanted someone to tell. Constant sex interrupted only by going to work was fantastic, but it was all body. Unless she had a conversation with somebody soon, she thought she would literally lose her mind. She sent Matt out to see a film, giving him the money for the ticket, which she felt slightly odd about even though she told herself it was only redistribution of wealth, not payment for services rendered.

Holly picked up her phone, trying to decide who to ring. Clare was obviously not the person although Holly owed her a phone call. She had rung to let them know that Ella had arrived safely, and then rung again, obviously wanting to talk. Holly had struggled to make appropriate noises as Matt was particularly keen on making out while she was on the phone. Not Mo either, although Mo had rung several times leaving hesitant messages like spoken postcards.

'We had a lovely time in Ireland. Hope you're well. Love Mum.'

'Hope you're OK. Give me a ring when you have a mo. Love, er, Mo.'

Simon didn't deserve to know about her affair, because he hadn't told her about his. Colette's answerphone was on.

'It's Holly. Ring me to find out whether I'm having a

passionate thing with a nineteen-year-old boy.'

Holly's phone rang the instant she put it down.

'You old tart,' said Colette.

'Why didn't you answer?'

'I'm monitoring my calls. I'm only speaking to Philip through my solicitor now.'

Holly had a fleeting vision of Colette with her face against a besuited lawyer's tummy and her ex-husband with his ear to the lawyer's back.

'Who is he, where did you find him, are there any more where he came from?' Colette demanded.

Holly told her.

'What does he see in you?' Colette asked.

'Thanks a lot.'

'You're old enough to be his mother . . .' Colette started humming the theme tune from *The Graduate*.

'I'm not that bloody old. Just because you're jealous . . .'

'Just because you're fast . . .'

'That's just what Mo would say . . .'

'You haven't told Mo?' Colette sounded alarmed.

'No, I haven't . . . I'm waiting to see where it goes . . .'

'Where it goes?'

Colette's voice confirmed Holly's instinct. In the privacy of her flat in the middle of the night when the streets outside had become eerily quiet she could look at the beautiful unlined contours of his sleeping face and the gold tips of his waxed hair and think why not? If it's gone on for two weeks, it could go on for two more, and then two more, and after a while he would be twenty, and that wouldn't seem quite so bad . . .

'Nobody complains when an older man goes out with a younger woman,' Holly argued.

'They always say that in articles about older women going out with younger men, and it's not true. People *do* mind older men screwing younger women. They mind a lot. I mean what did you think when Bill Wyman married Mandy Smith?'

'Inadequate jerk,' Holly admitted sadly.

Mo felt odd talking about it without having told Holly.

'I've left loads of messages,' she told Sonya, as they leafed through *Brides* magazine in the staff canteen, 'I hope she's OK.'

'Holly'll be happy to see you so happy,' Sonya said.

Mo wished she could be as confident.

'It's not as if I need her permission,' she joked feebly.

'A nice suit, then, or are you going for a dress . . . ?' asked Sonya.

'Do you think I can get away with white, I mean pure white,' Mo asked, 'because Laurel have some lovely separates with just a bit of gold on the button and I thought I could mix and match them afterwards, you know, so they wouldn't only get one wear . . .'

'Are we talking morals or skintone?' Sonya asked, giving serious consideration to the white question, before taking a bite of her sandwich.

'Goodness, nobody thinks you have to be a virgin any more, do they?' asked Mo.

'They wouldn't sell many white dresses if they did, I suppose,' Sonya admitted, giving Mo's face and neck a lengthy perusal. 'I think you'll need a tan for pure white,' she decided, 'you could always fake it . . .'

She and Mo exchanged a look and broke into girlish giggles.

'No, seriously, there's some lovely new preparations. No more orange streaks between your fingers. The secret is to exfoliate first . . .'

'Sounds rude,' said Mo, giggling again.

'Tell you what, I'll come over the morning of the wedding and do the whole thing. Body scrub, moisturize, fake tan, nails, a real top to toe. My wedding present to you. Be better than a wok, wouldn't it?'

'Be lovely,' said Mo, 'so you reckon white?'

'Perfect,' said Sonya.

Mo smiled at her.

'I'd better go and give Holly another try,' she said, her spirits sinking again.

Holly had always thought that the woman Kim Basinger played in *9½ Weeks* was a silly cow, but now, staring blankly into the ventilation shaft outside the window of her office, she understood how she felt. She didn't know whether it was love or just lack of sleep, but she couldn't stop thinking about Matt. It was mad to imagine it could last. He was from the generation they were always talking about in the newspapers before the election, the young people who had never known anything but Tory rule. If she were to ask him who his favourite Beatle was, he probably wouldn't even know all their names, because he had only been a toddler when John Lennon was shot. He wasn't even Julian Lennon's generation, he was Sean's. The fact was that he only knew who the Beatles were because of their influence on Oasis.

They had nothing else in common either. And yet she liked having him around. She liked the straightforward way he talked about food and films and football with no sense of what he ought to be thinking, or what other people thought. She couldn't imagine taking him to a work party even though part of her longed to, just to hear his views of the London media world afterwards, and to witness the perplexed shock on the other guests' faces when he gave his critical assessment of the latest movies he had seen: crap, alright or brilliant. He probably thought Almodóvar was a Columbian footballer, or the name of one of those ready-made freezer cocktails.

Were parties so very important to her, she asked herself, twirling idly round on her seat, questioning the very foundations of her social life. Had her life become a meaningless whirlwind of business and parties and drinking, with nothing at its core? Even if it had, the existential vacuum was hardly going to be filled by obsessive sex with a vain and sulky teenage boy, she told herself.

The night before he had brought back the video of *9½ Weeks* and they had watched it together. Afterwards, Matt had tied a scarf round her face as a blindfold and led her to the kitchen to re-enact the fridge scene, but apart from a couple of trays of ice-cubes and half a bottle of Frascati, there was nothing in Holly's fridge. The jar of chocolate spread had all gone in the first few days of their relationship.

'How did you know I would respond to you this way,' Holly had asked him in conscious mimicry of Basinger's sex-laden voice, as she lay on the kitchen floor beside him.

He ran a rapidly melting ice-cube down between her breasts to her tummy-button and left it there like a jewel. His face had the concentration of a small boy pushing along a toy train.

'You look dirty,' he replied simply.

He was totally honest, totally charmless, but it was one of the best compliments she had ever been paid. She was becoming dangerously fond of him.

With other men she had found that the better the sex, the more reluctant their willingness to be friendly to her. They behaved as if having given too much of themselves away in bed, they had to guard what was left preciously. She always associated love with worry and pain, but now people kept remarking how happy and well she looked and other men seemed to smell sex on her and smile at her in the street. Matt's undisguised enjoyment of her made her feel beautiful. She loved holding hands with him as they walked through the parks, and he could be sweetly chivalrous, although sometimes she wondered whether opening doors for her was his equivalent of giving up his seat for someone who needed it more. When they travelled together on a crowded tube she found herself pushing him down in the last available place, demonstrating that she could strap-hang as nonchalantly as the coolest teenager.

Holly began to leaf through her in-tray. Since the euphoria of making the deal for *The One*, things had been pretty flat at work. Perhaps it had been the zenith of her agenting career, she thought. As zeniths went, it wasn't bad to achieve a quarter-of-a-million-dollar deal for a virtually unknown scriptwriter whilst being fucked by a man half her age. She couldn't for the moment think how she could better it, and yet she felt vaguely dissatisfied with everything.

The summer was always quiet, with people away on holiday. She knew she should be using the time to catch up on all the novels she had not read, and reading all the unsolicited scripts that were piling up in the corner of her office, but she couldn't work up the enthusiasm. She had found that there was almost no point in coming into work if she did not feel like it. There was a lightness of touch that made difficult conversations a breeze and negotiations click into place, and if she didn't have it, problems that should have taken an afternoon to sort out took a week and still remained slightly unresolved.

She remembered thinking that if she sold *The One* for a lot of money to Hollywood her job would almost rate ten out of ten, but now that it had happened, in spectacular style, it didn't seem to have made a great deal of difference. It was still pretty good, as jobs went, but it still wasn't enough. The trouble with being an agent was that your success was measured in terms of your clients' success, and so it always felt slightly second-hand. Idly she jotted a calculation onto her notepad.

Job: 7 and falling.

Men: 9. Sex was definitely 10, but would it last?

Friends: 2. Colette was a bitch and Simon a traitor.

Family: 8. She couldn't in all honesty award herself 10 when she was cheating on her niece.

Flat: 10. As usual.

A total of 36 out of 50, which made 72%.

Holly stared at the figure. The last time the circumstances had been completely different and yet still it came out the same. Whatever she did, she was stuck at seventy-two per cent.

Perhaps she should go on holiday like everyone else. The papers were full of pictures of Princess Diana kissing Dodi Fayed on a boat in the Mediterranean. Holly imagined herself lying on the deck of a boat with Matt at the helm as they pottered from one Greek island to another, and then she remembered as the phone rang how sick she had been sailing.

She picked up the receiver wearily.

'Holly, it's Mo . . .'

'Hello, how are you, sorry I haven't rung . . . I've been a bit busy . . .' Holly sat up, slightly alarmed. Mo didn't like disturbing her at work and very rarely rang her there.

'I thought so,' Mo said, 'are you too busy to meet up . . . ?'

That was loading on the guilt a bit, Holly thought. It had only been a couple of weeks since they last spoke, hadn't it? It probably seemed longer because Mo had been away on holiday but whose fault was that? Surely she wasn't still annoyed about the cat?

'When were you thinking?' she asked, flipping through a virtually empty diary. At the beginning of each week that Matt was still miraculously there, she spent Monday morning clearing her evening engagements. Now that she had meetings with her clients in her office, not over a pavement table of a wine bar, she wondered why she had ever spent so much time working after work hours. As soon as you had a good excuse, work seemed a great deal less important.

'Tonight?' said Mo.

'Bit busy tonight . . .' Holly lied.

'Tomorrow . . . I could pop in on my way home . . .'

'Tomorrow's looking a bit . . .'

'Holly, there's something I want to tell you, but I can't tell you over the phone . . .' Mo interrupted. She sounded a bit desperate.

'You're not ill . . .' Holly was suddenly frightened.

'No, not ill. It's nothing to worry about . . .' Mo conceded.

'Well, what is it?'

'I don't want to tell you on the phone . . .'

'All right, tonight then,' Holly said, curiosity aroused, 'after work at my place.'

She could always give Matt a tenner to play video games at the Trocadero for an hour.

Mo looked different. Her long and lustrous hair, normally pinned up in a severe bun for work, was pushed loosely back from her head with a couple of grips, the top two buttons of her blouse were open and the sleeves rolled up.

'It's hot out there,' she said, sitting down on Holly's collapsed chair in front of the pedestal fan and kicking off her court shoes.

'Make yourself at home,' Holly said sarcastically, 'do you want a glass of wine?'

'Oh, go on then,' Mo said, 'how are you?' she called to the kitchen.

Holly splashed the chilled liquid into two glasses. She had no idea of how she was.

'All right,' she called back.

'Work?'

'Good.'

'Simon?'

'Haven't seen him for a while . . .' Holly walked back into her bedroom.

'Boyfriends?'

'Err. Not quite sure . . .' She looked at Mo and saw that she wasn't really paying attention, so it wasn't worth beginning to explain, 'so what's so important I have to cancel everything to hear about it?'

'I'm getting married,' Mo said.

'What? Oh, Mum, congratulations . . . who to?' Holly asked.

'Eamon, of course,' her mother replied, slightly crossly, looking at Holly directly for the first time since arriving.

'Eamon?' Holly repeated astonished.

'Well, who else?'

'I don't know. I thought you might have met someone . . . Eamon?' Holly asked again.

'Yes,' said Mo with slight impatience. Holly really could be very spoilt and difficult, she thought.

'You can't,' Holly said categorically.

'I haven't come to ask for your blessing . . .'

'I wouldn't bloody give it to you.'

'Well, I don't want it.'

A charged silence invaded the room as disagreement pivoted on the edge of escalation. Mo pretended to be very interested in the rim of her glass. Holly began to tidy her dressing-table.

'Mum, he's not good enough for you,' her back was to her mother, but she could see Mo's face reflected in the mirror, 'you never would have married him while Jack was alive . . .'

'That's probably true,' Mo admitted.

'So, are you glad Jack died, so that you could marry him?' Holly's voice was rising.

'Of course I'm not . . . but just because I held a candle for Jack all his life, I don't see why I should go on now . . .'

The logic was irrefutable.

'Don't you think it's a bit soon,' Holly tried another tactic, 'you're still in shock . . .'

'I'm not in shock.'

'How do you know?' Holly asked, then, seeing the exasperated expression on Mo's face, changed her tactics. 'Well, that doesn't matter, I suppose. Why the hurry?' she asked as patiently as she could.

'Why not?'

'You've known each other long enough . . .'

'Well, perhaps we're making up for lost time . . .'

'Don't be daft.'

'Is it being daft to want to be with someone who cares about you and makes you happy?' Mo asked.

'If the person in question happens to be Eamon, yes.'

'You little cow,' Mo said.

Holly's eyes filled with tears.

'Little?' she said, trying to make a joke to mask the sting of the remark. 'I'm nearly six feet tall and I'm thirty-six years old.'

'Well, behave like it then,' Mo told her, getting up to leave.

'I can't believe you went ahead and did something like that without asking me . . .' Holly felt wounded, furious, hurt. She stamped her foot.

'Holly, I'm happy. Why aren't you pleased for me?' Mo said, fighting tears herself.

'Because I know that you're settling for second-best . . .'

'What good did first best do me?'

'That's not a reason to settle . . .' Holly insisted.

'Why?' Mo asked her simply and turned to go.

With horror, Holly heard the turn of the key in the lock downstairs and the sound of Matt taking the steps three by three. She tried to compose herself. He was a friend, perhaps she should say the son of a friend, no, she remembered with relief, he was Ella's boyfriend. Mo knew about Ella coming to stay. If she just held her nerve she need not lie. Matt was Ella's boyfriend who was staying for a while in London.

'Hi sexy,' Matt said, leaning forward to kiss her. In his hand there was an ice lolly in a brightly-coloured cartoon wrapper. He looked about fourteen.

Mo looked, looked harder, then looked away.

'Mo, this is Matt . . .'

'Hello Matt,' Mo said and Holly heard the echo of her teenage years when she had brought boys back to the flat for tea so that Mo could cast her critical eye over them. It occurred to her that Mo had never met any of her grown-up boyfriends. The relationships usually finished before the time had come to introduce her mother. For Mo, it must seem as if nothing had changed, not even the age of the boys.

Holly suddenly saw her lover through Mo's eyes. A precocious teenager with an ice lolly. She felt ashamed of herself.

'I was just on my way out,' Mo said. The look she gave Holly was a horrible mixture of distaste and pity, and then she walked down the stairs.

'Why the hell did you do that?' Holly asked.

'Do what?'

'Kiss me in front of my mother?' She felt a fool as soon as she said it.

He looked bewildered.

'Mo's your mother?'

'Who did you think she was?'

'A friend. How should I know?'

Suddenly Holly realized that to him anyone over the age of twenty was old. He couldn't distinguish between thirty-five and fifty-five.

'I bought you something,' Matt told her.

'Oh?' Holly always brightened at the prospect of a present.

'Get your clothes off . . .'

'Oh, look, I've just had a bit of an emotional thing with my mother . . .'

'You need relaxing then . . .' With his body he pushed her back into her bedroom and down onto the bed.

Holly watched him as he unpeeled the wrapping from the ice lolly.

'Get your knickers off,' he said, watching her as he licked the drips of melting lolly from his fingers, and she realized what he was intending to do.

It was as if a switch inside her tripped, instantly shutting her erotic feelings down. She sat up and crossed her legs. They had done all manner of things with a tub of Haagen Dazs, but the lolly was so clearly suggestive it turned her off. She wouldn't have minded so much if it had been pure fruit juice, she thought, but it was one of those virulently-coloured stripey things in the shape of a rocket.

'Look, Matt, it's been good fun, but it's got to end,' she heard a very sensible-sounding voice saying.

He looked at the lolly, then at her, shrugged his shoulders and put it in his mouth.

'Pity to waste it,' he said.

She almost told him not to speak while he was eating.

He began to collect his various bits and pieces from around the room.

'I didn't mean you had to go now,' she said, suddenly regretting what she had said, but not regretting it enough to try to change it.

He stopped and looked at her and then said, with great dignity, ' "When the curtain falls, it's time to leave the stage . . ." '

She tried to place the quote. She knew she knew it, but she didn't know where it was from.

He stuffed T-shirts into his small backpack, then went to the bathroom to get his toothbrush.

'You couldn't lend me a tenner for my fare,' he asked, 'I'll pay you back.'

She took the money from her wallet.

'You don't have to pay me back,' she said, 'is ten enough?'

'I'll hitch.'

'You will be careful,' she said, like a worried mother.

'I'll be careful,' he said, smiling with his sloping eyes.

'You are very beautiful,' she told him, with nothing to lose. She would have liked to have taken a picture of him to somehow prove that he had been there.

'You're not so bad yourself,' he told her, and turned to go. She couldn't work out whether he was happy or sad, probably a bit of both, she thought, just as she was. He began to walk down the stairs.

'Matt?' she called after him.

He turned.

'How did you get your hair to go like that?' she asked him.

'It's wax . . .'

'No, I don't mean the wax, I mean the colour. How did you get it to look as if you'd been turned upside down and dipped in gold?'

'I bleached it. It grew out.' He looked at her as if to say, is that it, any more questions?

'Ahh.'

He shrugged and turned again, and this time she did not call him back.

Her eyes blurred with tears as the front door closed. She stared at the empty stairwell for a couple of seconds, then ran into her room and hung out of the window to watch him walking off down the street. He did not look round. At the bottom he turned left and was gone. Then suddenly she remembered where his parting quote had come from. It was what John Major had said when he resigned after the election.

Good God, thought Holly, I thought I was in love with a boy whose idea of sophistication is to quote John Major. What the hell has become of me?

Chapter 28

Ella was monosyllabic, which was usually an indication that she was angry, or about to cry. Clare was finding it difficult to drag information out of her. The induction course had gone well enough. Yes, she had made friends. One or two. The family she was allocated to were fine. They lived in a suburb quite a long way from the city. The house was very nice. Her room was very nice. The children were very nice. She couldn't talk much, she said, meaning that whatever she said could be overheard.

Clare tried to cheer her up telling her the funny things that Tom was now saying, then hearing his best *bons mots* repeated, Tom insisted on talking to his sister himself, and when Clare managed to wrestle the phone back from him she heard Ella sniff, and knew that she was on the verge of homesick tears.

'We're all fine here,' she said, not knowing how to comfort her daughter at so great a distance.

Ella asked if she had seen Matt.

'No, I haven't. Shall I give him your number? OK. And I'll ring you. It's not that expensive. And you ring if you need to. Reverse the charges. I love you.'

Clare replaced the receiver feeling vaguely unsettled. She had imagined Ella happy and she had sounded sad. Remembering with wincing clarity Ella punching the

air as she left the house and shouting 'I'm outta here!'
she had wanted to convey to her somehow that she too
was outta here. Not physically, but mentally. Yet when
she had heard Ella's small voice bouncing across three
thousand miles of ocean, she felt less confident.

Through the open back door, Clare watched Tom
making mud pies in the garden. He had learned to turn
the tap on the rain tank and could amuse himself for
hours filling his yellow plastic watering-can and emptying it. She picked up the receiver again and dialled
wanting to speak to somebody, if only Holly's answerphone, but even though it was early in the evening,
Holly answered.

'It's Clare.'

'Oh, hi! Look, I'm so sorry I haven't returned any of
your calls, I've been so busy . . .'

'Anything interesting?' Clare asked, keen to be
distracted from the sense of empty futility that was
descending on her.

Spurred by the adrenalin of almost being caught out,
Holly's mind scrabbled through the events of the past
few weeks, keen to find any memory that did not
contain Matt.

'I sold *The One*, did I tell you?'

Normally she kept the sums she negotiated for
her clients strictly confidential, but she found herself
naming the price she had achieved just to keep her end
of the conversation going for a while longer.

'Wow! I wish you could advise me how to make some
money,' Clare said, 'I don't know why it's taken me
so long to understand that money is freedom. When
we came to Cornwall I thought that having no money
at all was freedom, and now, just when the country
gets rid of the Conservative government, I become a
capitalist . . .'

'This lot are capitalists too,' Holly said. She
was beginning to feel slightly disillusioned with the

Government. They had been in power for a hundred days now and nothing had changed.

'. . . except that they're now going to charge fees for university . . .' said Clare. 'We're not sure where that leaves Ella because of her gap year . . .'

'I can't understand it,' Holly said, 'I thought it was all supposed to be education, education, education . . . I'm beginning to think Blair is a complete phoney . . .'

'They talk a lot about opportunity, don't they, but I don't think they understand what it's like somewhere like this,' Clare said, forlornly, 'of course people want to work, but where are the jobs . . .'

'You could start a business . . .' Holly suggested.

'Doing what?'

'You could sell your jam . . .'

'I've thought of that. Organic jam made from Cornish raspberries in little pots with linen covers . . . but I haven't got the money to set up, and anyway, I don't have a zeal for jam . . . I think you need to believe in your product if you have a cottage industry, like Body Shop, you know, and I just can't get excited about jam . . .'

Holly laughed. 'Can't you get some money out of Philippa?' she asked, then added quickly, 'sorry, I think I know the answer to that question . . . Do you think that if Jack had known he was going to die he would have left us something?'

Clare thought about it.

'He wouldn't have left me anything. He was always really mean with pocket money. He thought that because he had come from nowhere everyone else had to start off like that . . . I hate the way that people like Jack are held up as examples of what we could all achieve if we wanted to. The whole point is that they're the exceptions. They're famous because they're so unusual.'

There was silence at the other end of the phone.

Holly had bucked the system too, Clare remembered.

'God, now I'm beginning to rant like Joss . . .' she apologized.

'How are things with Joss?' Holly asked.

Clare hesitated. It didn't seem right to tell her on the phone, and she didn't know where Joss was. He might come in at any moment.

'Not great,' she said quietly.

'Well, probably your only option is prostitution,' Holly joked, getting back to the discussion about money before Clare had a chance to ask her a reciprocal question about her love life.

I'm already doing that, Clare thought. Except, instead of getting paid for it, she was buying time to allow herself to think. She didn't know what her position with the house would be. Joss had bought it and made it what it was, but she had kept it all going for years, so surely she must have a stake in it. She wondered if it was her right to get him to leave, but even if it was, even if she could imagine herself having the courage to ask him, she was absolutely sure that he would not go. And even if he did go, she didn't want to stay in Penderric, so what was the point. What she wanted was the house and garden miraculously transplanted to another place where nobody knew her and she could start again. The more she thought about it, the more elusive the dream of leaving seemed to become. She was going round in circles.

She desperately wanted to talk to Holly about it, because she was sure Holly would know about the legalities, but now was not the right time.

'Will you come down again soon?' she asked her plaintively.

'Well, there's a lot going on, but I'll try,' Holly lied.

Clare put down the phone. The conversation hadn't made her feel very much better.

'Tom, come on, we're going for a walk,' she called.

During the day it was too hot and crowded for the beach, but at this time in the evening, especially when the tide was up, the air felt cooler and most of the holidaymakers had gone back for their supper. Clare was pushing Tom's buggy along the sea front when she heard a man's voice a few feet away from her head.

'Clare! Hi!'

Seeing that he had made her jump, Matt leaned out of the ice-cream van. She had not recognized his voice, she realized, because she had never heard him call her Clare before. At first she had been Mrs Drummond, and when Ella had clearly forbidden him to call her that, he had stopped calling her anything, referring to her as 'your mum' in conversations with Ella and 'you' if he ever addressed her directly, which he didn't, often.

'Would Tom like a cornet? On the house,' he asked, then circling his eyes round his window, added, 'on the van . . .'

Clare laughed and bent down.

'Would you like an ice-cream?' she asked Tom.

'Yes!'

'What do you say?'

'Yes, please.'

'Thank you,' she said.

'Thank you,' Tom repeated dutifully.

Matt pulled a lever which disgorged a white whirl onto a cone.

'Flake?' he asked.

'No, he'll be fine with that,' Clare said, then on impulse she added, 'give me one though.'

He swirled a larger pyramid for her and stuck in two flakes. She handed him a pound coin. It was ages since she'd had a soft ice-cream and there was something sinfully synthetic about it. The taste made her think of childhood outings with one of the au pairs who used to buy her a 99 from the van in the car park next to

Hampstead Heath as a bribe to get lost for half an hour while she snogged her boyfriend on the grass.

'So, you're working here for the summer,' Clare said, trying to think of something to say. It seemed rude to accept free ice-cream and then walk away.

'I got back from London last week.'

'I thought I hadn't seen you about,' Clare said, biting into the chocolate flakes.

'Have you spoken to Ella?' she asked him.

'No. Is she having a good time?'

'Yes. I think so. She rang earlier.'

Clare looked at him as his eyes locked onto a yacht with a spinnaker out on the horizon. He was so clearly determined to look indifferent, she felt a little sorry for him. She remembered Ella's sad voice on the phone.

'I think she'd like to hear from you,' she said, hoping that she wasn't betraying Ella's confidence by suggesting it.

'I thought I'd write,' he said, looking deliberately over her head as a holidaymaker took up a position behind Clare as if she were the beginning of a queue.

'I'll leave you to it, then,' Clare said.

Joss was working when she came back. Since he'd had access to Ella's computer, he seemed to write a great deal more than he had ever done before. She could hear the soft rattle of the keyboard as he typed.

Holly lay on her bed in her underwear wondering how much worse her life could get. Her mother hated her. She'd wantonly betrayed her own niece and lied to her sister. Her best friend was a bitch. Her other best friend was ignoring her now that he had found a woman to bonk. Work was crap, her life was crap, everything was just crap. CRAP she scrawled on a piece of paper on which she had written:

Work: 5

Men: 0

Family: 0
Friends: 0
Flat: 10

She poured herself another glass of wine from a half-empty bottle on the bedside table. And her father was dead, she thought. It was all his fault. If Jack Palmer hadn't bloody died then Mo wouldn't have been getting married so they wouldn't have fallen out, and she would never have met Matt, and work would just have gone on as normal.

And she was going to be forty. Soon. Four years wasn't very long. She was going to be forty and at some point soon she was going to turn from Holly's-a-laugh to Holly's-a-sad-person. Perhaps she already had without realizing it, she thought, terror-stricken. But no, she reassured herself, Matt would not have been so willing to hold hands with a sad person, would he? The thought of him filled her with more self-pity. He was the best thing that had ever happened to her and she had thrown him out. What was wrong with her?

It was Mo's fault, she decided. If Mo hadn't been there, then the lolly wouldn't have been such a big deal. Who did Mo suddenly think she was, occupying the moral high ground with her fat-bore red-nosed fiancé who looked like an alcoholic and yet had the nerve to be a bloody teetotaller so he was never any fun either? Well, good bloody luck to them.

Holly gulped another glass and picked up the bottle, staring at its contents, trying to remember whether it was the last bottle in the fridge or whether there was another one. It was so hot she was drinking it like water, but she was still thirsty. She put the neck of the bottle to her lips and drained it, then got up, inadvertently kicking over her glass, and staggered through to the kitchen.

A few hours later, when she was calm enough to

let herself remember what followed, she wondered whether she would ever have encountered the rat if she hadn't at that moment had an urgent need for more wine. They might have gone on living together, never meeting, like ships that pass in the night, for months, or even years. Sooner or later, the rat would have realized that Holly was a rotten host and found somewhere more hospitable to stay. He had probably only been attracted in the first place by the appetizing scent of Matt's midnight snacks. The muffin, Holly thought with a flash of triumph as if she had just won at Cluedo, the rat was the explanation for the disappearing Canadian muffin. But all that was afterwards.

At the time, Holly simply screamed.

The rat was sitting on her toaster, its tail like an extra flex on the work surface. It probably wouldn't have moved if she hadn't screamed. She learned later that rats have very bad eyesight. It probably hadn't even seen her, but it heard her. Everyone within a square mile of Trafalgar Square heard her. Except herself. Holly was so drunk and so frightened that she thought that it was a bad dream where her mouth was open and no sound was coming out. The rat slid off the toaster and scampered down between the rubbish-bin and the sink, the bit of the kitchen Holly sprayed with Dettox occasionally and tried to ignore, and then she heard it scuttling somewhere she couldn't see, and the scuffling noise was even more frightening than the sight of it. The idea that it was there, somewhere very near, waiting to jump out at her . . . Holly's legs felt as if rats were scratching at them. Her body felt as if rats were running all over it. Banging the kitchen door behind her she fled down the stairs, slamming the front door and standing gibbering in the courtyard outside.

To his eternal credit Simon dropped everything when he heard her scream, and she was only in the courtyard for seconds before his own front door banged and he was looking at her, asking her to tell him what had happened.

'Rat, rat, rat . . .' was all she could say, so of course Simon automatically assumed she was talking about a man.

Imagining her assaulted, or raped, he put his arm around her very gently and helped her upstairs to his flat. Then he put a blanket around her and she shook and shivered on his sofa.

'Should I call the police? An ambulance . . .'

'No, I'll be all right,' she heard herself saying, like a brave victim in *Casualty*.

'Is he still in there?'

'Simon, it's a rat . . .' she told him, suddenly feeling very sober, 'I mean a real rat . . .'

'So why the underwear?' Simon asked bewildered.

'Oh, I do like to slip into something comfortable when I'm entertaining rodents . . .'

A slight breeze through the window made the newspaper on the floor rustle and Holly screamed again and put her feet up on the sofa.

'You don't like rats, do you?' Simon said, with a little amused smile.

'Completely phobic,' Holly admitted, 'I think I read *1984* too young . . . have you got the number for Rentokil or something? I've got to get it sorted right now . . .'

Simon looked dubious.

'I'm not sure that they can just sort it overnight. I think they have to lay poison,' he said.

'But I want it sorted now,' Holly wailed, flapping through the Yellow Pages in panic, 'I can't go back in there until it's sorted.'

'Let me call.' Simon took the phone from her, suddenly aware that she was the worse for alcohol.

He made several calls, taking quotes, patiently asking

about the procedures and writing down a list of telephone numbers and prices.

'Just get them round,' Holly kept hissing at him, but he would not be distracted from his methodical ways. Finally he made his report.

'You've got two choices. You can pay to get a private firm round now, but all they'll do is lay poison. Or you can get the council tomorrow, and they'll do the same for free.'

'I don't mind paying.'

'It's not that. It's that once you get in a private firm the council won't touch it. Which could be a problem if it recurs, you see . . .'

'Recurs?' It didn't bear thinking about.

'Either way they say it takes seven to ten days for the poison to work . . .'

'Seven to ten days? What am I going to do? Are you sure?' Holly asked him accusingly, implying that he hadn't asked the right questions on the phone, 'there must be some quicker way . . .'

'Apparently not.'

'What if I were the Queen? Surely she wouldn't have to put up with rats for a week?'

'There's probably someone called the Royal Ratcatcher with a shotgun . . .' Simon mused.

'Well, how can we get hold of him?'

'Holly,' Simon crouched on the floor beside the sofa, 'you're going to have to be brave. You've got a problem, it won't go away for a week or so, and in the meantime you've just got to pretend it's not happening . . .'

'Easy for you to say, you haven't got a bloody infestation of vermin in your flat . . .'

'Who knows? Believe me I want this sorted out as much as you do, it's a bit too close for comfort . . .'

'Oh God, you don't think it can get in here?' Holly hugged her knees, trying to make herself small in the corner of the sofa. In the kitchen, the kettle clicked off. She screamed.

'Come on, I'll take you back to your flat. We'll look everywhere. I'm sure it will have gone. I bet your screaming frightened it. It frightened me . . .'

'I'm not going,' Holly told him, shrinking even further into the sofa.

'Rats don't attack unless they're cornered,' Simon said.

'But what if I cornered one accidentally?' Holly wanted to know, thinking of all the nooks and crannies of her flat where a rat might think itself safe only to have her loom inadvertently above it.

'Come on . . .' he held out his hand.

'You can't make me . . .'

'Holly. Come on, even if I let you sleep here tonight, it won't be over for at least a week . . .'

'Simon, read my lips, I'm not going back into my flat . . .'

'All right,' he admitted defeat. 'There's no need to take it out on me . . .'

'Can I stay here tonight?' Holly asked him more humbly.

'Well, all right. But you'll have to sleep on the sofa because Tansy is coming round.'

'Tansy?'

'I know it's a silly name, but she's a very nice person . . . how's Matt?'

'Matt?'

'Ella's boyfriend. The one who looks like a pop star who's been staying at your flat.'

'He left last week,' Holly said, but even in the semi-darkness she could feel herself going red. 'Would you be a love and get me some clothes?' she asked.

'I heard that wherever you are in London, you're always within thirty feet of a rat,' Tansy said, after the introductions had been made and Holly's presence explained.

'I don't see how that can be true,' Holly said, logic battling with her desire to get off the subject. 'I mean, say if you're at the top of the Post Office tower?'

'Well, how many people are?' Tansy asked. 'Maybe there's rats in the walls,' she speculated.

Whenever Holly heard the word rat, she felt as if she'd seen one.

'When they jump at you, they're not going for your throat, really,' Tansy continued, 'they're going for the light.'

'That's comforting,' Holly said, shrinking backwards. If she became any smaller, she thought, she would pass for a cushion on the sofa.

'I don't think we're really helping Holly by talking about it,' Simon said gently.

'They're really very small,' Tansy said, 'it's their fur that makes them look bigger. If you took away the fur you could tread on one easily.'

'Oh just shut up!' Holly screamed at her.

'I was only trying to help.'

'Perhaps we'd all better get some sleep,' Simon intervened diplomatically.

Holly lay on the beige sofa fully clothed. It was a hot night, but she didn't want to take off the jeans Simon had brought over from her flat. With jeans and shoes on, she felt better able to cope. What was she going to do? Clearly she couldn't stay here another night. It wasn't fair to play gooseberry and anyway, she didn't think she could stand any more of Tansy's rat facts. There was no way Mo was going to welcome her home at this point, even if Holly had been prepared to ask her. Colette had lots of room, but her house was so far out of town, Holly might as well be away on holiday. Clare. No. But why not? Holly imagined Penderric like it was on the picture postcards. Sunshine, sea, not a rat for miles. She needed a holiday, she needed a rest, she needed to recharge her batteries. All the old clichés filtered soothingly through her head as her mind began to turn a vague thought into an imperative. She imagined the simple pleasure of building sandcastles with Tom, some good late-night girls' chats with Clare, and if she happened to bump into Matt, so what? They were both grown-ups. Well, she was, anyway. It wasn't as if they had parted on bad terms.

Clare had given Tom his supper, read him *The Teddy Robber* for the millionth time, and put him into bed. Then she had come downstairs and tidied up the kitchen. Overhead she could hear the boards creak as Joss walked from the bathroom to the bedroom. She wondered whether to make a batch of jam to avoid joining him while he was still awake, but she hadn't enough empty jars to make it worthwhile. She sat and flipped through the pages of Tom's book, wondering whether she had allowed Joss enough time to drift off. Yawning, she decided to risk it but when she was halfway up the stairs, the phone rang. Clare glanced at the kitchen clock. It was very late. The sound of the ringing irritated her as it was bound to wake Joss, or Tom, or both, and alarmed her because of the hour. Then she thought of Ella. It would be early evening for her. Clare leapt to the phone.

'Clare it's Holly . . . can I come and stay?' The whisper had a trace of desperation in it.

'Whatever's the matter?' Clare asked.

'I have to leave my flat. I can't explain . . .'

'But what's wrong, you sounded fine earlier . . .'

'I can't talk about it . . .'

'What about work?'

'Oh, stuff the bloody work,' Holly said.

Clare's brief annoyance that it was not Ella gave way

to pleasure at the prospect of having Holly there. 'Of course,' she said, 'when are you coming?'

'At first light,' Holly replied, melodramatically.

In the early morning, Simon could not disguise his relief at Holly's decision.

'I hate leaving it all to you to sort out,' Holly told him, trying to sound sincere.

'No, that's fine,' he said, 'if I can get through to the council when they open, I should only need to take the morning off work. Give me a list and I'll get whatever you need from your flat right now.'

Tansy appeared in the kitchen wearing just a towel and looking very at home considering she had only known him a month or so, Holly thought.

'They say they're very intelligent,' Tansy said, putting a couple of pieces of bread in the toaster, 'd'you want some?'

'No thanks,' said Holly – she didn't think she'd ever be able to eat toast again. 'Who?' she asked politely, trying to be friendly to Tansy, wondering why she had taken such an instant and irrational dislike to her.

'Rats,' said Tansy, 'you can't give them straightforward poison because they would soon get the idea it was doing them harm, so you have to give them this stuff that thins the blood. My dad had to have it for his heart.'

'Do we have to talk about it?' Holly asked, appealing to the woman's sympathy, 'it makes me feel really agitated.'

'I think you've got a phobia,' Tansy said, 'it seems to me that you're more frightened than you should be.'

'Where did you meet Simon?' Holly asked her.

'Didn't he tell you, I'm the personnel officer.'

'Ahh,' said Holly, thinking she might have guessed.

In her experience people whose job depended on putting other people at their ease were always notoriously bad at it.

'I mean we've fancied each other for ages, but neither of us realized, you know, and then, well, it just kind of happened . . .'

'A wink as you spooned out the Gold Blend?' Holly joked.

'How did you know?'

'Just call it intuition,' Holly said.

'Simon said you were funny,' Tansy told her.

'Did you see it?' Holly asked, trembling as Simon returned from her flat with another pair of jeans and a selection of T-shirts, 'oh I wanted the stripey one . . . not to worry . . .'

She could see that Simon's patience was tested to the limit.

'You hardly ever see them, they're not stupid . . .'

'No, I was just saying, they're very intelligent. That's why people have them as pets,' Tansy confirmed.

'Don't you think you'd better ring Mo and let her know what's happening?' Simon asked, as Holly prepared to leave.

Holly tried to think of a genuine reason why that would be a bad idea, but it was too early in the morning.

'Say if she rings when you're away, and gets no reply and then rings work and they tell her you've gone away. She'll worry,' Simon said reasonably.

'Oh, all right. How much does she bloody pay you to be on her side?' she asked him.

He raised his eyes to the ceiling.

'I'm going to Cornwall,' she told her mother in a clipped businesslike voice when she answered the phone.

'That's nice,' Mo replied, 'I think you probably need a bit of a holiday . . .'

Mo was a lovely kind mum and she had been horrible to her. Holly's voice began to well with emotion.

'Mum, there's a rat in my flat . . .' she sobbed, 'and my whole life's a mess . . .'

'Oh dear,' said Mo, remembering Holly standing screaming on the kitchen table when they'd once had a visit from a mouse. 'Do you want me to come and sort it out?' she asked.

'No, Simon's going to,' Holly blubbed into the phone.

'It'll be all right,' Mo assured her, adding with a slight, almost indetectable smirk, 'I bet you're sad you didn't have Frank Cooper now.'

Snapped back from little girl to grown-up, Holly was on the point of retaliating but stopped herself. It was Mo's way of getting even and she thought just maybe she'd better let it go.

Chapter 29

Clare was standing by the ticket barrier waiting for her. She was wearing cut-off jeans and a white T-shirt, but the T-shirt was so huge on her small frame that the shorts were barely visible. Her hair was pulled back in a pony-tail. From a distance she looked about twelve. Close up, she only looked about twenty-three.

'There's a bus in an hour,' she told Holly, taking her bag, 'let's go and have a coffee while we're waiting.'

'Can't we get a taxi?' Holly asked.

'All the way back? It would cost a fortune. Anyway, we're not in a hurry, are we?'

'No,' Holly agreed, as they emerged from the coolness of the station into a street humming with shoppers, 'no, I suppose we're not.'

She felt as if an almost infinite amount of time stretched ahead of her. She had informed them at work that she was taking two weeks' break, but if she wanted to there was nothing to stop her staying longer. Most of the senior staff had children on school holidays and were away – there was very little going on that Jemima couldn't cope with. In an emergency she could always be contacted at Clare's. Holly had forgotten to ask Simon to retrieve her mobile phone from the flat. On the way down on the train, when other people's mobiles had rung, she had sat up abruptly from her hungover doze with a guilty feeling, as if she had been caught truanting, then sunk back in her seat with relief remembering it couldn't be hers.

'There's one of those new cappuccino places,' Clare suggested. There was excitement in her voice. In London, Holly thought, it was almost impossible to get a bad cup of coffee any more, but down here the espresso machine was still a cause of wonder.

'I'm so pleased you've come,' Clare said, as they sat down with large white cups brimming with foam and powdered chocolate, 'I've been dying to talk to you for ages . . .'

'Where's Tom?' Holly asked, as if she had just noticed that he wasn't there. Whenever she pictured Clare she saw Tom around her legs. 'I've missed him,' she added.

Clare smiled. 'Yes, he does grow on you. I've left him with Joss for the morning.'

'And how is Joss?' Holly asked.

'I'll tell you later,' Clare said, 'first, you tell me why the surprise visit?'

'I've got a rat,' Holly announced gravely.

'What?'

'There's a rat in my flat,' she repeated, staring into the speckled froth of her cappuccino.

'Ugh, how horrible. Have you got poison down?' Clare asked.

'Simon's doing everything.'

Holly briefly recounted the previous evening's events.

Clare threw back her head and laughed, and then realized that she wasn't meant to.

'Sorry,' she said, 'good old Simon though. Actually, I'm quite good with things like that.'

'What do you mean?' Holly asked alarmed. How could you know you were good at dealing with rats unless you'd had experience of doing it?

'Well, of course, I don't like them, but you can't show your fear in front of the children, so you kind of get on with it . . .'

'Just a minute, are you saying that you've had rats in your house?' The sun-dappled picture-postcard cottage changed in her mind to a seething mass of rodents from *Indiana Jones and the Temple of Doom*.

'Not rats . . .' Clare said, 'we've had a few mice in from the garden . . . not recently,' she added quickly.

'You're positive no rats?' Holly said.

Clare saw real fear on her sister's face. It was rather endearing that someone as brave and tall as Holly should be so frightened by something so little.

'Cross my heart,' Clare said solemnly. They got up from the table and walked over the road to the bus stop.

'So, tell me all your news. What's been happening?' she asked, trying to move Holly on to a happier subject.

'Nothing much,' Holly said, and then remembering that she was meant to have been busy, added the first thing that came into her head. 'Mo's getting married . . .'

They clambered aboard and sat on the back seat.

'How lovely! Somebody she's just met?'

'Unfortunately not. No, he's her long-time boyfriend, faithful retainer, that kind of thing . . . I don't approve, but she won't take any notice of me . . .'

'What's he like?' Clare wanted to know.

'Eamon?' Holly thought for a moment, 'he's the kind of person who goes on holiday to Ireland and buys a sweatshirt with a shamrock on it . . .' she saw that Clare was mystified by this description, 'he wears cowboy boots and silver tips on his shirt collars . . . oh I don't know, he's just not good enough for her . . .'

'Would anyone be good enough for her?' Clare asked.

'Jack would have been,' Holly said indignantly.

Suddenly she was glaring at Clare as if it were her fault that Mo was marrying beneath her.

'Hmm. I'm not sure I would have wished Jack on anyone I loved,' Clare replied.

'So how come Philippa stayed with him so long then?' Holly asked.

'Philippa's a very strong personality. That's why he loved her. She was the only person he could not dominate, and he respected that . . .'

'Oh yeah, respected it enough to see Mo for all those years . . .'

'True,' Clare found she could neither support nor criticize. Curiously, the notion that he had had a secret friendship with Holly's mother had made her feel more warmly towards her father. It was touching that he had needed to keep a link with his roots. It made him seem almost vulnerable. It made her think how little she had known him.

'God, what a prospect,' said Holly, staring out of the window feeling extremely bad-tempered, 'Mo marrying Eamon and all their bloody friends asking me whether there's anyone in my life . . .'

For the rest of the bus journey she retreated into a silent gloom and although Clare was itching to tell her about her decision to leave Joss, she could see it was not the right time.

When they arrived back at the house, Joss and Tom were still out.

'Are you hungry?' Clare asked Holly.

'No. Actually, I'm really tired,' Holly told her.

'Why don't you go and have a nap. You'll feel a lot better. Have our bed. I'll wake you up for supper.'

Holly climbed the steep staircase with the bag Simon had hastily packed for her and dumped it beside the bed. The yellow room was filled with sunlight and the sound of a fly buzzing against the window. Holly opened the window to let it out and smiled as she saw the view. The sea was deep inky blue and the breeze blew up snatches of children's shouting from the beach. The air that billowed the cotton curtains was tangy with salt. She sat on the bed and took off her jeans, suddenly aware in this bright, fresh room how they stank of cigarette smoke. Like a pub smells at lunchtime, when you're the first customer, she thought, dropping them beside the bed and climbing in. Even though it was warm in the room, she pulled the sheet and blanket right up over her shoulders. The sheets were cool and newly laundered. It was lovely being in this bed, in this bright room, with the sounds of the seaside lulling away her fears. It felt as if no harm could come to her here with her sister downstairs in the kitchen. Sometimes it was nice just to feel that someone was looking after you. Holly closed her eyes and let herself sleep.

'Holly, are you a tree?'

Holly opened an eye.

'Do trees say boo?' she asked.

'No,' said Tom, cautiously.

'BOO!' Holly shouted at him, sitting up so that he fell back into the pillows giggling, half fearful, half delighted.

'Do it again!' he said.

'Boo!' said Holly.

'Do it again!'

'Are you OK?' Clare was standing in the door, 'I thought I'd leave you, but Tom wouldn't go to bed without seeing you.' She scooped his little pyjama-ed form off the bed and kissed his head.

'What's the time?'

'It's nine o'clock.'

Tom kissed Holly goodnight several times, then Clare put him into bed, and came back and sat down on the bed by her sister.

'I was so tired,' Holly said.

'You've been under a lot of pressure,' Clare said sympathetically, smoothing the covers around her as you would a sick child. 'Joss has gone out for a poets' meeting. We've had supper, but I've saved some for you.'

Holly got up and pulled a pair of clean jeans out of her bag. She sniffed them. They didn't smell as bad as the pair she had worn on the train, but there was still the definite odour of cigarettes. In this clean environment she suddenly understood why Matt had complained that she reeked of smoke.

'Can I borrow a T-shirt, or something,' Holly asked, 'so that I can give this lot a wash?'

'Of course. In the second drawer,' Clare pointed to the chest of drawers, 'I'll get your things in the machine. If we hang them out on the line tonight then they'll be dry by the time you want to wear them.'

She left Holly to get dressed.

It was lovely to be in a proper household with the smell of food cooking and a washing-line, Holly thought, selecting a T-shirt from Clare's drawer. Perhaps Clare had got it right. Perhaps these were the important things in life – nourishing food, the fresh smell of newly-washed clothes and a child's hug at night. She went in to look at Tom sleeping, wondering what dreams were puckering his little forehead in a frown. She smoothed his curls back from his face. He sighed and turned over, relaxed now, breathing so quietly she had to stand perfectly still to hear him.

Clare put a plate of macaroni cheese in front of her and pushed a large bowl of salad dotted with cherry tomatoes and tiny pink radishes across the table.

'I'm starving,' Holly said, 'I can't remember when I last ate.'

She looked thinner, Clare noticed, and her complexion was colourless. Her hair was growing out and it now fell over her eyes in ringlets which Clare had an almost irresistible urge to tie up with ribbon, as you would a small child.

'So, Joss is out,' Holly said with her mouth full. She was glad not to have to put on clothes to meet someone new. It was nice sitting in Clare's kitchen in just a T-shirt and knickers talking. It reminded her of the days when she had had flatmates.

'The poets meet up once a month or so. I used to go along, but I got sick of sitting in the kitchen talking about different things you could do with an avocado . . .'

Holly glanced at her. Clare was so pretty and sweet-looking it was easy to forget that she had a sharp tongue.

'What can you do with an avocado apart from vinaigrette?' she asked.

'Prawns with Marie Rose sauce. Very Seventies but now back in fashion,' Clare began to recite in a sing-song voice. 'Sour cream with fake caviar. You have to put on the caviar, or lumpfish roe as it's really called, right at the last minute otherwise the sour cream goes grey. Chilli and coriander and lime juice. A salad with grilled pancetta, cos lettuce and herb-infused olive oil . . . you didn't really want to know, did you?'

'So the women just sit around swapping recipes and the poets do whatever it is that poets do . . . what do poets do?'

'They read their work.'

'Lovely,' Holly said with heavy sarcasm.

'Oh, I'm so glad you're here,' Clare said, reaching forward and giving her a hug across the table.

Holly dreamed she was riding on a merry-go-round, a glittering golden merry-go-round with painted horses, like the one that came to Leicester Square at Christmas, round and round she spun with the wind on her face, laughing with the simple pleasure of the sensation and the tiddle-um-pom-pom of the music. Then she woke up, dream and reality mingling as she felt the coolness of the morning air blow through the back door into the living-room where she was sleeping, and heard an ice-cream van nearby tinkling 'I'm forever blowing bubbles' just as the fairground organ had done.

Deliciously unhurried, she spreadeagled her limbs to the four corners of the sofa bed, and yawned, and then froze mid-stretch as she became aware that a figure was standing in the kitchen door-frame watching her. As his face emerged from the half-light, she thought for a moment that she was still dreaming, or had stepped into a fairy tale, because when he smiled at her, his eyes glinting with amusement at her surprise, she had a feeling, like a premonition, that he was the One.

Bizarrely, her first instinct was to take a quick look under the sheet at her chest, unable to remember whether she had taken all her clothes off before getting into bed.

'Hello,' he said, stepping forward. There was a mug in his hand.

'How long have you been watching me?' she asked him.

'A while,' he said, sitting down on the foot of the bed, 'did you know that you laugh in your sleep? It is . . . enchanting . . .'

His voice was like Alan Rickman's. A low drawl so lazy that each word build up expectation for the next. She liked lying there listening to him, feeling his weight dipping the mattress beside her feet.

'So, you're Holly.'

He made it sound as if a fortune-teller had told him long ago that he would meet and fall in love with a woman called Holly, and finally she had appeared.

'You're Joss?' she asked, as her brain kicked into gear.

He was not meant to look like this. She had thought he was a shortish, grumpy man with thinning hair and, if not exactly a beard, then certainly sandy stubble on his chin. Joss was tall, slim, had dark, dark eyes and fine black eyebrows. His dark curly hair was threaded with silver. He looked intelligent, charismatic, like Byron or Shelley or someone, she thought, not the old Labour, Liverpool type of poet she had imagined.

'Is that for me?' She pointed at the mug.

'Oh, yes . . .'

He looked at the mug, then at her, his eyes lingering on hers, as if the sight of her had driven mundane thoughts from his head. Trembling with the intimacy of his gaze, she lay for a moment, letting him look at her, then shimmied herself up and took the mug from his outstretched hand, desperate to inject a sense of normality before the fantasy got out of control. She took a sip of the tea. It was still very hot.

'Where's Clare?' she asked.

She had meant it as a straightforward question, but somehow it came out sounding guilty.

He smiled at her again as if he knew what she was thinking.

'She's gone to the superstore with Tom. She didn't want to wake you . . .'

He made it sound as if she would be gone a long time. Holly suddenly felt vulnerable, having lain asleep unaware that she was being discussed and watched over, and now having to make conversation with a man whom she suspected she had just fallen in love with.

'So, you're a poet . . . ?' she said, reminding herself that she hated poetry, particularly poetry written by men. It was nothing more than the socially acceptable expression of misogyny, she had told Robert, the last time they argued about it over the coffee machine.

'Yes,' Joss replied, 'I write poetry.'

She heard a voice that sounded a little like hers saying, 'I'd love to read some of your work.'

'I'll leave you to get up,' Joss said, 'if you need anything, just shout, I'll be in my office.'

Holly lay for a while, trying to let the shock of meeting him filter away. Through the open back door she could see her jeans flapping on the line. Eventually she got up and went to retrieve the least damp pair, aware that Joss was watching from the window of the back room upstairs as she unpegged the washing in her underpants and vest. She waved at him, foolishly, and his face disappeared as the sun came out from behind a cloud and the little square of glass became a mirror of the sky. Then Tom appeared in the garden, running down the path and hurling himself at her legs. She was relieved to see Clare back.

'I thought we'd all have lunch, and then we'll take Tom down to the beach,' Clare said, cracking eggs into a bowl, 'spaghetti alla carbonara?'

'My favourite,' Holly said, folding up the sofa bed, 'is there time for me to have a bath?'

She stared at herself in the bathroom mirror, annoyed that she had not had a haircut before coming down to Cornwall. She was beginning to look like a ginger version of Ruud Gullit. Since Matt had left she had been drinking and smoking far too much and it showed. Matt! She laughed drily. How quickly guilty thoughts about him had been replaced by guilty thoughts about another man. What was wrong with her?

Holly leant forward, suddenly noticing that there was a long line going down one side of her face in addition to the laughter lines she had become used to at the sides of her eyes. It must be the way she had slept, she told herself, pinching her cheeks, but the line did not seem to go away. It must be the mirror. But if it was the mirror, it simply meant that the line had been there for a while but her own mirror had not shown it up. It was smoking, she decided. She was getting a smoker's face. She really was turning into Mrs Robinson, which was far more frightening than the idea of her lungs filling up with tar. It frightened her so much, her immediate thought was to have a cigarette. But she couldn't in this clean house. Even if she stuck her head out of the window, smoke would still blow back and taint the shower curtain and Clare would be able to smell it on her breath.

'Why is my life such a bloody mess,' she thought, stepping into the bath. From the kitchen she could hear the comforting chatter of Clare and Tom cooking, and the smell of grilling bacon wafted pleasantly up, mingling with the scent of baby soap and then overwhelming it.

'How do you make this, it's completely delicious,' Holly remarked, twirling the spaghetti round her fork. She'd once made the mistake of dating an Italian waiter from a trattoria in Soho. Unfortunately he'd become a bit possessive, so she'd packed him in, which was a pity because they did the best pasta in London, but at least she had learned how to eat spaghetti properly.

'The trick is not to use too much bacon,' Clare said, 'it's a flavour really, like all peasant meals, they taste better with less meat, because that's the way they were created . . .'

'Are you a cook, Holly?' Joss interrupted.

'Not bloody likely,' she said, 'I'm so useless I can't even get two ready meals hot at the same time.'

Holly waited for him to say something, but he did not. He was the sort of man who knew how to use silence.

'When Matt was staying . . .' Holly began to babble, 'there was absolutely nothing in the fridge and so . . .

and so . . . he was always popping out . . .' her voice trailed away. Clare was concentrating on spooning pasta into Tom's mouth. Joss was looking at her intently. She felt herself blush.

'I live just south of Chinatown,' she hurried on, trying to make up for the accidental hiatus, 'so I eat out most of the time . . .'

'How convenient,' Joss said, his slow, lazy voice pronouncing every syllable, filling the harmless phrase with innuendo.

'I told you about Holly's flat,' Clare said, rejoining the conversation, 'it's like a kind of dream student pad but with designer accessories. It's wonderful . . .'

'Not at the moment,' Holly reminded her. 'It's infested with rodents, so I've run away to you,' she told Joss. 'I hope you don't mind . . .'

'Mind? It's refreshing to have someone new to talk to, isn't it Clare? We get sick of each other, don't we?'

'Yes we do,' Clare agreed amiably enough.

'Clare always agrees with everything I say,' Joss informed Holly.

'Perhaps she's only being polite?' Holly challenged, beginning to see what a bastard he was.

Joss laughed. 'How interesting,' he said, looking from one sister to the other, 'one cooks, the other doesn't, one acquiesces, the other doesn't . . .'

'I think we're very dissimilar,' Holly agreed, undaunted, 'but Clare thinks we're quite alike.'

Clare looked down at the table. It was always this way when two people who didn't know each other first met, she thought. The way they got along was by talking about the person they both knew, because that was the only common ground. It wasn't personal.

'Salad?' she asked.

'Clare grows all our vegetables,' Joss said.

She didn't know how it was that he could make that sound like a put-down.

'I hate the way that Joss makes me out to be just a little woman,' Clare said as they pushed Tom's buggy down to the beach together. Holly was holding a string bag with buckets in it and a long plastic spade that seemed to keep getting tangled up with her legs.

'You shouldn't let him get away with it,' Holly said, 'he likes sparring.'

'I suppose not,' Clare said, suddenly depressed by the fact that after knowing him an hour, Holly knew how to deal with him better than she did.

'He is so different from what I expected,' Holly went on, hoping that if she talked about him the crush she was developing would go away.

It was the same intensity of feeling she had experienced seeing Robert De Niro in *Godfather II* for the first time. She vividly remembered coming out of the cinema vowing she would do anything to meet him. They would only have to meet, she had told herself as she stood in the rain in Leicester Square, and he too would somehow miraculously know that she was the One for him. The only time she had got close to him, at Cannes more than twenty years later, Bobby's eyes had met hers for a split second as his bodyguards had swept her aside, but there had been no flicker of recognition. But a long time had passed, she had consoled herself as she watched him duck into a waiting limousine, and she couldn't truthfully say that she felt the same way about him now either.

'What do you mean?' Clare asked, looking sideways at her and indicating with her eyes that she should be careful what she said in front of Tom.

'He's very good-looking, isn't he?' Holly said. If she acknowledged it openly, then she would not feel so ashamed about fancying him.

'What did you think?' Clare wanted to know, 'that I would plight my troth to some geek?'

'I just thought he would be more, more . . .' Holly searched for the right word, 'more vegetarian,' she finally said.

Clare looked at her in disbelief, then threw back her head in laughter.

'You're quite mad,' she said, 'did you know?'

'Holly MAD!' shouted Tom, leaping out of the pushchair and running towards the sea. Holly chased after him right into the sea where she picked him up and threw him into the air.

'I love Holly,' Tom shouted, running back up the beach to his mother.

'So do I,' Clare told him, smiling at her sister over the top of his golden curls.

They spread out towels and rubbed factor 25 sun lotion into Tom's skin and then their own. Then they lay back while Tom shovelled sand into the buckets, giving a running commentary on each step of the procedure and occasionally demanding that Holly empty one for him.

'What is it with Scandinavians?' Holly asked, turning onto her front after only a few minutes.

'What? Where?' Clare sat up, half-expecting to see a couple of Vikings walk along the sea front.

'Not here, I just meant how come Scandinavians have fair hair and go nut-brown?'

'I don't know,' Clare said, lying down again.

Holly lay back next to her.

'Do you ever tan?' she asked.

'Yes, if I'm careful.'

'I never do. It's Mo's fault, obviously,' Holly said, sitting up, 'I mean we've both inherited the red-haired gene from our father, but I've got another one from my mother too . . .'

'Is Mo red-haired?' Clare asked.

'Not really, but you kind of feel it's lurking there. Her hair is sort of springy brown, and really long.

She looks very Irish. Did I tell you she's getting married?'

'Yes.' Clare sat up. There was obviously going to be no restful lie in the sun with Holly fidgeting about beside her.

'I want ice-cream,' Tom announced.

'I'll get it,' Holly said, jumping up and taking his hand, 'do you want anything?'

'No, thanks.'

Clare watched as the two of them, one very tall, one very small, walked up the beach together. She could see from the movement of his head that Tom was explaining something important. He was one of the few people on earth, Clare thought smiling, who could give Holly a run for her money in opinionated chatter.

There was no-one at the window of the van.

'Hello?' Holly called, standing on tiptoe to peer right over the counter.

Matt suddenly stood up, almost colliding with her nose.

'Hello,' he said, smiling at her.

He had had his hair cut, almost shaved. Without the gold tips, he looked much more ordinary.

'What are you doing here?' he asked.

'I'd like an ice-cream for my nephew,' Holly said, gesturing frantically at Tom's head.

He pulled the lever that ejected a stiff white swirl onto the smallest size of cone. She looked away, pretending to see something going on towards the harbour.

'Changed your mind about the lolly?' he said as he handed it to her.

'As a matter of fact, I'm escaping from a rat that you tempted into my flat with all your bloody Canadian muffins,' she told him sharply, 'nothing good ever came out of Canada . . .'

He looked bewildered.

'Jacques Villeneuve,' he said.

'David Cronenberg, I suppose,' Holly admitted, '*Crash? The Fly?*'

He was too young to have gone to *The Fly*, she realized, as his face registered no trace of recognition.

'You got a job for the summer . . .' she said, more reasonably.

'Yeah. I do this every year . . .' he said.

'So you were always going to come back after a couple of weeks in London?'

'Yeah . . . I always work August . . .'

His look said what did you think? That I was going to stay with you? She had seen it before, many times, on the faces of men she had slept with.

'How much do I owe you?' she asked.

'Take it out of what I owe you. I'll buy you a drink as well if you're around . . .'

'I don't think I am really,' Holly said, with all the dignity she could muster, 'thanks all the same.'

She walked down the beach wondering whether his predilection for covering her breasts with ice-cream had been learned over many summers selling Mr Whippy on the Cornish coast and not, as she had previously imagined, by the adverts for Häagen-Dazs.

'Holly don't want a lolly,' Tom shouted at his mother.

Clare looked up and wondered why Holly was blushing furiously.

'Was it Matt?' she asked.

'Yes,' said Holly abruptly.

'I wonder if he's called Ella,' Clare said, fishing around in her bag for a tissue to wipe Tom's face. He looked as if someone had painted a white clown's mouth on his chin.

'How is she getting along?' Holly asked as nonchalantly as she could manage.

331

'I think she's a bit homesick, actually, but you know Ella, she'd never say that.'

'Missing Matt?'

'Perhaps. I don't really know what she sees in him, do you? I mean, he's all right, but he's not nearly as intelligent as she is . . .'

'No, that's true,' said Holly, desperately trying to suppress a fit of giggles and racking her brains for something else to talk about.

Simon rang in the evening to say that the poison was down. The pest-control officer had found a gnawed hole at the bottom of Holly's stairs leading from the flat downstairs which was unoccupied. He thought that the rat was probably still in Holly's flat but lying low. When they were sure that it was dead they would seal up the hole.

'But in the meantime, the rat can invite all his friends in for a party at my place?' Holly asked.

'He says they don't do that. They're opportunists . . . from the footprints, he thinks there's only one . . .'

'Footprints? No, don't tell me anything . . . how will he be sure that the rat's dead?' Holly wanted to know, but didn't want to know.

'Apparently, there's a smell. He says it's lucky it's hot weather. It'll smell quicker . . . I'll ring tomorrow with a progress report,' Simon said.

'I am grateful, Simon, even though I probably don't sound it . . .'

'I know,' Simon said, 'send my love to Clare.'

'And mine to Tansy . . .'

'That sounded so sincere,' Simon said.

'Oh, piss off.' Holly put down the phone.

'Why is it that when a disaster happens in this country we immediately start talking about luck?' she asked nobody in particular. 'E.g.: a bomb goes off killing two people, "Oh, lucky it wasn't the rush hour otherwise it would have been hundreds," we say, but it wasn't very lucky for the two who copped it . . . when Mo got mugged, everyone said she was so lucky that the muggers hadn't been carrying knives, so there's Mo in hospital with a black eye and no wages telling me, "I was lucky really . . ." And now I get a rat, and I'm supposed to think I'm lucky that it's summer because it'll putrefy quicker . . . shall I go and buy some wine? I think I need a drink.'

'I'll come with you,' Joss volunteered, adding, 'it's getting dark.'

His timing was just slightly out on the explanation, Holly thought. He'd given a reason for accompanying her just a little bit too quickly, and that had betrayed the fact that he fancied her. She suddenly knew that she could have Joss if she wanted him, and he was gorgeous. And he was her sister's husband and she was his son's aunt. She looked at him, and then at the silhouette of Clare's head as she sat watching television in the back room. Clare was the best thing that had happened to her for years. She was kind and sweet and she was family. And Joss was her husband, the father of Ella and Tom, whom she had stuck with through thick and thin for the sake of her children. She looked back at Joss and his sparkling eyes.

Dear God, if I deny myself this man, will you get rid of the rat for ever and make it so that I meet someone who loves me and live happily ever after? she bargained silently.

'Actually, I think I'll pass,' she said, 'I've been drinking a bit too much recently. It'll do me good to cut down.'

Joss looked surprised. 'Right, well, if there's nothing going on down here, I'll get back to my work,' he said, and the empty space that he left in the room was not entirely filled by Holly's feeling of righteousness.

As she sat down next to Clare on the sofa, Clare

patted her hand distractedly as if she were one of her children. They watched the news together and afterwards Clare went to check Tom.

'Both asleep,' she announced, when she came downstairs, 'shall we have some tea?'

She filled the kettle, then suddenly said, 'I'm going to leave him.'

'Who?' Holly asked.

'Joss.'

'You're going to leave Joss?' Holly repeated. She tried to form her face into an appropriate expression of sympathetic concern, but inside it felt as if she were jumping up and down screeching 'There is a God!'

'It's such a relief to finally tell you . . .' Clare said, drawing up a chair at the table and sitting down. 'I decided on my birthday. Just after Ella left, you know. I thought it would be so awful when she went and it was . . . is . . . but it kind of liberated me too, I can't explain . . .'

'But where are you going to go?' Holly asked, trying to think of something appropriate to say.

'I might not go anywhere. I might ask him to go,' Clare said.

'Is that possible? Isn't it his house?'

'I thought you might know. The thing is, I daren't speak to anyone round here . . . it's just so good to say it. It makes it seem so much more real . . .'

'But why now?' Holly asked. Just as she had begun to see the point of Clare's way of life, she was giving it up.

'Ella's gone, and Tom is still young enough to be portable. He doesn't start school for another couple of years, so I won't be disrupting anything. I'm too young to slide into middle age. I don't want to settle for putting up with my life. I want to see if there's something I can do, not just fade away . . . I thought,' she looked at Holly, disappointed, 'I thought you'd be pleased . . .'

'Of course I'm pleased,' Holly said, 'if you're sure it's the right thing . . .'

'If we decided to, could we come and stay with you, like you said?' Clare asked.

'I've got a rat, remember?' Holly replied.

'You won't always have one . . .' Clare said, a little desperately.

'Isn't it weird that we both see each other's home as an escape . . .'

'I suppose so,' Clare said, pouring boiling water into the pot. She couldn't pretend that she wasn't bitterly disappointed by Holly's reaction. She was talking about the biggest decision she had ever made in her life, and Holly was comparing it with a minor job for pest control.

'I'm just shocked,' Holly said, sensing that she had not delivered the correct response to the situation, 'it's just a bit confusing, that's all.'

'Don't worry,' Clare said, 'I probably shouldn't have told anyone until I'd thought it out a bit more.'

'I mean, what would you do in London?' Holly persisted.

'I don't know. Oh, let's not talk about it any more,' Clare tried to quash the panic that was rising inside her. She had thought that Holly would help, show her how, but she realized suddenly that nobody could help. She alone would face the consequences, and that was scary.

Clare lay awake staring at the ceiling. Sometimes a full moon would light the room with silver, but tonight the sky was black. She had put so much faith in talking to Holly, but Holly had nothing to say to her that she did not already know and she was beginning to realize that Holly saw things only in relation to herself, anyway.

Next to her Joss snorted and then rolled over, his arm flopping across her body like a large dead fish. A few days before he had rolled on top of her in the middle of the night and fucked her as she slept. Except that she hadn't been asleep, but he didn't seem to know that, or to care. Lying crushed beneath him, she had reflected that there had once been a time when she would have found such an act intensely erotic, imagining that the sexual pull between them was so strong it infiltrated his subconscious, driving him to make love to her even when they were sleeping. Now she found it almost necrophilic and it had killed any lingering feeling of desire she had for him.

She wriggled out from under the weight of his arm and went into Ella's room where Tom now slept. He was getting too big for his cot, but she had not moved him into the bed yet because she was glad of another bed to escape to herself. But it couldn't go on much longer, even if Joss continued to believe her story that Tom had woken in the night and needed her there.

She wondered why she found it impossible to imagine herself telling the man she had loved for so long, I don't want to live with you any more. Will you please leave?

People broke up every day of the week. She didn't think that Joss would really mind losing her, although he would find it inconvenient to have to look after himself. But she knew that he would not easily give up Tom. He had known a long time ago that Ella was lost to him, but Ella had always been a fiercely independent person. Tom was so affectionate, Joss had found it easier to love him, and would fight hard to keep him. In the darkness, Clare tried to imagine what could be the worst possible thing that could happen. In the past few weeks she had suffered a recurring dream in which Joss petitioned to have her judged unfit to look after Tom, and all their friends in Penderric rallied around him, bewitched by his tales of her insanity. And Clare would wake up shaking, wondering how her subconscious could be so frightened of the man she had shared her life with, and thinking that the dream contained its own logical consistency. Perhaps she was mad to have let it get to this point.

Holly lay on the sofa bed trying to sleep, her head a whirlwind of contradictory thoughts.

It didn't make any difference that Clare was about to leave him, she told herself. He was still Clare's husband and that was that.

And yet it seemed such a waste. One sister didn't want him, the other did. Surely they should come to some arrangement? However logical it sounded, she knew that things didn't work like that. She turned over. Just forget it.

Anyway, how could you be in love with someone you had only just met? She knew nothing about him and everything she did know was bad. He was moody, difficult and philandering and he was a bastard.

But so were most men, they just pretended not to be for the first few weeks until they had you hooked, and then they began to reveal themselves. Perhaps all the bastards she had ever dealt with were a sort of practice for this one. With Joss, the only surprises would be good things because she knew the worst already.

Even with Tom's benign and peaceful presence a foot away, Clare could not sleep. As dawn broke she went downstairs, put on her gardening gloves and crept through the back room where Holly was sleeping and into the garden. The dawn air was chill, but the ground was moist with dew. The weeds came up easily and the work calmed her, stilling the rushes of anxiety. Straightening up, she watched the sun beginning to break through the damp shroud of mist, then she walked over to inspect the trellises. This year she had planted runner beans and peas with sweet peas in between. The peas were ready. She crept back into the kitchen, then crept out again. Holly turned over and began to snore. Clare smiled fondly at her sister and pulled the duvet up over her shoulders. Then she picked a bowlful of peas for lunch and took them into the kitchen to shell, turning the radio on very low.

For the first few moments after she had heard the announcement, it seemed to her that she was the only person in the world who knew. It was unreal, another terrifying dream. Then they said it again. Clare stared at the radio, then she nudged the dial. The local radio station was in the middle of a weather forecast.

'Not as warm as it has been and there's a chance of some rain . . .'

Clare breathed a long sigh of relief.

'. . . And now let's see if there's more news about the reports we've been getting of the tragic death this morning of Diana, Princess of Wales . . .'

Clare crept into the back room and switched on the television, forgetting to turn down the volume.

'What's going on?' Holly awoke.

'Shhhh,' Clare said, crouching down at the foot of the sofa bed with her back to Holly.

The television cameras were outside the entrance to a hospital.

'. . . and it was here that Princess Diana was taken by ambulance earlier this morning . . .'

'What's the time?' Holly sat up rubbing her eyes.

'It's nearly seven . . .' Clare turned round. 'Princess Diana is dead,' she said, and suddenly she was sobbing uncontrollably, her small body made smaller by the seismic quakes of grief that seemed to be rocking it.

Holly looked at her uncomprehendingly, then leant forward and flicked through the channels. There was no doubt about it, Princess Diana was dead. Poor thing, Holly thought.

They sat staring at the news reports on screen. It was the strangest feeling, Holly thought, as if war had been declared or something. Clare sobbed quietly beside her, but Holly did not feel like crying. It was too unreal. She went into the kitchen and put on the kettle.

On the television there was a hasty montage of recent footage of Diana. Diana with Mother Teresa in New York, Diana with her children on a raft in a theme park, Diana walking through a minefield, Diana's dresses being auctioned at Christie's. How much more they'd be worth now, thought Holly as she poured boiling water onto tea bags. If the sale had been delayed a couple of months they'd have made tens of millions more.

Upstairs Tom woke up and started calling 'Mar Me, Mar Me' but Clare did not move from her position. Holly was about to go to the child when his cries abated and, moments later, Joss appeared carrying him. Joss was wearing a white cotton woman's dressing-gown which barely met across his chest.

'What on earth's going on?' His dark eyes flashed menacingly.

He looked utterly desirable with his hair ruffled and his child resting on his shoulder. The ridiculously feminine dressing-gown, which he had clearly pulled on remembering there was a visitor in the house, only seemed to enhance his masculinity.

'Tea?' asked Holly.

'You're an angel,' he said, his voice reverting to its usual smooth timbre.

Clare came into the kitchen, her face red and swollen from crying. She took Tom from Joss's arms. The child put his thumb in his mouth and closed his eyes contentedly.

'Princess Diana is dead,' Clare whispered over the top of her son's head.

'No! Assassinated?' Joss asked.

'Car crash in Paris. Accident. Stupid, stupid accident . . .'

Joss's eyes rolled very slowly and deliberately round the room.

'What are you doing?' Clare asked.

'I'm consigning to my memory exactly where I was when I heard the news. I'm sure that in a few years' time everyone will talk about where they were when they heard. I've always regretted not having taken more notice when Kennedy died. I'm the only person who can never remember . . .'

Holly tittered nervously.

'Oh, for God's sake,' Clare was suddenly angry, 'a woman is dead and all you can do is be facetious . . .'

'What am I supposed to do?' Joss asked.

'Show a bit of respect, actually,' Clare told him.

'Not my strongest suit, I'm afraid, not where royalty is concerned . . .'

'She's a mother of two children . . .' Clare's voice was rising.

'I'm sure that in the time it's taken you to say all this a dozen women with children in Africa have died but I don't see you weeping for them . . .'

'That's not the point and you know it,' Clare said, and then immediately started crying again.

Suddenly Holly knew what it must be like to be the child of rowing parents. She hated them doing this to each other and she felt as if she were invisible in the oppressive intimacy of their mutual contempt. She wanted to run away and leave them to it. She didn't know whose side she was on. Clare was her sister and she hated seeing her cry, but she thought she was being a bit melodramatic. Joss's reaction was similar to her own, except he had enough arrogant self-belief to be amusing about it.

'How about a nice cup of tea?' she said, mimicking Mrs Doyle in *Father Ted*.

Clare looked at her as if she had forgotten she was there.

'Thanks,' she said.

Joss merely smiled. The tips of his fingers touched hers as she handed over his mug.

Tom started demanding his breakfast. Clare seemed transfixed by the television. Holly found him some cereal, but it turned out it was not the cereal he wanted. Joss got cross and stormed upstairs to have a bath, and Holly felt a failure. Despite her indifference to the news, she seemed as magnetically drawn to the television as Clare was. Finally Joss came down, scooped Tom up, dressed him and announced he was going out.

'Can't you see it's upsetting him to see you crying like this?' he accused Clare.

'I can't seem to stop,' she said, 'I've tried to explain to him . . .'

'Oh, for God's sake, he's too young to understand about death or princesses,' Joss said impatiently. 'At least we'll have the beach to ourselves if the rest of the world is as mawkish as you two . . .'

'It feels like watching history, like we're all in it together, like the beginning of a war, or something,' Holly tried to defend herself, 'look, look, here's Tony Blair . . .'

'How convenient to catch him coming out of church. How very spontaneous,' Joss sneered, but sat down on the arm of the sofa to watch and listen to the Prime Minister as he paid tribute to the People's Princess.

'Well, that had to be the most carefully-prepared, off-the-cuff eulogy I've ever heard . . .' Joss said as soon as he had finished.

'You're so cynical,' Clare told him.

'It brought a bit of a lump to my throat,' Holly tried to tread the middle path, 'whatever you think, you have

341

to admit he does do this sort of thing well . . . he really looks as if he means it . . .'

'How do you know he doesn't?' Clare snapped at her, 'I mean, he's met her, his children have played with the princes . . .'

'Oh for God's sake,' Joss said, 'you're beginning to sound like a feature in *Hello*!'

'At least I feel something,' Clare retaliated.

'I can see you do,' Joss said, 'you've got all the early symptoms of a massive attack of hypocrisy . . .'

'Oh come on, guys,' Holly said, 'a woman's dead, isn't that enough for one day?'

Joss glared at her, took hold of Tom's hand roughly and led him out of the house.

Every channel had the same footage. They played it over and over again, interspersed with gloomy-looking royal reporters.

'Do you think they're genuinely upset, or are they mourning for the loss of their livelihood?' Holly asked.

Clare kept staring at the screen, saying nothing.

'I'd hate to have all my investments in magazines right now,' Holly commented later, 'I mean what the hell are they going to put on their covers?'

'Your humour may impress Joss, but it doesn't impress me,' Clare suddenly said.

Holly's mouth dropped open, and then closed.

'Are you unable to watch television without giving a running commentary?' Clare asked her.

'Well, excuse me,' Holly said hotly, 'perhaps you'd like to be left on your own?'

'As a matter of fact, I would.'

'Fine.'

Holly got up and walked out, slamming the door behind her.

All right, it was sad, but Clare was behaving as if she had known Diana. Holly stood at the garden gate trying to decide whether to walk to the clifftop or to the beach. It was a bit windy for clifftop, she decided. There was only so much fresh air city lungs could cope with.

If someone had asked her the day before whether she identified with the Princess, Clare would have laughed. Of course they had nothing in common. Diana was tall and statuesque, rich and famous, a fashion icon, who did a lot of silly things as well as a lot of good ones. Clare had never been one of Diana's detractors, although she had wondered recently what on earth she was up to visiting a clairvoyant by helicopter, but she wasn't a fan. Princess Diana really wasn't someone she was aware of feeling one way or another about.

Clare kept telling herself this while the tears continued to stream down her face. It was as if a tap had been wrenched on behind her eyes and the washer broken, making it impossible to turn off however sensibly and logically she tried to think about it.

When she saw the Royal Family attending church in their big black car, the princes sitting stiff with shock in the back, anger clutched at her insides making her desperate to rescue them from their wicked family, the only family in Britain in the Nineties to have escaped contact with popular psychology books. What would their lives be now? Motherless, secluded in castles and forced into clean slacks and pressed shirts even for the so-called informal photo-calls. It was too cruel. Clare sobbed because there was nothing she could do about it. They kept showing the clip of the Princess and the boys on the water chute at Thorpe Park. She looked so animated by her laughter and yet she was dead. The Royal Family looked dead, ossified in another time with different values, and yet, ironically, they were alive.

*   *   *

Holly was walking along the near-deserted sea front when she heard a muffled cry of her name. She looked around and saw Tom and Joss, their faces pressed up against the glass, sitting in the window of one of the little cafés that spewed out a vapour of deep-fat frying. The smell reminded Holly of her office.

'I couldn't stand it any longer,' Holly said, joining them at a formica table and picking one of Tom's chips off his plate.

'Put that back,' Tom ordered. He had a fat plastic tomato of vinegar-diluted ketchup in both hands and was endeavouring with huge concentration to swamp his chips in it.

Holly popped it into her mouth defiantly.

'Where's it gone?' Tom asked.

'Where d'you think? I'm eating it. What do you do with chips?'

'I seeing if they swim,' Tom announced, 'Daddy say that fish do swim.'

His eyes went from hers to the remains of a piece of battered cod on his father's plate as if to say, and you think I'm the one who's being silly?

'Do you think the Royal Family did it?' Joss asked as she sat down.

Holly found it easier to watch Tom's antics than to meet his eyes.

'Organized a car accident? Nah. They're too incompetent. Anyway, I thought you weren't interested . . .'

'I'm interested in news, not in sentimentality,' Joss retaliated, but it sounded a bit lame.

Holly laughed.

'Of course you are,' she said, congratulating herself on a hit. You see, she thought confidently, I do know how to deal with bastards.

It began to rain.

Joss went up to the counter and ordered an ice-cream

for Tom. He came back with coffee for Holly and the Cornish pasty she had selected from the heavy leatherette-bound menu.

'Tom likes anything with red sauce on it,' Joss said, looking at the cascade of raspberry-flavour topping on the sundae.

Holly took a bite of her pasty, made a face, then washed it down with a mouthful of bitter coffee.

'Well, that's nice,' she said, 'to know that there are still things you can rely on, like soggy Cornish pasties that taste of flour and pepper and cubes of not-quite cooked potato. You couldn't get this in London, you know,' she pointed with her fork at her plate, 'first of all it would be called a filo pastry parcel and it would be full of char-grilled vegetables. I'm so tired of the renaissance of British cooking, aren't you?'

'It doesn't interest me,' Joss said, coldly.

OK, round two to you, Holly thought.

It was still drizzling as they wandered across the beach. The tide was out and the sand undulated with even ripples.

'How does it go like that?' Holly wanted to know, 'so uniform . . . ?'

'Sometimes nature is very ordered,' Joss replied.

Tom ran on ahead, shouting. One minute he was a plane, the next a train.

'What are those little squiggles?' Holly asked, bending over to point at the sand.

'They're lugworm holes,' Joss crouched down in front of her, 'if you dug down a bit you'd find one.'

His face was very close to hers and, in the cold damp air, she felt the warm puff of his breath in her eyes.

'Do you want to?' he asked.

She met his eyes and was unable to remember what the question referred to. Then she stood up quickly and walked on.

'Brrmmm,' Tom came racing back to her and fell in the wet sand at her feet.

'What are you now?' she asked him.

'I'm a car crash,' he said.

Joss and Holly went to the pub for the evening. Clare stayed at home, glued to the documentary tribute to Diana. There were clips from the famous confessional *Panorama* interview. She remembered the first time round when Joss had mocked Diana's wide-open panda eyes and muted voice. She had sat watching the screen, wishing he would stop, but not daring to say anything, because of the diatribe that was bound to follow. Like thousands of other women who had been humiliated by their husbands when they were at their weakest, she knew what Diana had suffered, and, just fleetingly, far too embarrassed ever to admit it, she had wanted to be her friend.

In some ways their lives had been similar, Clare thought now. They had both lived unhappy childhoods in large houses where they rattled around like pennies in a moneybox. They had both been swept off their feet – someday my prince will come – by the first man who had taken any notice of them.

'Yes, I adored him. Yes, I was in love with him. But I was very let down . . .'

It didn't seem to matter that the person in question was a public-school twit called James Hewitt. Clare began to cry again.

Then the phone rang and Ella's voice said, 'Mum? Are you all right?'

Clare couldn't really speak, and then Ella was crying and Clare cradled the phone next to her ear, the hard plastic a poor substitute for her daughter's shoulder.

'I just feel so strange,' Ella was saying, 'I keep crying . . . I miss you so much . . .'

*　　　*　　　*

346

Clare went up to bed without saying anything to them when they returned. Holly sat down in the vacated sofa, and Joss slumped next to her. She tried to remember how much cider she had drunk. Was it three pints or four? It was much stronger than she had thought, anyway. Staring at the screen, she began to imagine all the news researchers in the country scrolling through their Psions desperate for another celebrity who had shaken Diana's hand who might not have already been grabbed for a sound bite to camera, or, even better, a fawning debate about Diana's qualities as a mother, ambassador and saint.

'How do you think she'll be remembered?' the presenters asked, again and again, striving each time to make it sound like an original question that had just occurred to them.

'Elton John'll be singing "Candle in the Wind" at the funeral before we know it,' Holly joked.

Emerging from the blur of scrumpy, she was beginning to be slightly appalled at the blackness of her own humour. It was as if she and Joss had set up in competition to see who could make the wittiest remark about the day's tragedy. Worse, she knew that she was only doing it to impress him. She felt Joss's arm along the back of the sofa behind her. Was this the beginning of a pass and how was she going to respond, or was it just a tall man having to stretch his arms? Slowly she turned to look at his profile. He was staring at the screen. Then suddenly he got up and said, 'I think I'll go to bed now. Sleep well.'

The television screen showed a montage of images of the Princess, ending with her coffin being taken off the plane at Northolt. On the A40 into London people stopped their cars to watch the hearse go past. This was no ordinary tragedy, Holly realized, it was history. The country was in shock, and yet here in this house in Cornwall three people were acting out a Pinteresque play only connected to the rest of the world by the flicker of a television screen. One part of her desperately wanted to return to London, where she could feel the heartbeat of the nation. Here, in this remote corner of Britain, she had lost all sense of how to behave.

As the strange, unreal week between death and funeral unfolded, the little house became claustrophobic with the palpable tension between Clare and Joss. He worked in his office most of the day, only venturing downstairs to glare silently at Clare and make himself a sandwich. Clare was untouchable in her mourning. There was a distractedness about the way she cooked and gardened, as if she was lost.

Holly fell into the routine of taking Tom out each day. A little way along the beach, beneath the cliffs, there were rock pools which became sources of endless fascination for Tom and for her. She discovered how relaxing it was to pass time just looking at water – the vast and ever-changing sea, or the tiny world of a sea-water pond with its fronds of lime green seaweed waving and tiny crabs scuttling away from Tom's curious fingers. For the first day or two she felt almost guilty to be so unoccupied, having no scripts to read, phone calls to make, nothing to do except amuse an easily pleased little boy. She stayed out of the house as long as she could, treating Tom to all the cheap plastic toys and ice-cream and chips he wanted.

Clare and Joss were obviously on the brink of splitting up, the distance between them exposed by the freak death of a woman that neither of them had known. It was horrible being a bystander in the domestic drama, her only role to indulge the child. In the evenings she would sit in the kitchen pretending to read the newspaper as Joss and Clare sat in tense silence, or bickered with one another.

The news was no longer the Princess's death, but the

depth of public feeling. Queues of people waited for hours to sign books of condolence. All over the country in shopping malls that Diana had opened, hospitals that she had visited, leisure centres and department stores, little shrines were laid to her memory with candles and flowers wrapped in cellophane. The aerial photographs of Kensington Palace reminded Holly of the swathes of land in the Canaries where they grew tomatoes under plastic. She could not understand why anyone would want to sign a book of condolence. Or write a message on a card. Or pay over the odds for a mixed bunch of horrid spray carnations that would wither and die in a heap of rotting blossom and plastic. But she looked at her sister, her eyes emptied by genuine grief, and she realized with shock that it was she herself who was out of sync with everyone else. To Holly, Diana was the woman who had made it all right for tall girls to wear high heels. She thought she'd done a lot of good for AIDS and land-mine awareness, and she was grateful to her for that, but that was about as far as her emotions went.

On the Thursday afternoon, Clare went into the garden and saw that the sweet peas were at their best. She cut a small bunch and was about to put them in a vase on the kitchen table, then changed her mind. Stealthily, she left the house and walked up the hill towards the cliff path. Checking that nobody could see her, she put down the flowers on the grassy hillock where she and Ella sometimes used to sit, chatting and looking out to sea. Then she closed her eyes and said out loud, but softly, 'Dear Diana, I wish you had known how much people loved you and how much all the good things you did meant to them. I wish you had had a happier life.'

As she opened her eyes, a wind picked up the frail blooms and carried them bowling over the turf to the cliff's edge where they remained for seconds caught in a tuft of longer grass, as if saying goodbye, and then a gust of wind carried them out over the sea.

On Friday evening, Joss announced that he had written a poem called 'Sea of Cellophane'.

'That's so typical of you,' Clare snapped at him, 'you write, you don't feel. You've always done that . . .'

'What?' he asked.

Sometimes his voice was like a knife, and he used it to terrorize, Holly thought. He liked people to adore him or fear him. He lived on extremes.

'You write because you have no compassion. You're a voyeur. Actually you're no better than the bloody paparazzi . . .' Clare said to him, shaking with her bravery which seemed to render Joss incapable of speech.

'It's the messages I think are so funny,' Holly said, trying to defuse another argument. 'I mean who on earth do they think is going to read them? "Dear Diana, you will stay for ever in our hearts." Do they really think she's looking down from heaven?'

'It's just a simple human need to do something,' Clare spat at her, 'why do you have to be so dismissive about it?'

' "Diana and Dodi, now you can be at peace together" . . . probably from the same people who last week were saying, "Surely she could do better than that Arab playboy . . ." '

'Honestly,' Clare said, getting up to leave the room.

'I wish I had a flower shop right now, that's all I can say,' Holly said.

'I wish it was all you would say,' Clare suddenly shouted.

If Colette had said such a thing, or even Mo, Holly wouldn't have been in the least bit shocked, but Clare didn't say things like that. Holly stared as her sister marched upstairs, her face quivering with unrepentant determination. The phone rang. Joss picked it up and handed it to her.

'There is a smell!' Simon's familiar, unneurotic voice brought homesick tears to Holly's eyes.

'Hooray.'

'No, not hooray, it is the worst smell I have ever smelled. Colin says it will dissipate in ten days, but I wouldn't advise you coming back before then . . .'

'Colin?'

'Our friend in pest control.'

'But I want to come back,' Holly said. 'It can't be that bad . . .'

'No, Holly, I'm telling you, it is really bad . . .'

'The rat is dead,' Holly told Joss solemnly as she put down the phone.

'Are you going to open a condolence book?' Joss asked.

She looked at him as sternly as she could, and then she felt the effort of being cross and the tension of the whole week welling up behind her face and she couldn't seem to stop it bursting through in laughter.

'Come on,' said Joss, 'let's go down to the bloody pub.'

Clare heard the door slam as the two of them departed. They were both so selfish it probably hadn't even occurred to them that they might wake Tom. She lay still for a moment on the top of her counterpane, listening to the sharp metallic tap of their footsteps on the tarmac road and Holly's giggling getting softer and finally fading away. Tom did not wake. Clare had not known that Holly was so selfish before. Holly had always said that the two of them were as different as Baby and Scary Spice, but she had not believed her. She had assumed that Holly's tough, ebullient exterior was a good disguise for a softer centre, but over the last week Holly's inability to feel anything about Diana's death had disturbed her. She hated the way that Holly laughed at the simple tributes that most normal people found touching. You can mock, Clare wanted to say, but you're lucky you don't know what it is like to marry a man who betrays you.

'. . . and so my friend Richard said to this woman, "This is Joss, we were neighbours in another life," ' Joss was regaling Holly, 'and the Italian woman says, "'Ow interesting, 'ow do you know zis?" . . .'

Holly laughed. '. . . she actually thought you meant another life? Like reincarnated . . . ?'

'Exactly.' Joss finished his pint.

'That's brilliant,' Holly said, congratulating him on his anecdote and trying to find something to match it. 'I'm waiting for the first sighting of the vision of Saint Diana, aren't you? Where do you think she'll appear? England? Ireland? Perhaps I could pretend to see her and set up a shop selling relics and things . . .'

'You always see the commercial possibilities,' Joss remarked, 'you always see a way of making money . . .'

'Yes, well, when you've grown up without money, you want it,' Holly replied, defensively, 'people like you get very righteous about not having money, but I bet you had a lovely middle-class upbringing, just like Clare did . . .'

For a fraction of a second his face showed that she had scored a hit.

'You're very like your father,' he told her, reaching forward and brushing a ringlet of hair from her face.

His touch was delicate. She felt herself flushing. Sparring with him was sexy. It was as if they knew exactly where each other's weaknesses lay. She had exposed something in him, and he knew how to reciprocate. It was like finding erogenous zones to stroke with infinite sensitivity, producing the electric tingle of one human being touching the core of another.

'Do you mean in looks?' she asked, flustered by the way he was staring at her.

'You have his eyes,' Joss said, holding hers for so long she had to look away, 'candid eyes.'

What did he mean by that? Were candid eyes attractive?

'But I meant his personality. You're very strong . . .'

'That's what he used to say. Holly, he said, the last time I saw him, you'll find it very difficult to find a man to marry you because you're so uncompromising . . .'

'Do you want to get married?' Joss asked her softly.

'Is that a proposal?' she shot back, delighted with her own wit.

'I don't think I make a very good husband . . .' Joss said, leaving the sentence open for her to add what she wanted to it.

'I don't think I'd make a very good wife,' Holly said, trying to maintain her ground, 'far too selfish, I'm afraid.'

They were talking in code. He was telling her that he wanted to be her lover, she was telling him that she would not cling, or maybe neither of them were saying anything at all, she told herself. If twenty years of flirting had taught her anything, it was that men and women saw it completely differently. Women listened and remembered, chewing over every word afterwards with their friends, assuming that men thought as hard about the messages as women did. Men just said the first thing that came into their head and sounded good and could never remember it afterwards. Or at least, that was their story.

'Come on,' Joss said, suddenly, 'let's go.'

She would have liked another pint or two. It was nowhere near closing time. Disappointed, she stood up and followed him. Outside it was very dark and her eyes took a moment to find him. He was walking towards the harbour. The tide was high and the sea was heaving, waves bulging against the harbour wall, occasionally tilting over the top, leaving a trail of white spume as they retreated again.

'Shall we walk along the top?' Joss asked.

'Isn't it dangerous?'

'Yes,' he said, his eyes meeting hers, daring her.

'OK,' she said.

They climbed up the steps and stood watching the churning sea. Then Joss began to run, dodging the waves as they broke, with Holly, unable to resist a challenge, following. They reached the end, soaked by salty spray, breathing loudly and fast, clinging to a metal post embedded in the stone. Suddenly Holly screamed as loudly as she could, throwing her face back, the noise swallowed by the elemental surge of the sea. Then he grabbed her with both hands, as if to shake her silent. She was laughing with the exhilaration of the danger. His eyes glowed with pure anger, as if he wanted to control her but could not. Then his mouth fell on her face, his hands in her hair, snapping her head back, and, as the waves soaked them, Holly thought, I am going to die. I am going to die. This is love.

Then, as brutally as he had started kissing her, he stopped.

'We'd better get out of here,' he said, and dashed, grabbing her hand, pulling her back along the now treacherously slippery harbour wall. It wasn't more than fifty yards but it felt like a very long way to safety.

As they stood catching their breath, the sounds of normality returning to their ears, a pub jukebox, the calls of drunken fishermen bidding each other good night, a car starting and the crash of the waves suddenly distant and soothing, the only proof of what had happened was their wet clothes.

'Do you realize how close we were to being swept out?' Joss asked her.

'Yes,' she said, staring at him.

'You would risk your life to kiss me?' he whispered.

'I was lost from the moment I saw you,' she said, unused to the total seriousness of true love.

He looked at her quizzically.

'Meryl Streep in *French Lieutenant's Woman*,' she reminded him.

He put his arm round her shoulders as they walked back up the hill and she let her body relax against his. Finally, she thought, I have found a man tall enough to rest my head on his shoulder without bending my knees.

As they came back into the house, they broke apart suddenly as if caught out by the light inside. The television was still on.

'Oh Christ, if I see that water chute one more time, I'm going to ring the BBC to complain,' Holly said, babbling to fill the embarrassed silence. What on earth were they going to do now? 'I've got friends who work there,' she told him as they both sat down on the sofa, 'and from time to time they have to go in at weekends in order to practise the routine for when the Queen Mother dies. Well, the old colostomy bag has been pipped to the post. If she died right now, no-one would give a fuck.'

Joss laughed.

It was the first time he had laughed at one of her jokes, she realized, and it felt good.

'Perhaps she has died and they're keeping her under wraps, embalmed until a more suitable occasion arises?' Joss said. Holly laughed back. How horrible they both were, she thought, how wonderfully, compatibly horrible.

'Let's pull out the bed,' Joss said, sliding his arm along the back of the sofa.

'But . . .' Holly's eyes travelled to the ceiling.

'She's asleep. I'll check if you like . . .'

'Yes . . . no . . . I mean . . .'

He left the room.

Holly sat stiffly, wondering what the hell she was doing. She couldn't seriously be about to fuck her sister's husband while her sister lay asleep upstairs, could she? But she was leaving the next day and she didn't know when she would see him again. She wanted him so badly. Clare did not want him at all.

Holly sat staring at the television, wondering whether to make up the bed, and decided not to. It would look too eager. Then, when he did not return, she reran the conversation they had just had, thinking that perhaps she had misunderstood him. Had he said that he was going to bed, before suggesting that they make up hers? Perhaps he was just being a considerate host. Was she feeling guilty about something that was not even going to happen?

Clare listened with dread to the characteristic sloosh and spit of Joss cleaning his teeth. The mattress dipped as he sat down on the bed to take off his shoes. Clare sensed him bending over to untie the laces, then he leaned right back to look at her. She could feel his breath on her shoulder and smell that he had been drinking beer. He would be randy and she felt she would not be able to bear it if he touched her. She braced herself, trying not to flinch, managing to maintain the evenness of her breathing long enough to convince him that she was asleep. As he left the room, she let out a long sigh of relief. She heard him padding downstairs, saying something to Holly, and then a muffled giggle. They had both been drinking. She heard the unmistakable creak and boing of the springs in the sofa bed uncoiling, and the thump of pillows. Holly was turning in for the night, which meant that

Joss would soon return. Clare tensed, then relaxed as minutes ticked by and he did not appear. Perhaps they had both dozed off in a drunken stupor. The television was still on downstairs. Clare closed her eyes and tried to sleep.

Joss took off his trousers and underpants. His body was thicker than Holly had imagined it, and he had grey hair on his chest and at the base of his spine. He was a man, she reminded herself, not a boy. He turned round, his penis hanging limp as he got into bed beside her. She could feel him hardening slightly as he put both arms around her and kissed her savagely.

'Lie on top of me,' he instructed as she struggled to break free for air.

She sat with her legs astride his hips, hovering above him. Then she started to lift and dip her body, brushing herself against him. He groaned a little and closed his eyes. She kissed his mouth softly, then ran her tongue down his body to his penis, licking the tip in little circles before taking it in her mouth and sucking. At last, the tissue began to respond. She sucked and he moaned, and from time to time she opened her eyes to look up his body to his face, but his eyes were closed. Her jaw was beginning to ache. Matt with his ever-ready erection had made her lazy. She had forgotten how much effort sex could involve, especially when you were tired and drunk. She was beginning to wish that she had never started, when she looked up again and saw first Joss's face frowning with concentration, and above, six feet away in the door-frame, the outline of her sister standing staring at them. Their eyes met.

Holly let the penis flop from her mouth.

Then Clare started shouting.

'GET OUT. GET OUT. BOTH OF YOU. JUST GO . . .'

For a few moments, no-one moved. Then Clare fled upstairs and suddenly Joss was on his feet, ripping the sheet from the sofa bed to cover himself, then leaping up the stairs after her.

Holly listened at the bottom of the stairs like a naughty child eavesdropping.

'DON'T TOUCH ME,' Clare shrieked, 'I HATE YOU.'

She broke down crying, and then stopped suddenly.

'What the hell did you think you were doing? In our house?' she asked him coldly, trying to keep her voice down so that Tom would not wake up.

'I don't know,' he faltered.

'You don't know . . . ?'

'I suppose I found the poetic symmetry of fucking the whore downstairs while the Madonna slept innocently above irresistible,' he laughed weakly.

'Is that supposed to be some sort of compliment? You're disgusting, you disgust me,' Clare hissed at him. 'I want a divorce.'

Chapter 30

There were thousands of people milling on the Mall, and yet it was quiet. A stillness had fallen, like the moment just before Mass in a great cathedral, interrupted only by an occasional wail from a baby too young to understand his surroundings, a sound that made strangers smile at one another, just briefly, acknowledging human frailty, then look away again, absorbed in their own private thoughts.

The department store had closed for the day. There had been a strange, hushed atmosphere there all week and very few shoppers. Outside, the pavements were awash with flowers. The staff talked about nothing else. Everyone had conducted their own inquest and reached their own verdict. Accident, manslaughter, murder or even assassination. Mo understood that people wanted to believe that it was not an accident. It seemed such a stupid, unnecessary end for Diana and Dodi, but she still thought it was the most likely explanation.

'Drink causes more deaths than all the other drugs put together,' Eamon said knowledgeably.

Mo had felt a special affinity with Diana right from the start, not just because she had bought the outfit she announced her engagement in from her department – she hadn't served her, but she'd recognized the blue suit when she saw it on television – but because she was the mother of a tall, slightly gawky girl almost exactly the same age. Over the years there were times when she had felt that Diana could have done with a mother like her to look after her a bit.

With hindsight, that first interview with Prince Charles had given it all away when he couldn't bring himself to say that he loved her.

' "Whatever that means?" ' she remembered repeating his words to Holly as they watched it, 'well what's that supposed to mean? Most people who've just announced their engagement do know what love means . . .'

'He's an emotionally repressed in-bred, royal git,' Holly told her, lolling on the sofa in jeans and a T-shirt with the name of a band on it, 'what do you expect?'

She had thought Holly a bit disrespectful at the time, but she had come to see that she was right. The Royal Family were out of another age. They were so blinkered they couldn't even see that they'd had a real piece of luck with Diana. She had made royalty modern, glamorous and caring and she'd produced two lovely boys. What more did they want? Mo couldn't see the point of them any more.

The edges of the Mall were six feet deep in flowers and candles. People had tied bouquets and pictures to the trees, somebody had even left his football shirt with a message written on it in felt-tip. Mo felt empty-handed. She would have liked to have lit a candle, although she worried a bit about the fire risk with all these people around and all that cellophane wrapping. She had laid a little spray of freesias outside Kensington Palace after work on the Monday. There were already flowers there then, but it was nothing like the huge shrine it had become later in the week. She wasn't quite sure why she'd done it, but she had felt better afterwards, although it had made her sad as the week went on, when she imagined her fragile flowers wilting and the fragrant floral carpet beginning to rot and smell.

Mo was wearing black. The Jaeger suit had been in the sale the year before, and she'd got staff discount on it. She'd thought it would come in useful. You couldn't really go wrong with black and a good cut, although she'd never envisaged that she'd wear it in mourning twice within the space of a year. This morning she'd put a pale pink blouse on underneath, because black next to her face did nothing for her, and checking her appearance in the mirror before she'd left, she'd felt a bit guilty for her vanity, but she didn't think the Princess would have minded. Most people around her were wearing jeans and T-shirts. Some of them had slept out all night, and looked like it. It shocked Mo at first, but then she thought how fitting that was. The Princess's life had all been about informality, so why not her funeral too?

Mo wished she were taller. There were so many people. She didn't think she'd be able to see when the coffin went past, even if she stood on tiptoe which seemed a bit undignified, more like a voyeur than a mourner. She decided to make her way up to the big screen in Hyde Park. She cut up beside St James's Palace where the princes were going to join the funeral cortège.

Behind the palace there were dozens of huge trucks with satellite dishes on their roofs, waiting to broadcast the procession all round the world. As Mo hurried on towards Piccadilly, she wondered whether Holly was watching it on television in Cornwall. It must be strange for her to be so far away when all this was happening just yards from her flat. She had thought about her so much this week, seeing the newsreel clips of the Princess's life, and remembering what Holly had been like at all the different stages. It wasn't that she had ever wanted Holly to be like Diana, although she had wished her daughter would do something about her hair, but there had been significant moments, rites of passage, when she hadn't been able to stop herself comparing the two of them.

Holly had still been living at home at the time of The Wedding. Mo had been all for going to St Paul's to watch the carriages arrive since it was only just down the road, but Holly had been disparaging.

'Watch the virgin being offered up for sacrifice? No way!' She had been in one of her black phases, where her mood seemed to match the colour of her ragged jeans and the kohl round her eyes.

When William was born, Mo remembered thinking that Diana looked very mumsy compared to Holly, who was by then sharing a flat with several other secretaries and wearing mini skirts that got shorter each time Mo saw her.

'I wonder what they'll do with her now that she's done her duty,' Holly had mused, looking at the photo on the front of the paper when she came to Sunday lunch.

'What do you mean?' Mo had asked naïvely.

'She's produced an heir, so she's fulfilled her function,' Holly had said, 'I expect they'll make her have a couple more and then put her out to charity pasture . . .'

Mo had scolded her for her cynicism, but now that she thought about it, Holly had been right all along. She'd tell her that when they next spoke. It was funny not to have talked to her all the week. Often weeks would go by without a phone call, but not when there was big news like this.

As she walked smartly along Piccadilly, Mo wondered whether Holly had been sad. With all the conspiracy theories changing by the day, Mo had missed her daughter's incisive comments on the whole thing. You could always rely on Holly for an opinion even though she pretended not to have the slightest interest in royalty. She had once let slip that she had phoned the Squidgy-tape line, and when Mo had visited her with the annual copy of *Hello*! that had pictures of all Diana's outfits, Holly had thoroughly perused the entire issue before disagreeing vehemently with the judgement of the team of fashion experts.

Mo reached Hyde Park just as the funeral procession was leaving Kensington Palace. The low murmur of the crowd suddenly ceased as the gun carriage carrying the draped coffin appeared on the screen, and silence reigned. Mo felt a lump rise in her throat. She had never heard London so quiet.

Thirst had driven Philippa into the first bar she found open in a narrow old street near the cathedral. The contrast between the glaring sunshine and the shade was so sudden, she had to push up her sunglasses to see where she was going. The suntan oil on her arms felt like a baste under the grill of the sun. The bar was the sort of place that usually had a bullfight on the television screen and men sitting on stools drinking fino, occasionally shouting advice to the toreadors. On the walls there were posters, bandillas with coloured streamers and a wreathed portrait of a local hero, all interspersed with faded colour photographs of the snacks available. Fried egg with chips, calamares in a roll, a circle of pink chorizo slices. Did people not know what a fried egg looked like, Philippa wondered, her eyes pausing on the unappetizing photo before being drawn to the screen. The sombre pageant taking place in London seemed a million miles away from this dingy place.

At first Philippa thought that the sound of the television set was turned off, but then she became aware of the clip-clop of the horses' hooves and the slow dull toll of the Abbey's bells as the coffin was pulled along the roads lined with people. There were three arrangements of white flowers on the top of the coffin. The round cushion of roses at the front had a card stuck into it. Infuriatingly the camera did not zoom in immediately to show what it said. The familiar landmarks of London sparkled in the morning sunshine, but South America had come to England since she had been out of the country. People had never wept openly and thrown flowers at a State funeral before. How green everything was there. She could imagine a BBC voice running a quiet respectful commentary over the pictures, giving sober information about the ermine on the Royal Standard, the height of the guardsmen and the exact distance their legs would cover today escorting the Princess on her last journey. The Spanish commentator had little to say. The horses trotted dutifully on. Finally the cameraman zoomed in on the card on the smallest wreath.

One word.

Mummy.

Philippa's sight blurred with tears.

Diana's death had shocked her, but it had seemed an unreal event, as far away as England, and as unconnected with her. She had seen the flowers and shrines photographed in the English newspapers, and read about the drunken driver and the paparazzi's chase much as she would read about a distant event, the Bosnian conflict, or the British withdrawal from Hong Kong. She had been too preoccupied with her own loss to be saddened by the loss of a woman she had never met.

Mummy.

Now she had seen it, she could not look at the progress of the coffin without focusing on the plain white rectangle stuck into the circle of rosebuds.

Mummy.

The most glamorous woman the world had ever known. The face that launched a thousand magazines, and yet one word would define her for ever.

Mummy.

The bartender came over to take her order. Philippa saw that he was startled by the tears rolling down her cheeks. They did not go with the elegance of her sleeveless black dress, the Loewe leather knapsack, the tortoiseshell RayBans perched on her forehead.

'*Agua mineral. Sin gaz.*'

The funeral procession was nearing Buckingham Palace. All eyes were on the Queen, but Philippa's mind was elsewhere.

Long ago, on her wedding day, she had received a warning.

'You cannot have a husband and a career and children.'

It was her boss who had issued it, smiling, but she had been deadly serious. She was one of the few women then who had reached board level in an advertising agency. She was the woman Philippa wanted to be. Her long painted fingernails were exactly the same red as the Campari and soda she was drinking.

'You can have two out of three, but you cannot have all three.'

Philippa had laughed, and pulled in her stomach, praying that her boss had not detected the small curve that lay beneath the tiny white shift, and looked across the room at Jack. He had not wanted a big reception but he had got the Ritz. He had not wanted to wear a suit but she had taken him to Simpsons. He despised her parents' wealth and class, and yet he was telling her mother a joke, a perfectly-pitched joke, for her mother was smiling, spellbound by her new son-in-law's charm. He had done all this for her. Watching him, Philippa loved him so much that she ached, and she had decided at that moment which two of the three options that lay before her she would choose.

Now she stared at the small rectangular card moving along the Mall, and in its wake two boys trying so hard to be brave.

Mummy.

Philippa had relinquished motherhood in a Faustian exchange for her career and husband long ago. And now her career was over and her husband gone.

Mummy.

The woman in the coffin was almost exactly the same age as her own daughter.

The cacophony of questions in Philippa's brain that had been clamouring for answers since Jack died grew suddenly quiet. You could not begin to repair the past, only the future. Long ago she had given up the right to be called Mummy and she did not know whether Clare needed or wanted her any more, but she knew that she needed her. Clare was the only person in the world she wanted to see.

Picking her leather knapsack from the chair beside her, Philippa made her way across the dingy bar to the payphone by the cigarette machine. She put in some coins but paused before dialling. How do you begin this conversation, she wondered, trembling. Losing her nerve, she replaced the receiver and was startled a moment later by the clatter of coins. She would ring from the Parador, from the privacy of her room. She glanced at the television again. Dignitaries were arriving at the Abbey. Everyone in England would be watching the service. If she rang now she would be almost certain of speaking to Clare, if she waited until she returned to the Parador the moment might have passed and having waited so long, she could not wait any longer. Philippa dropped the coins in again and stabbed out the number.

'Who's that funny lady?'

'Which one?'

'That funny lady with the funny hat . . .' Tom pointed at the screen where the camera had zoomed in on the latest arrival at the Abbey.

Clare laughed. 'She's called Mrs Thatcher.'

'She's funny.'

It was wonderful to have a child's innocent perspective on the funeral and when you were trying to think of answers to the constant stream of questions, it was almost impossible to cry.

Why are those horses going so slowly?

Why are those men wearing big black hats?

And, when the procession was joined by people representing Diana's favourite charities. What is the man doing in that pushchair?

They were both sitting on the sofa, Clare's feet on the floor, Tom's just reaching over the edge. They had eaten biscuits instead of breakfast and the crumbs were everywhere. She put her arm round his shoulders and squeezed, thinking how nice it was, just the two of them, together, chatting and watching an event that in years to come might be his first remembered memory.

'The day my father left us,' Tom might say, 'it was the funeral of the Princess of Wales . . .'

Clare did not know where Joss had gone.

The night before, when they had finished shouting at each other, she had come downstairs to find Holly gone. On the table the Yellow Pages lay open at Taxis, so Clare assumed that she had called one and checked into a hotel. For a moment she felt oddly sad that they had not said goodbye. And then she remembered Holly's face frowning with concentration on the task of pleasuring Joss, and she was glad neither of them had suffered the indignity of her apology.

Seeing that the sofa bed was vacant, Joss had said he would sleep there. Clare had not wanted him in the house, but, suddenly coldly rational and exhausted by their row, she could not see what would be gained by making him leave in the middle of the night. She had returned upstairs without speaking to him.

Early in the morning he had brought her tea, as if nothing had happened, and sat down on the edge of her bed.

'How do you feel?' he asked, as if she were convalescing from flu.

She had slept better than she had for weeks and her brain felt as if it had been rinsed with clear spring water. She finally saw how he always manipulated history to make her somehow the culprit and him the victim of his poetically uncontrollable urges. And she understood as she never had before that to stop him she must refuse to engage with the run of his questions.

'You can see Tom whenever you want by prior arrangement, but I do not want to see you, or to talk to you except to discuss Tom's well-being or Ella's, should that be necessary,' she told him.

The pleasure it gave her to see Joss's surprise was immeasurable, and she marvelled at her use of the words 'prior arrangement'. It made her sound as if she had been talking to a lawyer.

'And don't even think about telling him that Mummy made you leave, because if you lie to him, I shall be forced to tell him the truth. Do you understand?'

He had merely nodded, and for a moment he looked beaten. She fought the Pavlovian urge to feel sorry for him. It must be awful to live your life on an illusion of strength, she thought, and then to be exposed as weak. Far better to think you are weak and discover you are strong.

Wearily he had started to put a few things into a bag,

very slowly, as if expecting her to relent with each pair of socks he added, but she did not.

He went in to say goodbye to Tom and she jumped out of bed to stand outside Tom's door listening.

'Daddy's going away for a little while,' he told him.

'To a poet thing?'

'Yes, something like that.'

'Can I still go to the beach?' Tom had asked, with a child's glorious selfishness.

'Yes, with Mummy.'

In the end, he had done as she asked. If she had asked before, would he . . . ? Standing outside her son's bedroom door, Clare had gulped back tears. It was too late now. It was over.

The funeral cortège had finally reached Westminster Abbey.

'What are they doing now?' Tom asked.

'They're taking that box with the flag on and carrying it inside,' Clare told him.

'But WHY?'

'Because they're going to sing some nice songs and remember the nice lady.'

'Oh. That OK then,' Tom allowed.

At that moment the phone rang.

Surely it couldn't be Joss. Surely even he had enough respect to wait until the funeral was over. She decided not to answer it, then Tom slid off the sofa and said, 'I'll get it.'

And Clare leapt up to reach the receiver before his little hands could.

'Clare? It's Philippa . . .'

'Philippa, where are you?' She sounded a long way away and in distress.

'In a bar in Granada. But I'm coming home.'

'When?'

'As soon as I can get a flight . . . Could I see you?'

'Of course.'

'Are you all right? I'm thinking about you . . . I wanted . . .'

And then her mother's money ran out, and the congregation in the Abbey rose.

It was a bit like the Oscars, Holly thought. When the Prime Minister arrived she had assumed it was a plain-clothes policeman behind him who looked just like Tom Conti, then the commentator said, 'And there's Tom Conti . . .'

Richard Branson waved at the crowd. She was surprised that everyone so far had resisted the temptation to sign autographs. Chris de Burgh was there looking even more pious than ever. George Michael was in the Abbey, and Elton John really was going to sing 'Candle in the Wind'. It was going to be the campest funeral showbiz had ever seen.

Holly tried to get comfortable on the beige sofa.

Simon had been right about the smell in her flat. When the taxi that had driven her all the way from Cornwall had dropped her at seven in the morning she had been relieved to be home at last. It felt as if she had been away for months. Her key slid into the lock with a satisfying click and then she had pushed open the door. The smell that assaulted her nostrils had an initial sweetness that made her think, oh, it's not so bad, and then suddenly it was so searingly disgusting, like an infinite multiplication of rotting cabbage and blocked drains, that she knew she would throw up if she took another breath. She banged the door shut again and stamped her foot in frustration. The one place that she had made her home, where she felt safe, had been taken from her and she had nowhere left to go.

Then Simon and Tansy had appeared in the court-yard, arm in arm and looking cloyingly couply. She was the sort of woman who blow-dried her hair even at this time on a Saturday morning.

'Where are you going?' Holly asked them.

They looked at her oddly.

'To watch the funeral,' they said simultaneously.

'Am I the only person in this country who hasn't gone mad?' Holly asked.

She had just been stuck for six hours in a car with a cab-driver who wanted to air his particular theory which was that Diana and Dodi were not really dead at all, but that there had been a getaway car, and look-alike bodies had been placed in the Mercedes.

'Anything's possible these days,' he had told her in his annoying West Country burr that sounded like a cider advert, as they sped over Dartmoor.

'Do you mean that French doctors gave heart massage to a look-alike before pronouncing her dead, or that there are several dozen people in on the escape plan?' Holly asked, never able to let a theory go untested, although as soon as she'd said it she wished she hadn't.

In the rear-view mirror, the driver's face fell.

'I'm not saying it happened,' he said, 'I'm just saying it's possible.'

'I think I'll try to get a bit of kip if you don't mind,' Holly told him, lying down across the back seat. She had woken up on Salisbury Plain and sat up with an aching back.

'Nobody's traced that white Fiat Uno, though, have they?' the driver asked, and she wondered whether he had been droning on all the time that she had been sleeping without noticing that he was getting no response.

'So, where do you think they are?' Holly asked, wearily.

'On some paradise island, I shouldn't wonder,' he said, as they pulled into a lay-by for a coffee break.

'Well, if that's true, the *News of the World* will find them soon enough,' Holly said.

'Not if they're not looking for them,' he replied sagely, unscrewing his Thermos flask.

'Think of all the people who'd see them on the way . . .' Holly argued.

'Plastic surgery,' he said.

'Yes, but then you're adding a surgeon and at least a couple of nurses to the picture,' Holly said, 'and do you really think that all her family and Prince Charles who presumably saw the body, would either be fooled by a look-alike, or be able to keep the secret?'

'Well, they didn't let her sons see her,' said the driver as if that constituted irrefutable proof.

Holly lay down again. The next time she woke up they were on the Chiswick flyover.

'We've made good time,' he told her, 'is there anywhere near where you live I could park up? Now I'm here, seems a pity not to watch the procession . . .'

And Holly suddenly realized why it had been quite so easy to negotiate a cab journey to London in the middle of this particular night. He was being paid two hundred pounds to do something he dearly wanted to do.

'What's the point of watching a coffin with a look-alike in it?' she asked him as she got out of the car. He pulled away muttering something about lack of respect.

And now here were two people who favoured beige and pastel shades standing in front of her dressed in black at seven o'clock on a Saturday morning, when anyone with a brain would be asleep in bed. If they had a bed to go to. Holly seized her opportunity.

'If you're out, could I have a sleep in your flat?' she asked Simon.

'Of course,' he said, 'you've got a key, haven't you?'

Tansy's face fell dramatically.

'I think so,' Holly said, diplomatically, as if it were something she'd never used before.

Simon smiled gratefully at her.

Even though she felt exhausted, she hadn't been able to resist turning on the television.

The sister did well, but she felt Tony Blair tried to stay a bit too long in the limelight. Holly sat staring at the screen unmoved by the Prime Minister's words.

And then Elton was sitting at the piano and, hearing the first so-familiar chords, Holly's heart began to beat very fast, pounding with vicarious stage fright, but he sang out, the professional he was, his voice rising to the occasion. As Holly let herself breathe again, suddenly something very strange happened. A flood of unstoppable tears began to pour down her cheeks, and her shoulders began to shake as her whole body was racked with grief, and she did not even hear the end of the song because the room was filled with great gasping howls.

On her own for the first time since Diana had died, Holly wept for the Princess who had done so much good, and for the princes who had walked behind the coffin refusing to cry for the world, and most of all she wept because even with all those clothes and all that money, surrounded by all those celebrities, Diana had been lonely.

Earl Spencer began his oration, standing like Mark Antony on the biggest stage on earth. Holly suddenly stopped crying, unable to believe that she was hearing the words he was speaking and the extraordinary insult to the Royal Family contained in them. As his speech unfolded, she drew closer to the television, now eager to participate in history being made, suddenly understanding the significance of the week's events – that things would never be the same again. When the applause of the people rushed through the doors of the Abbey like the sound of a torrential hailstorm, Holly found herself on her feet applauding too. And then, as the ethereal notes of Tavener swept the coffin along the aisle, Holly was filled with remorse at the shameful way she had behaved.

The coffin paused inside the Great West Door of the Abbey for a minute's silence. Holly stood with tears rolling down her cheeks wishing that she had bought flowers, lit a candle, or done something, just something, to recognize the life of this woman, whose death had changed the life of a nation for ever. She watched silently as the hearse drove through London's streets and people applauded the Princess on her last journey, and threw flowers in her path. She watched the car all the way to the gates of Althorp, where it suddenly, unceremoniously, disappeared, carrying the Princess towards the island in a lake where she would remain alone for ever.

PART SIX

September

Chapter 31

Clare stood on the doorstep holding Tom's hand, waiting for the bell to be answered. Tom thumped the shiny black paint with his fist, and then discovered the polished golden letter-box.

'Does Postman Pat put the letters in here?' he asked.

'I expect so.'

Clare could hear footsteps tapping across the polished wooden boards of the hall and her heart began to thump in her chest as she braced herself for the meeting. The imposing Georgian house with its eccentric battlements topping the white stucco façade had always been a place of confrontation. Then the door opened and Philippa was smiling. Her hair had turned completely white.

Tentatively, Philippa opened her arms and it was such an uncharacteristically vulnerable gesture, Clare responded, clasping her mother, feeling the boniness of her ribcage against her own. After a couple of seconds they disengaged, embarrassed to be so close.

'Hello Tom,' Philippa said.

'Are you my grandma?' he asked.

She looked surprised and Clare calculated that her mother had not seen him since he had started talking.

'Yes, I am,' she said.

'Oh, that OK then,' he replied stepping over the threshold uninvited, eager to see what was inside.

Philippa exchanged a glance with Clare as they followed him in.

There was a sadness in her eyes that Clare had not seen before and her body, which had always been slim but very strong, had lost its confidence. Philippa had been the epitome of presence, facing down the world with a glare, or pulling adoring men into her orbit with a look, but now she seemed partly absent. Clare found herself fighting an almost maternal urge that rose spontaneously as she watched her wander into the kitchen, as if she did not really know where she was.

'Coffee? Or a drink? What would you like?'

'I think Tom is hungry. Have you got anything in?' Clare opened the fridge and found it completely empty.

'I only got back yesterday,' Philippa said apologetically.

Her mother had called the night before, asking if Clare could come up to London straight away.

'Why the rush?' Clare asked.

'I wanted to see you . . .' her mother faltered.

Clare wrestled with the adolescent rage rising in her body. It was so typical of her mother to think only of her own needs, and yet she appeared to have changed. The woman Clare had last spoken to on the day of the funeral would never have let her hair go grey.

'Is there a supermarket?' Clare tried to remember what was on Hampstead High Street. She could recall clothes shops, booksellers, coffee bars, but no food shops.

'I thought we could go out . . .' Philippa said.

'But Tom's too tired to go to a restaurant . . .'

'Of course he is,' Philippa said, defeatedly.

'I'll pop out,' Clare said, finding herself unable to be cross with her.

'Just a minute . . .' Philippa said, walking through to

the hall, 'they're always dropping stuff through the door about pizza delivery. Does he like pizza?'

'Pizza, pizza, pizza,' Tom jumped up and down.

'There's your answer,' Clare said.

When he heard that a man on a motor bike was going to bring the pizza round, Tom insisted on sitting on the doorstep to wait for him. Later, as they ate slices with their fingers, Tom declared it was the best food in the whole world, which Clare found slightly galling.

'Which bit do you like best?' Philippa asked, pointing at the pieces of olive and sausage and mushroom.

Tom gave the question due consideration.

'The big box,' he said.

Clare put Tom in the middle of the large double bed where she would be sleeping too, then made a moat of pillows all around the edge.

'Why are we sleeping in Grandma's house?' he asked.

'We're having a holiday,' Clare told him.

'But why?'

Before Clare could think up a suitable answer, he was asleep.

She left the door open so that she could hear if he woke up, but blocked it with two chairs so that he could not go exploring the unfamiliar house in his sleep, then she went downstairs.

In the huge back room with its wall of glass that overlooked the garden, Philippa was drinking a tall glass of something clear and fizzy.

'Can I have one of those?' Clare asked.

'Of course. It's just water . . . I gave up drinking alcohol in Seville.'

Clare raised an eyebrow.

'The quantities I needed to deaden the pain seemed to make the pain worse the morning after,' Philippa laughed shortly.

Clare poured herself gin from a bottle in a cupboard full of bottles in the kitchen, and plopped ice-cubes in from the dispenser in the fridge. There was no tonic water. She topped up the spirit with mineral water.

'I've phoned Lucinda. She's going to do a shop tomorrow and cook us something wonderful . . .' Philippa called.

'Oh, really, I can do that,' Clare began to protest.

'No, you are my guests . . .'

'We're your daughter and grandson . . .' Clare walked back into the dining-room.

The familiar pattern of argument was beginning to assert itself again.

'Do you know how difficult it is to indulge you?' Philippa asked her, half-exasperated, half-teasing.

Curiously, Clare felt more comfortable now that they were back at the point of a row. The sad, repentant Philippa terrified her far more than the sharply aggressive one. She smiled at her and sat down on a large sofa opposite the one where her mother was sitting.

'What did you do in Spain?' she asked her.

'Nothing. I don't really know. Just existed, I suppose . . . I did a lot of thinking. I learned quite a lot about Spanish history, as a matter of fact. Have you ever been?'

'No. I've always wanted to.'

'I never understood the pure pleasure of learning,' Philippa turned and looked out into the garden. 'I suppose when I was at university I saw it only as a means to an end. It can be very distracting . . .'

'How do you feel now, I mean, about . . . about Jack?' Clare asked.

One of them had to mention his name sooner or later. She hadn't thought it would be her.

'Just as raw as I ever did . . . I wake up sometimes feeling fine and then suddenly I remember and I'm choked . . . what about you?'

Clare was surprised by the question. She had never felt included in her parents' life, nor in his death.

'I cried a lot last week. I just couldn't seem to stop myself,' she admitted, 'and I think maybe some of it was for him. I didn't cry when he died. Not once. I don't miss him exactly, but I regret . . .'

'Yes. It somehow gave a focus, didn't it?' Philippa said, and Clare was astonished that her mother had chosen the exactly appropriate word. Diana's death had given a focus to everything that was sad in people's lives. Perhaps people had felt able to cry because it did not seem as selfish to cry for someone else as for all the insignificant little tragedies that made up their own existence.

'You are her age,' Philippa said.

Then Clare began to understand, seeing the tears welling in Philippa's eyes. Even Philippa, cold, hard Philippa had been moved. She did not think she had seen her mother cry before and she did not know what she would do.

Philippa looked away, staring out towards the pool.

'What a bad mother I've been to you . . .'

Clare watched her mother's thin little body trembling with silent sobs, and she did not know whether to comfort her or to leave her. The oddness of it frightened her. Then Philippa stretched back a thin arm towards her and Clare could not bring herself to take it, unable to find it in herself to forgive so much so soon.

'I've left Joss,' she said, in the strange silence that followed, 'or at least he's left me, at my request, but it feels as if I've left him . . .'

'When?' Philippa sniffed.

'Saturday morning, ironically.'

'But you seemed so very happy together . . .'

As soon as Philippa said it she knew it was not true. How painful it was being honest. On the rare occasions she had thought about Clare's life, she had consoled herself that her daughter had chosen two options, just as she had. Two different options. Clare had chosen the man and the children. Clare's love for Joss was all-enveloping, as hers had been for Jack. Now she knew she had lied to herself about that too. She had known that Joss was not half the man that Jack was. Jack could be difficult, no-one more so, but his power derived from his quick intelligence, and Joss's from his inferiority, which made him a bully. Over the years she had seen how her daughter had been ground down, but it had been easier to believe Clare's proud story that they were very happy and not to see them much. Far easier that way than to admit that her daughter had chosen a pale imitation of her real father because she had lost the love of the real thing.

'I'm so sorry,' she said.

'I'm not,' Clare replied, 'I feel liberated . . . although I don't know what the hell I'm going to do, where I'm going to go . . .'

'You can stay here . . . always . . .'

'We'll see,' Clare said, unwilling to leap from one oppressive household to another. That would be going backwards. In the days since Joss left, she had felt gloriously, irrationally optimistic, and she did not want to let go of her freedom so soon.

They both sat in silence, then Philippa said, 'Clare, there's something I have to tell you.' The sentence started off loud and then dropped, as if she was unused to hearing her voice and the sound of it frightened her.

Philippa looked so stricken, Clare's heart began to thump in her chest. Not cancer, she thought, please don't let her have cancer.

'There's no easy way of saying this . . .'

'What?' Clare interrupted, impatient for the news that seemed to weigh so heavily on her mother's shoulders.

'Your father had another child, a daughter . . .' Philippa stared out of the window.

'How long have you known?'

'Since the night he died . . .' The relief of saying it was immense. Philippa looked at Clare for the first time directly. 'You knew?' she said, accusingly.

'Only since the funeral . . .' Automatically, Clare began to defend herself.

'Who told you?'

'She did. I met her at the funeral.'

'She was at the funeral?'

'I just told you,' she sounded like a sulky teenager.

'How old is she?' Philippa demanded.

'She's my age,' Clare said, thinking what an odd question it was, then suddenly understanding.

'Why didn't you tell me?' Hysteria was beginning to rise in Philippa's voice.

'You didn't give me much of a chance . . . why didn't you tell me for that matter?' Clare shouted back.

'What?'

'You said you knew the night he died . . . so why didn't you tell me then?'

'Because . . . because . . .' Philippa's angry expression melted into fear. 'Because I thought that telling me had killed him . . . I thought I had killed him . . .' she said, at last speaking the thought that had harried her subconscious since Jack's death.

The pale, petrified face and the white hair finally broke down Clare's defences. She got up and crossed the room to Philippa's sofa, sat down next to her, and put her arms around her.

'Of course you didn't kill him,' she said, stroking her mother's hair as she wept into her shoulder, 'he lived for you. He loved you . . .'

In the end, she thought, it doesn't really matter who gives and who receives comfort. It is the exchange that is important.

★　　★　　★

'Do you think you always take other women's men because your father was taken from you?' Colette asked.

Colette's brand of amateur psychology always seemed to make Holly feel worse rather than better.

'I don't always take other women's men . . .' she protested.

'Matt, Joss . . . and don't let's forget Piers . . .'

It was a shameful list.

'I didn't really do anything with Joss . . .' she offered lamely, 'but he's the only one I feel bad about. Matt didn't mean anything, it was a kind of one-night stand that went on for more than a night, and I've always thought that if Piers hadn't had me he would've had someone else, and since I was never a threat, I kind of think I did his wife a favour . . . I feel bad about Joss, though . . .'

'Your own sister,' said Colette, underlining the sin, and confirming Holly's suspicion that Colette had been rather jealous of her relationship with Clare. 'There's an article in one of the glossies this month called When Your Best Friend Fancies Your Man, I thought of you . . .' she added helpfully.

'I can't remember fancying any of your men,' Holly retorted. 'I think I've been a bit mad since Jack died . . . and it was so weird being away from London in that week . . .'

'It was an extraordinary week.'

'All I wanted was a bit of peace and tranquillity and I landed in the middle of a marital minefield and then Diana died, and it all turned weird, and if you think I'm bad you should meet Joss . . .' she defended herself.

'What's he like?' Colette wanted to know.

'Gorgeous to look at, and really . . . *bad*,' Holly tried to think of a way of describing the sheer bastardness she had found so intoxicating, 'it was a bit like when you're with someone who's so drunk it makes you feel practically sober. They're falling over and slurring their words and you're still standing up, so you think you're fine, and you lose count of the number of glasses of wine you're knocking back because you think you're so in control because they're so pissed?' Colette was nodding. 'And then you leave the party, congratulating yourself on how un-drunk you are, and out in the street you try to tell the taxi-driver where you live and the words get all tangled up and then you pass out in the cab . . . ?' She checked to see that Colette was still with her. 'Well, Joss was like that, except with flirting. He flirts so outrageously and he looks at you so intensely that by comparison I thought I was only fluttering my eyelashes, except I wasn't, I was licking his dick . . . d'you see what I mean?'

'Sort of,' Colette replied, 'any more of this?'

She held up the empty bottle.

'There's another one in the fridge, you get it,' Holly said, 'I don't like going into the kitchen now . . .'

'The smell's not nearly as bad as you made out,' said Colette.

'What d'you mean? There isn't a bloody smell any more . . . Simon bought a face mask and rubber gloves, found the offending item behind the sink, wrapped it in about fifty plastic bags and buried it in a rubbish-bin at a secret location somewhere on the other side of Soho . . .'

'God, he's nice to you,' Colette said.

'Well, he knew it was either that, or me on his sofa for ten days . . . he sealed up the gnaw-hole too. So hopefully that's the end of it, but the flat's not the same to me now. Every sound makes me freeze . . . Nothing's really the same now. I feel as if I've come to the end of a phase, and I can't see what's next . . .'

'I can't recommend my dating agency highly

enough,' Colette said, as if she were in an advert for washing-powder, 'you might as well know that I'm seeing a guy called Nigel.'

'Nigel? That's worse than Piers, and he's a . . . ?'

'Financial manager of a sports-equipment supplier . . .'

'An accountant.'

'Well, all right.'

'What sort of sports equipment?'

'Athletic supporters.'

'What's an athletic supporter?'

'A jockstrap, if you must know . . .'

'And how much athletic support does he need, if I may ask?'

'No you may not, nor will you attempt to find out,' Colette told her.

'Don't worry. I've had enough men for one summer,' Holly said, 'anyway, it's not really about men . . . it's about the direction of my life. I've got all these contradictions. My life is full, but essentially empty. Any success I have is not my success, it's the success of my clients, except if they're not successful, then somehow it's my fault. Where will I be in ten years' time? Will I still be doing the same thing, living in a glorified student flat, just me, the odd affair, cirrhosis of the liver and a cat . . . ?'

'You hate cats.'

'True, but they're what single middle-aged women have . . . and rats don't like them.'

'The trouble with you is that you do want a man, but you're just not prepared to compromise . . .'

Same old tune, thought Holly, different band playing it. Why the hell was everyone so keen for her to compromise?

'The only reason I want a man is I've got to find someone to take to Mo's wedding,' she said briskly. 'I just can't bear the thought of everyone asking if I'm going to be next. They wouldn't dare if I had someone with me . . .'

'Try my dating agency. What have you got to lose?'

'My dignity . . .'

Colette just looked at her.

'I've only got a month . . .' Holly said, tacitly agreeing to the idea.

'Has to be the agency then. If you put an ad in a mag, by the time it's gone in and you've sifted the responses, you'd probably only just have met the first batch . . . and you can't start off "Hello, you look OK, will you come to my mother's wedding," can you?'

'True.'

'Unless you're planning on finishing what you started with Joss . . . ?'

'No,' said Holly wistfully. She couldn't deny that the thought had crossed her mind that he would follow her to London. It had been such a romantic moment down on the harbour wall, but somehow the romance had evaporated on the sagging sofa of Clare's living-room. 'It was a bit like me and Robert De Niro . . .' she said.

Colette arched the thin lines of her eyebrows.

'In the flesh, he was a bit of a disappointment,' Holly said with a dirty laugh.

'So Jack had a wife and a mistress,' Philippa said when she had heard everything Clare knew, 'except he chose a mistress for a wife, and a wife for a mistress. Typical of him to be so contrary . . .' She said it almost fondly, but there was a bitter edge to her voice.

'I hadn't thought about it like that,' Clare said.

It was dark outside now. She could see her own reflection bouncing back at her from the glass side of the room.

Perhaps that was what all men wanted, she thought. Perhaps one woman could never be both things as she had tried so hard to be with Joss. In the end what men wanted was a madonna and a whore. Just as Joss had said that night. The memory was still raw enough to make her wince with physical pain. Madonna and whore. It had not occurred to her before that she and Holly had simply followed the pattern that their mothers had set, and the idea filled her with horror.

'A shop assistant,' Philippa said, disgusted.

'She was his childhood sweetheart,' Clare rose to Mo's defence. 'She didn't have the benefit of rich parents and a good education. That doesn't mean she's stupid . . .'

'Stupid enough to get pregnant . . .' Philippa said.

'But you were pregnant when you got married, weren't you?'

Clare had worked out the dates in her early teens and it had explained then why both her parents seemed so indifferent to her. She had not been wanted in the first place. But now, even in the darkness, Clare could see the depth of her mother's blush and she knew that she had not got the story quite right.

'Oh, I see,' she said.

'What do you see?' Philippa asked, but she knew that she had already given herself away.

'You weren't stupid enough to get pregnant, so you must have done it deliberately . . . I didn't realize that contraception was so sophisticated then . . .'

'It was, if you knew where to go. And if you had money . . . but it's always been easy to get pregnant . . .'

'But why?' Clare asked. Clearly her mother had never wanted to have a child.

'I had to have him,' Philippa said, 'and I knew that he was working-class enough to do the right thing. Everyone wanted him. I had to make sure . . .'

'But he adored you . . .'

'Did he? I thought so, but now I'm not so sure . . .'

'Of course he did,' she couldn't believe she was

reassuring her mother of such a transparent truth. What about me, she was screaming inside, what about me?

'So I was conceived as a trap for you to get your man . . .' she said, 'and so you and Jack both kept secrets about your children . . .'

That thought had not occurred to Philippa before. Hers was only one little lie, she told herself, not a lifetime's lying.

'I understand about you,' Clare said, 'but why didn't Jack love me either?'

Philippa looked up, clearly surprised.

'But he did. He adored you when you were little. You were a real daddy's girl. He was always buying you things . . .'

'Buying things is not the same as loving . . .' Clare interrupted, but Philippa took no notice.

'. . . when you grew older I think he found it difficult. You were so different from either of us. So quiet and secretive . . .'

'Secretive?'

'You were in a world of your own with your fairy stories and your imaginary friends . . .'

'And by that time he had Holly . . .'

'Is that her name?'

'Her mother named her after *Breakfast at Tiffany's* . . . She looks like Jack, if you can imagine that, and she always lets you know what she's feeling. Always. No wonder he loved her. She's the exact opposite from me.'

'You sound as if you know her quite well.'

Clare laughed drily.

'A bit too well,' she said.

Her overwhelming feeling about Holly now was disappointment, not so much for the betrayal, although that hurt, but because she had fallen so swiftly and eagerly for Joss's charm. She had thought that Holly was different from everyone else, and she had turned out to be just the same.

'I think I'll turn in,' Clare said, 'Tom gets up very early, I'm afraid . . .'

'Oh . . .' In the darkness Philippa's voice sounded very small and as Clare stood up she said, 'Thank you, Clare.'

'What for?'

'For coming. For explaining. I know I don't deserve it, but it has helped me . . .'

'That's OK,' Clare said.

She lay in bed listening to the sounds of the house that had not changed in twenty years, the creak of the fifth step on the first flight of stairs, water flowing down the pipes as Philippa drew her bath, the screech of car brakes on the unexpectedly sharp corner at the bottom of their road, the rustle of leaves in the tall trees. The sounds were potent memories that made her a child again, and tears dribbled down her cheeks, soaking the pillow on either side of her face.

Anji said that her next script was going to be called *Never Enough*.

'It's about this really ambitious woman who gets everything she ever wanted, but it's never enough. You know, job, money, man . . . what do you think?' she interrupted herself.

Holly didn't know what to say.

'Sounds good,' she managed.

Sounds like me, she wanted to say. I used to think that sitting around in a West End office with my feet on the desk, having a cigarette with an interesting and talented client would be enough. But here I am, and it isn't. I used to think that a salary that took me into the forty per cent tax bracket would make me rich, but I'm just as broke as I've ever been. Just a week ago, I thought that fucking Joss Drummond would be enough but . . .

'I've got to run,' Anji said, 'I'm having lunch with Charlie Prince.'

I used to think that being friends with someone like Charlie Prince and his wife would be enough, Holly thought. But she hadn't even seen them since the dinner party, and the wonderful feeling of having met kindred spirits had been as ephemeral as any other sensation in the illusory world she inhabited.

She took a long drag on her cigarette as Anji left the office, and stubbed it out. Then defiantly lit another, daring anyone to come into her office and tell her off in the mood she was in. She rearranged the papers on her desk, thought about making some calls, picked up the phone, put it back, swore at herself, and decided to go and buy a sandwich.

The notice on the cash machine said:

'In our continuing effort to provide our customers with an efficient service, this express till was operational 98.6% of opening hours during the month of August.'

The screen below said:

'Sorry, due to a fault, this machine is temporarily out of order.'

Why did her decision to withdraw money always seem to coincide with the 1.4% of opening hours when the machine broke down, Holly asked herself. The statistical likelihood had to be infinitesimally small and today it seemed emblematic of everything that was wrong with her life. Outside the bank the queue for the cash till was seven deep. She didn't even have enough cash for a cheese roll.

The only way to cheer herself up in the circumstances, she decided, was a bit of shopping, or retail therapy, as Colette insisted on calling it. Marks and Spencer first, because she could buy a sandwich, or even a triple pack, with a debit card, and while she was there have a quick look at lingerie. Who needed anti-depressants when you could have a rainbow pack of pretty knickers all folded neatly round cardboard in a space-saving box, and while you were about it, sweet little colour-co-ordinated cotton bras, a couple of vests that really worked as T-shirts, a nightie that could pass as a John Galliano dress, and a matching negligée in case anyone were ever to invite you away for the weekend on the spur of the moment at a Friday night party, leaving no time for you to shop beforehand. Holly felt better already. She was almost glad that the cash machine had broken now, because it was much more fun shopping when the balance left in your account was a figure in your imagination, as opposed to a considerably smaller and more accurate livid green number on a screen.

'One hundred and thirty-one pounds and ninety-nine pence,' said the shop assistant.

Perhaps she had gone overboard with the triple pack, Holly thought, tearing open the plastic triangle and selecting a prawn and mayonnaise, but now she was in the mood, she thought she might as well go and have a quick look in Selfridges for an outfit for Mo's wedding. It was pointless to go overdrawn for a piddling amount. Simon had once explained to her about the proportionate charges. If you overdrew ten pounds and the charge for going overdrawn was ten pounds then you had an overdraft of twice as much as you'd taken out, but if you overdrew one hundred pounds the charge was still ten pounds which was only ten per cent of what you'd gained. A thousand made it even more of a bargain. As Holly walked towards the main store through avenues of fresh pasta pyramids, inhaling the cool smoked scent of delicatessen, she wished she had been a bit more organized about things. If she had known she was going to do a serious shop, she would have left out the sandwich and downed half a dozen oysters at the bar in the Food Hall.

Even though the weather was still warm, in department-store seasons it was officially winter. The last bargains of the summer sales had been ruthlessly banished, along with anything bright or cool or remotely suitable for a wedding. There were some gorgeously rich purples and charcoal greys but even with the suggested addition of a toning feather boa they looked more funeral than wedding, and she had had enough funerals to last her a lifetime. Mo's wedding was a watershed, not just for Mo, but for her too, she told herself. She must be positive, looking towards the future, laugh and the world laughs with you, and all that sort of thing. Holly stared at herself in the mirror and smiled. Purple turned her face very white and the feather boa made her look like a bit part from *Interview with the Vampire*. More Bride of Dracula than bridesmaid. Holly envisaged the look in a magazine spread. The Undead Gorgeous Look. In her haste to get the outfit off, several dyed purple feathers drifted to the floor.

Holly walked towards the escalators down. Never mind. There were only two sorts of shopping days. On good ones, everything you tried on looked better than you imagined and was miraculously reduced by thirty per cent when you took it to the till. On bad ones, they never had your size in the items you picked out, and so you tried other things in the futile hope that they might look better on, but they never did. Then you found yourself in an increasingly desperate chase in and out of every shop on Oxford Street, and further afield, getting assistants to ring other branches, and ending up thoroughly exhausted and demoralized, having spent all your cash on taxis as you hopped from Knightsbridge to Covent Garden and back to the Kings Road.

She had been fooled by her initial fillip in M & S into thinking that this was destined to be a good shopping day, which was ridiculous because it was impossible not to make a successful purchase of lingerie in M & S. Holly had made up her mind to quit while she was ahead, when, like a mirage in the dark desert of winter woollens, she spied the Christian Lacroix section dancing with mismatched colours and eccentric fabrics.

The dress was long and lycra, it felt like a bathing costume and it fitted her like Michelle Pfeiffer's catsuit fitted in *Batman 2*. The pattern was a funky combination of Greek vase painting and go-go girl in turquoise and yellow. Holly stepped outside the fitting-room and twirled, admiring herself, so pleased with the look she decided to see if they had a jacket that went with it.

'What do you think?' she asked the assistant, as she flipped through the rails. It was a rhetorical question. She knew she was going to have the dress. It was made for her. And then she saw the assistant's face, and even though it did not have writing on it, Holly could clearly read the words 'mutton dressed as lamb'.

'Yeah, great!' the assistant said, but seconds too late.

Holly turned and went back to the fitting-room. Now, when she looked in the mirror, she saw that her breasts were not quite as high as they used to be and the tops of her arms not as thin. The lines on her face became crevasses as she stared. A couple of years before she had one day, without really noticing, passed the age where she could buy stuff from Miss Selfridge and pass it off as designer. (Suddenly angora just didn't look like cashmere any more, and she was too old to show her midriff). Now another important rite of passage had gone by without her being aware of it. She had passed the age where she could buy designer that looked like Miss Selfridge. It was all downhill from here. She should have known, Holly told herself. It was a bad shopping day. First vampire, then mutton. In the cool pastel cube of her changing-room, Holly sat down and wept.

Tom had just learned to pedal the tricycle tractor Philippa had given him.

'Not near the pool!' Clare shouted.

It was a dangerous garden for a child, filled with steps and climbing roses with sharp thorns.

'He loves his tractor, doesn't he?' Philippa said.

The miniature farmyard machine complete with trailer looked ridiculously out of place in this sophisticated, long-established garden.

'He loves everything you've given him. He's been thoroughly spoilt,' Clare said, smiling.

On the first day, Philippa had swished them off in a taxi to Brent Cross where she had purchased everything Tom pointed at in the Early Learning Centre. The house was now scattered with brightly coloured plastic, and the dining-table had feathers of paint with flat edges where Tom's brush had swept over the side of the giant-size sugar paper.

'Perhaps he'll want to come again,' Philippa said tentatively.

'I don't think I'll ever get him to leave . . .' Clare said. Their bag was packed and waiting for them in the hall. They had said their goodbyes, and promised to visit again soon, and then Tom had asked for just one more go on his tractor.

'Why not stay a while longer?' Philippa asked as the two women watched him hurtling around.

'I've got things to sort out . . .' Clare said, 'I have to make arrangements with Joss . . .'

She still did not feel comfortable in Jack and Philippa's house. There were too many memories there. She and Philippa had managed to keep the ceasefire, but it was a delicate truce. Sooner or later resentment was bound to ambush them. She did not want to be her mother's enemy again, but it was too soon to be her friend.

The house in Cornwall could not stand empty for too long in case Joss decided to move back in. She wondered if he was staying with Pepe and Vivienne and what mischief he had been making in her absence. All the poets and their wives would have fallen upon this juicy morsel of human distress. She could imagine their comments as they chewed it over, salivating . . . I never thought Clare was strong enough for him. Surprised it didn't happen ages ago . . . and, with a grudgingly admiring laugh, Joss is so bloody capricious . . . Clare didn't think that there was much chance of her job in Vivienne's shop still being open when she returned.

'Are you OK for money?' Philippa asked her suddenly.

Clare just laughed.

'I'd like to give you some . . . a lot . . . however much . . .'

'No, I'll manage,' Clare said.

'Why won't you take anything from me?' Philippa asked despairingly, 'you accept presents for Tom, why can't you see the money as a gift for Tom . . . ?'

There were times when Philippa's tone could send Clare's temperature from cool to boiling-point in seconds.

'Because I won't be bought by you,' she insisted through clenched teeth.

How did this start, she asked herself. We almost managed to get away without an argument.

'But that's ridiculous . . .' Philippa argued, 'that's the sort of rhetoric Joss always came out with. It's very Old Labour, I'm afraid . . .'

It was an attempt at lightness, but Clare refused to laugh.

'As a matter of fact, Joss would have loved to get his hands on your money. It was me who always refused . . .'

'But why?'

'You virtually abandoned me as a child, you ignored me as a teenager until I got a drugs conviction and then instead of helping me, you let Jack throw me out. You could have stood up for me. Instead you just stood by and watched . . . it was as if you wanted me to go . . . I was always in the way . . .'

It was a child's anger, held back for many years. Philippa looked at her, astonished that she should have blurted out something neither of them had acknowledged for twenty years. It seemed so uncalled for when all she had been doing was offering support. But it was all true. This was the moment she had returned for, she realized. This was the reckoning. She took a deep breath.

'I know . . .' she said, 'I've thought about that a great deal, over the last few days and in Spain. I thought about you all the time in Spain . . .'

Her tone was all wrong. She managed to make it sound as if Clare had been an unwelcome intruder in her thoughts. She tried again.

'I know that money can't make up for that, but surely it would help you now?'

'You mean that it would help *you* now. It would help you salve your conscience . . .' Clare was stiff with unresolved anger. She saw Tom look over at the two of them. The constant low-level tension at home, occasionally spilling over into furious argument, had made him very sensitive to changes of mood.

Philippa sighed heavily.

'So what if it would? Would that be so unbearable? Or is my punishment so important that you're prepared to make your child suffer . . . ?' she challenged Clare.

'How dare you offer me advice on caring for my child
. . . HOW DARE YOU?' Clare screamed at her
mother. The words echoed around the pool.

Frightened by the noise, Tom got off his tractor and
came running over, hurling himself at his mother's legs.

'It's OK, darling,' she said crouching down to his
level, trying to sniff back the tears that were streaming
down her face, 'it's OK.' His head was buried in her
shoulder, his arms tight around her neck. She looked
up at her mother. There were tears running down her
face too as she stared at Tom's protective embrace with
bewildered envy. Then suddenly Clare began to laugh.
Her body was still shaking with sobs, but her face was
strangely lit by laughter, a rainbow in wet grey sky.

'What?' Philippa asked, uneasily.

'I can't believe I just said that. I promised myself I
would never say "how dare you?" to anyone . . .
especially not here . . .' she gestured vaguely at the
pool.

Philippa did not understand.

'It's what you said to me . . . twice . . . it's one of
your favourite expressions,' Clare explained.

'Is it?'

'Oh, for heaven's sake!' Clare said, unable to muster
any more anger. She stood up.

'Can I have JUST ONE MORE go on my tractor?'
Tom asked her.

'Oh all right,' Clare said, looking at her watch, 'well,
I think we've missed that train now. And the next one
gets us in too late. Would it be OK if we did stay
another night?'

'It would be a pleasure,' Philippa smiled with relief.

Clare heard the words and saw her mother's face as
she spoke, and suddenly Clare understood something
that she had not understood before. Philippa came
from a background where people did not hug one
another or say affectionate things. The language she

used was dictated by form and politeness. She simply did not have an emotional vocabulary. But that did not mean that she did not feel.

As she lay in bed that night, hearing the swish of wind in the tall trees and the screech of brakes at the bottom of the road, she thought about her father, and where he came from. His background, though completely different from Philippa's, also frowned on displays of emotion, especially from men. Perhaps that explained his great attraction to Philippa and their hunger. for each other's bodies, which had been so obvious and so excluding. And maybe the reason Clare had dreamed of being swept off her feet by a handsome prince long after she had grown too old for fairy stories was because that was what she had witnessed all through her childhood, Jack scooping Philippa up and their bedroom door closing behind them, and that other sound, which the house had lost, the sound of her parents making love.

In the morning Clare felt as if sleep had unravelled the tight coils of anxiety in her brain and made it calm and smooth again. She had a moment of panic when she found Tom no longer beside her, but then she heard his chattering voice coming from downstairs. Philippa was already sitting at the breakfast table trying to feed him his cereal. She had a large box of tissues beside her, and one in her hand to dab immediately at the splashes of milk caused by the entry of Tom's spoon into the bowl at high velocity. Tom was still in his pyjamas and his face and chest was covered in softened Weetabix.

'You're enjoying yourself, aren't you?' Clare asked him, planting a kiss on top of his head.

'This is how you make a sandcastle,' Tom demonstrated.

'We thought we'd let you sleep,' Philippa said.

'What's the time?'

'Nearly ten o'clock.'

'That's the longest lie-in I've had for two and a half years!'

Philippa looked pleased. White hair suited her, Clare decided. It made her face softer. She hoped that she would not dye it again, but she did not think that they were yet friends enough to tell her that. There would always be some boundaries best left uncrossed.

'About the money,' Philippa said with a kind of determination Clare knew it was going to be impossible to deflect, even if she wanted to.

'Yes?' She felt light today, refreshed by her sleep.

'Why don't we go to the bank today and sort something out for the interim . . .'

'For the interim?' Clare repeated suspiciously.

Surely her mother was not now going to impose conditions, not after all that had passed between them the day before?

'Well, I don't want to load you up with the lot before you're divorced . . . you are going to get divorced?'

Clare looked significantly at Tom, but then saw that Philippa had chosen her words well. Tom did not know what divorce was yet. She had not mentioned his father's name.

'Yes I am,' she said.

Curiously, her mother's determination filled her with courage. She had been dreading facing Joss.

'I don't want him having a claim on it,' Philippa said, 'and Jack would be appalled . . .'

'He hated him, didn't he?' Clare asked, sitting down beside her son, idly spooning some of the contents of his bowl into her mouth out of habit.

'He did. He didn't think he was good enough for you . . . but of course, no man ever thinks that anyone is good enough for their daughter. My father was the same, although he did acknowledge that Jack was very clever . . .'

Philippa's father had died when Clare was a baby. She had never known him. The wedding picture had him looking very straight and stern, but Clare had always assumed that that was his formal pose for photographs. He had been an ambassador. There was a portrait of him looking just the same in Philippa's office. There were so many things she did not know about her mother that she now wanted to learn about. She was intrigued by the knowledge that Philippa's father had disapproved of her shotgun wedding, and by the realization that she herself had slipped into another family pattern without even knowing it. How strange it was that families seemed not to learn from past mistakes but to repeat them endlessly.

'I think Jack always believed that you would come home and throw yourself on his mercy, you know . . . sounds so Victorian, doesn't it? If you had, he would have been kindness itself, you know . . . but of course you were just as proud as he was . . .'

'Yes, I know that now,' Clare said, 'and I regret it,' she added.

Philippa looked up at her with great gratitude in her eyes.

'You will take some money?' she asked.

The money had become hugely symbolic to both of them, Clare realized. To refuse it now would give it far too much significance.

'Oh, all right then,' she said, trying to kill the sting of acceptance with a joke, 'I'll only get it when you die, won't I?'

Philippa laughed.

'Do you know,' she said, 'that was going to be my next line of attack . . .'

Both saved faces smiled at one another.

Chapter 32

'A word of advice,' said the woman leaning across the desk, 'men don't like hats.'

She nodded at Holly's head.

Holly removed the straw cloche. On the tube on the way there, she had been aware that people were looking at her. The hat she had put on to divert attention beckoned it instead. She was sure that if anyone she knew had seen her going into the building, they would have shown far more interest than usual. Oh look, there goes Holly in a hat! I wonder what she can be up to.

'Oh, you've cut your hair!' The woman, whose brooch said Barbara, Personal Counsellor, looked at the old photo that was paper-clipped to the top of Holly's application form and then at Holly's dreadlocks with clear displeasure.

'Yes?' said Holly, 'oh I see, well, I'm growing it out. That's an old photo, but I think it's quite good of me. Normally I look terrible. The camera always seems to catch me between expressions . . .' She pulled a face to illustrate what she was talking about.

'Yes, well, I suppose there's nothing you can do about it now. It's just, well, generally men prefer long hair . . .'

'Look,' Holly leaned forward, 'if all you've got are men who want Charlie's Angels, I'm in the wrong place. In case you didn't notice I'm nearly six feet tall, my hair is ginger and I've got an unfortunate habit of saying what I think. That's three more things men don't generally prefer. If I was petite, blonde, GSOH, loves animals and wants to travel I'd probably already be hitched up and on holiday in Malaga right now, wouldn't I?'

Barbara let out a short, hollow laugh.

'You're a real individual, aren't you?' she said, making an illegible note on her clipboard. 'Now, the credit check was fine . . .' She smiled at Holly as if she were announcing the result of a smear test.

What did you expect, Holly asked herself. You came here to find a date, not to become friends with a woman who makes her living out of other people's loneliness. Colette had told her that it was a bit embarrassing at first. This was probably what she meant. She wished that Colette would use language a bit more precisely sometimes.

'Do you like animals, by the way?' Barbara asked.

'Frankly, I wouldn't care if I never saw another animal in my life,' Holly replied, 'but I tend not to like people who own dogs. I didn't see a box on your form about that. Maybe you should have one. A bit like smoking . . .'

'But it says here that you do smoke,' Barbara interrupted.

'Yes, I was thinking of the other way round. Habitual non-smokers won't usually go near smokers, which is fine because people who have never smoked in their life are usually pretty boring. What I mean is, I would as soon go out with a dog-owner as a non-smoker would go out with me. For me, it would be on the level of a beard. A bearded, non-smoking, dog-owner is my idea of the date from hell. Does that help?'

Barbara smiled at her. The strain was beginning to show.

'Well, let's not waste any more time sitting around chatting,' she said, brightly, 'I'm sure what you really want is to get your fingers on some profiles. If you can just sign this confidentiality agreement . . .' She shoved a piece of paper across the desk, which Holly picked up and began to read.

'It's just . . .'

'I make my living negotiating contracts,' Holly told her, 'I'm not about to sign something without reading it.'

'Well, I'll just go and find you some suitable men!' Barbara's voice rose at the end of every sentence and she spoke a little too loudly, as if she were dealing with a child or an elderly person. It was a bit like being with an evangelical charity-worker before she handed out the soup. And Holly was paying her. It was all the wrong way round, she thought as Barbara disappeared into another room, leaving her alone with the confidentiality agreement with its list of conditions including the explicit statement that there would be no refund of the joining fee after signature.

How much did she want to meet a man? Holly asked herself for the umpteenth time, chewing on the top of the Bic Barbara thoughtfully provided. Several times her hand hovered above the declaration and signature section, then snatched itself away as if the clause were an open flame. Apart from the question of Mo's wedding, not really very much at all, she decided. Even less after her little chat with Barbara, who would have about as much chance of knowing the sort of man Holly would like as Mo or Colette would. But perhaps that was the point. Perhaps the closest people to you were the most useless at matchmaking because they had all sorts of other investment in you. Perhaps it was the very fact that Barbara was someone Holly would never ever have as a friend that made her perfect for this sordid job. Hmmm.

What have you got to lose? Colette had asked. The answer was simple, a) pride, and b) four hundred pounds. The four hundred pounds Holly could cope with, although she wondered whether she wouldn't rather spend it on the English Eccentrics dress she had spotted in Fenwicks the day after the bad shopping day. Would the pleasure of appearing in it at the wedding negate the need for an escort? Just lolling around on her bed in the dress might be far more satisfying than sex with any man the dating agency had to offer. But sex was not what she was here for, exactly, she reminded herself.

Barbara came clicking back into the room with a sheaf of plastic slip folders in her hand. Holly had expected about three, but there were at least thirty. One of them surely might be OK. It would be a laugh. What the hell? If she put it on Access, she could buy the dress as well. Holly took a deep breath, bent forward and put her signature on the confidentiality agreement.

The faces were as different as those of men in a tube carriage, but you didn't spend your tube journey wondering whether you'd like to go to bed with the person reading the *Standard* opposite. Or perhaps some people did, Holly thought. Perhaps that was why Colette didn't mind travelling all that way up and down the Metropolitan line every day. Perhaps her own preference for taxis was actually symbolic of one of those psychological barriers Colette was always talking about. She could see it as a question in a magazine quiz entitled Do You REALLY Want A Relationship? Question 1. Are you a) 18–24, b) 25–34, c) far too old to be reading this kind of crap? Question 2. Do you a) travel on public transport, b) walk or jog, c) always take taxis?

When they had first started doing those quizzes at school, it had been a simple choice. Were you an a) b) or c) kind of person? Usually b) was the best kind, a kind of medium line between ballsy and insipid, but the other two had their good points. Holly nearly always ended up with equal amounts of a) and c) which Colette said proved how interesting she was. Then when you graduated onto the grown-up women's magazines it started getting more complicated and you had to score each answer from the chart that was usually on another page, so that flipping back to see what you had marked became very tiresome. And then, Holly thought, trying to concentrate on the forms in front of her, when you grew out of that, you joined a dating agency, and you got to look at the quizzes other people had filled in, which in itself was quite fun.

After the photo, she found the first thing she looked at was the box for cinema. The ones that mentioned anything with Eddie Murphy she put to one side immediately. There was one man who listed *Terms of Endearment* and *Truly, Madly, Deeply* but she discarded him, because she'd seen both films with men, and she knew that they just didn't get those films. This one was clearly only writing what he thought would appeal, and you couldn't start a relationship like that.

She had got about halfway through making one pile into two piles of NO and MAYBE when Barbara returned to the room.

'Sometimes it's a good idea to cover up the photo until you've read the details,' she suggested, leaning over Holly's shoulder, adding in her singsong voice, 'you don't have to, but it's different . . .'

You don't have to but it's different, Holly mouthed at her back as Barbara began to click her long red fingernails importantly over the plastic-coated markers in a drawer filing cabinet.

Oh hell, why not, Holly thought. It was quite a quick way of getting through the rest of the pile. Nearly all of them eliminated themselves on the basis of politics (not interested) or sport (rugby, rowing, darts) without her even having to deliberate what it would be like waking up next to that face. Except one. On paper, he was absolutely perfect: several inches taller than her; honest enough to say that he had only just given up smoking and was finding it tough, which led Holly to believe that he certainly had the occasional puff of someone else's, if not his own packet of ten. Under profession, he had put 'writer (not rich and famous)' which she thought was rather sweet, if potentially a little mean. He loved all the movies she had loved recently. It was the words 'Tarantino, but I have my hands over my eyes at the nasty bits' that really won her over. Holly was almost in love. Feeling excited and nervous, she slowly drew back the form she had been using to cover the photos, praying that the face on this snapshot was unbearded. It was. She gasped as she found herself staring into the familiar eyes of her client Jeff.

Barbara looked round. Holly put her face in her hands.

Of all the worst, humiliating things she had thought might happen, she had never envisaged the possibility of finding someone she knew. Holly stifled a horrified scream as her mind worked through the logistics and she realized that even worse than this worst thing was the idea that someone she knew, particularly one of her clients, might find her form in this desperate place.

'It's no good,' she said, standing up, 'I'm just not up for this.'

'Too much in one day, I know the feeling, believe me,' Barbara chimed. 'We're open till eight, you know, and Saturday mornings . . .'

'No, I mean, I just don't think this approach is going to be right for me,' Holly said.

'No? If you like I can make the choices for you. Sometimes it works better that way, and we're always getting new people. I'll give you a call, shall I, just as soon as . . .'

'No. You don't understand. I want out,' Holly interrupted.

'Have a think about it. I won't put your profile into the files just yet if you'd prefer . . .'

'Oh God, just shut up and give me back my bloody form, will you?'

'Oh well,' said Barbara, suddenly losing her cheery good nature, 'if that's what you want.'

'It is.' Suddenly Holly saw why it would have been better to take the you've-been-very-kind-but approach. It was too late now.

'Seems such a waste of four hundred pounds,' said Barbara with a smirk.

The front door was difficult to open because of the pile of post behind it. Clare pushed hard, a space big enough to allow Tom through. He stepped over the envelopes into the hall and shouted 'Daddy?' and Clare's spirits plummeted. She had told him on the train that Joss would not be there when they got back, but he had not believed her. Every time Tom enquired where Joss was, or what he was doing, she asked herself how she could be denying this little boy his father. She had always criticized her mother for neglecting her, and now she was doing the same, except worse because she was lying to Tom constantly now, pretending that things were the same when for him they were about to be very different. They would work something out, she told herself. They would find a way. But the more she reassured herself, the less confident she became.

It was bill season. The electricity was not too bad because it was summer, but the phone bill was more than twice as big as it had ever been. Calls to Ella, Clare thought. But there had only been one or two. Their long conversation about what had happened between her and Joss had been at Philippa's expense from the Hampstead house and was too recent to appear on a bill. It had been a frustrating call. She had found it difficult to know what Ella thought. Part of her had been expecting enthusiastic approval, but all Ella would say was 'it's up to you, Mum,' in a resigned voice. They had promised to write to each other.

Clare turned to the itemized listing. The same number appeared again and again, and it was a number she did not recognize. She would have to make a list of things to discuss with Joss. If she did not then he would direct their conversation and he was useless at detail, pretending a kind of artistic impatience with trivia. She was about to put the bills on the kitchen table when she saw the envelope with her name written on it.

It was just one piece of paper and his sloping handwriting covered it neatly, leaving approximately an inch frame all round. Her initial reaction was to wonder whether it had just come out like that, or whether this perfectly centred page was the result of many drafts. She sat down to read it, then realized that she could not with Tom dancing around her, knowing somehow that reading the letter was going to be a pivotal point in her life that demanded a certain concentration and quiet space. She remembered feeling exactly the same way on her wedding day, when she arrived at the register office alone, excited, but fighting the urge to run away, wanting somehow to duck the responsibility of changing her life irrevocably.

There was pasta sauce in the freezer. The date label said 1st May 1997. The day she had made a wish for change. Clare stared at it with a sad, ironic smile. Her wish had been granted, a hundredfold, but if she had been able to see the future then, she did not know whether she would wish it again. Like all fairy stories, the moral was not to underestimate the power of magic. Unless you locked your wish in with conditions, as she could remember doing whenever she won the pull of a wishbone or caught a falling leaf when she was a child, then your gain might well be balanced by loss. She had lost her husband, which was what she supposed the original wish had been all about, but she had lost her father too and in doing so discovered a sister. And then she had lost her sister. And then she had found her mother. It was all very peculiar. She made Tom his supper then put him to bed, holding him very tight when he gave her his good-night hug.

Clare,
I see you in my class that first day of term. Your hair spotlit white-gold in the shaft of sun, and your face wistfully watching the sky through plate glass, paying no attention to the notice about canteen facilities I was obliged to read to the class. How other-worldly you were, a mermaid washed inland, floundering in the dust of the city and how I longed to take you back to the sea, to set you free again. You flourished here and bore my children and suckled them on the seashore, Madonna of the Rockpools, and every time I see you now, I think of your shining hair and its affinity with the sun. Clare running along the beach, Clare hiding among the raspberry nets, Clare on the clifftop path, thinking herself unobserved, betrayed by her phosphorescent tresses.
My love,
Joss

The piece of paper in Clare's hand shook as she began to weep. She stared helplessly as tears fell on the page and the letters blurred like chalk pavement pictures in the rain. She remembered that first encounter. How he had looked directly into her eyes and she had shivered with *déjà vu*, as if their souls had touched before and now recognized each other. The feeling was so powerful she had not been able to meet his eyes again, and so she had stared out of the window, hearing the lazy drawl of his voice, but not what he was saying. And she remembered, as if it were a photograph, the scene on the beach that he had written about so vividly before. The first time they went out after Ella was born, the three of them together. Clare had been dazed from lack of sleep but so proud. They had meant only to go for a short walk, but it was such a beautiful evening and they had found themselves far down the beach, just wandering, holding hands, with Ella strapped to her chest in a sling. Then Ella had yelled with hunger and Clare had sat down on a rock to feed her, bathed in the golden evening sunlight, while Joss skimmed stones out to sea.

Is that it? she asked him silently, reading the prose poem again. Is that all you thought of me? A mermaid, a Madonna, a head of golden hair.

But perhaps it was no different from what she had thought of him. A prince who rescued her, the black curls, the lulling enchantment of his voice. Perhaps that first impression was what remained, and if it lived for ever you called it love at first sight, and if it failed, you called it infatuation.

She thought about the terrible weeks she had nursed him through pleurisy, and the moment she had confronted him with his affair with Joni, and the pain she had suffered with the first ectopic pregnancy, and the rush to hospital with her second. She thought about the moment earlier that year when the letter arrived from University College Hospital offering Ella a place, when both of them had been such embarrassingly triumphant parents they had made their daughter's cheeks fire. And she thought about the constant gift that was Tom. She began to weep again as memories of their life together collided in a kaleidoscope of acute pleasure and pain. And she knew that if he were here now she would forgive him as she had always forgiven him, knowing that no-one else would ever be

411

able to make her touch the extremities of sensation as he did.

Where was he, she wondered, gulping for breath. With Holly? She did not think so. The very things that attracted them to one another would even now have put them asunder. Holly was as competitive as he was and as quick and as manipulative. Neither of them would relinquish centre stage for very long. He had referred to her as a whore, which said more about him than about Holly, but it showed that she was only another woman he would use and discard, probably just because she was so very clever, and therefore threatened him.

Joss must have come into the house after she and Tom had left for London, because he had placed the letter on the table. And he must have done that a few days before, because the post had built up behind the door since anyone had been into the house. She went upstairs again. The drawers in which he kept his clothes were empty and their one good suitcase had gone. In the tiny room he used as an office his most recent manuscript had disappeared. Ella's laptop computer sat on the desk, with a pile of paper on top of it.

Clare stared at the typewritten note on top of the pile.

Dear Clare,

I have decided to visit Italy, with a view to settling there. I am writing to Ella to tell her that she will always be welcome wherever I make my home, and Tom of course, when he is old enough. But the children have always been yours, and you will do as you think best. There are some poems on my desk, some of them about Tom, some not. Perhaps you could read them to him with my love. Joss.

As a PS he had added his address, and an E-mail number.

'You bastard,' Clare said to the empty room.

'Did you fancy Robert Carlyle?' asked Colette, as she and Holly emerged into Leicester Square after seeing *The Full Monty*.

'He's sex on legs,' said Holly, 'very short legs, of course, but somehow he's still sexy . . . he's the first knowingly-short man I've ever gone for . . .'

'What do you mean, knowingly-short?'

'Most actors are short, but some are so short that all the special effects in the world can't make them look tall . . . the computer programmer who comes up with digitally-enhanced on-screen height is going to be a rich man . . .'

'Loads of short men are sexy,' Colette argued, 'd'you fancy a Mexican? I'm starving . . .'

'As long as it's not Taco Bell. What about that place off Long Acre?'

They both turned and started walking towards the opposite side of the square.

'Such as?' Holly was back on small men.

'Gary Oldman . . .'

'Gary Oldman is sexy because he's weird and un-knowable and he sounds like all the boys we grew up with. Height doesn't come into it . . .'

'I'm not saying that he's sexy because he's short, just that being short doesn't stop him being sexy . . .'

'All right,' Holly conceded, 'why didn't any of the boys we grew up with become film stars, do you think?'

'You've forgotten the boys we grew up with,' Colette said. 'What about Dustin Hoffman?'

'What about Dustin Hoffman? Dustin Hoffman is not sexy,' Holly stated categorically.

'He is!'

'Just one film . . . after *The Graduate* they did their best to promote him as a pin-up, so why does he end up playing a crippled alcoholic tramp with TB, a middle-aged housewife and an idiot savant?'

'Because he's a great actor,' Colette said.

'Because he's short, that's why . . .'

'You're so bigoted,' Colette told her, as they sat down at a table under a ceiling fan.

Sometimes Holly wondered why she and Colette still called themselves friends. They bickered all the time and at some deep level didn't really like each other very much any more, but they had known each other so long they were a bit like family which went even deeper. They knew so much about one another that they never had to explain or put on a show, which was vaguely relaxing, and, also like family, their pasts were so entwined they would never get rid of the other one, even if they wanted to.

'I'm just tall. It's all right for you, little Miss Average Height . . .' Holly retaliated, 'now shall we have a pitcher of beer or margarita?'

'Margarita,' Colette took a quick look at the menu and sat back in her chair, 'so how did you get on?' She knew Holly was employing her usual technique of aggressive, rapid-fire banter to avoid talking about something.

'Get on?' Holly enquired disingenuously.

'At the agency . . .' Colette persisted.

'Decided against,' Holly told her, lighting and drawing on a cigarette. 'It wasn't so much the shame of having to find someone that way, as the idea that someone, one of my clients, even, might find me there . . . what are you having?' she asked, looking at the menu, 'have you ever noticed how it looks like you have the most enormous choice when you pick up the menu in Mexican restaurants, but when you actually read the descriptions they're all exactly the same . . . it's all tortillas and refried beans, even the do-it-yourself ones . . . how's Mr Jock Strap?'

'We're thinking of going on holiday together . . .'

'How tall is he?'

'Err . . .'

'Too short for me to borrow for a day . . . ?'

'Sorry,' Colette said.

'So, he's short, then . . .'

'You're so judgemental . . . no wonder you never find anyone,' Colette sniped.

'I may still find someone,' Holly said, rising to the challenge, 'there's two and a half weeks to go. Anyway, I've bought my dress . . . by the way,' she retaliated, 'you can't be judgemental about something like height which is an objectively measurable quantity. Why do you think it is you always choose short men?' she added, with the implication that there might be some deep psychological explanation for Colette's behaviour.

'Why do you always choose married men?' Colette shot back.

'Married men can get divorced,' Holly told her, 'short men never grow.'

As soon as she said it she knew she had gone too far. Having said that she was ravenous, Colette would only have a starter and then declined her invitation for more beer at the flat. Holly wandered back alone through the thronging crowds in Leicester Square.

She saw Simon before he saw her. He was walking up the street from the Trafalgar Square end, looking a little preoccupied, but the moment he identified her in the darkness he stopped and smiled broadly.

'Long time, no see . . .' he said.

'Whose fault is that?' Holly asked tetchily.

'Mine, I suppose,' he conceded.

His disarming pleasantness made Holly instantly ashamed of her petulance.

'I'm sorry, I sound like a nagging wife.'

He smiled.

'Coming up for a drink?' Holly asked.

Simon looked at his watch, then at her. It was after midnight, so she expected him to decline.

'Yeah,' he said, 'why not?'

It seemed like ages since they had done this. Holly opened a bottle of white rioja she had bought with Colette in mind, but forgotten to put in the fridge. They drank it warm.

'How's insurance?' she asked him, hoping that for once she had remembered his field of expertise correctly.

'Fine. How's the agency?'

'Pretty dull at the moment. Or maybe it's me that's dull. I feel a bit stale, need a holiday, that sort of thing.'

'You just had a holiday . . .'

'When? Oh, you mean Cornwall . . . that wasn't much of a holiday . . .' she let out a brief, rueful laugh, realizing that they had not spent much time alone together since her precipitate return.

Simon raised an eyebrow.

'. . . what with Princess Diana dying, and all that . . .'

Simon said nothing, but she knew he knew she was hiding something.

'I misbehaved . . .' Holly admitted, then because he still said nothing, 'with Clare's husband . . .'

'My God, Holly, first the boyfriend, then the husband . . . what's got into you?'

'What boyfriend? Oh, Matt . . . how did you know?' she asked.

'It's summer. You open windows in summer . . .'

'All right, don't go on. It's embarrassing enough . . . I only gave the husband a blow-job,' Holly said, in her defence.

Simon threw back his head and roared with laughter.

'Clare hates him anyway . . .' her brain tried to spark some more mitigation, but failed, 'still bad, isn't it?'

'Very bad,' Simon said, but he sounded more amused than critical.

'How's Tansy, anyway?' Holly asked him.

'All right.'

The conversation seemed to be petering out, but Holly was desperate for him to stay. She knew that if he went she would only finish the bottle on her own, and maybe start the next, and she knew that it was bad to drink alone, although she was never quite sure why it was so much worse than drinking with some other wreckhead.

'I bought a dress for Mo's wedding,' she said suddenly, 'will you tell me what you think?'

'Of course.'

She disappeared into her clothes room for a few minutes, then came back wearing the English Eccentrics dress she had stopped off at Fenwicks to buy on her return from the dating agency. It was almost floor-length and made of devoré velvet in soft sea colours. Who needs a man when you can look like a Thirties film star? she had asked herself, twirling in front of the mirror. The dress fitted her like a mermaid's skin. It was made for her. Problem solved, Holly had thought triumphantly as she handed over her credit card.

'You don't like it,' she said, dismayed, as she saw Simon's face.

'No, I do like it . . .'

'But? I can tell there's a but coming . . .'

'Well, I just wondered what Mo's wearing and what time of day the wedding is and all that . . .'

'Noon at Camden Register Office,' Holly said impatiently.

'Why Camden? You can get married almost anywhere nowadays . . .'

'Eamon lives there. I don't know. What does it matter anyway?'

'Have you ever been to Camden Register Office?' Simon asked.

'No.'

'It's right outside St Pancras . . .'

'So?'

'Well, to me that dress says champagne and caviar ball at the Ritz, and, well, Camden Register office is more mug of tea at a greasy-spoon café opposite a sleazy main-line station . . .'

'Oh . . .'

Crestfallen, Holly tried hard to hold back the overwhelming urge to cry. Whatever was the matter with her these days? It had always been a point of principle for her not to be the sort of woman who cried, and now she seemed to cry all the time. Recently, all the things that used to give her pleasure had become hurdles to jump. She couldn't seem to get up the enthusiasm to work, no-one wanted to play, and whenever she drank she wondered whether she was becoming an alcoholic. There were articles everywhere about totally normal people who were alcoholics and they seemed to drink far less than she did.

'I mean, it is fantastic. It makes you look so glamorous . . .' Simon tried to backtrack.

His eyes travelled up and down her body in a way that made her feel slightly self-conscious, as if there were a draught blowing round her waist.

'All right, no need to sound so bloody surprised . . .' she said, swallowing the tears.

'You look really, well, slinky . . . it's just that you're so tall and Mo isn't and . . .'

'And you think she might think I was upstaging her . . .' Holly slumped into the low armchair. 'Oh bloody hell!' she said, 'I don't even want to go to this fucking wedding . . .' She looked up at him desperately as the tears began to course down her cheeks. 'You wouldn't do me a big favour, would you?'

'Of course I would,' Simon said immediately. In all the years he had known her, he had never seen Holly cry.

'Come with me?' Holly pleaded.

Everyone else in Penderric had known for weeks about Joss's affair with the Italian woman from the poetry festival. Apparently Joss had told Jeremy, Olivia's husband, during one of the poets' meetings. When she heard that, Clare wondered briefly, why Jeremy? She didn't think he and Joss had ever been particularly close and she was almost certain that Joss and Olivia had been having an affair earlier in the year, but, of course, that was it! The juicy titbit had been tossed in Jeremy's direction as a kind of consolation prize for Joss's dalliance with his wife. Jeremy had always been rather a weak character. Clare could imagine him preening with the knowledge that he had become Joss's confidant.

She learned all the facts sitting in Amelia's tea shop after dropping Tom at his playgroup. Amelia was overbearingly concerned about Clare's welfare at the same time as being visibly cross that Clare had completely forgotten to deliver any jam for the past two weeks.

'I do think you might have called,' she chided Clare.

'I'm sorry,' Clare said.

'I had to buy a few jars of Tiptree to tide me over,' Amelia said, looking hurt. 'I will be getting my usual order this week, won't I?' she asked with a slightly threatening edge to her voice. Deliver or die was the message.

'No, I'm afraid you won't,' Clare heard herself saying, 'I'm not making any more jam . . .' Her hands were shaking with the shock of her unexpected resolve. She drained the willow-pattern cup. Amelia did make a

419

very nice cup of Earl Grey, she thought, as she stood up and walked out.

Vivienne was equally concerned, and dying for the opportunity to bitch about Joss. Clare was not surprised by the level of support when it was so clear that Vivienne felt Joss had betrayed her too.

'We wondered what had happened to you,' she said.

'I've been in London . . .' Clare told her, 'but what I don't understand is how? How did they communicate?'

'Apparently they wrote each other poems,' Vivienne said.

'But I'm always up earlier than Joss. I always see the post . . .'

She thought of the large phone bill, but she couldn't imagine Joss extemporizing poetry or even reading it on the phone, and she could not recall any awkward moments when she might have caught him talking.

'E-mail,' Vivienne said. 'We feel so guilty about it because when he asked Pepe about Internet servers and all that we had no idea . . .'

It took a while for the information to sink in, then the thought of Joss using Ella's computer for his billets-doux made her feel physically sick.

'Are you going to be OK?' Vivienne asked.

'I'm going to be fine,' Clare assured her.

As they walked back up the hill towards the little cottage, Clare asked Tom, 'How would you like to go to nursery school in London?'

'London is a big city,' Tom told her, 'Philpa, who called Granma, live there.'

Clare didn't know how much Philippa was going to like being called Grandma all the time.

'Yes, but how would you like to live there too, for a while?'

'Will my tractor be there?' Tom asked.

For one moment as he said the first two words,

Clare's heart stopped. She thought he was about to say daddy rather than tractor and she needed more time to work out what to tell him.

'Oh yes,' she said, picking the child up and hugging him, 'your tractor will most definitely be there.'

Chapter 33

'I, Maureen O'Mara, do solemnly swear that I know not of any lawful impediment . . .'

Mo's voice was strong and clear. The confidence of it moved Holly as she understood for the first time that this was something her mother truly wanted to do. It was quite romantic really, she thought, fighting back the urge to cry. Mo's obvious happiness radiated from her and made the tasteful plain white dress and jacket she had chosen to wear almost luminous in the functional room. Her skin looked fresh and glowing with health, as if she had just returned from a wonderful holiday. A simple Alice band of tiny white rosebuds and forget-me-nots held her long hair away from her face, and it fell around her shoulders looking as if it had been brushed a hundred times that morning. When she reached the end of her vows her smile lit up the room.

It was the first time Holly had seen Eamon in a suit and she had to admit that from the back he looked what her mother would call a fine figure of a man. She imagined that Mo had had a hand in choosing the suit, which was dark navy and well cut. His voice was less certain than Mo's and he jumbled some of the words up and had to say them again several times which made everyone in the room smile. Holly watched as her mother's hand reached out for her new husband's, and, encouraged by the touch of her small palm on his, he managed to say the sentence correctly, and everyone spontaneously started clapping.

Just before Holly signed the register as Mo's witness, she caught her mother's eye. Mo's look said a whole lifetime of things to her. It said, I know that this is all the wrong way round and that I should be giving you away, but thank you for coming round to it. It said, I hope that you'll find a nice man to look after you. It said, just because I'm marrying him doesn't mean you're not still the most important person in the world to me, you know that, don't you? Holly nodded and tried to speak significantly and silently back, but all her effort was used up trying not to cry. Her hand shook as she wrote her name and she had to wipe her eyes with the soft sleeve of her jacket because, as usual, she didn't have a tissue, and although she knew Mo would have a packet in her handbag she couldn't ask at this moment, nor could she let her tears smudge the signatures.

In a second the moment had passed. Holly sniffed and was able to smile again. The wedding party moved outside where there was a ghastly concrete garden with a pathetic dribble of a fountain, like the centrepiece of a run-down shopping mall, but somehow it didn't seem to matter because Mo and Eamon's happiness transcended the surroundings and the photographs would recall only their smiles.

Holly thought about the English Eccentrics dress hanging on the rail in her clothes room and was unendingly grateful for Simon's astute warning. In this setting it would have looked not just eccentric but stark raving bonkers. In the end she had gone to Emporio Armani and bought a silver grey chenille jacket with black velvet buttons to go over plain black trousers she already possessed. The jacket combined understated elegance with a hint of festivity.

'You look very grown-up,' Simon had said when she opened the door to him that morning, which was exactly the compliment she wanted to be paid, and it had got the day off to a good start.

There was a banner strung above the entrance to the main hall that said Congratulations Eamon and Mo! The members of Eamon's band, the Old Flames, changed their suits to jeans and their ties to bootstrings and hurried to their instruments to strike up the first number. The room had been set out like a dancehall with a horseshoe of tables all around the central floor where Eamon and Mo would start the dancing later.

Holly and Simon joined the bridal couple at the top table and although he had never met him before, Simon fell easily into conversation with Eamon about England's qualification for the World Cup and the car that had broken the sound barrier in the Nevada desert days before. Holly watched Mo greeting friends who came to offer their congratulations. In the more subdued light of the hall, her skin seemed almost to have a golden tan. It made her teeth look very white as she smiled and laughed and held out both her hands to her star pupil who came up to present her with a bouquet of flowers. The girl then ran back to the group who had collected on the floor to perform a display of Irish dancing while everyone settled themselves down for their lunch.

'Did folk used to get married in the early morning?' Eamon asked nobody in particular, 'why else would it be called a wedding breakfast, do you think?'

He had a gift for putting people at their ease, Holly thought, trying to find reasons to like her new stepfather more. There was nothing wrong with Eamon, she knew that. It was just that she didn't think he was good enough for Mo.

'Isn't it marvellous to see your mother so happy, Holly?' Sonya asked her.

'Yes,' Holly replied, forcing herself to smile.

'Seven hundred and sixty-three miles per hour, wasn't it?' Eamon asked Simon.

Other members of Mo's classes, dressed in their white school shirts and black skirts, brought plates to the table with slices of ham, chicken drumsticks, and bowls containing potato salad and coleslaw. The older girls took orders for the bar. Most of the men in the room were drinking pints of Guinness and the women sweet white wine.

'I expect you'll be next, will you?' Sonya asked, nodding significantly at Simon.

'I very much doubt it,' Holly said.

'Well, never give up hope,' Sonya told her, 'Mo's living proof of that.'

My mother has not spent her entire life waiting for the moment some bloke would ask her to marry him, Holly was about to reply, when it occurred to her that she did not really know if that was true. When she was younger, she had taken it for granted that Mo had been happy enough living with her, but maybe she had always wanted to have a man around?

'Is this the boyfriend you've been keeping so quiet about?'

Mrs Draper, who had lived on the ground floor of their block of flats for as long as Holly could remember, was using the back of Holly's chair as a zimmer frame as she queued to kiss the bride and shake the groom's hand.

Holly's heart sank as it gradually began to dawn on her that she had overestimated Mo's friends by assuming that if she arrived at the wedding accompanied, they would be discreet enough to shut up about her marriage prospects. In fact, the novelty of a man at her side, particularly such a nice, approachable kind of a man had made them more curious than ever. It would have been better to come alone and suffer alone, she thought, than to subject both herself and Simon to this scrutiny. Simon's presence alongside her also made it much more difficult to lie.

For a moment she saw him as others must see him. Tall enough, good-looking enough, nice enough to be the sort of man to whom any woman would be fortunate to plight her troth. She wondered if he would marry Tansy. Simon dutifully kissed Mrs Draper's proffered cheek that smelled of stale face-powder and mothballs as old ladies' skin often did.

'Oooh, if I were fifty years younger, I'd snap him up!' Mrs Draper squealed.

'I don't mind if I do,' Simon told Eamon who was asking him if he wanted another Guinness.

'Have you ever been to Ireland?' Eamon asked him.

'No, always wanted to though . . . they say the Guinness tastes different there . . .'

'It does . . . it's a long time since I've tasted any, mind you. You should take Holly one day. She's not been, have you, Holly?'

'No,' said Holly, impatiently, 'but Simon and I are not in the business of going on holiday together. We're just neighbours, as you know, Eamon . . .'

Simon's face said that he didn't mind, but Holly was determined to spare him further embarrassment. Why was it, she wondered, that perfectly nice people who normally would not dream of asking personal questions became brutishly insensitive when there was a single woman in her twenties or thirties around?

'Any chance of a gin and tonic?' she asked one of the waitresses, 'large?'

'Holly's in the film business,' Eamon was telling one of his friends. He pronounced it fillum just as Mo did. Holly gulped the gin and tonic as if it were water.

426

'What's your favourite film, Eamon?' she said, making an effort to join in.

'Ah, now that would have to be *Nashville*,' he replied.

The answer could not have surprised Holly more. It was one of her favourite films too.

'Really?' she asked.

'If it ever comes on telly, I can recommend it unreservedly,' Eamon said, for the benefit of anyone who was not familiar with the movie, 'it has some lovely songs . . .'

Holly couldn't work out from his twinkly eyes whether he was teasing her, or whether he had actually experienced the biting satire about American politics as a simple musical. It *was* a musical, she reminded herself, and it did contain some lovely songs. What did it matter what reasons Eamon had for liking the film anyway. She hated tight-assed poseurs who couldn't enjoy themselves without going into some big intellectual analysis, and now she was becoming one of them. Holly stared at her empty glass wondering whether it was alcohol that filled her with self-loathing, or whether the self-loathing was hidden there all the time and the alcohol merely released it.

'Yes, I'll have another,' she told the waitress.

Eamon made a simple speech thanking everyone for being there, and one of his friends acted as best man and gave a potted history of Mo and Eamon's relationship. They had met at a line-dancing class, he informed anyone who did not know, and he hoped that their future would be filled with music and rhythm and that their bodies would move in perfect time together. Mo blushed so pink it looked as if she were sunburnt. While he was speaking the waitresses charged everyone's glass with the champagne that was Holly's contribution to the feast.

'The bride and groom!'

Everyone stood up, drank the toast, sat down and began to applaud.

'Do you think I should say something?' Holly whispered to Simon.

'No,' he told her, 'I think Mo would be embarrassed.'

'No, I think I must,' Holly said, chiming her fork against her glass.

The room fell silent again. Holly glanced at Mo and saw pure fear on her face.

'I've known Mo for a long time,' Holly said, and there was a ripple of laughter, 'and anyone who knows her can see that she's very happy today, and all I wanted to say was I'm really pleased about that, and I hope you'll look after her, Eamon, because she deserves the best . . .' Stranded mid-sentence, not knowing where to go next, Holly decided to sit down, and everyone clapped again.

Mo smiled at her.

'That was very nice,' she said, relieved.

'I'm sorry,' Holly told her, 'I just thought someone should speak for you . . . Mum, am I drunk, or have you been on a sunbed?'

'Is it that bad . . . ? Oh come on . . .' She took Holly's hand and they scuttled off to the Ladies together.

'Jesus!' Mo said looking in the mirror, 'I thought Sonya was laying it on a bit thick . . . she gave me a self-tan treatment this morning . . .' Mo turned on the tap and started scrubbing at her skin.

'I don't think that's going to do it,' Holly said, looking at herself in the mirror next to Mo. The bare light bulb was not kind.

'It just keeps getting browner,' Mo said desperately, staring at herself as if she would stop the tone deepening if she looked at it disapprovingly enough.

'Don't worry, everyone'll think you've gone to the Bahamas for your honeymoon . . . where are you going, by the way?'

'Ireland . . . flying out tonight, staying at the Shelbourne Hotel, if you please,' Mo hesitated and took a deep breath. There was never going to be a good moment for what she had to say. 'And tomorrow we're driving across to Galway to look at properties . . .'

'You're going to move to Ireland?' Holly's tone was immediately hostile.

'Not right away,' Mo tried to back off. How cowardly she was to try to slip it in at a time when it would be virtually impossible for Holly to make a fuss.

'Well, there's no point in us keeping two places here and you'd be surprised what Eamon's little terraced house is worth now . . . he's got the offer of early retirement. It's a good package . . . and his brother says there's tons of work there these days . . .' She found herself disclosing all their plans in Holly's stunned silence.

'So Eamon's going to move into our, I mean your, flat?' Holly asked eventually.

'In the meantime, yes . . . oh come on, Holly. We'll probably see each other as much as we ever do. There are flights every hour and it doesn't cost a fortune . . .'

The words had the strange echo of a plea Holly herself had made years ago when she left home. It's not like I'm moving to the other end of the earth, she had told her mother. It's only a tube ride away. She remembered Mo's sad, brave look, and she now understood how lonely her mother must have felt. For all her insistence on independence, Holly realized that Mo's flat had always been there for her, a bolt-hole in times of trouble.

'I'll miss you a lot,' Holly said.

'We'll still see each other, of course we will . . .'

Mo stretched out her hand, and Holly took it. The two women looked at each other in the mirror above the row of sinks.

'Do you think if Jack hadn't died you'd still have

429

married Eamon?' Holly asked her mother's reflection.

'No, I don't suppose I would,' Mo's reflection admitted, after a long pause, 'but I'm glad to be free to marry Eamon. We are happy together . . .'

'But if I told you that it was all a joke and that Jack was sitting outside in a white Rolls-Royce waiting for you, like in *Pretty Woman*, or something, what would you do?'

'Oh Holly,' Mo's reflection laughed and turned and Mo took her by both hands, 'why do you always ask such difficult questions?'

How was it that Mo's body was so neat, Holly wondered, as she watched her mother take to the floor for the first dance. If people thought that dancing was all about using your body to express emotion, they should look at Mo, because it was just the opposite. With Mo, it was as if the dance was using her body, not the other way round. Her long practice of Irish dance had made her precise and obedient. Where Eamon led, she followed, making him look as graceful as she was. It was a great gift.

'Can you two-step?' Simon asked Holly.

'Not really,' Holly said, 'Mo always tells me I'm too bossy to be a very good dancer.'

'Shall we have a go?'

'Can you dance?' Holly asked him, suddenly remembering the karaoke bar in Brighton and Simon's amazing ability to sing.

'A little bit,' he said.

'Oh, bloody hell, why not?' Holly said.

She trod on his toes a couple of times before they got the hang of it, but when they did, the feeling was pure triumph as they grew confident enough to look where they were going rather than at their feet. The band twanged away, banjo, Hawaiian guitar, fiddle all taking their turns and if she closed her eyes Holly could imagine herself as Debra Winger in *Urban Cowboy*, a film she had always liked more than the reviewers.

Formal dancing was a turn-on, she realized, throwing off her jacket in the direction of her table and revealing a black jersey vest and bare arms. They circled round again. It involved total concentration, co-operation and consent. It was like giving your body up to a greater purpose, and if you got it right, the feeling of triumph did something to your pheromones or hormones, or whatever mones they were that made you feel sexy. Whoever put a stop to it in the Sixties had been crazy if they thought it was sexier to strike poses by yourself and spin about with your long hair whacking anyone who came too close in the face.

Holly hated the way that people went on about the Sixties. All that crap about changing the world that middle-aged left-wing intellectuals were so pleased with themselves about, oblivious to the fact that there was still war and nuclear weapons and torture and famine. The only visible difference the Sixties had made, Holly often thought, was that it was now acceptable for big businessmen to have beards. People like Louis Gold were always telling her that you had to be there. It was a revolution, a total break with the past. You mean the Pill, Holly would argue, that miraculously profitable invention by the pharmaceutical companies that turned sexual harassment into free love. You don't really mean that, they would say. No, I don't, Holly would think, but it's fun to see doubt cross your smug face.

'What's up?' Simon asked, seeing Holly's frown.

'I was just thinking how much I hated the Sixties . . .'
Simon looked perplexed.

'You were only a child . . .' he said.

'No, I don't mean . . .' She was going to explain but she knew he would think her barmy if she did. 'Oh, it doesn't matter,' Holly said, laughing breathlessly as the number came to an end.

'Shall we have a rest?' Simon asked.

'Yes, but we can dance more later?' Holly pleaded like a child.

'I don't believe it . . . you're enjoying yourself, aren't you?' Simon said.

'I really am,' Holly replied as he handed her a drink, 'thanks. Thanks for coming, Simon . . .'

'My pleasure . . .'

Holly had always considered Simon nice but a bit boring, and she wondered now how it could be that she had not found out until recently about the significant accomplishments he had kept secret for all the years they had been neighbours. He could sing and he could dance, and now he was behaving like the perfect gentleman as he noticed that Sonya was alone and asked her whether she would care to dance too. They whirled round the room, with Simon managing to avoid collisions and make small talk to a virtual stranger at the same time. Sonya always had the latest information about blocked pores and moisturizing colour-fast lipstick, but Holly couldn't imagine what titbits she might have to interest Simon.

Holly realized that she had never before seen him at a party. In her experience, the attractions of most men paled when you suddenly saw them through the eyes of friends or family, but it was just the opposite with Simon. For the first time since she had known him, she found herself wondering what sort of lover Simon would be, but quickly dismissed the thought. Every man she slept with she lost, and she had lost enough men for one year. Her friendship with Simon was far too valuable to chuck away out of curiosity. And there was Tansy, she reminded herself.

Mo's face was the colour of caramel by the time she and Eamon left the gathering.

Holly hugged her really tight before letting her get into the car.

'You're not losing me, you know,' Mo whispered in her ear, 'I'm harder to get rid of than that.'

'Just don't tell me I'm gaining a stepfather,' Holly whispered back, 'Eamon's all right, but I'm too old to want his opinions about the way I conduct my life.'

'You've never taken any notice of anyone's opinion about the way you conduct your life,' Mo chided, giving her one final squeeze, 'why should you ever start now?'

'True,' Holly admitted, 'have a lovely time.'

The others cheered as Eamon started the grubby old Metro. It pulled away slowly, trailing beer cans and green and white balloons. Holly ran alongside it down to the main road, not wanting to let her mother go. They had said goodbye to one another a million times, but this time it felt different. This time Mo was on her way to a truly separate life which did not involve her at all, and she didn't want to let her go. She ran until the car was going too fast for them to hold hands, then stood panting, waving until it disappeared from sight, and a moment longer.

Then she turned and walked back towards the rest of the crowd.

'Shall we go and get something to eat?' Simon asked as the hard core of the wedding party sauntered back into the hall. 'If we stay here, we'll just go on drinking . . .'

'What's the time?' Holly had no idea.

'Quarter past seven.'

'I thought it was about four . . . yeah, why not?'

Better really. She knew that the rest of her mother's friends would go on drinking until one or other got up to sing, and then they would all take their turn, becoming more and more maudlin as the evening went on. Simon had done his duty spectacularly well. It would be unfair to impose on him further.

'If you've got other plans . . .' Holly began, politely offering him the opportunity to be shot of her for the evening.

'No.'

'How about the Chuen Cheng Ku then?' Holly immediately suggested.

'How about Mr Kong?'

'Good idea,' on this particular evening, Holly couldn't be bothered to argue over the merits of their two favourite Chinese restaurants, 'it's on me,' she said firmly.

'Taxi or tube?'

'Stupid question,' said Holly, sticking her arm in the air at the sight of an orange light and only remembering as the cab screeched to a halt beside them that she had still to collect her jacket and bag from inside the hall.

The great thing about eating Chinese food with Simon was that he never said, 'Don't you think that will be enough?' when the waiter was taking the order. She didn't know whether it was the saltiness or the sweetness or simply the monosodium glutamate that gave Oriental food its addictive qualities, but she knew it must be something that was bad for her. Simon didn't mind as long as her choices included something loaded with chilli. Simon was a bit of a vindaloo man, if truth be told, but he never forced his predilection for an Indian upon her. Nor did he ever complain about the huge bills Holly always ran up. So many men let themselves down with meanness, Holly thought, but not Simon. He was a man of few complaints. When Simon had a cold, he either struggled manfully on, or he said that he had a cold, and that was that. Most men Holly had known were incapable of having anything less than an itis. A sore throat was tonsillitis, indigestion was suspected appendicitis and a headache sinusitis. They would emerge in a cloud of steam from under a towel with bleary eyes and a self-pitying expression, leaving the room stinking of eucalyptus for days. Simon just made himself a Lemsip and went to bed quietly without bothering anyone.

'So, how's Tansy?' Holly asked for no good reason.

'Fine,' Simon replied.

'Right.'

The food arrived.

Steamed scallops, salty spicy squid, Singapore fried noodle. Two bottles of Tsing Tao beer.

'If I had to eat just one food for the rest of my life it would be salty spicy squid,' Holly announced.

'No, you'd get sick of it . . .'

'I wouldn't. What would yours be?' she asked him.

'My favourite food?'

'No, not your favourite food necessarily, the food you would eat if you had to eat the same thing every meal until you die . . .'

It was important to get the rules absolutely straight in this sort of pointless game.

'This is not the same as if you were food, what would you be?' Simon asked warily, remembering the occasion when Holly had pronounced him mashed potato and gravy, after he had put great thought into a description of her as *crème brûlée* with exotic fruit.

'Quite different,' Holly said.

'OK then, how many veg am I allowed?' Simon asked.

'As many as you want, within reason, but you can't start slipping in dishes that are really main courses and saying that they're veg . . .' Holly warned.

'Right. Well, I suppose, roast chicken, new potatoes and runner beans and butter.'

'God, how boring!'

435

However hard Simon tried to succeed at one of Holly's games there was always something wrong with his response. He couldn't decide whether that was his fault or whether it was just Holly's unbelievable competitiveness.

'Dessert?' Holly demanded.

'You first.'

'I think it would have to be ice-cream, no, wait a minute, lemon meringue pie . . .'

'I once had a lemon meringue ice-cream in Devon,' Simon suggested.

'You're a genius! I'll have that then.'

'You haven't even tried it.'

'I trust you.'

He was delighted to have been of some help.

'You?' Holly asked.

'I'm not really a pudding kind of person.'

'I always forget to say pudding,' Holly mused, 'I know it's what posh people say, but where I grew up it was posh to say dessert. It's the one thing that makes me sound like Mo . . . anyway, you have to choose something . . .'

'Why should I?' Simon asked. But she could see that he was enjoying the stupid game as much as she was.

'How about a selection from the cheeseboard?' he said finally, and they both burst out laughing.

'I'm sorry about Mum's friends, you know, all that crap about us being the next and everything . . .' Holly told him.

'That's OK. That's how people are at weddings . . .'

'How come you're so sweet?' Holly asked him.

'Did you know that sweet is about the worst compliment you can pay a man?'

'Sorry. I just meant, you know, you're nice, pleasant, reasonable . . .'

'All nearly as bad as sweet . . .'

436

'Sorry. I would love it if somebody thought I was sweet . . .' Holly said, toying with her beer bottle.

'Only because you're not. Well, you are, but, you know, it's underneath. Shall we have another beer?'

'I think the combination's beginning to catch up on me. I've had gin and tonic, champagne, now beer . . . oh, all right then.'

Simon waved the waiter over.

'The trouble is, I'm a cow,' Holly said, suddenly gloomy.

'You're not a cow. You're incredibly bright, tough and difficult . . .'

'Oh. And I love you too.'

'I'm sure there's a soft centre there somewhere.'

'Don't count on it.'

'Actually,' Simon took a long slug of his beer, 'I do.'

'Count on it?'

'Love you.'

Mr Kong just wasn't the kind of place you said things like that. It was too bright and the tables were too close together, and it smelt of spring onions and hoisin sauce. Holly felt a little panicky.

'Are you saying that because you'd like to fuck me, or is it one of those I love you but we're no good for each other kind of admissions, or was it just a joke?' Holly asked, calculating that she had covered all angles.

Simon laughed. 'None of those,' he said, 'well, except the first . . .'

'What about Tansy?'

'Tansy didn't like me going to the wedding with you . . .'

'Oh, Simon, I'm sorry. You should have said . . .'

'Doesn't matter,' he told her, pushing some rice around with his chopstick in the awkward silences.

'So, did you hear what I said?' he asked her eventually.

'Yes,' she told him, 'I just don't know what to say. I mean, it's lovely, but we're friends and I don't want to lose you, I really don't . . .'

Simon sighed and took a sip of beer.

Holly remembered him two-stepping and tried to rekindle the rumblings of desire that watching him dancing with Sonya had aroused.

'Oh what the hell?' she suddenly said, 'things will always be a bit awkward after this conversation anyway, so we might as well give it a go . . .'

'You're so overwhelmingly romantic . . .' Simon exclaimed laughing and waving at the waiter for the bill.

The pavement of Lisle Street seemed narrower than usual. It was impossible for them to walk along beside one another without touching and yet every time their sides bumped Holly felt embarrassed, not knowing whether the agreement they had just entered into meant that they should be holding hands, or arm in arm, or just walking determinedly single file like two grown-ups who had struck a deal. Neither of them had said a word since except to thank the waiter. She could still get out of it, Holly told herself. And so could he. Maybe it was just a joke. She didn't know now whether she would be relieved or hurt to find out that it was. It might have been better, she thought as they turned into Wardour Street, if he had waited until they were back home with a bottle of wine, and then they could just have fallen into sex without either one of them really acknowledging what was going on. But at some point in life you had to grow up and stop using drunkenness as an excuse for a decision. Alcohol made it easier at the time, but afterwards there were still all those terrible unasked, unanswered questions about whether it had just been a one-off, or the start of something, and all those hazy memories about what you had done and hadn't done and whether either of you had enjoyed it.

'Your place or mine?' Simon said as they reached the entrance.

'Yours,' Holly said immediately, not wanting the memories of what might be a big mistake to haunt her own flat for ever, 'no, mine . . .' She changed her mind as she envisaged Tansy and Simon making out under Simon's maroon and beige duvet, knowing that it would be almost impossible for her to get turned on in that colour scheme.

'It's up to you,' he said, shrugging his shoulders.

'Don't pressure me!'

His face fell.

'All right. Mine. Look, do you still think this is a good idea?' Holly asked.

'I think it's a lovely idea, but it's OK if you don't . . .' he told her.

She unlocked her door. On good days, the sight of the dusty staircase made her think of Matt. On bad days, it reminded her of the rat who must have scampered up the threadbare carpet. Now she thought of them both and it wasn't a happy combination in the circumstances.

'Yours,' she said, shutting the door again. She had made love to lots of men in her flat and to no-one in his. That was what finally decided it.

She sat on his beige sofa trying to relax.

'Coffee?' Simon asked.

'Have you got any beer?'

He went into the kitchen and came back with two cans of Stella. Then he sat down beside her on the sofa and they both pulled the rings on their cans.

'I feel really nervous,' she admitted.

'Me too.'

Silence as they both sipped their beer, staring at the television as if it were on.

'Simon, can I just ask you whether you see this as a one-off or something more than that?' Holly finally enquired.

He threw back his head and laughed.

'I wouldn't be this nervous if I saw it just as a one-off.'

'Really?'

'Holly,' he took one of her hands and held it in both of his, 'I've been in love with you for years, you must know that . . .'

'I knew you loved me, sort of, well, I mean, we get on, don't we? We just get on really well . . . we have a laugh . . .' she was babbling to try to hide her confusion.

In love. He had said 'in love', which was lovely. But she wasn't in love with him. In love meant you had a kind of slight nausea in your stomach all the time and you tingled when he touched you. She wasn't tingling.

But Simon was about a million times nicer, kinder and more reliable than any man she had ever been in love with. And he understood her, and had seen her at her worst, and still he loved her. Most of the others had only ever seen her at her best, and that still hadn't been enough.

On the very same day Mo had decided to settle for second best, was she going to do the same? She had seen how happy Mo was. Never happier. So why not? You could wait for ever for the One, and even then you might get it all wrong. She thought of the grey hairs at the base of Joss Drummond's spine and his reluctant penis. And yet she had felt more powerfully for Joss in that strange week that she had known him than she ever had for Simon in all those years. But that just proved how silly 'in love' was.

Even if by some strange quirk of fate you met the man you were destined for, like Meg Ryan listening to the radio in *Sleepless in Seattle*, meeting was just the beginning. You never got to see what Meg Ryan felt about Tom Hanks five years later. Pretty fed up, Holly suspected. But at the end of *When Harry Met Sally* you did know that she would be happy with Billy Crystal, because they knew each other. That was it, Holly suddenly thought, wondering why she hadn't seen it before. It was a sign. She had been living in the middle of one of her favourite films without even realizing it. *When Holly Met Simon*. Even their initials were right.

'Can we have some music on?' Holly asked suddenly.

'What would you like?'

'*Frank Sinatra's Greatest Hits*.'

'Haven't got it . . .'

Holly's face fell.

'But I can sing one for you . . .' he offered.

'How about "It had to be you"?' she suggested, her expression suddenly demure as she looked at her hand in his, then looked up.

Simon smiled into her eyes, and she knew that he understood not just the request but the subtext. He took a deep breath.

'It had to be you,' he leaned towards her and kissed her softly on the mouth.

'It had to be you . . .'

Longer kiss.

Then there wasn't any space for the singing. They kissed for ages before going further, tasting and exploring each other's mouths and faces and laughing a lot, not out of embarrassment, exactly, but with surprise that they hadn't done all these nice things before. Then they slowly undressed one another and went into the bedroom. He was careful with her body, but gloriously competent, as if he had read the manual and knew how each bit worked.

Afterwards she lay cradled in his arms, feeling complete and contented.

'Will you marry me?' she asked him.

'Yes,' he said, as usual, then added, 'but will you marry me?'

'I think I'd better now,' she said, as if she had just lost her virginity.

The ringing woke them both up, but the phone was on Mo's side of the bed. Eamon grunted, turned over and pulled the sheet over his head.

'I am sorry to disturb you,' said the weary voice of the receptionist, 'but I have your daughter on the line . . .'

'Put her on.' Mo sat up, trying to find the light-switch to see what the time was. Two thirty. What on earth could be wrong? She didn't even remember telling Holly where they were staying. Oh yes. Mo's brain clicked into gear. She remembered now. She had been asleep. Now she was awake and her heart began to thump with fear. Why on earth would Holly be ringing the Shelbourne Hotel at this hour, on this night of all nights?

'Mum!'

'Yes? Are you all right?'

'Mum, I'm with Simon.'

Holly certainly sounded all right. A bit drunk and overexcited, perhaps.

'Are you OK?'

'I'm fine. We're fine . . .' There was a lot of giggling and shushing in the background, then finally she heard Holly saying, 'Stop it, I'm trying to tell her . . . Stop it!' then into the phone, 'Mum, Simon has asked me to marry him, and I've said yes . . . Mum? . . . I just wanted you to know . . . Mum?'

It was silly to cry when you were happy. Mo wiped her face on the stiff, clean sheet.

'I'm here,' she said, 'oh, Holly, that's marvellous news. You've made my day.'

442

PART SEVEN

November

Chapter 34

'All men are shits,' said Ella.

'No, really, they're not,' Clare tried to assure her.

'So, name one who isn't . . .'

Clare thought of all the men she had known: Jack, Joss, the other poets . . .

'Well, Matt's a nice boy,' she said eventually, 'have you heard from him?'

'Yes, he wrote me a letter describing in great detail his fling with an older woman. He said it got me out of his system and he thought we could now be friends . . .'

'Oh. I see . . . have you met anyone out there yet?'

'There's some guys who hang out in the bar we all go to downtown. Some of them are OK. But I'm not about to be a notch on someone's bedpost. I don't mind thrashing them at pool though . . .' Ella's voice had already picked up an American twang. Clare was relieved that she sounded so sanguine after all that had happened.

'So, you've found some friends anyway . . . are you having quite a good time?' she asked hopefully, but knowing what the answer would be.

'Mum, I'm having a desperate time. I'm stuck out here with these spoilt brats all day and when I'm allowed out at night the only people I see are other au pairs. I'm learning more about Scandinavian culture than American. And since the trial, the only thing anyone wants to talk about is Louise Woodward. It's like "Oh, so you're an English au pair, so how many babies have you shaken this week?" My kindly hosts leave the paper open on the kitchen table like a kind of warning to me . . .'

'Oh, Ella . . .' Clare bristled at the implied insult to her daughter.

'It's OK . . .'

But Clare could tell by the sudden monosyllables that she was on the verge of tears.

'You know you can always come home?'

'Yes. Don't want to though. I'd feel I'd failed . . .'

There was a long transatlantic silence, then Ella sniffed.

'Anyway, the good thing about being bored is that I'm not even spending my wages. When I'm through here, I'm going to put on my Hawaiian shirt and jump on a Greyhound bus and go wherever it takes me . . .'

'That's what I've always wanted to do,' said Clare, 'except I wanted to drive a Chevrolet from coast to coast . . . hey, you don't fancy . . .'

'What?'

'Shall we drive across America together . . . with Tom of course . . .'

'In a convertible?'

'Yes!'

'Next summer? Oh Mum, that would be fantastic . . .'

'D'you mean it?' Clare asked anxiously, 'I mean I don't want to cramp your style . . .'

'Mum, you've never cramped my style. I might cramp yours . . . but I'd be there to babysit Tom . . .'

'Oh, don't be ridiculous.'

Their laughter echoed across the Atlantic.

'Why next summer?' Clare suddenly asked, 'why not now?'

'It's getting a bit cold for convertibles . . .'

'Well, we could go south first. I've always wanted to see New Orleans. I can't bear to think of you stuck in some snowbound suburb all winter . . . listen, I must run. Philippa and I are going to a screening of Jack's film.'

'*Paying for It?*'

'Yes.'

'I've seen the trailers. Sounds terrible.' Ella put on an American accent, 'He went looking for his daughter and he found himself . . .'

'Oh God, really?' Clare's heart sank.

The screening theatre was in the quiet area north of Oxford Street that people had recently started referring to as Noho. Philippa and Clare emerged from the darkened room and walked through the brightly-lit empty foyer, then stood outside the entrance, disorientated, unable to decide which way to go. A sudden burst of an ambulance siren approaching a nearby hospital smashed through the silence and unlocked their voices.

'I read that there's a wonderful fish restaurant somewhere round here,' Philippa said, 'shall we try to find it?'

She didn't want to go home just yet. She needed to wander a little, breathe a little air before returning to the house.

'I'd like to ring Lucinda,' Clare said.

Philippa handed her her mobile phone.

Clare rang the house. Tom was fine. He hadn't stirred since they left.

'Sorry,' Clare said, handing back the phone, 'it's just that I've never left him with anyone but Ella before . . .'

They walked along side by side, each absorbed in their own reflections about the movie. Finally Clare said, 'What did you think?'

447

'I thought it was very brave,' Philippa replied, after long consideration, 'to put so much of himself into it. I don't know whether I would have thought that if he had been alive. I think I would have seen it completely differently.'

She had wanted the movie to contain a message for her. A farewell from beyond the grave, and she had sat on the edge of her seat waiting, but it had not come. And yet, it had told her much about the preoccupations of the man she thought she knew so well. This was the one film he had struggled to make and she could now see why. He had used every cent of the box-office clout he had achieved to persuade the studio to undertake this movie – they had not originally wanted to. The endless rows about the final cut had kept him in Hollywood, and eventually he had won the argument. It was almost as if he had known that it would be his last film. Ironically, he had even said that, she now remembered, the night he returned from the States. The night before he died.

'At this rate, it may be the last thing I direct.'

She could still see him smiling at her with that wicked smile he had when he knew he had triumphed.

'I suppose I admired it, more than liked it,' Philippa said to Clare. 'What did you think?'

'I didn't know what to think . . .' Clare said.

Paying for It was set in the bleak landscape of the homeless. In America, the early reviews were billing it as *Missing* meets *Midnight Cowboy*. It was about a man whose daughter runs away from home. In his search for her, he encounters a prostitute the same age as his daughter who refuses to tell him what she knows unless he pays her the normal rate for her time. As the story unfolds, the relationship between the girl and the man develops, and through her he begins to recognize not only his own deficiencies as a man, but also the failure of society to protect the vulnerable.

'I couldn't decide whether it was very moralistic, or just voyeuristic, and it felt uncomfortable being his real daughter . . . I mean, what on earth was he trying to say?'

For a moment Clare wished that Holly was there beside her and not Philippa. Holly would have known what to think.

'You mean the love affair . . .' Philippa said, 'I think perhaps he had to put that in for the studio. A controversial sex scene was like Jack's signature on a movie. I think that was the trade he made for doing the picture . . .'

It was the only tenable explanation for the very graphic, torrid sex scene between the man and the young prostitute at the end of the film, which had made her squirm in her seat, not with prudishness, exactly, but with the thought that there might be other areas of Jack's life that she had not known about.

They found the fish restaurant. It was late and most of the specials had gone. They both ordered homemade gravadlax. The waitress brought a basket of bread and a little pot of herbed butter.

'I think I need a drink,' Philippa said.

The cold wine seeped through her body like anaesthetic.

'So do you think I should give my blessing to the première?' she asked Clare.

Jack's films had always attracted controversy, and *Paying for It* was clearly going to stir up a debate about whether Jack Palmer had merely exploited the plight of the homeless in order to make a sugar-coated, soft porn movie, or whether his intention had been to draw maximum attention to the problem by making a film that people wanted to see. Anticipating a mixed reaction, the studio had decided that a première that raised funds for one of Princess Diana's chosen charities, would be a suitable way of generating publicity for the opening in London. They needed Philippa to turn up to show her approval.

'It's up to you,' Clare said.

'Would you come?'

'No. I'm going away,' Clare said firmly. She knew she would not be brave enough to arrive at such an event. She had made a kind of reconciliation with Jack and she would not do it again in public, not to promote this film at any rate. She had found the ending disturbing. The girl in the film was younger than Ella.

'Oh?'

'Ella and Tom and I are going to drive across America,' Clare announced.

'Oh . . .'

'What's wrong?'

Their gravadlax arrived. It was thinly cut and very good.

'I was thinking of going away myself . . .' Philippa said, 'but I just don't know if I have the energy to do it alone. I was thinking of India . . .' She said it almost as if she had expected Clare to come with her. Clare had a fleeting vision of her mother lurching along on a ceremonial elephant.

'Why India?' she asked, trying to suppress the smile the image produced.

'My father was brought up there, you know. It's always interested me, and I rather took to backpacking when I was in Spain . . .'

'Backpacking?' Clare repeated, astonished.

'Just jumping on a bus and seeing where it takes you, without all the bother of luggage . . .' Philippa replied, 'obviously, I'd want to stay in good hotels . . .' She grinned at Clare.

It was one of the rare occasions Clare had known her mother to make a joke against herself. She thought of her earlier conversation with Ella and how odd it was that all three generations of women should simultaneously harbour the desire to be blown like driftwood to foreign shores.

'Well, you must go . . .' Clare said.

'Perhaps. I feel I must do something. I haven't really *done* anything for months. I hate being underemployed. But I shall wait until after Jack's première. I might as well agree to it.'

Philippa ravelled a translucent slice of cured salmon round her fork. Then put it down. She was clearly preoccupied.

'Should I invite the other daughter?' she asked, 'to the première. Do you think that the other daughter ought to be invited?'

'You mean Holly?'

Clare had not told Philippa about the part Holly played in her split with Joss. It was too uncomfortably symmetrical. She had not wanted Philippa to appropriate Clare's betrayal as an adjunct to her own. What had happened was a fluke, and she resisted the conclusion that it might be part of a pattern laid down by their history. If you let yourself believe that the past determined what happened, then there was no future. And the future had become desperately important to Clare.

'I think it would be a lovely idea,' she said, relieved that she had already informed Philippa that she would not be going to the event.

'I was thinking that I ought to give the other daughter some of Jack's money . . .'

'She wouldn't take it,' Clare said immediately.

'But I should offer,' Philippa said.

'See what you think when you meet her,' Clare said.

'What about the other woman? Do I have to invite her too?' Philippa asked wearily.

'Mo? I think it would be generous of you. And fitting . . .'

'You would approve?'

'I would.' Clare smiled, thinking how odd it was that Philippa should seek her endorsement.

'Oh well then,' Philippa said, clearly quite liking the notion of herself as a generous and fitting benefactor, 'I suppose I'd better.'

Chapter 35

'It's sort of *Sea of Love* with laughs,' said Jeff.

Holly raised an eyebrow.

'It's a sitcom about the lonely hearts industry,' he went on as if his pitch had made that perfectly clear, 'there's this man and this woman who would be perfect together but they keep missing each other. First they try the personal ads, then they try teledating and then they join an agency, but even then they don't meet up, except perhaps in the last episode. Then there might be another series . . .'

'Oh, so you were just doing research?' Holly said without thinking.

'What?' Jeff blushed.

'Nothing . . . great idea. I like it . . .' Holly covered quickly, sensing herself blushing too.

'Smoke?' Jeff asked her, leaning across the desk.

She wondered if she ought to tell him that a regular wash under the armpits might be all it took to find someone nice.

'No, I don't any more. My future husband won't allow it . . .'

She never knew how to refer to Simon. Boyfriend sounded so teenagey, fiancé was just an awful word, lover was a bit intimate, partner was so politically correct, and friend didn't do it. It wouldn't make sense to say that your friend wouldn't allow you to smoke. It was the first time she had tried future husband, and she wouldn't use it again.

'I'm covered in patches.' Holly rolled up her sleeve to prove it.

'So you like my idea . . . ?'

'I do. I really do. I think you'll have to write an episode, though, but not the first one. People always make the mistake of trying to do the first episode. If you know your characters well enough, you should be able to do one of the middle ones, and then you don't spend the whole half-hour introducing people and producers will be able to get an idea of the voice . . .'

'OK. I'll do that. Thanks.' Jeff stood up to leave.

There was something very different about him today, Holly thought, and then realized that it was that he was smiling. It was the first time in months that she had liked one of his ideas.

'Good luck,' she said to him, as he left her office.

Jemima walked in and stuck a couple of yellow post-it notes in front of her.

'Charlie Prince would like to take you to lunch,' she said, 'and Simon rang to ask what time tonight.'

'Oh. Right. Thanks.'

'He sounds really nice,' Jemima said, looking at Holly as if she couldn't for a moment understand how she had managed to land such a charming man.

'He is,' Holly replied shortly and picked up the phone to dial his number.

Her hand toyed with the message from Charlie Prince. A few months ago, she thought, she would have been in a state of great anxiety about what two invitations to lunch in the space of six months might signify. Did it mean that he fancied her, and what was she going to wear? Now she didn't have to worry about things like that, and life was so much easier.

Simon answered his phone.

'Hi honey . . .' Holly said. She didn't know why she had taken to calling him honey, but she felt the need for an endearment to indicate the shift in their relationship. Darling sounded daft. It was weird to get to the age of thirty-six and suddenly have to learn a whole new vocabulary, like a foreign language in which she was not yet fluent.

'I think I said eight, at the club,' she told Simon, 'and we've got to eat there because Colette says Nigel can't stand hot food. I don't think somehow we're destined to become best buddies . . . no, you're right, it will be nice to meet him. He's probably not that bad . . .'

Simon was having such a positive effect on her, Holly thought as she put down the phone. Under the influence of his love, she made Jeff smile and toned down her bitching about Colette. Tonight they were going out as a foursome. Colette and Nigel, Holly and Simon.

She couldn't remember going out with Colette and two blokes since the time Tony and Alan Thomson had taken them to Margate in the summer of '76, the summer they all grew up. They seemed to get away with a lot that summer, Holly remembered, because it was so hot nobody's parents had the energy for a row. Holly remembered their screams on the roller-coaster and Colette throwing up all over Alan's hair. She had been so pleased that she hadn't been the one sitting in front of her. Then Tony had got done for pickpocketing. No wonder they hadn't gone out as a foursome since, Holly thought.

'I've done your typing.'

Jemima put a large For Signature book in front of her and waited as Holly checked and signed her letters. There were only a couple of mistakes, and Holly corrected them with her pen before handing back the folder.

'You can go now,' Holly told her.

'But it's only twenty past . . .'

The look of surprise on Jemima's face as she left made Holly aware of how horribly strict she must usually be.

'Time for a drink?' Robert stuck his head round the door.

'Not really. I've got a letter to write.'

'You're no fun any more . . . don't tell me you're giving up drinking as well as smoking?'

'No, but I'm going out tonight. I don't want to be drunk.'

'Why change the habits of a lifetime? Oh, don't tell me, because you're getting married. Look, I'm as pleased as everyone else about that . . . well, actually, I'm not . . . I much preferred you as a tortured old maid to a happy spoken-for . . .'

Holly laughed but refused to move from her seat.

'Don't go boring on me, Holly,' Robert pleaded, 'you're my only friend here . . .'

'Any other evening, Robert, but I have to write this letter . . .'

'Oh well, fuck off then.'

The office emptied for the evening. Holly closed her window. It was getting dark outside and the air was chilly, autumnal.

She looked at the piece of paper in front of her, then began to write.

'Dear Clare,

'I know that there are no excuses, but . . .'

She tore the piece of paper in two and threw it at the bin. You couldn't say there were no excuses then start listing them.

'Dear Clare,

'I don't know what to say to you . . .'

So why was she writing?

'Dear Clare,

456

'What happened with Joss . . .'

No, she must not mention Joss. No point in trying to blame him. This letter was all about taking responsibility herself. And, if he happened to read it, she did not want Joss thinking that she thought about him for even a second.

'Dear Clare,

'Words cannot express . . .'

Bin.

The clock ticked on. She had to send it tonight. If she didn't, Clare would not get it in time.

'Dear Clare,

'I've thought of a million reasons why I did what I did, but none of them excuse it, so I won't waste your time, but I am very sorry. I don't suppose that I even deserve to be forgiven but I loved having you as a sister. I'm finally doing something I know you will approve of, see enclosed. We'd both love you to be there, but it's probably too much to ask.

'I got an invitation from your mother to Jack's première and I was really touched to be included, but obviously won't be coming because I'll be on my honeymoon. I am going to write to her separately to tell her that.

'I hope we may be able to be friends one day. I would like that a lot and I know Simon would too. He sends his love, as does

Holly.'

Holly read it through, then wrote out an envelope and put it in along with a printed wedding invitation. They were getting married in a restaurant in Holland Park with dinner for about twenty afterwards. She was about to seal it up when she remembered she had forgotten to say the most important thing. She unfolded the letter and scribbled at the bottom:

'PS I will be moving out of my flat because we're going to buy a house in Brighton, but I can't bear to give up the tenancy, so would Ella like to have it with some of her mates when she comes up to medical school?'

'What are you going to wear?' asked Colette.

They were standing chatting in the cramped space between the sinks and the cubicle doors in the Ladies' room at Holly's club. Colette was retouching her lipstick.

'I thought the English Eccentrics dress. When I saw it I knew it would be perfect for a wedding, I just didn't realize which wedding,' Holly replied.

'But hasn't Simon seen it?' Blot.

'So?'

'It's unlucky . . .' Colette bared her teeth at the mirror.

'I don't believe in all that old and new and borrowed and blue stuff . . .'

'If you don't believe in it so much, why are you bothering to get married at all?'

'Because we've known each other so long as friends, and now it's different from how it was, d'you know what I mean? It's like we're making a statement to the world. Things have changed. We're now bonking too . . .'

'What colour is it, the dress?'

'Sort of bluey, greeny turquoisy, you know how devoré velvet is . . .'

'Married in green, wish you'd never been . . .'

'Oh shut up.'

'What's it like, anyway?' Colette extracted a tissue from her handbag, carefully folded it to a point, licked it, then removed a smudge of mascara she had detected under her right eyelashes.

'I've just told you.'

'Not the dress, the bonking . . .'

'Gorgeous,' said Holly, 'what's the word? I know,

458

consensual . . . it's the most consensual sex I've ever had . . .'

One of the doors to the toilets opened and two women emerged.

Colette and Holly exchanged looks. Women's toilets were a bit like a confessional, you could do or say almost anything there and nobody would tell.

'Don't you mean sensual?' Colette asked.

'No, I don't, although it is that too. It's like really enjoying each other . . . and I mean *really* enjoying,' she said, in case she hadn't made it sound sexy enough.

'Don't you normally enjoy it then?' Colette wondered.

'Well, usually I'm trying so hard to be the best they've ever had . . . with Simon I can just relax . . .' She saw that Colette had no idea what she had been talking about. However intimately you knew someone, Mo would say, you never knew what they did behind closed doors. For a moment Holly wondered whether Colette was a lie-back-and-think-of-England kind of girl, even though she spent half her life reading articles with titles like Ten Great Ways to Turn Him On.

Colette lit up.

'How's Nigel in that department, then?' Holly asked, staring at the cigarette.

'Very nice, thank you,' Colette said and blew out through her nostrils.

'We've seen the virtues of purpose-built,' Nigel was telling Simon, when the women returned to the table, 'you get the garage and a downstairs loo thrown in if you're prepared to forego a few period features . . .'

'True enough,' Simon said.

Colette's divorce was finally through and she was having to vacate the marital home she had occupied for so long. She and Nigel had decided to look for somewhere together, and Holly was glad that Simon had

459

managed to introduce house-hunting into the conversation after the interminable talk over the first two courses about their professions. Movies, insurance, jockstraps and skin diseases. Skin diseases had won out for longer than the others because Nigel was troubled by psoriasis and Simon had recently been suffering from a very stubborn case of athlete's foot. Apart from minor illnesses they seemed to have very little in common that you could talk about without the help of a few drinks, and they weren't being allowed a few drinks because Colette had announced firmly as they sat down that it wasn't fair for everyone else to get drunk because Nigel was driving.

Holly and Simon were recent converts to house-hunting because that was how they now spent their weekends. They'd decided on Brighton because Simon's boat was there and there were enough clothes shops and decent restaurants in the Lanes to keep Holly happy, as well as bowling, sleazy nightclubs and a permanent funfair. Simon talked about commuting, but Holly knew herself well enough to acknowledge that leaving a party she was enjoying in order to get herself to Victoria to catch the last train back was unrealistic, so they had decided to keep the lease on one of their flats. In the end they had tossed a fifty-pence piece and Simon's flat had won, which was probably sensible because it was at the back of the courtyard, quieter, and had been kept in better decorative order over the years, but Holly had felt the wrench when the coin fell tails up, and she had struggled with the urge to say 'best of three?'

It was fun snooping round other people's houses and laughing about their bathrooms afterwards, but they had not yet walked into one where they felt immediately at home. Mo said that you knew when you had found the place, you just knew. Even though they had seen several little terraced houses that Simon favoured, and one top-floor flat with sea view that Holly liked, neither of them had been convinced enough yet to take the next step of lobbying the other seriously.

Mo was back from Ireland with a photograph of the pink cottage on a harbour wall that she and Eamon had bought. It seemed a miraculous trade for the two up two down in a grimy street near King's Cross that was Eamon's home in London.

Everyone was moving on, Holly thought suddenly. Everyone was leaving the city and going into semi-retirement. She looked across the table at Simon, and his smile gave her strength.

They lay in bed together chatting that night. Holly loved the chatting almost as much as the sex. It was nice just having somebody there.

'Well, I can see why Colette's always accusing me of being judgemental these days,' Holly said.

'What d'you mean?'

'Well, if you were her, you wouldn't really want me to judge Nigel, now would you?'

'He wasn't that bad.'

'Simon, he's the sort of man who buys Lynx bodyspray . . .'

'Do you think so?'

One of the few minus points about Simon was that he just wouldn't be drawn into unfair criticism.

'Anyway, I think Colette's madly jealous of me,' Holly said with great satisfaction as Simon switched off the light next to the bed later that night.

'You say that as if you're pleased.'

''Course I'm pleased. There's almost nothing nicer than the jealousy of your best friend.'

'How can you say you're best friends, when you're so nasty about her behind her back?' Simon said.

'You can do that with best friends. In fact it's a

measure of your friendship how horrible you can be, and still be best friends . . .'

In the darkness, she heard Simon sigh. She thought she might have heard him mutter 'Women!' under his breath, but she told herself she hadn't. 'Have you ever muttered "Women!" under your breath?' would be one of her make-or-break questions.

There had been a time when Holly could drink coffee before bedtime and still fall fast asleep as soon as her head hit the pillow, but recently she had noticed that if she forgot to say 'decaffeinated' before 'double espresso' she was awake half the night. It was another thing she probably ought to give up. Her list of sins was becoming so short she could hardly dignify it with the term list any more. Smoking, no. Well, not really. You couldn't count a puff on Colette's Silk Cut just before re-entering the restaurant. 'Exhale,' Colette had reminded her, before pushing open the door. That was the sort of thing that made someone your best friend, Holly thought, although she couldn't see how to explain that to Simon. Excessive alcohol consumption, no. Even though there had been occasions that evening when Holly would have welcomed the freedom of speech that several very dry Martinis would have given her, she was glad that she had stuck to a couple of glasses of wine. Sleeping around, of course not. Not that she had exactly slept around before, Holly reminded herself, but that was more through lack of opportunity than restraint. It was amazing how easily you could give up all these things when you were happy, she thought, unable to resist doing a quick happiness calculation.

Work: 8. So it wasn't everything she wanted, so what?

Family: 8. She was friends with Mo again which felt much better, but Mo was going to live a long way away, and there was still the residual guilt about Clare.

Flat: 9. It had never been 10 since the rat, but now that she was leaving it she had become prematurely nostalgic.

Men: 8, almost 9. She loved Simon dearly and he was great in bed and she thought that one day she might feel passionate, but in the meantime, it was lovely.

Friends: 10. Technically she didn't know whether she could still count Simon as a friend, but she decided to anyway, because he was.

Holly did the mental arithmetic. Eighty-six per cent. Higher than it had ever been. And that was if she counted Simon as 8 not 9 in the men stakes. By settling for second best she hadn't just levelled out, but had actually given herself a ten per cent rise in happiness. Amazing, she thought, smiling to herself. Perhaps she should write an article for *Cosmopolitan*, with pseudo-scientific graphs and bullet points, call it something like 'Why Settling Down is Really Settling Up'. She turned over and drifted pleasantly into sleep.

Chapter 36

The weeds had already begun to take over the garden and some of the vegetables had gone to seed. How quickly nature reclaimed what was hers, Clare thought, absently deadheading the last of the yellow roses as she fumbled in her bag for the key.

'Are we going to see Daddy?' Tom asked.

'No. Not today. Daddy's gone on his holidays,' she hated herself for lying to him, 'and we're going too. We're going to America to see Ella . . .'

'Oh.'

She waited for him to say 'That OK, then,' but this time he did not. Children had favourite little not-quite-correct sayings that they repeated for days, or weeks. Then one day for no apparent reason they just stopped and moved onto something else and it was the adults who missed the phrases that had become part of the family's vocabulary, and who wished that they had recorded that little bit of development before it vanished without warning.

Clare stroked her son's dark gold curls, wondering what went on inside his angelic head. Did he have any sense of time? Did he know that Daddy had been away longer now than he ever had before? Would the conscious part of his mind forget one day that he had once had a daddy who chased him along the beach and made up better stories than his mummy ever could?

The anger she felt towards Joss on Tom's behalf was more painful than any hurt he had inflicted on her. She pushed open the door. The house was cold inside, uninhabited. They had lived there almost twenty years but all that time was as nothing now. Ella's life was the only proof that it had ever happened.

It disturbed her to realize that she had spent so much time with someone she had not known. She could not have lived with him if she had known that he was capable of leaving Tom so casually. She had racked her brains to understand it from Joss's point of view but she could not. Even if she had driven him to go, even if all the responsibility for their break-up was hers, he had still abandoned his son and, even in the deepest depths of her guilt, she could not find a way of blaming herself for that.

The house no longer felt as if it belonged to her. There had been times in the past few weeks in London when she had found herself missing the sounds of the sea, the distant drag of water on pebbles, the mournful cry of seagulls at twilight. Philippa's house was not home. There was no space there that she felt was her own. But this house was not home now either. She wandered round the rooms viewing them almost as an outsider, feeling no nostalgia for the kitchen where she had cooked so many meals, nor the bedroom where she had slept so many nights. The way they had split had negated the time that she and Joss had spent together. It was as nothing. Perhaps Joss had decided that the only way he could start again was to pretend that it had not happened. But, in doing so, he had denied her a past and denied their children's lives. She could not get her head round that.

Standing on a chair, she pulled down the children's paintings from above the cupboards, leaving white rectangles on the wall that had been stained ochre by years of cooking. She realized that she had come back not just to get the birth certificates for their passports, although that task seemed profoundly symbolic, but to pack up their things and move out. There was nothing to be said any longer. The solicitors could talk to one another. They could handle the sale, and do the sums. It did not matter now. Only in the garden did she allow herself tears, as she looked at the tangible products of her labour disappearing, the vegetables yellow and overgrown, the bean rows suffocated by convolvulus.

That night, when Tom was asleep, she began to clear out Joss's office. There were heaps of the unpaid bills he had snatched from her hand as they arrived, scowling at her as if she had been deliberately squandering fuel, insisting, 'I'll deal with it'. But after a while, when the red-bordered copies had arrived, it had been left to Clare to go to the bank, negotiate with Matt's father for a little more on their overdraft, and write out the cheques.

There were cardboard boxes of Joss's notes and unfinished poems, and at the bottom of one of them she found the manuscript of the novel he had once written. It was about a man who lives with his wife and child in a cottage by the sea and fantasizes about other women. Sitting on the floor, Clare read the first page: an image of a seagull poisoning itself by preening feathers covered with crude oil. With the objectivity of time, she was surprised how disturbing and beautifully written it was and she wondered why it had not been published. Then she felt a needle of guilt in her chest as she remembered secretly wishing it would be rejected, unable to bear the idea of her marriage being literally an open book for everyone to read.

She carried the boxes downstairs and piled them up in the garden for a bonfire. But then she brought them in again, choosing the sweeter revenge of sending them to him. She imagined his lover's face as she opened the door to the tatty pile of heavy boxes that would clutter up their life together with evidence of his past. Burn it yourself, she thought. I have cleared up after you for the last time. It took several journeys down the hill to the post office the next day, using Tom's buggy as a trolley, and many raised eyebrows in the town, but the great feeling of catharsis made the trips worthwhile.

Afterwards, she and Tom walked to all their favourite places to look at them one last time. She wondered if, when the little boy had become a young man, he would arrive in this godforsaken place one day in a camper van with some friends, and feel the pull of *déjà vu*.

'Holly sitted there,' Tom told her, pointing at a smooth rock beside a pool.

'Did she?'

She wondered whether it was the same rock that she had sat on to feed Ella that golden day long ago, but she thought not.

'Is Holly on holiday?' Tom asked.

He thought it was what you said when people you liked were no longer there.

'I expect so,' Clare told him.

'With Daddy?'

Chance, or had he sensed their attraction to one another?

'No, not with Daddy, with a nice man called Simon.'

'Simon,' Tom repeated.

The letter had arrived that morning, almost as if Holly had known it was her last opportunity to contact her. Clare did not know what to do with it. The hook of the offer to Ella of the London flat made it impossible to do nothing. She couldn't decide whether Holly was being manipulative, or whether it was simply a generous thought that had occurred to her as she wrote, and which she had spontaneously jotted down at the end. Whatever, it was an offer that Ella would find difficult to turn down.

Their lives seemed inextricably linked. But they had always been. It would be ridiculous now to pretend that she did not have a sister, when for so many years she had pretended she had one without knowing it was true.

'Shall we go and have some tea at Amelia's?' Clare asked Tom.

'Treacle tart?' he negotiated before giving his consent.

'Treacle tart,' Clare agreed, smiling.

'We'll miss you,' Amelia said.

'Yes,' Clare replied, unable to bring herself to lie even for the sake of politeness. She would not miss Penderric, not for a long time anyway.

'Is Ella all right out there? We've all been thinking of her because of Louise Woodward. I couldn't help wondering how you would feel if that was happening to Ella.'

'She's fine,' Clare said, adding in case she had sounded rude, 'thanks.'

'We're going to MERICA in a BIG CAR!' Tom informed Amelia.

'Really?'

'Well, we're going in a plane, actually,' Clare smiled, but inside she wished that Tom had not revealed their plans. She wanted to box up her past and leave it in Penderric. Even though she would not be there to hear it, she knew there would be speculation about what exactly she was up to. Was Ella in trouble in the States? Had Clare met an American man? How could she afford such a holiday when she and Joss had always complained about having no money?

'We will miss your treacle tart,' Clare told Amelia truthfully as she pressed the last crumbs onto the pad of her thumb and licked it.

Amelia smiled gratefully. She wasn't so bad, Clare thought. She was just another lonely woman married to another selfish man. She gossiped because there was nothing else to do. Perhaps they should have been better friends. But it was too late now.

'We'll miss your jam. And Tom's smile . . .' Amelia said.

Neither of them bothered to suggest that they keep in touch.

The furniture would be sold with the house. The one decent piece was the brass bedstead that Joss had restored in the early days of their marriage, but she did not want that to follow her to her new life. All she wanted to take with her were the children's things, their books and favourite toys, and the bagful of little dresses she had made each summer for Ella which she unearthed from the back of the cupboard under the stairs and found she could not throw away. Each garment produced more memories than any photograph could. Images of Ella growing up ran through her mind like frames on a video as she folded the little smocks and shifts and party dresses carefully into one of the boxes the storage company had provided.

The things she wanted filled a dozen boxes that would be driven to Philippa's house. The rest was going into storage. Tom stood in the little front garden wearing his yellow hard hat and watching the men move their stuff out. In an hour, all evidence of their life there had been transferred into the back of a truck. Clare picked up the little boy so that he could wave it all the way down the street.

She looked at her watch. She had timed it almost perfectly. The cab would be there in fifteen minutes. They went back inside. Two cases and her African shoulder-bag stood in the middle of the kitchen floor.

'Where's all the boxes gone?' Tom asked surprised.

'Into that big truck. You saw them.'

Their possessions had already become just boxes to him and his simple question filled her with optimism. Children adapted quickly and survived. They were going to be OK.

'Can I have an ice-cream?'

He had heard the tinkle of the van in the distance seconds before she did.

'OK, then,' she smiled at him and took him by the hand.

The ice-cream van climbed up the hill towards them on its way to the factory to fill up with its frozen cargo. Clare recognized Matt at the controls and waved him down.

'One last cornet for Tom?' she asked through the driver's window.

He smiled at her, switched off the engine and climbed into the back.

'Where's your white coat?' Tom asked suspiciously.

'I'm not on duty right now,' Matt told him, 'so this is a really special ice-cream for you.'

He squirted a trickle of red sauce all over the white pyramid and Clare instantly regretted not having packed a spare T-shirt for Tom in their bag for the journey.

Tom took the cornet and looked at it in wonder.

'I heard you were moving out,' Matt said to Clare.

'Yes. We're going to see Ella.'

'We going to MERICA in a BIG CAR!' Tom confirmed.

She saw from the envy in Matt's eyes that despite what he had written to Ella, he had not entirely got her daughter out of his system.

'I'm surprised you're still here,' Clare said, suddenly feeling awkward.

'I'm auditioning for a new band in a couple of weeks.

I decided to put college off again. Don't know whether I'll bother . . .'

'Oh, you should . . .' Clare said immediately, feeling very middle-aged as she heard herself, 'you'll regret it if you don't . . .'

He gave her the arrogant, insolent look she had always found so irritating.

'How's Holly?' he asked.

'Fine, I think,' Clare said, 'getting married . . .'

'Married?'

The surprise in his voice made her look at him again.

'Oh well, I'd better be on my way,' Matt said, closing the window in front of his face, so that she was left staring for a moment at peeling transfers of lollies in all shapes and lurid colours.

She looked down. Tom was holding his cornet solemnly in both hands as if it were a posy and he were a very conscientious page-boy.

'See you around.' Matt started the engine then pressed the button which blasted a speeded-up snatch of 'I'm Forever Blowing Bubbles'. They watched as the van chugged up the road and disappeared over the brow of the hill. And then their cab arrived.

Chapter 37

It was Holly's last day in the office before the wedding.
They'd decided to take a week off straight after to give
them time to sort their living arrangements out. Weekends were not long enough to make real progress
finding a house to buy, partly because Holly refused to
spend Saturday nights on Simon's boat, and so they
seemed to spend half their time on the train. Simon
had suggested that they check into a hotel in Brighton
for a week for what he called a working honeymoon and
she had agreed on condition that a) they would have a
real honeymoon in the Caribbean at Christmas and b)
when he said hotel he meant the Grand.

Holly stared out of her window, then back at her
desk. Even though she would only be away for five
working days, she found herself looking at everything as
if for the last time, wondering whether she would see
things differently when she was married. On her screen,
she scrolled through a list of the ongoing projects she
represented and their status. *The One* was now in
production, *Never Enough* was under option to a British
independent, *Soul Mates* was out on multiple sub-
mission . . . All of them were about single people in
their thirties. It had never before occurred to her that
agents represented their peers. She thought of her
colleagues in the offices down the corridor. Serena

Bean, a mother of two in her mid-forties, handled all the cooks and gardeners; Robert's novelists were nearly all youngish gay men; Louis Gold's screenwriters had been angry young men when he founded the agency in the Sixties, and now they were mainly self-satisfied older men who only got angry when they couldn't find a parking space; the ancient agents' clients were mostly literary estates.

Holly began to wonder whether she would now find herself representing situation comedies about newly-weds. Would she, in a few years' time, discover the next *Teletubbies*, or, God help her, *Barney*? Would the feature films she would then be touting be *angst*-ridden dramas about middle-aged adultery starring the leading actors of her generation, their once-beautiful faces sagging with age? She was trying to imagine Neil Pearson and John Hannah with thickening bodies and thinning grey hair when her phone rang and she picked it up straightaway, relieved to be distracted from the increasingly alarming train of thought.

'There's a Virginia Prospect here, says she hasn't got an appointment but she'd like to see you.'

The receptionist made it sound as if the person in reception had been making a nuisance of herself.

'I don't know any Virginia Prospect,' Holly said.

'She says try Ginger,' the receptionist said, wearily, as if this were a ruse she'd heard many times.

'Oh yes, of course,' said Holly, 'send her down.'

She waited outside her office as Ginger pushed a twin buggy the length of the corridor.

'What a lovely surprise!' Holly said, 'haven't they grown!'

Guy and Rose Prospect Prince were both asleep.

'We walked all the way here,' Ginger told her, 'and they finally conked. I'm just about conking too.'

She collapsed into a chair.

'I'm so pleased you're here,' said Ginger, 'I kind of

knew you would be, and if you weren't, it was going to be a sign . . .'

'You almost missed me,' Holly told her, 'I was just about to go and get myself made-over. I'm getting married tomorrow.'

'Married? Oh, I'm so pleased. When you left after dinner I said to Charlie we must find someone for Holly, but of course, you didn't need my help . . .'

For a moment Holly was about to say no, go ahead, find someone for me. She was certain that if anyone could find a suitable man for her, it would be Ginger. But she didn't need that any more, she reminded herself, she was marrying Simon.

'Sign of what?' Holly jerked herself back to the conversation.

'I've written that screenplay we talked about . . .' Ginger pulled a large manila envelope out of a string bag that was slung across the back of the buggy.

'What screenplay?'

'About the two sisters, born on the same day, you know . . .'

'Bloody hell!'

'You didn't mind, did you?' Ginger asked, her little elfin face puckering with anxiety.

'No, no, of course not. I thought it was a joke, that's all . . .'

'Well, here you are. I've called it *Jane and Mabel*.'

'*Jane and Mabel?*' Holly repeated, pulling the script out of the envelope.

'You don't get it. Oh dear. That's another tenner I owe Charlie. He said nobody would,' Ginger looked downcast.

'What do you mean?' Holly asked.

'Well, it's Cain and Abel, isn't it, the female version . . . except they don't kill each other . . .'

Holly burst out laughing, read the first page aloud.

'*Scene One: One candle on a perfectly iced cake in a*

Harrods box. Two shadowy adults in the background sing Happy Birthday unconvincingly. Baby stares at candle about to cry . . .'

'I thought of Rose in the starring role,' Ginger said, anxiously waiting for Holly to make some comment.

Holly read on.

'*Scene Two: One candle on an obviously cheap bought cake. Mother and baby giggle together then mother sings Happy Birthday with gusto and they blow it out together . . .*

'*VOICE-OVER*

'*Once upon a time there were two little girls.*

'*One lived with her mother in a tower in the middle of a big city where the lifts did not work and the garden was made of concrete. Every day, after school, she would climb one hundred and eighty-two steps to their flat, and let herself in with her key. She would throw down her satchel and gaze out at the chimneys and rooftops below and the great grey river that shone in the sun like a trail of silver, dreaming of being rich and famous . . .*'

'You would see a child doing all that on screen too,' Ginger interrupted, 'except I didn't know how to put that in the directions. I know I could have asked Charlie, but I didn't want him to read it, you see.'

'So, I'm the first person to read it?' Holly asked.

'Yes, 'cept for Pic, of course, but she's not the most unbiased critic in the whole world . . .'

'How is Pic?'

'Fine. She's going out with a particle physicist, whatever that is. He's very clever but a bit old for her . . .'

Holly looked back at the script.

'. . . *The other lived with her parents in a big white house that looked like a castle. Every afternoon she would lie on her bed in her smart school uniform listening to the rustle of the leaves in the tall trees that lined the street outside, dreaming that one day a prince would come to rescue her . . .*'

Holly stopped reading and smiled broadly.

'I love this beginning,' she announced.

Ginger looked relieved.

'Any other weekend, I'd read it straight away, but I just don't think I'll be able . . .' Holly began to apologize.

'For heaven's sake,' Ginger said, standing up, 'I don't care when you read it. It's enough for me to have handed it over . . . well, almost enough. I'm so pleased you were here. It had to be you, you see, because you gave me the idea . . . and Charlie says you're the best agent of your generation . . . God, he's so pompous sometimes . . . so I sort of can't wait to know what you think, but now that I've handed it over, at least I feel it's real . . . it's been such a struggle . . .' She paused for a moment. 'Do you think I know you well enough for me to give you a piece of advice on the eve of your wedding?' she asked, only semi-joking.

'I need all the advice I can get . . .' Holly told her.

'Make sure that you've done everything you want to before you start having these . . .'

Ginger pointed at her children's heads.

'They're lovely, but they're all-consuming and your brain turns to fluff, and you kind of lose confidence about doing anything else . . .'

If this was Ginger with a fluffy brain and no confidence, what on earth had she been like before she had children, Holly wondered.

'Charlie sends you his best,' Ginger remembered at the door to Holly's office, 'and says he wants lunch. Oh, and have a lovely day tomorrow!'

'So, how's the man in your life?' Danny asked.

It was the moment she'd been waiting for.

'I'm marrying him tomorrow . . .' she said, smiling triumphantly at her hairdresser in the mirror.

'Oh, that's nice. So you eventually decided to tie the knot?'

Eventually? We only started bonking a month ago, she wanted to say, realizing aghast that he asked the same question of every woman whose hair he styled and never even listened to their answers. She could have told him that she and Ralph Fiennes were getting spliced and he would have said oh, that's nice, so you eventually decided to tie the knot, and the next time she got her hair cut he would ask, so, how's the man in your life?

Or was it possible that Danny was really psychic, as he always claimed, and he had known, just as many other people seemed to have known, that Simon was the perfect man for her?

'Very nice,' she said as he held up a hand mirror so that she could see the back of her head. She'd asked him to do a kind of Thirties bob because she was growing her hair and she thought it would look better with her dress than the untidy dreadlocks that seemed to be her hair's natural state. He'd done an OK job, but she wondered why she always said very nice when the only time she had really liked her haircut was the day she'd had it all cut off. It was just what you said at the hairdresser. Somebody should record a loop of tape that you could slot in as soon as the hairdresser started cutting, which would blurt out meaningless dialogue while you relaxed:

'How's the man in your life? . . . We're getting married . . . Oh, that's nice, so you eventually decided to tie the knot . . . Going anywhere nice on holiday this year? . . . St Lucia, how about you? . . . We thought we'd try Tunisia . . . Is that OK? . . . Very nice.'

It would mean you could read in peace while he concentrated on snipping. Holly was dying to get back to Ginger's script, but tradition demanded that she try to be as beautiful as possible by the next day and Colette's wedding present to her was a Pampering

Experience at the Sanctuary and she was already half an hour late.

Holly couldn't face an hour's guilt-inducing talk about T bars and clogged pores so she cancelled the facial booked in her name and decided to spend the time reading the script, lying in a white towelling dressing-gown beside a pool filled with koi carp.

It was the most wonderful feeling to discover a new writer. Holly could go for months reading scripts without finding anything that gave her that buzz, and she would begin to wonder whether she was being too critical, or whether her luck had failed her, then suddenly a script would simply jump off the page, and she would know with certainty that she was onto something. She often thought that the only skill required to be a good agent was patience. In quiet times you just had to trust that good things would come to you and that you would recognize them when you saw them. It was tempting to clutch at perfectly acceptable but ordinary scripts and try to build them into something special, but it never worked. The writer either had a voice, or they didn't. Ginger did. A brilliantly funny and honest voice.

There were moments when the story was uncannily like Holly's own and she shifted around uncomfortably on her padded leather bench as it became increasingly clear that the working-class sister was going to sleep with the upper-class sister's husband. But there were a series of deftly handled mishaps before the moment, a couple of which made Holly laugh out loud, which was something you didn't do in the Sanctuary. She was three-quarters of the way through when she looked at her watch and realized that she was going to miss her massage if she didn't stop reading immediately, and she knew that she couldn't do that and look Colette in the face that evening. Holly locked the script in her locker and made her way to the treatment rooms. At least with massage you could pretend to fall asleep to stop the masseuse talking to you.

What did you wear to your husband's glittering première when your husband was dead and one of the major themes of the film was the gaping divide between rich and poor in today's society? For the hundredth time, Philippa wondered whether she had been right to agree to the première. However hard she tried to work out what Jack would have made of it, she could not decide. Sometimes she visualized him thinking that the whole thing was a great kitsch joke. He'd always had a fascination with tacky glamour, and nothing delighted him more than rubbing shoulders with the stars of catwalk and soap opera at Hollywood fund-raisers. At other times, she could see him raging with indignity at the trivialization of his work. The worst thing was not knowing, not being able to tell what his reaction would have been. It was as if he were slipping away from her.

She decided on black, then changed her mind to navy, not wanting the première to look like a memorial service, then she wondered about purple, but it was so unflattering, especially in colder weather. She decided to go to her favourite department store and have a mooch round Ladies' Fashions. It was the first time for as long as she could remember that she did not know exactly the shapes and colours of the season.

Wandering through the designer rooms, she recognized the assistant who'd been so kind to her the last time she had shopped there, and smiled at her. A flicker of alarm passed across the woman's face. Philippa remembered how distraught she had been when she was last there. Then the woman smiled back cautiously.

'Can I help you?' Mo asked.

'I wonder if you could?' Philippa replied, 'I've got an event. I need to be smart but not glamorous. I suppose a dress and jacket. I don't really want black, not just black anyway . . . I don't really know what I want . . .'

Mo realized immediately that her customer was buying something for Jack's première. She struggled with the impulse to thank her for the invitation she had received via Holly. She had declined it formally, but she wanted Philippa to know how grateful she had been. But all that was in the past now. She had a new life.

Eamon would not have objected if she had wanted to go, but she knew with absolute certainty that Jack would. It made Mo sad that the secret he had kept for so long from the woman in front of her had come out in the way that it had, sadder still that Philippa had turned out to be more forgiving than Jack had credited. To invite Holly to the film première was one thing, but to include Mo as well, that showed real class. All the times she had nagged him to be honest flooded through Mo's mind, and his response:

'She would never forgive me. No, I'm sorry, Mo, you don't know Philippa. What's the point? Everyone's happy this way . . .'

He was such a good persuader, it had taken her a long time to work out that no, everyone was not happy. He was happy. Everyone else in the equation was being deceived. But she had never been able to find a way of winning the argument. And if she was really honest with herself, half of her had wanted him to tell Philippa in the hope that she would kick him out, and Jack would finally come home to her.

Now she looked at Philippa with her shock of white hair and had the strongest urge to embrace her. If Philippa had asked for her advice when Jack was alive, Mo would not have been able to resist steering her towards something unflattering. On quiet days, the women who worked in the department would sometimes amuse themselves by choosing the garment they hated most and trying to flog it to some unsuspecting customer, usually a man buying for his wife or mistress, with no idea of style. But Philippa would never have asked her advice when Jack was alive. It was only without him that she needed help. Her confidence had drained away like the colour of her hair.

'Is it for evening?' Mo asked, knowing the answer, but trying her best to be professional.

'Yes.'

'How about velvet? Perhaps black with a nice rich colour over . . .'

With her hand outstretched, Mo walked towards a line of velvet jackets in rich, luxurious dark colours with black frogging.

'A bit too military,' Philippa said, absently stroking the silky soft pile, 'if there were something plainer . . . what about that?'

She pointed at a short dark red velvet jacket with large covered buttons.

'It reminds me of the skaters in Central Park,' Philippa said wistfully, remembering all the times she and Jack had stopped to watch the quintessentially New York winter scene on their Sunday morning walks in the city that for so long had been half-way between them.

'Do they do that in real life?' Mo asked.

Philippa looked at her, surprised.

'Of course,' she said, not unkindly.

'Oh, I thought it was only in the movies,' Mo said.

'Well, you're right in a sense. In the movies, they would wear a jacket like this. In real life probably more of a grey sweatsuit.'

'But you couldn't wear a grey sweatsuit to a film première,' Mo said, laughing.

'No,' said Philippa, looking at her oddly, 'no, you couldn't.'

*　　*　　*

It was their last night in England. Tom was in bed asleep, their suitcases were packed in the hall. Tom had insisted that they bring the tractor in and put it beside the suitcases and all that remained for her to do was to find a way of forgetting it that would not lead to an unhappy departure. Clare looked at her checklist again. Every item was ticked.

'What do you think?' Philippa asked, walking downstairs with a bias-cut black dress underneath the red jacket. It was the third combination she had tried on.

'I liked the black velvet trousers best,' Clare told her.

'Yes, so did I. Jack never liked trousers, though,' Philippa replied with a sigh.

Well, he's not around to see them, Clare felt like saying but stopped herself. Her mother's indecision and vanity were beginning to irritate her.

'Look,' she said, 'would you mind babysitting Tom for an hour or two? There's something I want to do in town . . .'

'But it's seven o'clock, everything's closed . . .'

'I won't be very long . . .'

'No, it's fine,' Philippa said, remembering her new, conciliatory self, 'be as long as you want.'

When Colette had suggested a nice quiet dinner, just the two of them, so that they could chat and reminisce and not get too drunk, Holly hadn't believed her for a second, but when she came to pick her up and they began walking in the direction of the Criterion where Colette had said they were going to eat, she had a moment's sinking feeling that her friend had grown so boring, that was really what she had planned.

Then, just before the Trocadero, Colette suddenly stopped in her tracks.

'Oh, I forgot to tell you, I changed the venue,' she said, 'we'll need to take a cab.'

Automatically, Holly's arm shot into the air as

several black cabs raced past them, turning down the Haymarket. She had to step quickly out of the road as a white stretch limousine approached her.

'Hey! I exist too, you bastard!' Holly shouted, banging her fist hard on the front of the vehicle.

The driver stopped the ridiculous car, jumped out and leapt round to the front.

'Yeah?' Holly asked with as much aggression as she could muster. Surely he wouldn't dare to hit her in the middle of Piccadilly Circus?

'Your carriage awaits,' the driver replied, with exquisite timing, and behind her Colette screamed with laughter.

'We're in this?' Holly asked.

'Yup! Although I didn't quite plan it like that,' Colette said.

'God, you really show your roots sometimes,' Holly told her, 'this is so vulgar, you know what I mean?' She looked at the enormously long limo in disgust.

'Says the woman who swears in the street,' Colette said, 'you do love it, don't you?'

'Yeah!' Holly laughed. 'Size does matter . . . Secretly I've always wanted to go in one of these . . . how did you know?'

Lounging inside were Holly's best friends from all stages of her life. Norma, her first boss, who taught her how to walk with a tray full of ice-cream round her neck, Debbie who had worked with her at the rock promoter's office, and, lying all the way along the back seat sipping champagne from the bottle, there was Robert.

'I'm a token girl for the evening,' he told her, 'all your shameless secrets are safe with me.'

'Right,' said Colette, pulling out an itinerary, 'I've got venues all over town. Thought we'd better make use of this wagon, so I drew up an itinerary. First stop is a vodka bar in South Ken. Drive on!'

Clare pressed the entry phone beside the entrance gate several times. There was no reply from either Holly's or Simon's flat. She thought now that it was probably unrealistic to expect Holly to be at home the night before her wedding. It had been a spur-of-the-moment decision to come. In her imagination she had seen the two of them making up with a great hug, like the closing frames of a film, but real life was not so neat.

She wandered up the street towards Leicester Square feeling vaguely disappointed and empty, chiding herself for not having come sooner. She did not feel like returning to Philippa's house straight away. It was the last evening of her old life. Tomorrow she and Tom would fly off to a new beginning, drifting for a while, seeing where the wind blew them. It might just be an extended holiday, or it might turn into something more, but right now she wanted to do something that she would remember, that would bring this stage to a feeling of conclusion, but she did not know what. Outside one of the places where Holly bought her cigarettes there was a spinner of postcards. Red telephone boxes, an aerial view of the Tower of London, Diana's face, and a teddy bear wearing a policeman's uniform. Clare stared at each one of them before deciding on the telephone boxes. Then she borrowed a biro from the shopkeeper and wrote.

'Not a very appropriate wedding card, but I wanted to tell you in person how happy I am for you. Congratulations! Haven't our lives changed since we met! Tom and I are going to America now to see Ella, and I don't know when we'll be back, but I hope that we'll be in touch again. Have a lovely day, and a wonderful life. Clare.'

Then she ran back down the street and began pushing all the buzzers hoping that someone would buzz her in and enable her to put the card through Holly's letter box.

'Do you mind if I ask what you're doing?' Simon's voice said.

Clare spun round.

He was standing behind her with a brown paper bag in his arms.

'Oh, sorry,' he said, recognizing her, 'I was just doing my Neighbourhood Watch impression.'

'Hello,' said Clare.

She didn't know whether or not to kiss him. People in London kissed each other much more than people in Cornwall did. After a moment's hesitation, they both went to kiss the opposite cheek, ended up kissing nothing and laughing nervously.

'Did Holly know you were coming?' Simon asked.

'No. No. I didn't even know until I got here,' Clare replied, thinking how silly that sounded.

'She'll be so sorry to have missed you,' Simon said.

'Really?'

'Very much so . . . she's gone out with Colette. Hen party.'

'Oh, of course. What about you? Stag night?'

'No. No, I was just about to celebrate my last evening as a bachelor by doing bachelor things. I've got four cans of Stella, an individual curry from the chilled cabinet and a video of *Independence Day* – well, the title seemed appropriate!'

Clare laughed. 'Do you think the curry's such a good idea?' she suggested nervously.

'What do you mean?'

'Well, you know, it kind of lingers on your breath, on your wedding day . . .'

'Oh my God! That hadn't even occurred to me . . .'

'Holly would kill you,' Clare giggled.

'You've just saved my life then,' Simon smiled at her. 'Have you eaten? Would you like to have dinner?'

'This evening? No . . . well . . .'

Clare hesitated, sensing somehow that Holly would not approve, but not knowing why she thought that. There was no rational reason why she should not have dinner with Simon.

'I'd love to,' she agreed.

'Not Indian, though,' Simon said, 'and by the same token not Chinese, Thai or Malaysian. What do you like to eat?'

'Anything, really . . .'

'OK. Let me just dump this lot.' He pointed at the bag of provisions.

When he returned, they began to wander across Leicester Square in the direction of Covent Garden in silence. It was difficult to know how to begin a conversation with Simon, Clare found, because although she had heard so much about him that she felt she knew him, they had only met very briefly once.

'How about this place?' Simon said, stopping suddenly outside a restaurant called Brown's. He glanced up and down the menu. 'Doesn't look too offensive, does it?'

'It looks lovely,' Clare said, peering through the door. There were potted palms everywhere and ceiling fans that made the vast room seem like a colonial club.

'How's your boat?' she finally said, when the waitress had placed them at a table near the grand piano.

'Very well, thank you,' Simon said, as if the boat were a relative after whose health she was politely enquiring.

'Shall we have a bottle of champagne? You can't get drunk on champagne, can you?'

His eyes had a lovely scrunched-up look when he laughed, Clare noticed.

'All right,' she said, suddenly beginning to enjoy herself.

They both ordered salmon fishcakes and salad.

'I think I'm going to be very sensible and have a milk shake too,' Simon said, 'to dilute the alcohol, of course.'

'Of course,' Clare said, 'I'll have one as well. They sound delicious!'

'How are your children?' Simon asked, slurping on his straw.

'Both very well, thank you.'

'And your husband?' Simon asked.

How much did he know of what had happened, Clare wondered, unwilling to land Holly in it by saying something amiss.

'He left me,' she decided to reply. It was the simple truth. Technically, she had thrown him out, but, as usual, Joss had gone one better. She sometimes wondered how long he would have gone on having clandestine sex in cyberspace if the events of the first week of September had not pushed them past breaking-point.

'Oh, I'm sorry,' Simon said.

'I'm not,' Clare said.

'I knew about . . . Holly told me . . . I thought perhaps . . .'

'No,' Clare said, understanding immediately what he was trying to say. 'Don't worry. The thing with Holly was nothing really, just the catalyst. It should have happened ages ago. It's fine.' Unwanted tears sprang to her eyes. She dabbed them away with her napkin.

'Oh, I'm . . .'

Their waiter arrived with two large white plates.

'No. Really it's fine. I don't know why I'm crying. I'm actually very happy,' Clare said, staring down at the table. 'I suppose you're the first person I've told who didn't know him, you see,' she said, trying to explain her tears, 'everyone else just thinks, oh, well, what did you expect with Joss? And that sort of makes me feel more of a fool for asking myself what I did to deserve this. D'you see what I mean? I don't know which is worse, being left by a shit, or realizing that you've lived with a shit for almost twenty years . . . oh, I'm sorry, this is not great talk for your wedding eve, is it?'

On balance, Holly was relieved that her single life was almost over. She couldn't deny that seeing a male strip show had never crossed her mind, but now that she was at one, it just seemed so desperate. Even Robert, who had matched her shot for shot in the vodka bar, added a camp spin to the outrageous flirting in the singles telephone bar, done a magnificent John Travolta impression in the Seventies disco, hadn't the stomach for the sleazy finale Colette had organized in a kind of converted concrete garage somewhere on the way to Essex.

Holly and Robert stood in the entrance sharing a cigarette like two schoolchildren who'd been sent out of class. It was raining. In the dripping darkness the white limousine looked vaguely sinister parked alongside the rows of Vauxhall Astras, like something out of *Goodfellas*.

'I thought you'd given up,' Robert said, as he passed her the last drag.

'I have,' Holly said, inhaling so hard the embers burnt right down to the filter.

'Given up buying them,' Robert said sulkily.

'No wonder you're gay,' Holly said, jerking her thumb back towards the hall, 'when you see that lot. It's not that they hate men, it's that they think they're laughable. I've never been to a strip show with female strippers, but I bet it's completely different. I mean, for us, this is a kind of team sport, but I bet with men, they think she's doing it just for them . . .'

'I'm as inexperienced as you on that subject,' Robert said wearily. 'You're in a very philosophical mood. I'd have thought you'd be out there screaming with the best of them. You're not even drunk. What's wrong with you?'

'I really think I've changed in the last few weeks,' Holly told him, 'I'm much happier, don't you think?'

'If you say so . . .'

'The thing is, I started reading this script today and you know when you're onto something good, you just can't wait to get back to it . . .' Holly explained.

'Oh I see,' Robert said, understanding perfectly, 'someone new?'

'Friend of yours, as a matter of fact. Ginger Prospect. You know, married to Charlie Prince?'

'Oh yes, I know Ginger . . .' he made it sound as if they had shared an interesting past. 'Has she really written something?'

'It's very funny . . .'

'I've no doubt about that . . . now, we have to stop. I'm under strict instructions not to talk about work. I don't want to be torn into little pieces by your friend Colette and the others. There's something rather uncomfortably Bacchanalian about this gathering . . .'

'Do we have to go back in there?' Holly whined.

Robert poked his head round the door to the bar.

'They're down to their jockstraps, and everyone's singing "YMCA", so there can't be long to go,' he informed her.

Clare couldn't remember the last time she had talked so much. In Penderric she had grown used to not talking. It was the only way she had of preserving her sense of self. Experience had taught her that if she revealed her thoughts to anyone there she would not own them any more, and there had been so little that was exclusively hers, it was the only way she had of keeping something. She could tell from the way that Simon was looking at her that he was listening to what she said, not just lying in wait, as Joss used to, impatient for the first opportunity to jump in and demonstrate his brilliance in a put-down.

They had eaten their fishcakes, drunk their milk shakes, but half the bottle of champagne remained in its ice bucket.

'Do you want any more of this?' Simon asked, picking it out.

'Actually, I don't. Do you mind? I just feel pleasantly relaxed, I don't want to be hungover for my seven-hour flight with a toddler . . . What I would like more than anything is a cup of tea,' Clare said. 'God, that sounds so middle-aged!'

'I suppose we are middle-aged. I mean we're old enough to have children who could vote . . .'

Clare laughed. 'I do have a child that age, remember?'

'Sorry!'

'Ella was very annoyed she couldn't vote this time . . . half of her was wanting a hung parliament so that there'd be an election soon after her birthday . . .'

'Yes, I can imagine that . . . she's very determined, isn't she? Are you really going to drive across America together?' Simon asked, picking up on what she had been talking about.

'Yes. It's something I've always secretly wanted to do. And now there's nothing to stop me. Not Joss, not lack of money. I'm really extremely lucky . . .'

Simon looked at her childishly animated face and smiled.

'I've always secretly wanted to sail round the world . . .' he confessed, a little wistfully.

'Mmm. That would be wonderful,' she agreed. 'One of the things I always regretted about life in Cornwall was that I only went sailing a few times. Joss didn't really get on with the sailing set, you know . . . I loved it. I loved the exhilaration, and the hugeness of the sky. Well, you've got a boat, so what's to stop you?'

'It's not big enough for going round the world, but fine for popping across the Channel,' Simon laughed, 'not that I imagine I'll be allowed to very often . . .'

'What could you mean by that?' Clare asked in mock innocence.

'Holly is not a good sailor . . .' he sighed, then looked at her, 'you're so different . . .'

'In what way?'

He thought seriously about his answer for several seconds, then said, 'Holly always seems to be on the move, and you have a kind of stillness, serenity . . .'

In the mirror, behind his head, she saw herself smiling slightly coquettishly at him. Her eyes were shining. Stop it, she told herself. Stop flirting with him.

'I think I'd better be getting back,' she said, picking up her bag from the floor.

'I've an idea,' Simon said, waving at their waiter for the bill. 'Why don't you come and have a cup of tea at my place?'

'Well . . .'

'Holly might be back,' he suggested.

'Are you sure? I don't want to intrude on your last evening . . .'

'I'm enjoying myself. This is far better than sitting worrying about whether I'm doing the right thing . . .' His voice was unconcerned, but there was the hint of a question mark at the end of the sentence.

'Of course you're doing the right thing,' Clare told him, 'but I know what you mean. It's daunting, isn't it, the idea of making vows . . . I remember being really nervous . . .'

'Were you?'

'Absolutely. I almost ran away at the steps of the register office. I just didn't know where to run to . . .'

They walked back along a quiet street on the north side of the National Gallery.

'It must be lovely living here, being able to pop in

and out of the gallery,' Clare said, breaking the moment of silent reflection.

'I don't think anybody who lives here ever does that stuff. Holly went to a lecture there once on a Sunday morning, and came back all evangelical about it, insisting that we *must* go *every* week . . .'

Clare laughed as he imitated Holly's unique brand of prescriptive enthusiasm.

'But usually I'm out of town at the weekends, and, as a matter of fact, I can't remember Holly mentioning it again . . .'

'Perhaps she still goes but doesn't tell you?' Clare said.

'Yes, I think that's highly likely,' said Simon, which made them both laugh a lot.

'Home?' screeched Colette, 'you must be out of your mind. You'll miss the Full Mountie . . . oops!' she knocked over her vodka and orange with the extravagance of her gesture.

'The Full Mountie?'

'He's Canadian, he wears a uniform and he's hung like a horse . . .'

'I'll get the driver to take us home and come back for you, all right?' Holly shouted above the roar of applause as a troupe of young men who called themselves All Sinners finished their act.

'What's your problem?' Colette screeched back.

'You know I hate Canadians,' Holly replied, 'I'll see you tomorrow, and thanks for . . . well . . . it was great, it really was . . .'

'You all right?' Colette asked.

'Yeah . . . just can't believe I'm prepared to give all this up,' Holly gestured around the room. The walls were made of breeze-blocks and there were fluorescent sun shapes hanging from the ceiling, detailing the price of misspelt bargain cocktails in black felt pen.

Colette was too drunk to recognize sarcasm.

'We can still do stuff like this, if you like,' she said, tearfully, 'it's not like anything's going to be different . . .'

'I'll see you tomorrow,' Holly said, bending to kiss her, 'be good.'

'He's sleeping like a baby,' Philippa said, 'he woke up once, but I sang "Bye Baby Bunting" and he went straight off . . .' She sounded proud of herself.

'I'm just having a cup of tea, and then I'll be off,' Clare told her.

'Stay out as long as you like,' Philippa offered generously.

'Tom's fine,' Clare informed Simon.

'Oh good.'

'Philippa's been singing him lullabies . . . I'm surprised she remembers the words.' She tried to imagine her mother's strident voice softened, and laughed to herself.

'What?' Simon asked, putting a mug of tea on the coffee-table and sitting down next to her on the beige sofa. For a moment, Clare felt slightly uncomfortable and wished that there was another chair in the room.

'I was just thinking of the words to "Bye Baby Bunting".'

'And they are?'

Clare sang softly, ' "Bye Baby Bunting, Daddy's gone a hunting . . ." '

'Oh.'

'You sort of think that they don't listen to the words, but of course they do. The other day I was singing "Dance to your daddy, my little laddie", and Tom suddenly said, "I can't. My daddy's not here." '

She looked up. Simon was staring at her.

'He must be mad to have left you,' he said simply.

'Oh, I'm sure that there was fault on both sides . . .'

Clare was unused to receiving compliments, and flustered by the way Simon was looking at her.

'No, you're really lovely,' Simon told her.

'No I'm not . . . everyone thinks I'm a softie, but really, I'm not . . .'

Very gently, he put his finger against her lips to silence her.

'Don't . . .'

His voice was gruff and sounded as if he were issuing an instruction to himself as much as to her.

The sensation of his finger against her mouth was as intimate as the most tender kiss. They sat very still, the space between them a magnetic field of longing. She knew that if either of them moved a millimetre towards the other their bodies would be drawn inexorably together.

Finally, she broke the intense silence.

'Look, it's late, I'd better be going . . .'

'But . . .'

'Send my love to Holly. Erm . . . have a lovely wedding . . .' she couldn't think of the appropriate polite formula. 'I'm sure you'll be happy . . .'

Before he could get to the door, she had closed it behind her.

As she put her key in the gate, Holly heard a door shut on the other side of the courtyard. Then a female figure walked towards her, and Holly braced herself. Not a prostitute, please. She knew it was his stag night but . . . and not Tansy, please not Tansy . . . she couldn't decide which would be worse. And then suddenly the person she least expected to see emerged from the shadows.

'Clare?'

'Holly! I'm so pleased I didn't miss you. I came to wish you well, and then Simon and I went out to dinner and . . .'

'It's one o'clock in the morning,' Holly said, stunned.

'I waited for you,' Clare replied.

'God, it's so nice to see you,' Holly finally said, 'I'm so sorry about what I did. I just can't believe . . .'

'Let's not talk about it here,' Clare said.

They were speaking to each other from each side of iron bars as if one of them were in prison.

'Would you like to come up to my place? I mean, have you got time? Where's Tom?'

'With Philippa . . . look, it's too complicated . . .'

Holly unlocked the gate and let herself in. Then she embraced Clare with such force she lifted her feet off the ground.

'I'm so, so, so pleased to see you . . .' she said.

'He's Cyrano of the bloody Internet!' Holly said when she had taken in what Clare had told her about Joss's international love affair.

'What?'

'Oh, doesn't matter . . . just a movie that one of my clients came up with . . .'

'They say that truth is stranger than fiction,' Clare said.

'Yeah . . .' Holly agreed automatically, then thought about it, 'but who are *they* that say that? Does anyone know? As a matter of fact, I've never heard anyone say that truth is stranger than fiction . . . *They*, whoever *they* are, also say if you put it in a movie no-one would believe it, which is also utter crap . . . So, like we wouldn't believe that a guy's conducting an affair in cyberspace, but we accept that a giant lizard is roaming the streets of New York . . .'

Clare laughed. 'I've missed you,' she said.

Holly looked at her and smiled.

'Look, I'm really sorry about Joss . . . I'm sorry that he's gone and I'm sorry about what I did . . .'

'It's OK,' Clare said.

'No, it's not.'

'All right, it's not, but in the end, you probably did me a favour. Without that, I don't know whether I ever would have got up the courage to confront him . . . it might have gone on for years . . . what you did kind of gave me the courage. You, and I suppose Princess Diana . . .'

Holly looked aghast.

'Well, that's the one and only time my name and hers will figure in the same sentence,' she said, 'hey, that could be a game, couldn't it . . . you know those games where one person has to go out of the room and everyone switches identities, well everyone could switch identities with the person least like them in the whole world, and then you'd have to guess what had happened . . .' Her brain began to mull over whether it would work.

'Who would mine be?' Clare asked, reluctantly joining in.

'Me, I suppose. I mean, you're the sister who's good and beautiful and true, and I'm the big, bad, ugly one . . .'

'You're not ugly,' Clare protested.

'I'm not beautiful though, am I? My face has got *so much character* . . .' Holly began to quote from the long list of backhanded compliments she had received over the years, 'I look fun, sexy, dirty, up for it . . . not exactly overwhelmingly romantic, are they?'

'Who said you were dirty?' Clare asked.

'I can't remember,' Holly replied quickly, flushing so pink Clare thought it must have been Joss.

'What does Simon say you are?' Clare wanted to know, feeling the slightest pang of guilt. If Holly had seen her half an hour before, she might not have thought her quite so good and true.

'Simon says that I'm incredibly bright and tough and difficult . . .'

Clare couldn't disguise her surprise.

'. . . and that he loves me. So that's all right,' Holly laughed, but when she looked up Clare could see that there were tears in her eyes.

'D'you know, nobody, except Mo . . . and you . . . and Tom, but that's different,' Holly took a deep breath, 'nobody, by which I mean no man, has ever told me that he loved me. Except Simon. I mean, I've slept with dozens, literally dozens, and they've said that I'm wonderful in bed and all that, but nobody has ever told me that they loved me . . .'

'Well, you're marrying the right one then,' Clare said, gently reaching out to touch her arm. Holly smiled and sniffed.

'Yes. I suppose I must be,' she said, 'he loves me, and he got rid of the rat. D'you know, of all the horrible things that have happened this year, I think that bloody rat was the worst. Can you believe that?'

'No,' Clare said, 'I think you probably transferred all the insecurities and fears that you already had deep down, about Jack dying, and where you were going in life, and all that, onto the rat, so it just seemed like it was the problem . . .'

'Or perhaps it's that I'm just a really shallow person,' Holly said, only half joking.

'Oh no, absolutely not . . .'

Holly stared at her.

'What makes you so nice?' she asked, 'you're even defending me against myself.'

'You do love him, don't you?' Clare asked, suddenly desperately needing Holly to say yes.

'Simon? I do. Yes, of course I love him. I'm not *in love* with him. D'you think that matters?'

'I think it's probably better,' Clare said, remembering exactly what *in love* felt like. In love was when you suspended all your critical faculties. It was a state of altered consciousness, rather like dreaming,

497

but far more disorientating when you woke up.

'How's Ella?' Holly asked, feeling slightly uncomfortable with the run of the conversation.

'We're going to see her tomorrow . . .'

'You and Tom?' Holly couldn't disguise her surprise, 'how?'

'I've made my peace with Philippa. She insisted I have some of Jack's money, and you know, it wasn't so very hard to take after all . . .' Clare gave a rueful smile at the easy loss of her own principles. 'She would like you to have some too . . .' she added quickly.

'Oh no. That's very kind, but I couldn't . . .'

'That's what I told her. So which one of us is the honourable one now?' Clare asked.

'You've got children . . . you need to look after them . . .'

'Thank you,' Clare said, feeling as if Holly had granted her absolution. She saw that Holly was shifting around uncomfortably in her chair.

'Look, since we're getting all confessional, you might as well know, if you don't already, that I slept with Matt too,' Holly suddenly blurted out.

'Matt? Not Ella's Matt?'

''Fraid so,' Holly replied.

'You're the older woman? He wrote to Ella about an older woman. How sweet!' Clare roared with laughter.

'Are you shocked?' Holly asked.

'I don't think anything you could do would shock me,' Clare said, suddenly understanding why she had found the boy's manner overly familiar since Ella had left, 'you wanted to from the moment you set eyes on him . . .'

'How did you know?'

'You told me!' Clare said, which both of them suddenly found hysterically funny.

'So, who'd have thought you'd be the one off to do a *Thelma and Louise*, and I'm left here playing . . .

playing . . . d'you know, I can't think of a film with a happily married woman as the central character . . .' Holly said, 'do you think that's a good sign or a bad one?'

'Good, because you can write your own script . . .' Clare suggested.

'Oh, very funny,' said Holly, wondering whether to tell her about Ginger's take on the theme of two sisters who meet in their mid-thirties, but Clare was standing up, about to go. She didn't want to complicate the moment.

'It's been lovely,' Clare said, 'and I do wish that I was coming to your do tomorrow. I'll drink a glass of champagne to you at thirty thousand feet.'

'I'm scared,' Holly suddenly blurted out. Clare was the first person she'd felt able to admit that to.

'Oh, Holly, it'll be fine. He's a gorgeous man, really kind . . . and I shouldn't be telling you this, but he's really scared too . . .'

'Is he?'

'Yes.'

They hugged each other for a long time.

'D'you think we're going to be friends, again?' Holly asked when they finally separated.

'Yes,' Clare replied instantly, 'why, don't you?'

Chapter 38

Holly woke up at about eleven o'clock feeling luxuriously relaxed. Normally, on waking, her brief sense of pleasure at being alive was almost instantly replaced by anxiety about what the time was, what clothes she was going to wear, whether she had any clean underwear, what problems lay in wait for her at work, and how she was going to staunch the headachey nausea that flooded through her body as her hangover began to kick in. Today, she felt as if all her demons had been laid to rest.

Bright sunlight flooded through the windows. It was one of those crisp, cold, autumnal days that made her almost look forward to winter. She wriggled down further under the duvet so that only her head was peeping out, and looked around the room she loved. This fourteen-by-ten-foot rectangle was the story of her life so far. The walls were papered with the film posters she had nicked when she worked at the Odeon; the bedspread had been created by Mo from pieces of her childhood dresses. The mirror on the dressing-table was strung with beads of all descriptions, dating from the long strings of tiny love beads from the first and second hippy eras to the big fake ruby crucifix she had worn during her Madonna period. There were book-shelves made from bricks and planks nicked off skips when she had no money, and a candelabrum dripping with bunches of Venetian glass grapes which she had bought herself as a reward for doing her first six-figure deal. There were 3D postcards with religious scenes blu-tacked around the mirror and ashtrays stolen from all sorts of different venues on every available surface. On her bedside table there were five alarm clocks, a half-empty bottle of Evian and Ginger's script.

Holly got out of bed and rummaged around in her handbag before pulling out a single Marlboro that had snapped in the middle. She had cadged it from Robert just before she clambered out of the white limousine at the bottom of her street. Her last cigarette. She had intended to smoke it before going to bed, but Clare's presence had made her forget. This must mean, she told herself, lighting up the bit with the filter left on it, that she was no longer addicted. Inhaling deeply, she picked up Ginger's script and read the rest of it, and when she had finished she got up, showered, put on jeans, a T-shirt and a big jumper, and went out to Patisserie Valerie for breakfast.

There was only one chair left at a table for six. Holly sat down, breathing in the wonderful steamy scent of fresh croissants. Three people at the table were hidden behind newspapers, the other two men, both smoking Marlboro, were discussing the ban on tobacco advertising and their disillusion with the Labour government.

'Do you mind if I cadge one of those cigarettes?' Holly asked. 'I'm getting married today,' she explained, as they gave their assent with an irritated wave.

The day stretched ahead of her, gloriously empty. Life stretched ahead of her, waiting to be enjoyed. Ginger's script was so good, she just knew she would sell it for a great deal of money. She thought of the bonus she would receive at Christmas and smiled, and then her face set into a frown. It would be large, possibly five figures this year, but would she feel it was finally enough? Maybe now was the time she should break away from Louis Gold Ltd and set up on her own? It was what people did when they became successful.

But would it really make so much difference, she wondered, ordering a second cup of coffee. More of the money she made would go into her own pocket, but she would still be an agent and she would never really feel she had achieved anything except as an intermediary.

Anyway, now was not the time to make any big decision like that, she thought, stubbing out her final, final cigarette and picking up her *pain au chocolat*. Getting married was enough for one year. The wonderful thing about getting married that no-one ever told you was that it freed you up. You didn't have to spend all that time worrying about whether you really wanted a man, whether you could get a man if you did, where, how, whether you should have gone to bed with him on the first date, whether he was too old, too young, married, misogynist, repressed homosexual, or just too boring to spend the rest of your life with. Marriage sorted out your personal life in one stroke. That, she decided, was enough for one year. Her professional life might take a little more consideration and, like Scarlett O'Hara, she couldn't think about that today. Perhaps other things in her life would become important, like even, maybe, one day, they hadn't made any definite decision yet, children? Enough. Holly stood up and paid her bill. It was noon. There was still a whole afternoon of her single life left to her before Colette came round to help her get dressed and made up. She wanted to make the most of it.

Holly walked towards Covent Garden. There was a flower stall at Seven Dials that looked as if it should be in a painting. She hadn't intended to bother much with flowers, but seeing all the colours dancing before her in the sunshine, she could not resist, and spent ages choosing a selection of brightly coloured blooms which the man tied into a packed hemispherical posy for her.

'Oh, but my dress is sort of a bluey, greeny colour,' she suddenly remembered, looking at the predominantly orange choice she had made.

'Well, this will go with your hair,' he said, winking at her, 'I love a redhead. Tell your husband he's a lucky man.'

'Oh, I do,' Holly replied, 'all the time.'

She wandered around Neal's Yard sniffing essential oils and eventually buying a small bottle of something that promised healthy-looking skin in seconds, then she bought a hot dog in a bun and ate it leaning over the railings in Covent Garden market, watching a string quartet playing in the well below.

The Christmas decorations were already up, and in the piazza there was an old-fashioned carousel with golden horses. Holly had loved carousels ever since seeing her first film which was *Mary Poppins*. Climbing aboard, she thought how silly she must look, nearly six foot of her, alone, up there with all the five-year-olds. I'm getting married, she wanted to shout, as she went round and round and round in a glittering gilded whirl of lights and music.

Afterwards she walked down to Waterloo Bridge to look at the view of the city she loved. New York had the skyscape and Brooklyn Bridge, Paris had the Ile de la Cité, and this was London's view. She gazed down to St Paul's and beyond towards the concrete tower where she had grown up, and then turned and looked up the river to the Houses of Parliament. The sun was going down already and all the buildings were tinted with rose gold.

Holly remembered with nostalgia all the times in her childhood she had hung from the top bar of the railings by her knees, terrifying Mo, not because she was about to fall into the river, but because she was showing her knickers to the world.

And she remembered walking back across the bridge with Jack on the morning of 2nd May that year, after the victory party at the Festival Hall. She couldn't recall how the subject had come up but she remembered with great clarity him saying, almost affectionately, 'You'll never find a man strong enough to marry you, Holly.'

'Well, Jack, I just did,' Holly whispered into the wind.

By the time she was back at her flat it was getting cold outside. Holly went into the bathroom and turned on the hot tap to fill the room with warm steam before her shower. She was just about to step in when the doorbell rang. Cursing Colette for being early, she put on her towelling bathrobe and padded downstairs.

Simon was standing outside.

'Have you lost your key?' she asked him.

'No. I just didn't want to use it . . .'

'Didn't want to? Look, come in, it's bloody freezing. Colette'll kill you if she finds you here. I'm sure it's meant to be unlucky or something . . .'

He followed her up the stairs, then stood awkwardly in the doorway of her kitchen.

'Coffee?' she asked, 'I haven't got any milk, but if you're really desperate you could nip back and get some . . .'

'No thanks,' he said.

'I've had a wonderful day,' Holly began to tell him as she poured boiling water onto brown granules in the bottom of her cup, 'first, I had breakfast at . . .'

Then, sensing something was wrong, she looked over to where he was standing.

'What's up?' she asked him.

He looked at her for a few moments.

'Cheer up,' she laughed, 'it's your wedding day!'

'I'm sorry,' he said, 'I just can't go through with it.'

'Can't go through with what?' Holly asked.

'The wedding.'

'Oh come on, Simon, it's not such a big deal. That's why we kept it small. It'll just be like having a nice dinner with friends. I may make a speech, but you don't have to . . .'

'No . . . I didn't mean . . .' he tried to interrupt.

'. . . we're not even having a proper cake . . . look, I couldn't resist these flowers, and the man told me to tell you . . .'

'Just shut up a minute,' he suddenly said, exasperated. 'I'm trying to tell you that I can't marry you,' he added gently.

There was a moment's silence as she wondered whether she had heard him correctly.

'Can't marry me?' she repeated.

'It won't work. I'm very sorry . . .'

'Sorry? What d'you mean it won't work? Who says it won't work?'

'I do . . . oh, we might go on pretending for a few months, even a year, but after that . . .'

'After that we could get divorced,' Holly interrupted, 'everyone gets divorced for God's sake . . .'

She waited for him to laugh, but he didn't.

'I'm sorry,' he said.

'What the hell do you mean?' she suddenly turned on him, 'I'm the one that's settling for second best. Not you. You're the one getting what you always wanted, remember?'

'Well, that's one of the reasons it won't work,' Simon said calmly, 'because you're not the sort of person who settles for second best, as you put it so charmingly . . . are you?'

'Hang on a minute,' Holly held up both hands. 'Don't make this my fault. You're the one who's calling it off. Not me. Just don't try to make it me . . .' She began to shake.

Simon went to put his arms around her.

'Leave me alone!' She shrugged him violently away.

She stood with her back to him, her mind a mass of contradictions.

'Oh bloody hell!' she stamped her foot, 'why d'you have to call it off today, of all days. Why couldn't you just have waited . . .'

'Until when?'

'Simon, we've got twenty people sitting down to dinner in . . . in about an hour. Some of them are probably there already. I know Mo will be . . .'

'So you'd rather get married, then split up?' he asked disbelievingly.

'Yes!' she said, with a bright smile, then saw that it wasn't an offer.

'Oh God, you really mean it, don't you?' she said.

'I'm sorry . . .'

She knew that she should be crying or something, but she just felt blank.

'So, when did you decide this?' she asked coldly.

'Last night. I've been thinking about it all day, trying to find a way round it . . . but I can't . . .'

'What happened last night?'

'Nothing . . . it just suddenly went from being a dream to being reality, and . . . well, I thought . . . I thought that you were everything I wanted, and I realized . . . well, I suppose I realized that you weren't . . .'

'So, what's wrong with me all of a sudden?' Holly demanded, turning round again. He could look her in the face to tell her that.

'Nothing's wrong with you . . .' he pleaded to be let off the hook.

'There's someone else then,' she looked straight at him.

506

There was no denial.

'There's someone else! I don't bloody believe it . . .'

'There isn't anyone else . . .' he began.

Suddenly, in an imaginary bubble above Holly's head, a light-bulb went on.

'It's Clare, isn't it?'

There had been something about the way the door closed behind the person leaving Simon's flat last night that had made her think of sex, Holly remembered. And then she had seen who it was and the thought had disappeared.

'How did you know?' Simon asked, blushing.

'Because I bumped into her on her way back from your midnight tryst . . . We had a wonderful chat, or so I thought. I can't believe it. Clare! You went and fucked my bloody sister!'

'We didn't fuck. We didn't even touch each other . . .' he protested, then added quietly, 'but I was shocked by how much I wanted to . . .'

'You bastard!' she shouted.

'Holly, don't . . .'

'Clare, beautiful too-good-to-be-true Clare . . . I'm sure she must have been delighted to get her revenge . . . duplicitous little bitch . . .' Only rage held her back from the brink of tears.

'It wasn't like that,' Simon broke in, 'it wasn't like that at all. Don't blame her. She wasn't interested. She fled . . .'

'All right, all right, shut up. Just shut up. I believe you. OK?' Holly shouted, unable to bear the passion with which he was defending her sister.

She suddenly laughed drily.

'Well, thank heaven I didn't give up the lease on this place,' she said.

'I think I'm still going to move to Brighton. Be nearer the boat . . .' Simon told her.

'Well, don't give up your lease either, because I've

promised mine to Ella. She can have yours instead,' Holly instructed, unable to resist adding, 'it'll be OK once that bloody awful sofa's gone.'

They looked at each other. There was surprisingly little to say.

'I'm sorry,' Simon offered.

'You can go to the restaurant and tell everyone what a shit you are. And pay the deposit,' she told him as if meting out a punishment.

'Of course,' said Simon. Sensing that he'd been dismissed, he turned around, then stopped. 'Look, I know now's maybe not the right time, but I hope we can still be friends.'

'Trouble is, we can't. We can't be friends any more. Not now that we've had sex. It would always be there, lurking around, and I don't want to play all those bloody mind games with you. I can't go through all that with you . . .' she said, looking defeated. Then, visibly pulling herself together, she added, 'Anyway, right now, I don't even like you very much.'

He looked so stricken, she almost relented.

'I told you I'd lose you if we did it, didn't I?' she said, trying to lighten the atmosphere.

'Yeah, you did,' he said, with a sad smile.

'Well, why the hell didn't you take any notice?' she asked him as the doorbell rang.

He turned and went downstairs, and in a moment the space he had left in the kitchen was filled by Colette.

'Anything wrong?' she asked.

'Yeah,' said Holly, 'I've got no alcohol or cigarettes in the flat. Let's go out and get plastered.'

Chapter 39

The film had been received in silence. A shocked silence that was charged with thought and emotion and went on for several minutes, unlike the minute's reverent silence at the beginning called as a mark of respect to the film's director, which had been filled with several coughs, the odd rustle and the almost indiscernible noise of people trying silently to masticate the handful of popcorn they had just put in their mouths.

Philippa stood in the red velvet foyer greeting a line of people she had not seen for six months.

'Wow. Strong stuff!' they said, and

'Brilliant. That's given us all something to think about . . .' and

'Darling, you look wonderful. What an amazing film. You must be so proud.'

Her sense was that the reviews would tend to kindness because Jack was dead. Had he been alive, she thought that the knives would have been out.

'Philippa Palmer?'

The confident London accent startled her as she focused on the last person in the line, who was holding out her right hand to be shaken.

'Hello. I'm Holly. I decided to come after all.'

It was as if Jack had been reincarnated as he was

when she first met him, but in female form. The woman's eyes were his, and she was long and lean as he had been.

'I'm so glad,' was the only thing that Philippa seemed to be able to say.

The two women stared at each other, conducting a silent assessment, then smiled.

'Did you enjoy the film?' Philippa finally managed.

'I thought it was a bit like all those movies about Vietnam,' Holly said, 'they were never about what America did to Vietnam, always about what Vietnam did to the American psyche. *Paying for It* isn't about what society does to the homeless, it's about how guilty the homeless make people feel. If you want my honest opinion,' she went on, as if she had kept it quiet so far, 'I thought it was a middle-aged, middle-class wank . . .'

The pale blue eyes dared Philippa to contradict her.

Philippa's mouth pursed. Inside, she felt as if she was about to explode, and suddenly she could control it no longer and her laughter burst out and bubbled around the murmuring crowd. Many eyes looked at her. Philippa looked only at Holly.

'Are you free for dinner?' she asked.

Holly nodded.

Ignoring everyone around them, the two women began to walk towards the exit.

'What do you do?' Philippa asked her, with the formulaic politeness of a good hostess.

'I was an agent,' Holly told her, holding open the huge, heavy door, 'but I've recently decided to become a producer.'

'Really?'

'You see, one of my clients wrote this script and I liked it so much, I bought an option myself. It helps that her husband's got an independent production company which I'm using as my base. Now all I have to do is raise some money . . .' she laughed.

'Well, that's very interesting,' Philippa told her, as they walked across Leicester Square together, 'because I may be looking to invest myself . . .'

'If you read this script, you'd know you were onto a winner . . .'

'Really?' Philippa asked, looking up into the clear, candid blue eyes.

'Trust me,' said Holly.

THE END

A SELECTED LIST OF FINE NOVELS
AVAILABLE FROM CORGI BOOKS

14060	0	MERSEY BLUES	Lyn Andrews	£5.99
14516	5	SOPHIE'S SCANDAL	Virginia Blackburn	£5.99
14323	5	APPASSIONATA	Jilly Cooper	£6.99
14261	1	INTIMATE	Elizabeth Gage	£5.99
14447	9	FIREBIRD	Iris Gower	£5.99
14537	8	APPLE BLOSSOM TIME	Kathryn Haig	£5.99
14385	5	THE BELLS OF SCOTLAND ROAD	Ruth Hamilton	£5.99
14566	1	THE DREAM SELLERS	Ruth Hamilton	£5.99
14553	X	THE BRASS DOLPHIN	Caroline Harvey	£5.99
14686	2	CITY OF GEMS	Caroline Harvey	£5.99
14220	4	CAPEL BELLS	Joan Hessayon	£4.99
14535	1	THE HELMINGHAM ROSE	Joan Hessayon	£5.99
14207	7	DADDY'S GIRL	Janet Inglis	£5.99
14543	2	THE COLOUR OF SIN	Janet Inglis	£5.99
14332	4	THE WINTER HOUSE	Judith Lennox	£5.99
14599	8	FOOTPRINTS IN THE SAND	Judith Lennox	£5.99
13910	6	BLUEBIRDS	Margaret Mayhew	£5.99
14492	4	THE CREW	Margaret Mayhew	£5.99
14498	3	MORE INNOCENT TIMES	Imogen Parker	£5.99
14499	1	THESE FOOLISH THINGS	Imogen Parker	£5.99
10375	6	CSARDAS	Diane Pearson	£5.99
14577	7	PORTRAIT OF CHLOE	Elvi Rhodes	£5.99
14549	1	CHOICES	Susan Sallis	£5.99
14636	6	COME RAIN OR SHINE	Susan Sallis	£5.99
13845	2	RISING SUMMER	Mary Jane Staples	£3.99
14507	6	SPECIAL DELIVERY	Danielle Steel	£5.99
14640	4	THE ROMANY GIRL	Valerie Wood	£5.99